Rob took the scope, swept its view around to get his bearings, and saw a hard, bright yellow-green dot that gleamed unmoving near the next lake. Eventually he saw the bear as well, moving farther from the trail but circling that point of light.

It was obvious that the infrared glow of their campfire embers was the source of that hard dot of light in the scope—and that the bear, elevating its muzzle now and then to test the air, was growing bolder in its approach to their camp. Bolder, that is, until it stopped, frozen with one paw uplifted, muzzle pointed campward.

Then, with a burst of fluid grace the bear pivoted and doubled back on its tracks in an astonishing lope that could have been comical. it failed to be funny to Rob because, near the edge of the green tableau, a bright, almost white line swept their campsite from somewhere off to the left.

Gooseflesh marched up his arms because his left eye did not register a flashbeam at the campsite. Something was scanning their camp. Something with a powerful infrared signature, and no visible flashbeam.

A human figure stepped carefully from behind a tree, the light emanating from its head, and again the beam swept from mummy bag to hammock as the figure approached their camp. Rob realized that the stranger was using expensive night-vision goggles with a good IR illuminator, and for a moment he considered shouting at this man who was reaching to point toward his hammock.

He reconsidered abruptly as a brilliant flash erupted from that outstretched hand, and another; a third; a fourth, though no sound carried to him.

Praise for Dean Ing

LOOSE CANNON

"Man-on-the-run thrillers are a dime a dozen, but fresh ones are substantially rarer. Readers looking for something new will be happy to crack the covers of Ing's latest offering. . . . Featuring well-drawn characters and reasonably sharp dialogue (Ing avoids most of the cliches of the genre), the novel reenergizes the on-the-run theme without straying too far from the familiar conventions."
—*Booklist*

THE NEMESIS MISSION

"An exciting techno-thriller. . . . Ing maintains masterful control of his storyline. As each subplot is resolved the reader sighs with regret, only to be swept forward into an even more suspenseful situation. The dialogue is crisp and the main characters convincingly portrayed, including a well-developed supporting cast."
—*Publishers Weekly*

"Beyond the thrills and humor, Ing's high tech designs fly miles above his imitators. Some of us read him to see what we'll be developing tomorrow."
—Leik N. Myrabo, author of *The Future of Flight*

"Ing, author of the best-selling *The Ransom of Black Stealth One* has written another excellent high-tech thriller. . . . Rich in plot detail and unforgettable individuals, Ing creates a build-up of suspense until the Mexican jungle explodes into a war zone of destruction."
—*Library Journal*

"High-tech machinery and low-life schemes keep the action moving in this thriller. . . . Fast-paced and all-too-believable, bouncing skillfully from one country to another, and from one set of characters to the next, Ing keeps you guessing till the end as to the final outcome."
—*West Coast Review of Books*

THE RANSOM OF BLACK STEALTH ONE

"The Hellbug ignites a new generation of stealth technology. . . . Stunning, high-potential stuff packed into a thriller I couldn't put down . . . and I wasn't a fan of thrillers."
—Joseph Vasilik, Manager (ret.),
Advanced Development Section,
Hughes Aircraft Company

"Has the reader hanging on to each page . . . Ing has successfully blended the elements of an old-fashioned chase with a Cold War spy thriller and the almost-science-fact of stealth technology that is making headlines today."
—*Associated Press*

"The novel is tightly plotted with interesting and attractive characters. In a season crammed with technothrillers, Ing reminds us of the poetry and joy of flight, which give this subject its enduring fascination." —*Library Journal*

ALSO BY DEAN ING

The Big Lifters
Blood of Eagles
Butcher Bird
Flying to Pieces
The Nemesis Mission
The Ransom of Black Stealth One
Silent Thunder
Single Combat
The Skins of Dead Men
Spooker
Systemic Shock
Wild Country

LOOSE CANNON

DEAN ING

TOR®

A TOM DOHERTY ASSOCIATES BOOK
NEW YORK

This is a work of fiction. All the characters and events portrayed in this book are either products of the author's imagination or are used fictitiously.

LOOSE CANNON

Copyright © 2000 by Dean Ing

A Tor Book
Published by Tom Doherty Associates, LLC
175 Fifth Avenue
New York, NY 10010

www.tor.com

Tor® is a registered trademark of Tom Doherty Associates, LLC.

ISBN: 0-812-57631-4
Library of Congress Catalog Card Number: 00-031808

First edition: November 2000
First mass market edition: June 2003

Printed in the United States of America

0 9 8 7 6 5 4 3 2 1

For Carolyn and Emmay;
IT MUST BE IN THE GENES

LOOSE CANNON

CHAPTER 1

ROB TARRANT SUSPECTED THAT THIRTEEN-YEAR-OLD KENNY was jerking his old man's chain with the claim that a naked lady was polishing some guy's Porsche across the street. Rob adjusted his magnifying goggles, tenderly clamped what looked like a very large dragonfly wing in a fixture, and smiled as he looked around to the boy, who was hovering at Rob's shoulder. "Yeah, right," said the father. "I suppose you're borrowing that three-in-one oil to give the lady a rubdown."

The boy shook his head. "Gonna fix my bike out back," he said, and paused on his way into the hall. "But straight deal, it's a bitchin' black 928." A moment later the back screen door slammed.

Yeah, right, Rob repeated to himself. If Kenny were serious, he would've described the lady, not the car. Or maybe not yet, but in another year, for sure.

Still, it seemed worth a glance while the cement dried on Rob's latest hobby project, as long as Corrine didn't catch him. "Ogling," she would call it, bugging her bedroom eyes and drawing out the "ooooh" syllable in derision. It wasn't as if she'd lost her looks, she would say, cocking a provocative hip; and he would earnestly agree. He had learned to avoid rejoinders along the lines of: *Since you seldom play the game these days, you shouldn't mind my enjoying spectator sports.* But Corrine minded just the same. On the other hand, she was shopping in the San Jose suburb of Cupertino at the moment.

Rob figured it wouldn't hurt to check out the kid's bizarre report from the kitchen window while he nuked a cup of coffee, but he was wrong about that. Given Rob's tendency to string ideas together like firecrackers, the view from his window turned deadly in distinct steps.

At thirty-six, Rob used magnifying lenses only for the gossamer bits of his hobby projects. He didn't need glasses to appreciate that the woman across the street, really no more than a girl in her late teens, wasn't entirely nude in her string bikini. Close enough, though. She was put together like a blow-up doll of Kim Basinger, just a wee bit overinflated, and in ten years she'd probably look like the Michelin Man. But right here, right now, in a Silicon Valley suburb on a sunny Saturday afternoon in May, she made a man feel guilty just watching.

The fact was, Rob decided, this girl seemed to be getting off on her chore, using a swatch of orange parachute silk the size of a pillowcase against the gloss black of that Porsche 928, actually climbing onto the damn thing, writhing in joy, probably doing more harm than good to the car's glossy finish. Well, California girls were notorious car nuts and this sight was one to take back to his fellow engineers at General Standards, if only he had a video camera; better still, a camera small enough to mount on one of his tiny mantis aircraft. He could imagine standing on the front porch, guiding a mantis with his Futaba transmitter so that it flitted unnoticed with its electric drive whirring in almost perfect silence over hedges, car, and girl, recording every languid whisk and voluptuous shimmy with—what, a standard videotape rig?

Nope, far too heavy. A CCD with its own microtransmitter was a better match, if he could afford charge-coupled devices on the salary of a GenStan engineer. His grin became less guilty, more calculating, as he thought about it, coming nearer to the point that would detonate his entire life.

Colleagues called his toys "models," though the flying mites weren't models of anything. They were UAVs, "unmanned aerial vehicles." When a winged critter is no bigger than a man's hand, the rules of aerodynamics begin to change. Air that seems almost intangible to a Boeing can seem thick as pancake syrup to an insect—or to a minuscule flying machine. For some years, toys of this sort had been almost entirely the province of a few hobbyists.

Some of Rob's UAVs looked like insects, wings covered by

plastic film, landing gear stripped from bundles of carbon fiber, their propellers sweeping a circle scarcely larger than a silver dollar. Corrine's father Gus, who built conventional radio-controlled models spanning four feet and more, had given Rob a flyswatter as a gag, in case his bugs got the better of him. Both men pursued their hobby using a minimum of funds and a maximum of ingenuity. *Okay, since a CCD is too spendy I could build a still camera*, Rob thought. *Or I could install a company chemchip right now and find out whether she's wearing perfume.*

At that point the Porsche's owner came outside and raised hell with the zaftig Miss Teeny-Weeny Bikini, grabbing her polishing rag and, as she retreated, popping the rag in the direction of her butt, where a lot of guys would have been snapping at it like a collie. Rob had to renuke his caffeine again, sipping thoughtfully as he returned to his study and the carrel he'd built for his tiny UAVs. If you put one of the company chemchips into a mantis, you could run chemical analysis of perfume—*no, make that insecticide spray patterns instead*—over a hundred acres of apricot orchard for a few dollars, and do it in ten minutes flat: what microchip nerds called a "killer application."

And GenStan would make a bazillion bucks, and the guy who developed this killer app would be switched onto the fast track, maybe even rekindle some respect from his bored wife. All a man had to do was build a prototype and demonstrate it to bean-counters who'd never thought seriously about aircraft that would circle in your living room; who might snicker at the very mention of it unless proof was literally flitting down Mahogany Row over their expensively styled haircuts.

Most of the managers gave lip service to creativity but thought it was antisocial to color outside the lines with anything that hadn't been created already. And if you proved something new, these same guys would try to steal the idea.

Rob recalled a slogan, one of a score that Gus had pinned up over his workbench when Kenny was four or five, before Gus retired. It said,

A LIE BY THE COMPANY IS A MATTER OF POLICY.
A LIE BY THE EMPLOYEE IS GROUNDS FOR DISMISSAL.

So, rather than get caught up in charges and counter-charges, a smart employee wouldn't spread such ideas around until he had the demo ready, but Corrine's dad Gus was a special case. He could help with the circuitry, too.

And that was the moment when Robert Paul Tarrant, class of '84 from Oregon State University, went from being a harmless hobbyist to a man who needed killing.

CHAPTER 2

ROB PLANTED THE SEEDS OF HIS OWN DESTRUCTION WITH THE innocent curiosity of a toddler checking out a loaded revolver. Sunday evening he laid out his brainstorm for his father-in-law, Gus Kallas, sharing Haake Beck nonalcoholic beers in the old house trailer that Gus kept in his driveway. As Gus put it, "to call that goddamn old bucket of bolts a mobile home would be putting on airs." In common with many machinists, Gus Kallas was a man who took his facts neat, no ice, no seltzer.

Rob firmly believed that Corrine's best-ever decision was her choice of dads. A professing pessimist with a sly grin, a doting grandparent prone to barracks language, a man of firm habit who had given Rob his only tailored suit after retirement to drive home a point, Gus Kallas had moved the stinks and bangs and balsa shavings of his hobby outside his Santa Clara bungalow when Corrine was still a teenager and his wife was still alive. Big radio-controlled models needed a portable hangar, he said, and Gus could tow that old trailer halfway across the country to attend a model competition without leaving his workshop behind—kitchenette and machine tools included.

By now Rob was more at home in Santa Clara, in Gus's tacky sanctum on wheels, than he was in his own study in nearby Sunnyvale; here, he didn't have to apologize to Corrine for the odors of solvents and soldering flux.

". . . So I thought if I could stuff a GenStan chemchip between the wings of a mantis," Rob was saying, "I could use it as a chassis for the radio-control bits."

"Nah you didn't," Gus argued, stifling a belch. "You figured you c'd con me into doing it. RC servos need good mounts;

I've never seen one of these chemchip doodads but I'll take a crack at it."

The slender tab Rob drew from his shirt pocket was narrower than a business card and just as thin, laminated from sheets of clear plastic, with an odd assortment of tiny channels and circular voids clearly visible inside the plastic. One corner of the tab had been creased by some mischance. "I spotted a bunch of these rejects in the surplus yard a month ago," Rob confided. "You never know what they'll toss out."

Gus understood. GenStan wasn't the only corporation that, through sheer thoughtlessness, sometimes sold scrap that would horrify top management and delight an industrial spy. "Doesn't have any electrical contacts," Gus complained.

"Not supposed to," said Rob, "though some do. It isn't an electronic microchip, it's a chemchip. For my demo, it doesn't even have to work. The lines are hollow passages. This one was a telltale for nitric oxide before someone broke it; the little bulge at the bottom is a pump with a one-way valve. You squeeze it with a finger to pump a sample in."

"Hell you say," Gus muttered, donning his magnifying headset. He swung a cantilevered lamp near with a *skrinch* of protesting springs and peered closely at the device for a long silent moment. Then, "It inhales an air sample, does it?"

"About a picoliter; trillionth of a quart. And hauls it past reagents and ignores everything but what it's built to detect. If there's any NO present, that last little circle turns pinkish. This is a very simple one; some of the new ones need a power source. Would you believe, they can give you a digital readout?" He laid the tiny device down. "By the way, just because some idiot threw this away doesn't mean we should be talking about it to anybody."

"Goddamn thing is a one-gram chemistry lab," Gus mused. "But why does it need to fly?"

"Okay, say you've got fifty acres of apricots and you want to know if some particular bug is threatening them."

"I've got fifty acres of—" Gus began, a familiar gleam in his eye.

"Don't say it," Rob interjected quickly, knowing that Gus

was capable of repeating the whole damn sentence just to play the fool. "Now, there are chemical sensors that can tell you if that kind of bug is in your orchard, and to be certain of it, you can pay some guy to visit every tree and it could take a day or two. It'd be a lot quicker to send a mantis cruising just above fifty acres of treetops, one row at a time. Half an hour or so, tops. It could return a radio signal so you'd even learn which corner of the orchard you need to spray first."

A moment's silence as Gus visualized it happening. He grinned. "Son of a bitch," he said with a nod. "If you tried it with a rented copter, you'd damage the crop. But you're not just talking apricots here, Ro-bo." The nickname had stuck after Rob showed Gus one of his early mantis devices, with tiny robotic pincers that snapped forward when it touched down.

"Right. Tomatoes, grapes, whatever. But even with a chemical microchip the marketing hotshots would want to mount it on a Buick. I know how those guys on Mahogany Row think."

"They *do* think, then? I wouldn't bet a nickel on it after meeting one of their wives; friend of Corrie's. Funny name. Drives one of those turd-ugly Beemer roadsters," Gus muttered.

"That'll be Deirdre Lodge," Rob said, "and for God's sake don't quote me to Corrine, but I think you've got that classy lady pegged. Stand Deirdre in front of your microwave oven and she'd wait an hour for the picture to come on."

"I'll never understand my daughter. Why does Corrie do volunteer work with such a dumbshit?"

"Deirdre married into GenStan's management cadre so, in Corrine's view, Deirdre Lodge must be smart and worth following," Rob shrugged. "Matter of fact, it's Ethan Lodge I intend to spring this on. I only know him through a few company parties; he's not in my branch. So if this idea gets a close look, we can thank Corrine for climbing the right social ladder."

"Ethan Lodge; yeah, I've heard the name. You don't think he'd take your baby and run with it?"

Rob sat back, his rattan chair squeaking. "Possible, but he's Deirdre's hubby and I think we hit it off. Besides, the word on Lodge is, he knows his limitations. Got the right degree and connections even if Princeton is more theory than practice, got the right spiffy wife, got sent to that Harvard management class they call 'charm school,' all that crap. And if he tried to pass my chemchip mantis off to the tech staff as his idea, he'd be out of his depth like that." A fingersnap punctuated Rob's assertion.

"You gonna tell him at work tomorrow?"

"Nope. I'll wait till we have it flying. You think we can get it up in a week?"

"Not even with Viagra," Gus joked. "But who knows? Show me those airframe sketches."

BY FRIDAY MORNING, ROB KNEW HIS GUESS ON THE SCHEDULE had been good. Gus had yet to affix tiny controls to the chemchip, but with equivalent weights cemented to its frame the little mantis had flown uncontrolled across Gus's backyard on Thursday evening—flown so well, in fact, that they'd needed Kenny to retrieve it from the Kallas avocado tree. A device that small, that weightless, could be destroyed between thumb and forefinger but, flying no faster than a man could jog, it could impact a branch without damage. Gus had claimed he would have it ready for radio-controlled flight by the weekend.

Rob suffered through the usual morning traffic clots on Lawrence Expressway and chose the south gate into GenStan's sprawling, fenced square mile. With his thumb, he lifted the security badge clipped to his jacket collar so the gate guard could scan past his Saturn station wagon's windshield decal to his personal ID without pause; got the hand-wave that said, *Pass, friend,* even as the guard flicked his gaze toward the Toyota behind Rob. His dashboard clock read 7:36, just about right for his quarter-mile walk from the vast GenStan parking area.

It was shaping up to be a warm, sunny day, the kind of day that made Rob wish he were still an Oregon State undergrad at Corvallis. In those days he could've cut the day's classes in

favor of trout-fishing on the nearby Willamette. Here in the
Santa Clara Valley of central California there weren't any wild
trout and, working inside a building with windows that
wouldn't open, you seldom thought about what kind of day it
was. Maybe, he thought, that was why they built 'em this way.

Production Engineering, Rob's branch, took up one wing of
an addition to the GenStan shops. He nodded to several acquaintances and dodged two hurtling green company bicycles
ridden by couriers before entering the building, where he
showed his badge again and got a nod. Striding past rows of
cubicles, he made a point of touching base with his section
head, Guy Halloran.

The rotund Halloran tried to be nice but he knew where his
check was printed. And he tended to forget where he got his
ideas. "Yo, Rob," he said as the engineer passed.

"Hey, Guy."

"That progress report?"

Rob paused. "Draft's nearly done, you'll have it by five. I,
uh, may have to run over to Marketing but it won't take long."

Professionalism, according to GenStan, meant you didn't
have to punch a time card. It also meant you were at your desk
by eight wearing a tie and coat always—excepting mathema-
ticians and programmers, who succeeded in ignoring all
known dress codes—and you worked overtime without expecting extra pay for it. It meant a hell of a lot of other things,
too, including your signed promise that anything and everything you thought up while on GenStan's payroll belonged to
the company, and for six months after you left. Rob's name
was on two patents, each of which he had dutifully signed over
to GenStan ". . . for the sum of one dollar and other valuable
considerations." Those "valuable considerations," as every engineer knew, were nothing more than continued employment
by GenStan.

This was a galling satire on the original intent of the U.S.
patent system, but that's how you played the game. If the
company valued those ideas, you eventually got promoted;
Rob was now a Senior Production Engineer. If this flying
chemchip made the suits happy on Mahogany Row, Rob might

make Production Engineer Specialist before he turned forty. His paycheck would rise to roughly half that of, say, Ethan Lodge. Speaking of which . . .

Rob found Lodge in the company directory, which had over nine thousand entries, and punched the number. You could get an outside line, but you could also get your tail in a crack if your call was other than GenStan business. They monitored calls at GenStan, and told you so up front.

"Market Research," said a cool, modulated soprano. That would be Edwina Doyle, whom Rob remembered as the kind of secretary (*Whoops, now they're "associates,"* Rob reminded himself) you got when you met customers on a regular basis. Face a bit on the square side, but Ed Doyle fairly dripped smarts, had dynamite dimples, a shy smile, and a bod that . . . He realized he was smiling at the receiver instead of talking.

"Rob Tarrant in Prod Engineering. I need a face-to-face with Ethan; ten minutes, fifteen at most." Using Lodge's first name was the gentlest of reminders that Rob Tarrant and Hizzoner Lodge were on good personal terms.

"Hi, Mr. Tarrant. Um, company priority?"

He wished it were so. "Not yet, Ed, but it could be."

"His calendar's pretty jammed today. Monday morning good for you? Early is good—but you knew that."

Rob knew that. Tuesday through Friday, the Mahogany Row boys got their business done early, on priority, and often disappeared "into the plant" during the afternoons. If they showed up on golf courses in Palo Alto or South San Jose, it wasn't a lowly engineer's business. But Monday morning found many of the hotshots late, missing, or surly as Rottweilers. The fact that Ethan Lodge accepted appointments on Monday mornings suggested that he wasn't one of the hard-living types. Rob agreed on a Monday eight-thirty slot and Ed Doyle promised to call if someone canceled sooner.

And Rob submerged himself in work, adroit with the combination lock of his desk's file drawers, careful with the pages in his spiralbound work log. GenStan still required that personal computer logs be backed up with written entries because GenStan twice had suffered major glitches with the mainframe computer—failures which were absolutely, positively, impossible until they happened. As every production engineer had long known, pencil and paper beats a blank screen every time.

Rob was negotiating schedules on the phone with a Republic Steel man in Youngstown, Ohio, when his second phone line began to blink. He properly ignored it, producing a busy signal to the in-house caller. Within a minute his computer signaled that he had in-house e-mail; this, he could handle during his call.

Moments later he was tapping out a reply, then wrapping up his business in Youngstown. One edoyle@mkt had sent him an internal message:

Mr. Lodge has a no-show @ 10AM. Can you make it?

He could if he hurried.

CHAPTER 3

MANAGEMENT OFFICES, FAMILIARLY KNOWN AS MAHOGANY Row, took up the second floor of GenStan's showy executive building. Rob chose the nearest of two company bikes, in varying shades of green, from the rack outside and pedaled briskly toward Mahogany Row a quarter-mile away. Because the cafeteria and the tech library were unclassified areas in the same big structure near the main gate, he needed his badge only to trot upstairs toward Ethan Lodge's corner office.

Edwina Doyle made dimples for him as he stepped into the anteroom. "You must've found a bike," Ed said, turning away from her computer screen as he nodded, glancing down at a button that glowed on her telephone. "Himself knows you're coming; should be off the phone shortly."

Something about the tightness of her words, and the way she said "Himself," formed the warp and woof of a small flag that waved invisibly before her. Rob said, "Isn't this a good time, Ed?"

"I'm not having one, if that's what you mean." She gave a faint toss of her head toward the closed door. "When someone cancels on him it puts him in a fulminating snit, so the next few minutes get, um, interesting. He gets over it so you'll be okay. They call that 'mercurial,' I think."

Rob gave her a blinky wide-eyed look of bogus innocence. "And what do you call it?"

"You don't—want—to know," she said primly, but she was only half a dimple away from a smile now.

He brought the full sunburst out with, "Well, if I have to dance away from his left jab, at least I'll know it's not personal."

"You do a mean samba, I'll hand you that."

"That's right," he said, after a moment's confusion; recalling it now, pointing a finger at her. It had been half a year since the party when he'd danced exactly one number with Ed Doyle, and paid for it later.

"How soon they forget—whoops, he's through," she said, and toggled her speaker to announce Rob.

IF ETHAN LODGE WAS SIMMERING, HE HID IT BEAUTIFULLY, standing to welcome Rob, motioning him to one of the Danish chairs that were several cuts above company standard. As the two men exchanged the usual inquiries about health, Rob wondered where a man went to be trained into this kind of easy grace, displayed even to underlings. It wasn't all on the surface; when you had the attention of Ethan Lodge, you had it all. It was a quality that Rob wished he knew how to cultivate.

"I came to you because I have an idea," said Rob when the Marketing man had sat back in his burnished Eames. He continued, unrolling the sketches from his inside coat pocket. "Actually, it's a working demo. I think if GenStan wants to run with it, well, it could make millions; maybe thousands, who knows, even pennies may be involved."

Maybe it was exactly the right tack to take, or maybe Lodge was just in a mood to relax and have a laugh. The Marketing man smoothed out the sketches, placed a Steuben paperweight on one corner with perfectly manicured fingers. For some minutes he studied one page, then another, then the last, nodding as Rob described how a mantis might be used. Finally: "You'd put a chemchip in this?"

"I already have a reject chip at home for a proof-of-principle demo, and it's rigid enough to double as a chassis. It works."

"Of course they do," Lodge smiled.

"No, I mean, it flies. It could be mass-produced, and it could be a must on every farm and orchard, and maybe every pollution monitor team, in the country. Notice the dimensions?"

Lodge considered for a moment before saying, very slowly, "But this would fit in here." He indicated the carved humidor, flanked by pipes: briars, honey-tinted Meerschaums, and even a corncob, on his satiny rosewood desk.

Nice touch. That corncob saves him from raw elitism, thought the engineer.

Almost coyly, Lodge cocked his head and added, "You're certain you can do this?"

"I'm certain I had to get it down from a tree," Rob grinned. "I can make it fly around inside a good-sized conference room while some dude's telling me it can't work. Haven't got the controls adjusted, but that's just . . ."

He fell silent because Lodge was studying him closely, silently, rolling the sketches and handing them back. Lodge spoke only after Rob pocketed his sketches. And he spoke as if talking to himself. "Why me?"

"I know you," Rob said, displaying his palms. "I haven't told anybody in Prod Engineering because frankly, there are too many idea thieves around; they get known for that. You're not. And you'd know whether GenStan might be interested in marketing the system. Jesus, Ethan, *you're* Marketing!"

The manager put up a hand as if to quell an expected outburst. "And I could get the ears of some R&D people down the hall for you. Are we on the same page?"

"Right, sure. You can be the guy who realized its full potential," Rob said, realizing too late that it sounded like exactly what it was: an offer to share credit; a bribe.

Lodge's smile was gentle, understanding. And perhaps tainted with faint regret. "Wouldn't dream of stealing your thunder, Rob, even if I thought it would be of interest down the hall."

"You mean it wouldn't?"

A long judicious pause. "If GenStan were aiming toward flight systems, it might. One day, it might still. I'm not at liberty to explain in detail, but for the immediate future I'm afraid your mechanical hummingbird isn't the direction the company is taking. I'm sorry, I really am."

There was too much firmness in that managerial headshake, and Rob knew a feeling all too familiar to him, as if all of his usual optimism were leaking out onto the carpet. Rob shrugged and blurted out what he was thinking: "Still, as you say, someday it might be useful. Wouldn't hurt to start a patent application. We could have Tech Pub take a couple of photos. Can't hurt."

"I'd have no objection," said Lodge, after a moment of reflection, as though his endorsement were needed. A few engineers made a hobby of patent applications, shotgunning ideas in the hope that all that paperwork amounted to brownie points. "In point of fact, Rob, I feel bad about this because a patent application is often another way to pigeonhole a good idea. It's just possible that I could get McAdams in R&D interested if he saw a working model. If he shows no interest, there's plenty of time for a disclosure afterward. When were you thinking of bringing this demonstrator model to the plant?"

Rob's spirit-ignited again. "Um, will next Monday be too soon?"

"Tuesday morning would be much better. Give you time to perfect it. Even if it's not debugged, Mac will want to see the real thing and if we disappoint him the first time—well, you know how he is."

Rob *didn't* know how McAdams was, but that's one of the things managers were for, knowing when and how to finesse colleagues. "Tuesday's fine; sooner, the better." He caught the manager's quick glance at his Rolex; stood up, thrust his hand across the expanse of rosewood. "Hey, I've got a report to massage and I've taken enough of your time. With luck, we can both be glad you bothered."

"Hold that thought until Tuesday morning," said Lodge, smiling as he reached for a folder of in-house memos. Above a certain level, GenStan's managers still made do with real paper. And perhaps a computer screen was low-caste; until now, Rob had never thought about it.

SOMEONE HAD TAKEN THE BIKE: FIRST COME, FIRST SERVED. Another two-wheeler was locked to the stand with a green combination lock. Only couriers with priority deliveries were issued those locks for a given task, another of GenStan's ways to assure that management was always first served.

Rob enjoyed the sunny walk back to his workplace and spent the balance of the day on his progress report. Because fresh details of his mantis design kept sneaking up on him and clamoring for attention, that report wasn't his best work. He kept flashing on brief scenarios in which his tiny flying mite performed additional tasks for the Research and Development man. If he could entice McAdams outside, Rob would show how a mantis resisted wayward breezes, climbing until it was virtually invisible over the parking lot.

Those scenarios were just wishful thinking, though, and he knew it. Far more important for a proof-of-principle demo was the tried and true engineering principle called "KISS": "Keep it simple, stupid!" He would bring extra lithium batteries, fully charged, and a spare propeller. Those damned little batteries were worth their weight in precious metal, but the investment might bring a handsome reward. Before he left work that afternoon, Rob had penciled a list of details to be covered before Tuesday.

SATURDAY, THE MANTIS FLEW UNDER RADIO CONTROL—BUT IT wouldn't fly in a circle small enough for a conference room. Gus patiently waited while Rob adjusted his gossamer mite, modifying its wings, enlarging its rudder. They sent Kenny off for Safeway sandwiches in clear plastic containers, and found that Rob could carry the mantis and its spare bits in a coat pocket, protected by one of those throwaway containers. On Sunday they flew it around that avocado tree of Gus's, the older man kibitzing because Rob had never been very adroit with an RC transmitter.

And Monday, Rob Tarrant was all but useless in his usual work, thinking of the following day and the triumph he expected. He worked late to atone for it, keeping his expectations to himself, relentlessly cheerful at first when Corrine bitched about his tardiness.

"Sorry, honey, but there are times when I must render unto Caesar," he said, sliding into his chair at the dinner table. It was set for one, Corrine and Kenny having eaten on time.

"You could've called," she said shortly, his plate of reheated pasta clattering as she served it.

"I did. Isn't the messenger working?"

"I didn't check it," she said—and added, "Don't," as he patted her rump. "It's not a good example for a teenager," she explained.

As if Kenny isn't a mile away, he thought. *Say what you mean, Corrie. Say you're pissed about nothing much, certainly nothing I could avoid, and a love tap makes it worse—and if I know that's one of your little eccentricities, why the hell do I do it?*

She left him to eat alone and to silently answer his own question. He still did such things because, fifteen and ten and perhaps as recently as five years ago, they had served as signals of affection, received with a smile and sometimes a wink: *I'm okay, you're okay,* like as not to be followed later by an innocent smooch behind Kenny's back and later still by a loving, lustful tussle in their California king-sized bed.

But that was before Corrine judged her husband by his peers and the wives of peers; and those days had begun to fade like a summer sunset not long after Corrine met Deirdre Lodge, once described by another engineer's wife after three martinis as "the trophy that walks like a woman." The corporate pecking order, Rob decided, seemed much the same everywhere.

He entertained a vagrant wish, and not for the first time, that he had gone on to grad school and from there to an academic life. Rob still believed the collegial myth that the life of a professor was free of petty politics and old-boy networks. He had applied three times in ten years for graduate engineering courses, which GenStan occasionally permitted a favored employee at the company's expense, but by now it was clear that you had to be on the corporate fast track to get those courses. Well, a good demonstration of his mantis might be the magic wand that waved him onto the fast track.

Buoyed by this thought, Rob deposited his dinnerware in the dishwasher and changed into his oldest sweats, which bore the Halloween-orange–and–black colors of Oregon State University. A three-mile run twice a week wasn't enough to stay in shape, but as a reminder that he *wasn't* in shape, it never failed. Usually it helped him sleep later, though this time, impatient for the morning, he lay awake for an hour.

Tuesday morning, Rob had to forgo breakfast because he had changed ties half a dozen times. He wondered which tie Ethan Lodge would choose. He wondered whether standing in a dither before a mirror was going to make him late. Above all, he wondered why GenStan or any other industrial firm would insist that one sure mark of professionalism was that a man must wear a silk rope dangling from his throat, when he might later be inspecting enormous machines that were constantly waiting to snatch that rope and make him truly a part of the machinery.

Lockheed, according to rumor, had dropped the requirement after an engineer, his own perspiration ruining a blueprint when the air-conditioning failed, removed his tie one breathless summer afternoon. "Ties will be worn," he was told.

The engineer returned the following day wearing a determined look—and a red tie and a green tie, one over the other.

On inquiry, he repeated the dictum. " 'Ties,' plural," said he. "I'm the only son of a bitch in this outfit who's properly in uniform." Told that his attire was perhaps drawing a tad more notice than was absolutely necessary, he thought it over; perhaps more notice was exactly what "Ties will be worn" needed.

During the following weeks he wore a foulard a foot wide, with a Warhol print of such horrendous hues that it could not be viewed without sunglasses. He tied a Windsor knot so near another tie's broad end that the tail pendulum'ed to his knees—aided by a small fishing weight. He fabricated a tie of honest-to-God fur that made it seem he was smuggling a raccoon into the office. He got someone to turn a tie around so that it hung down his back. And more: He wore ties with such beatific panache, such creative abandon, that staff scientists made special trips to marvel at this inspired lunatic.

And always the sartorial rebel stayed within the letter of Lockheed's antiquated, counterproductive dress code. One scientist made book on whether and when this engineer would take up the matter of "sport jackets." Shooting jackets, jeans jackets, and sequined coats of rock stars were all undeniably sporty.

Management, it was said, hoped the engineer would run out of ideas and subside. Perhaps he did. The day he wore *two dozen* bow ties clipped here and there on his suit coat—one of them with blinking lights—the engineer resigned. During his exit interview he assured them, "Groucho was right. I wouldn't work for weenies who would put up with what you deserve."

Lockheed, they say, no longer hews to that dress code, but GenStan was made of sterner stuff, and Rob, of more amiable stuff. Wearing a tie of subdued earth tones, he hurried from the parking lot to his work station with the borrowed radio-control transmitter openly displayed under his arm, the mantis and its container in his pocket.

On occasion, GenStan made unannounced security checks, and this seemed to be one of those occasions. Standing next to the guard at the entrance to his building was a large gent with a piercing gaze and a special red badge, and employees had queued up to pass this bottleneck, moving slowly past the Security man, some holding their clip-on badges between thumb and forefinger for easier inspection. Rob, impatient to be about his business, followed suit.

Until Mr. Redbadge motioned him to one side. "Here it is," said Rob, waggling the badge clipped to his coat pocket.

"Would you mind showing me that thing," said Redbadge, indicating the transmitter under Rob's arm. It wasn't really a question.

"An RC transmitter," Rob explained. "Personal property. For models," he went on, feeling foolish under the scrutiny of others streaming past.

Redbadge knitted his brows. "What models would those be?"

"Oh Christ. A demo I'm showing. I really haven't got time for this, buddy," he added in exasperation, tugging the plastic container from his pocket. "*This* model. It isn't really a model of anything, it's—Whoa, careful!"

As Redbadge saw the mantis and its chemchip chassis inside

the clear plastic, his entire attitude changed. "What have we here?" He wrenched the packet from Rob, popped the cover off. "You'll tell me this is personal property, Mr. Tarrant?"

And with that, Redbadge took the chemchip between thumb and forefinger of one hand, ripping away the delicate wings and control links with his free hand. That's when Rob swung on him.

CHAPTER 4

AN HOUR LATER, ROB STOOD IN THE OFFICE OF GENSTAN'S DIrector of Security Services. The mediation was not going well. Seated near him was Ethan Lodge, facing the director who lazed behind his desk in a three-piece suit. "I do wish you'd sit down, Mr. Tarrant," said the director, whose framed endorsements included a law degree and a previous career with the FBI.

"Too wired," Rob growled, combing his hair with shaking fingers. He pointed to the shreds of his mantis that lay on the desk, the old transmitter lying nearby. "I've told you three times now, that chemchip is my property; I bought it two weeks ago with other stuff at the Surplus sale yard. There must've been a dozen more of 'em there at the time."

"My man had no reason to suspect that. It's a shocking lapse of business sense to have experimental hardware on what amounts to public sale. You can prove it?"

"I save receipts; I can probably find that one."

"Even granting your claim," said the Security head, "there's still the matter of assaulting one of my people. That's grounds for dismissal."

"It's just not done, Rob," Lodge said gently. "You know that. I understand how you feel, but there's such a thing as diplomacy."

Now Rob did sit down on the edge of a chair, his right leg bouncing as if to a metronome. "Sorry. You don't think about diplomacy when the product of weeks of work, on your own time and intended for the company, gets marmaladed by some thoughtless yahoo."

"Certainly *you* don't," Lodge shrugged, leaving a silently damning implication.

"*Not* a yahoo," said the director firmly. "Our man has a degree in police science and, not incidentally, martial-arts training. He'll be sporting a mouse under his eye tomorrow yet he tells me he only put you in a headlock. He could have put you in traction." He saw Rob stiffen, and raised a hand like a Hollywood Indian. "That's part of his job, Mr. Tarrant. It is not part of your job to discipline him. At the very least, this will go in your file as a Class A reprimand. Men have been escorted off the premises for less. Permanently." He seemed to take pleasure in saying it.

"I would hope not, in this case. You have my word that Mr. Tarrant is not a scofflaw or—ordinarily—a hothead," Lodge put in. "Actually, Robert Tarrant is not in my branch and I may be stepping on some toes by responding in this matter, but I can see why he asked that I be consulted. I feel a certain culpability here," he said, with a look toward Rob that added, *You poor lamebrain.*

"I can grant mitigating circumstances, I suppose," said the security head. He glanced quickly back to Rob, his gaze darkening. "But your next brush with security at GenStan will be your last, Mr. Tarrant. I promise you that." He turned his attention to the manager again. "Take him away and have a talk with him, Ethan, before I change my mind."

Rob stood, feeling Lodge's gentle grip on his arm, and was almost to the doorway when he wheeled. "Just a minute. All that stuff is still mine."

"You have a lot of chutzpah," said the security head, not smiling, handing over the transmitter and the container with its savaged contents.

"You had a lot of my property," said Rob. Most of it belonged to Gus, of course, but why bother to explain? He felt extra pressure from Lodge's grip and walked out.

Moments later, Rob was being steered toward the company cafeteria, jokingly called "the Choke and Chuck," though its fare was in fact better than average. "You didn't cover yourself with glory or respectability on your exit back there," Lodge remarked as they decanted coffee into porcelain cups. "Rule number umpteen: Always leave them on a cheerful note."

"Thanks for the help," Rob said. "I'll never be a politician."

"You were almost unemployed; perhaps unemployable," Lodge said. That was very close to an admission that corporations shared blacklists. Then, with a sudden change of tone that implied, *Let's think nicer thoughts*: "So! How long would it take you to produce another of those things? I confess, it doesn't look like something that could fly. Not that I'd want to bring this up to McAdams again anytime soon," he added quickly, his smile an apology.

Rob placed the container between them, stirring Equal into his coffee, frowning as he thought. "A few weeks," he said at length. "Below a certain point, the smaller these things are, the longer it takes to craft them by hand. Now, with mass production—," he said.

Lodge chuckled. "Spare me, I beg you. Let me take your word that they could be stamped out like cookies. I should think it would require respectable lead time to develop the methods?"

There was that word again, "respectable"—one of Lodge's favorites. "No doubt," Rob said. "Miniaturization is a field that's growing in grad schools. I don't know about San Jose State, but at Stratford for sure," he added, naming a prestigious school not far from San Francisco. "There must be someone in GenStan who's had the coursework."

Another brief silence as Ethan Lodge sipped, the picture of elegance. As the cup left his lips: "You should've applied for those courses."

"I did, and I named Stratford. Several times." Rob's shrug said the rest.

At that point, Lodge asked how the Tarrant boy was doing; obviously he had forgotten Kenny's name. Rob supplied it, and recounted the tale of "Porsche with Naked Lady," to show that Kenny was not yet a sophisticate, and presently the two men separated—on a cheerful note.

IF NOT FOR ETHAN LODGE, ROB SAID TO GUS AS HE MOURNfully picked through the debris that had once been his mantis, the Tarrant household would be without an income.

"But you pasted the fucker a good one, didja?"

"Oh yeah, but only because I wasn't thinking and he wasn't looking for it," Rob admitted. The two of them disassembled linkages, placed batteries aside, tested the servos and agreed that another mantis could be built from what was left. The next time he brought one to GenStan, said Rob, he'd get a permit. Building another mantis of the same design shouldn't take quite as long as the first; two weeks at most.

Had Rob been fully alert to his intuition, it might have suggested unseen forces at work a few evenings later, when Corrine returned from planning a bake sale with Deirdre Lodge. "Somehow I don't see milady greasing a cake pan," Rob remarked.

"She doesn't have to," said Corrine, "these fund-raisers are—by the way, she passed on something nice about you."

"You're kidding."

"Ethan evidently thinks you're 'a man of vision.' That's what Deirdre said he said: 'a man of vision.' "

"It's good somebody noticed." He had said nothing about the trouble at GenStan. Corrine would have asked for details, and then lectured him about what he should have done instead of whatever he did. The most aggravating thing about Corrine's lectures was that she was sometimes correct. No, that was only the second-most-aggravating thing; the *most* aggravating thing was that since entering her Deirdre era, Corrine displayed such total confidence that she was *always* perfectly correct.

DESPITE THE EVIDENCE THAT HE'D MADE A FAVORABLE IMpression on Lodge, no little flag waved in Rob's mind. Accordingly, he was first nonplussed and then elated the following day while completing the cost analysis of a product improvement with Guy Halloran. "We could have a pilot batch running by early fall," Rob said at last.

"Who d'you think I should put on it?" Halloran asked.

"Uh . . . why not me?"

Halloran blinked. "Not if you're a college boy again," he

said, and smiled when he saw Rob's confusion. "You haven't seen it yet, have you?"

Rob shook his head, mystified.

"Your application, Tarrant. The grad courses you wanted?" He grinned; snapped his fingers twice before Rob's silent gaze. "Wake up. You got approved, man. I saw the status-change request. . . . Ah—you did want me to approve it, I assume."

"Hell, yes," Rob blurted, a sudden awareness flooding him. He had made no new application, but hadn't Ethan Lodge said he was a man of vision? Applications, like medals, could be made from above. Someone else had made this one, and from far above, because it had been approved at higher levels. The employee's section head's approval was by far the least important, and therefore last to be sought. Guy Halloran would have needed a damn good reason to refuse to sign.

Rob wasn't worth a lick to GenStan for the balance of the day. Ostensibly he was checking the impact on his section of his working half-days; in truth, he was staring at walls and making guesses. Ethan Lodge, as the force behind this thing, was hardly a guess at all. Rob's own department head had probably seen upper-level signatures and signed with reluctance; his attitude on half-time employment was implicit in his oft-quoted growl, "We need all the engineers we can get." At the branch-manager level, it probably wasn't too hard for Lodge to jolly another company bureaucrat into a favor, a quid pro quo of some sort.

In any case, it would be no skin off Ethan Lodge's back, so long as Robert Tarrant made good in his studies. Rob had been a strong B student, but that had been fifteen years ago and by now, a lot of his undergrad stuff was little more than a warren of dusty crevices in his memory. If he was going to make the summer quarter, he'd have to start brushing up, scrubbing up, frantically *polishing* up those near-forgotten skills they would expect at Stratford. He hadn't doubted for a moment that the application had been to Stratford, until the company mail carrier dropped a "brownie," a sturdy tan company envelope, at his desk in late afternoon. He had a moment of prickly-heat fear then: *What if the application is to some lesser university?*

It wasn't to anyplace less. The form specified Stratford, a master's-degree program, and an emphasis on mass-production methods. It wasn't exactly what Rob would have specified, but in GenStan's terms it was more congenial than he had any right to expect. And it wasn't a one-year permission on his own expense. It was the nearest to a full ride GenStan offered, all expenses paid for a full two years at three-quarters pay, on extended leave. He wouldn't be working half-days; though still employed, he wouldn't be working at GenStan at all for a full two years.

It was the fast track.

Rob found his vision dimming; wiped at one eye with a guilty glance toward his co-workers. He resisted the impulse to call Corrine, thinking how sweet the moment would be, what joy they could share, when he broke the news to his wife face-to-face.

SHE KNEW BEFORE HE TOLD HER; HAD PROBABLY KNOWN BE-fore he did, thanks to the rumor mill that churned out bulletins among GenStan's upper crust. "You can't accept it, of course," she said, facing him in the living room, fists on her hips instead of taking his hands.

He pulled his tie off to have something to do with his empty hands. "What's wrong with you, Corrie? You used to piss and moan worse than I did when my applications didn't go through. Now, when I get a full ride—"

"A full ride off the main track for two years? At less than full pay? I'm not so naive now, and I know how these things work," she said tartly.

You know whatever Deirdre tells you, and the woman is giddy as Woody Woodpecker, he thought. "It was probably Ethan Lodge who got me the chance," he reminded her.

"I know it was," said Corrine. "And Deirdre has seen these things happen, and as soon as she heard about it she tried her best for us, tried to tell him you'd be a forgotten man by the time you graduated. But Ethan's mind was made up," she said.

For the second time in one day, Rob was thunderstruck. "You tried to get someone to bump me out of a graduate program?"

"I did nothing of the sort. It was all done before I heard about it," said Corrine, "but it's not too late for you to—"

"I'm going to Stratford, Corrie," he said, and removed his coat with such a flourish that she took a step backward. His gaze was disbelieving. "Jesus Christ, did you think I was going to slap you? It's that goddamn Barbie doll, Deirdre Lodge, I want to slap, but I tell you what: I won't interfere with your friendships if you won't get in the way of my career.

"I know it won't be easy—my God, Corrie, for the next two years I'll be flailing in textbooks, competing against bright young guys who still remember things I've forgotten! Yes, we may have to scrimp and save for a while, but it won't be forever. Lodge is offering me a leg up the ladder."

"So he thinks," said Corrine.

"Right. And just about anybody else in this hemisphere would think the same." More calmly now: "Even if I didn't want it, Corrie, ask yourself what would happen if I turned it down."

The shift in her expression said she hadn't thought about that. After a moment she said, "You'd still be drawing the same pay, at least."

He nodded. "Forever. Adjusted for inflation. I don't think you want that, Corrie. I sure as hell don't."

"I don't want a college kid for a husband, either," she said.

He looked long and steadily at his wife of fifteen years. "But that's what I'll be. Maybe you'd rather I moved into some little apartment so the midnight oil won't keep you awake."

"Maybe nothing," she spat. "Or would you rather take the roof away from over your son's head?"

When she glanced toward the living room, he looked, too, and saw for the first time that Kenny had been quietly reading in there, hearing every word. Corrine had known. It would have been so easy to postpone what she knew would be an ugly confrontation. "You are really a piece of work, Corrine.

No, I wouldn't do that to either of you. And you think a one-
parent household would be better for him?"

"Much better, for the time being." When she put her chin
up like that, nothing less than 9.7 on the Richter scale would
shake her from a position.

CHAPTER 5

ETHAN LODGE HAD NEVER EXPECTED THAT HIS ISRAELI SPY-master would actually demand any action of him beyond the reports for which he had been so well paid, for so many years. From time to time, Ethan had played what-if games with himself, and the most common of them was, *What if they insist I commit some kind of real spying, or even sabotage?* A realist up to a point, he admitted that his response would depend on the demand.

The point at which Ethan slipped below the waves of reality, to choke on wishful thinking as abysmal as that of some ordinary American president, was in his definition of *spy*. To Ethan, a spy was not a successful executive whose Christian idealist college roomie later had emigrated to Tel Aviv but kept up auld acquaintance. A spy was not a man persuaded to supplement his taxable income with untaxable cash while he provided harmless little technical news items to stalwarts of a friendly nation, and bought yuppie roadsters for a wife who was boring even in bed.

No, a spy was a swarthy little fellow wearing an overcoat of dreadful fit, with shifty eyes, a sloppy Windsor knot, and a tiny camera, who conspired with his nation's enemies and informed on courageous men destined for some foreign torture chamber. The only similarity, in Ethan's mind, was that both sorts of men made regular contact with someone known in the trade as a "handler." Ethan was not even familiar with the fate of Jonathan Pollard, convicted years earlier of spying for our friends the Israelis.

Until the past week it had not occurred to Ethan that sticking his finger into another man's life and stirring briskly might create a whirlpool of unintended consequences to the victim,

including separation from the man's family and, in the case
of Rob Tarrant, a small domestic torture chamber called an
"efficiency apartment." Now it was becoming harder for
Ethan to keep his trouser cuffs above the grime of the "spy"
label—since the very day he had passed on the information
that a low-level GenStan engineer would soon be offering an
operating, sensor-equipped micro-UAV to the company.

Ordinarily, Ethan's handler made contact on a monthly basis, but with a matter this timely, the meetings became a flurry.
The two usually made contact during happy hour because
Ethan Lodge had a democratic habit of downing a drink or so
in one of a dozen trendy bars before driving home to Los Altos
Hills. Often he met colleagues for that drink; just as often, he
passed an amiable half hour with strangers. On this evening,
by prearrangement, he would meet his handler in Palo Alto at
one of the bars that wasn't trendy enough for his colleagues.

Palo Alto is really too small to be so many towns: site of a
major university, ringed by think tanks, home to the demirich
and to quiet retired couples, adjacent to a ghetto where
"honky" was the mildest greeting an Ethan Lodge could expect. Ethan parked his Taurus in plain sight near a decent El
Camino waterhole and, on entering, immediately made eye
contact with his handler, who already had a booth. Ethan
looked around, seeing no empty booths, and asked charmingly
if he might take the opposite seat. There was, of course, no
objection.

Ethan got his order, though he had to explain it to the waitress. "I always wonder why you swill those things," said the
handler.

"A Cin-Cin? Because it's half dry vermouth and half sweet,
looks like a Manhattan, and I can toss off several with a clear
head," said Ethan. "It's actually a woman's drink. I'd think
you would appreciate my choice; if I weren't meeting you I'd
be having a martini."

A shrug. "I do appreciate it; for that matter, you might
consider laying off booze completely until the shit settles in
this little aquarium. How's our fish?"

"Floundering for the past week," said Ethan. "He's not taking his separation well, but as soon as the summer quarter at Stratford begins he'll be too busy to think about it." A judicious sip, a judicious nod. "He's already boning up on his math; I think he'll be fine in a month. I've dropped in on him a couple of times."

"Twice might be once too many. You're not holding his hand too much?" The Israeli handler essayed a faint smile. "You're a handler of sorts yourself now, and believe me, it's not easy."

"Tell me about it," Ethan said wryly. "I advanced him some cash, with the proviso that I'd deny it if anyone asked. Would you believe, he insisted it was at six percent interest?"

"Don't drop in on him so often. He could wonder why. Besides, he needs to feel he's getting on with his life without too much help. And the busier he is, the less he'll think about the damned micro-UAV toys."

Ethan nodded, uneasy with all this micromanagement, and upended his Cin-Cin. "Dealing with people is what I do, Mike," he said. "Let me do it."

"Brings up another point. I mention it only because you may not always know everything about the man you're dealing with. If we should ever meet in some other context, then, and only then, will you have the need to be curious. That isn't the same as a need to know. Swallow that curiosity. We're strangers. That's all I intend to say about it."

Ethan blinked, then nodded. He had taken cryptic orders from Mike before, and knew better than to demand more.

After a few more exchanges, they agreed on the next meeting—something they usually did before anything else—and Mike ended their session with their terminal code phrase: "Let's have no more about that"—which, to casual ears, justified Ethan's abrupt departure.

On his way home, Ethan drove past the dreary apartment complex in Sunnyvale where Tarrant had moved a week before. Its lights were on but Ethan didn't stop. In truth, he fought with faint pangs of guilt unfamiliar to him. Well, that was just part of the big game; he would deal with it. In two years Tarrant would be past this rough spot, once again dissolved into GenStan, probably enthused over some new idea completely divorced from micro-UAVs, possibly divorced from the self-absorbed Corrine. It was all for the best, as some hero of the classics had once said. Especially for the Israelis, who obviously did not want any competition in the field of micro-UAVs.

Mike—not the handler's true name, of course—had said very little about that, though Ethan Lodge would have been a total fool to miss the implications. Israel depended crucially on American aid, both financially and technically, so any field in which the Israelis honed a cutting edge of their own became doubly crucial. If they needed some lower-echelon American techie on ice for two years, the technology in question was probably being developed in some Tel Aviv lab.

During the past week, without mentioning his curiosity to his handler, Ethan had spent a few hours researching the open literature on UAVs. Evidently, after begging well-developed Northrop UAVs from the U.S., the Israelis had improved them before developing their own. By now, the U.S. Navy and Marine Corps both operated Israeli-developed UAVs. Though pilotless, the little aircraft are almost large enough to carry a human as cargo.

Ethan vaguely recalled a recent news piece describing the surveillance and assassination of two Hamas guerrillas by Israel. The surveillance had been done by means of small Israeli UAVs loitering over the guerrillas, even though one of the miniature aircraft had crashed nearby during surveillance. The smaller the robotic aircraft, the less hue and cry would result from such accidental crashes.

Ethan smiled to himself. From what he'd seen of Tarrant's insectlike creation, a hundred of those could crash on a Hamas terrorist's roof without rattling a teacup below. Given a year or so of further development by aerospace labs in the Negev Desert, Israel could have micro-UAV technology worth trading to its American friends—infinitely better than having to beg, borrow, and steal it. *We profit, Israel profits.* I *profit. Even Rob Tarrant will profit*, Ethan thought comfortably as he steered the Taurus up the driveway that snaked through an acre of manicured lawn.

IF DEIRDRE GAVE ANY THOUGHT AT ALL TO ETHAN'S UNUSUAL interest in the Tarrant family, it was probably delight to find him interested in her chatter. Corrie Tarrant, she said, now had more time to handle worrisome details of Deirdre's social life. Deirdre had given the woman a few of her castoff designer outfits, and she had blossomed with fresh cheer, no longer so much the frumpy engineer's Frau. Depressed? Not at all, said Deirdre, though Corrie did seem irked after brief confrontations with Rob when he'd dropped by his home to borrow linens, boxes of his books, and an old pot or two. In Deirdre's opinion, the change in Corrie was all for the good. It was a pleasure to see the pretty little thing getting on with life—and by implication, Deirdre's life.

"I do hope you can avoid too much fraternizing," was the nearest thing to restraint that Ethan voiced as he prepared his first martini. "It's one thing to show a little Christian charity, but, ah, socially—"

"What a quaint idea," Deirdre said, striking a pose. "Don't be tiresome, Ethan. Do you think I'm an imbecile?"

And her husband admired the jut of her hip, the length of her calf, the tilt of her patrician smile, and wisely avoided the least hint of a truthful reply.

It was an easy matter for Ethan to keep tabs on Rob Tarrant, simply by putting himself on the list of those in management who were interested in Personnel records of certain lower-echelon employees. Ethan gave himself a silent pat on the back for just happening to mention, to Rob's division manager, that GenStan might ensure the future loyalty of this Tarrant fellow with a little bump in the pay grade. It almost made up for the reduction Tarrant would suffer while on extended leave.

Not a status change or an absence day could occur without the nod from Personnel, and Ethan knew not only what Tarrant's reduction in salary would be, to the penny, but also the date when Tarrant would begin his extended leave. He knew before Tarrant himself knew it. Because universities kept their own schedules, and because Stratford was encouraging Rob Tarrant almost daily with signs that its graduate engineering faculty was impressed, Ethan carefully avoided any direct inquiries to the university.

After two more weeks, Rob Tarrant would begin his extended leave. It seemed certain that he had been shunted safely onto a track that would keep him too busy to think about what Mike had called "those damned micro-UAV toys."

This being the case, Ethan Lodge had no warning that Stratford University would cancel Tarrant's enrollment one day before its summer quarter began.

CHAPTER 6

"THE WORD THEY USED WAS 'DEFERRED,' LAKE," ROB HUSKED into the phone. If anyone could help him understand this bolt of summer lightning, it would be his old friend Lake Bowers, now an associate professor in San Luis Obispo two hundred miles away. Cal Poly was a good school, but it wasn't the class act of a Stratford. Rob's voice was choked with suppressed emotion. "They can't do that on twenty-four hours' notice!"

An old hand at the games academia plays, Bowers knew better. "They're not state-supported as we are here, Rob. And they're everybody's choice, they can do almost any damn thing they like, but they usually give reasons."

"Not in the letter," Rob said, staring at the single folded sheet of paper that shook in his hand. "But I called Dr. Jonas, thinking it was a mistake, and he gave me the oddest runaround I ever heard."

Bowers fell silent for a moment. Then, with a truncated chuckle: "Are you going to tell me or do I get to guess?"

"Oh. They thought they'd have twenty openings in the grad program. Overnight, at the last minute, it was collapsed to five."

"It happens. The regents probably gave some engineering money to Humanities, Business School, something like that. But with GenStan behind you, I'd think you could've made it over the bar." Bowers, six foot six, had jumped his height at Oregon State.

"There's more. This year, two black students can fill any one available slot."

"Ouch. Well, there aren't that many African-American engineering students applying at the graduate level. That might account for, oh, say a couple of slots; maybe more at Stratford, though. In any case, there's a backlash to that. I don't think they'll be doing it for many more years."

"Terrific," Rob went on, "and meanwhile, I can fucking well wait! Only, I probably can't. And one more little item: Jonas said they're giving special attention to 'qualified Third World students.' "

"An idea whose time never came; I know that old story, Rob. Stratford expects its advanced graduates to go back to Nigeria and Paraguay, and help turn their countries into little copies of this one. 'The infection theory,' we call it. Sounds great, but you can see the flaw. I see it all the time."

"Lay it on me, then, Lake, I could use a little clarification. Hell, and here I am with an armload of expensive new texts."

"The flaw is, your Paraguayan hotshot doesn't *intend* to take his advanced degree back home, whatever he may say now. If he has the clout to get here, he can probably find a way to stay. But Rob"—and now Bowers's tone became more dulcet, the voice of a patient academic—"it wasn't a refusal. They're telling you to wait a year. I hate to say this, but it's probably worth it, imagewise."

"This is a narrow time window at GenStan, pal, and if it shuts now it might never open again. Jesus, I can't tell you how this is gonna play at home. Corrine will . . . Never mind, I've already told you about that, and you're free to imagine the rest."

"Your problem with Stratford," said Bowers, "is that while you had people outside pushing you in, you didn't have an uncle on the faculty, so to speak, *pulling* you in. State school or private school, on the grad level it's hell when you're nobody's baby. Orphans don't get to read the fine print, they have to infer it."

"It shouldn't work like that, goddamnit!" The thump of Rob's fist on the desk was audible through the receiver.

"But it always has. And if you're not molded by that uncle, you'd better let him think you are. It's ego transference; it's cronyism; it's horseshit. In a word, it's academia."

"So I'm pretty much out of options," Rob said.

"Boy, are you slow. You have an option," said Bowers, but gently, gently. When Rob did not reply, he added, "Cal Poly offers some pretty decent master's programs."

"It's gotta be too late, Unc."

"Our timetable isn't joined to Stratford's at the hip, I'll have you know," said Bowers, with detectable pride. "I imagine, if you happened to know somebody here, and kissed his backside just right—and got a transcript and so forth down here post-haste, ol' Uncle Lake just might even get you in late. Best if you come down here and try to look bright of eye and bushy of tail while I tell lies about what a good student you were."

"—who let you crib off his paper in Organic Chem," Rob demanded.

"I forget," Bowers lied. "Anyway, as I recall, that was the blind leading the blind. So how about it? You might let your company know what you're doing, and I can't absolutely swear I can swing it this summer, but call it ninety percent likely . . . okay, eighty-five. You have about ten days."

Rob ran a scenario through his head, fast-forward. "It'd be better if I got the full, no-bullshit acceptance from you guys before I broke the news at GenStan. Even then they might not—"

"Are you a half-miler or a pussy?" asked Bowers, abruptly recalling their college days: an old challenge, a goad for reaching down into your reserves.

"I'd be hours away from my kid, and my wheels are the old Bronco Corrine won't drive. It'd mean finding another apartment down your way—"

Lake Bowers seemed prepared to steamroll over any objections, and interrupted again. "Hey, we can put you up in the spare room for a month or two. Come on, Rob, it's time to get down in your starting blocks. Or not; I'm only trying to help."

"I know, and it's a wonderful offer. Look, give me a few days—I need to feel out the family, see how they'll receive this. Especially Kenny."

Bowers cautioned his friend against too much delay, but agreed that Rob would have to work out his own priorities.

When Rob fumbled the phone into its cradle, he was staring at his desk calendar and feeling less like pulling his hair out in frustration.

Most men might have told themselves that kids are resilient, and would let a thirteen-year-old roll with whatever punches life delivered. Rob was not among that throng. He would try to explain these profound changes to Kenny in ways that the boy could accept, and only then would he break it to Corrine. *Break* might be the operative word; Corrine was not one to accept changes she didn't initiate. GenStan? He would take his case to them—starting with Ethan Lodge—if and when all else was decided.

Rob did not know when he first thought of fly-fishing with Kenny for a few days. The idea coalesced from his awareness that he needed some quality time with his son, a few days alone, uncomplicated by freeways and TV and cell phones. He needed to talk things out with the boy in an open, timeless environment, down to basics, with no need to worry about who might overhear them. Damn it, they needed to pack into the Sky Lakes of southern Oregon!

SETTING IT UP WAS SIMPLER THAN HE THOUGHT. HE SAID NOTH-ing to Corrine about the Cal Poly option, and Corrine left it to Kenny to decide whether he wanted to lie on sharp rocks and slap mosquitoes for several days. To her estranged husband she waved her take-no-prisoners flag, pointedly leaving the house before Rob arrived to dust off his backpacking gear from the garage.

Kenny's mood was buoyant, and no wonder: The day before, he had sailed through his finals to pass into the eighth grade. That meant ten dollars for each A, five for every B, and a crisp fifty from his grandfather for making the honor roll.

Rob hadn't meant to be mysterious in his choice of fishing locations, but Kenny reacted to the fly-fishing proposal with the kind of excitement that seemed to call for surprise. Corrine was not a backpacker, and had no desire to see Oregon and even less desire to be seen in his ancient Bronco which he'd had for twenty years.

Hardly an ideal vehicle for city driving, the Bronco was built for hard times: half pickup, half small station wagon, ugly as a full spittoon, and lucky to get ten highway miles per gallon. Bronco devotees described it as "a tank that climbs trees." It needed an auxiliary fuel tank to get far from a service station, and with its outlandish suspension underpinnings, it weighed as much as some Cadillacs. But it would run until the blast of Gabriel, and Rob Tarrant blessed his earlier decision not to sell it.

Kenny viewed the Bronco as a punishing ride to rewarding places, but he knew Oregon only from stories Rob had told about his undergraduate days. Asked whether they would head beyond Fresno and east into the Sierra, Rob only winked and said, "You'll see." It would be slow going in the sturdy old Bronco, but eight hours would carry them up Interstate 5 to Medford, Oregon, and after that their windshield view would be full of very large rocks with names like Grizzly Peak and Mount McLoughlin.

It was nearly dusk before they finished stuffing their backpacks. Kenny's small pack had been bought when he was a third-grader and Rob, sighing, watched marshmallows, pretzels, and chocolate-chip cookie dough disappear into it without comment. Rob's stained blue Himalaya pack weighed in at only forty pounds with the fly rods stowed in aluminum tubes, because they would not carry a tent.

Gus had borrowed Rob's dry flies and camp saw during a previous summer, so his bungalow was their last stop before the freeways. "I would've asked you along," Rob told his father-in-law as they searched out the little cloth wallets full of hand-tied dry flies, "but it used to be a pretty rough hike." That wasn't his primary reason, but Rob loved the old man too much to say, *Three would be a crowd*.

" 'Fraid I'd show you up," said Gus, taking the Sierra range as a given. "If you're heading up around Devil's Postpile, you better check the snow line."

"Not going that high this early." Rob's glance told him Kenny was off checking batteries for his favorite techie toy: the night-vision monocular Gus had given him for Christmas.

He lowered his voice. "And he's never seen Sky Lakes, which aren't all that high. I want to make it special."

Gus patted Rob's shoulder en route to the Bronco. "Been thinkin' about what you told me on the phone this afternoon, Ro-bo. I don't know what advice to give, but I know you're doin' the right thing, unwinding with Kenny in that kidney-busting ol' tacklebox on wheels. This will all turn out okay." Gus never had been much of a prophet.

"Oh, I've got both feet planted firmly in the air, all right," said Rob, as Kenny gave his granddad a hug. He swung into the driver's seat, buckled up, started the Ford's burly V-8 as Kenny secured his harness. "See you early next week," he called. Gus diminished in his rearview, smiling with arms folded as he watched their departure, a man who had come to terms with solitude. *Or if he hasn't, he won't let us know it,* Rob's insight whispered.

Near Livermore, after dark, Rob turned north. Kenny had his Walkman playing and did not notice their direction. When he did, it was because of the freeway signs as they neared Sacramento. "Whoa, Dad, we're a bazillion miles off course," he exclaimed, sitting bolt upright.

"No we're not," said his father imperturbably, waiting to see whether the boy would adopt his mother's stance, arguing about it, or his father's, with hard data.

"Da-aad"—Kenny began, expending three tones on one syllable—"yes we . . ." Then he stopped, reached for the glove compartment, unfolded the tatters of a Chevron map, and let it bathe in the glove compartment's light. "Yes we are, Dad. Sacramento's up here, and Fresno's down here."

He's half Corrine and half me. God, but I love this kid.

"That map is older than you are," Rob shrugged.

"Uh—yeah, but, but, but . . ." said Kenny.

"Your engine's dieseling," said Rob.

"You're saying they've *moved* Sacramento?"

"No, I'm saying Sacramento's the capital of California. And we aren't headed for California."

"We're *in* Calif— Say that again?"

"I won't. You've browned me off now," said his father—in

tones making it obvious that he was joking. "If you're so smart, which direction are we heading?"

Kenny could play those games, too. "Not south. And not east or west. Pick one," he challenged.

"No, you pick a place, north of California. Not too far north," Rob teased.

"Oh, jeez, we're going to Ohio?" And when Rob jerked his head around, appalled, Kenny made a pistol of thumb and forefinger. "Gotcha back. It's gotta be Oregon," he crowed, and for the next two hours Rob recounted stories of that state during the decades before urban growth and logging destroyed half of it and imperiled the rest. They sought a motel near the interstate on the outskirts of Redding, California, fifty miles short of a sight that first-time viewers usually greet in slack-jawed silence. Kenny had never seen the frosted immensity of Mount Shasta, and Rob did not want his son to pass this solitary sleeping volcano in darkness.

The more powerful of two locator beacons, magnetically affixed beneath the Bronco's chassis, caused a pointer to swing eastward in a vehicle a mile behind. The same vehicle glided past as Rob strode to the motel office, stretching kinks from his shoulders. It was parked, lights out, a hundred yards away when Rob reparked the Bronco nearer to the room he had taken.

CHAPTER 7

THE GEOMETRICALLY PERFECT CONE OF OREGON'S MOUNT MC-
Loughlin could hardly compete with the early-morning sight
of Mount Shasta, with its county-wide girth, but McLoughlin's
classic Fujiyama shape kept a grin on Kenny's face as the
Bronco approached it on the blacktop road, tires giving an
occasional faint squeal. Though Rob had bought fishing li-
censes in Medford, expecting a procession of other anglers,
they had not met another car for ten minutes. Only rarely did
the grille of a following vehicle appear in his rearview, after a
half-mile or so of straight blacktop through a high meadow,
and Rob gave it no particular attention.

Kenny glimpsed the mountaintop again over a forested
ridge. "You mean there are actually lakes up on that thing,
Dad?"

"Not on its upper slopes. A few big lakes down below the
treeline, though, and several groups of smaller ones. We're
going around McLoughlin now and if I miss the turnoffs to
Lost Creek or Cold Springs Trail, well . . ."

"I thought these were your old stomping grounds," Kenny
said, his amused *"nyah-nyah"* implicit.

"Keep a civil tongue there, kid. It's been fifteen years since
I did any stomping in these— Ah, here we are." Rob interrupted himself and slowed, turning from the surfaced road,
shifting down as they passed a rustic road sign.

Kenny applied his attention to the remains of a map so old
its creases had made three smaller maps of it. "Wh-whoa, I
can't read these nu-umbers wi-i-ith all the bumping."

"Doesn't—matter," Rob replied. "I rem-member this." In
truth, the primitive condition of the road satisfied something
deep within this engineer, spoiled daily by six-lane concrete

ribbons. If these access roads were no better than they had
been a generation ago, fewer people would brave the endless
jounce and plunge that brought them to the trail's end a mile
above sea level. To the brick-solid little Bronco, of course, any
road at all was a luxury to be spurned.

At the final turnoff, Rob held up a palm and Kenny
slapped it. "Trailhead by—noo-hoon," he managed to say.
Kenny grinned again, gripped the windowframe, and gamely
hung on.

A few other vehicles had made recent tracks to the trailhead,
but Rob felt a vast satisfaction to find no others present as he
backed up a slight incline to park. Here and there on the north
side of boulders, traces of snow lingered, and the air kept its
gentle bite in the shadows of towering conifers. Rob helped
Kenny adjust the bellyband of his pack before shrugging into
his own larger rig and securing the Bronco. With its removable
steel hardtop bolted in place, the Bronco could be locked as
securely as an ordinary vehicle.

"Easy on the salty stuff," he cautioned, noting that Kenny's
cheeks were stuffed with pretzels. "We won't see water for a
while."

Kenny was one of those lucky few who grew acclimated to
modest altitudes almost instantly. Moreover, in his daily use
of a bike, Kenny was in better condition than his father. He
spurted ahead up the trail, calling back his discoveries, and
stood fidgeting whenever Rob paused to lean against an out-
crop. One of the best things about the Sky Lakes region was
the gentle slope of the trails, so they made good time for perhaps three miles.

Then: "It says 'Sky Lakes Trail' here," Kenny called from
fifty yards beyond.

A vagrant memory nudged Rob, who knew what lay just
ahead. "You go on, son. Find us a campsite." The boy was no
longer trotting, but disappeared with man-sized paces. No
more than a few minutes passed before whoops echoed again
and again from up the trail. It told Rob that the boy had arrived at Lake Natasha, always a joy to behold, one of those

shallow mountain ponds so limpid that its bottom was clearly visible.

But no sooner had Rob started to remove his pack at a prominent campsite, when Kenny beckoned him onward. "Everybody on the trail will see us here, Dad. Let's look for someplace neat."

This early in the season there might not be any competition for campsites, but Rob agreed that the first location was the backpacker's equivalent of building your house on a freeway. He let the youth lead for another mile as they completed part of a rough oval that encompassed a half-dozen lakes, but at last even Kenny's energy flagged. The boy sat down heavily on a fallen hemlock and, for a moment as they gazed across the nearest pond that lay below them, neither made a sound. "Dy-oh-*mite*," the boy said at last, in a virtual whisper.

It was Kenny's guess that they'd hiked ten or fifteen miles; Rob told him it was only five. If they continued on this trail for another mile they would be back at the Natasha campsite, and Rob urged the boy to choose a site. They'd seen several inlets where pan-sized trout lazed among the submerged branches of fallen firs, and Rob hadn't flicked a dry fly in too many seasons.

The site Kenny chose was not ideal, though its view over Lake Liza couldn't be faulted. Kenny stretched his groundcloth out before unrolling his mummy bag while, nearby, his father chose a pair of foot-thick pines from which to sling his hammock. The latest word in light camping a decade before, the hammock sported a guyed, rainproof cover with zippered mosquito netting. The things were cheaper now; if Kenny expressed enough interest in it, thought Rob, he might find one under the tree next Christmas.

That presumes I'll be able to afford it, Rob reminded himself. The expenses of driving back and forth from San Luis Obispo, and eventually renting an apartment, might loom much larger in another six months. Meanwhile, Kenny would be the man of the house in Sunnyvale: Another topic to be squarely faced during their time on the lakes. Dealing with a sundered family unit was a rite of passage that few boys welcomed, and that fact accounted for much of Rob Tarrant's guilt.

By midafternoon they had begun a slow circuit of little Lake Liza with fly rods, at first tentative and clumsy, losing several dry flies with their faulty backcasts to nearby trees. It was fly-fishers' conventional wisdom that if you can see the little bugger, he can see you; and Rob's belief that if you moved nothing but your wrists, the trout would soon forget he ever saw you.

Yet it was Kenny, never still for more than a few moments, who finally hooked the ten-inch bundle of electricity that was a brook trout. Kenny's gleeful shouts could have startled every fish in the adjoining lakes as well, and they caught nothing more until they moved across the few hundred yards that separated Liza from the much larger Isherwood Lake, a quarter-mile in length.

Combing his memories of a single geology course, Rob shared them with his son while they failed to interest any more trout. None of the lakes, he pointed out, had inlets or outflows of any size, which suggested they were very young lakes, as recent as the last glaciers that had gouged furrows through the Cascades range. They were so shallow, a man might walk much of the way across some of them, which meant the sun would warm the shallow parts enough to swim in.

"Did we bring swim trunks?" asked Kenny, seeing his father remove his hiking boots.

"Yep, the ones we were born with," said Rob. "Who's going to complain of skinny-dipping up here?"

"Those women on the trail," Kenny replied with a nod; and, as Rob snatched at the jeans around his ankles: "Gotcha again"—with a wink as Rob chuckled at his own gullibility. There were, of course, no other hikers; at least, no others to be seen.

If the water was bracingly chill at the surface, it was liquid ice a few feet down. Rob surfaced without yelling, a marvel of self-control, and as he thrashed around he saw that Kenny was staring into the sky, evidently following the path of some bird or insect that Rob could not see. Then Kenny switched his attention to his father who vented a few "huh . . . huh" gasps and announced that it was warmer below. Eventually this suckered Kenny into stripping down, and then into a shallow dive from which he emerged with a yodel worthy of an Alpine guide. They laughingly called a truce, a limit of one "gotcha" per day, and soon dried themselves as they sunned on a lakeside boulder.

Presently, Kenny looked toward the sky again. "Dad, do you know of any birds that hum? Bigger than a hummingbird, I mean."

"How much bigger? Some moths are bigger than some birds, and their wings might have a soft hum. I assume you have a reason."

A silent nod before, "Just after you jumped in a while ago, something went over the lake." He swung a pointing forefinger across, east to west. "It was in sight about five or ten seconds and it was higher than the trees."

Rob knew, and Kenny knew, that the tiny mantis craft emitted a faint hum from its whirling propeller. He affixed his son with a wary eye. "Not a bird. It was a bug."

"Bugs don't get that big, Dad."

"This kind does. And it hums. In fact, that's what they call it," Rob said, the half-smile giving him away.

Kenny wrinkled his nose, squinting. "Wha—?" And then he got it. "*Humbug*. Yeah, right. I thought we had a truce."

"I thought so, too, Baron Münchhausen. Your old man may be dumb, but not that dumb."

Kenny solemnly crossed his heart, and Rob turned the query into an exercise in critical thinking. If the thing had really been above the trees, it couldn't be a bug. A hundred and fifty feet up, a bug would be too small to register in the best human eye as more than the tiniest dot. And according to Kenny, it hadn't veered in sudden changes of direction, which bugs usually do; small birds, less often; large birds, seldom. Given that data alone, the thing had probably been at least the size of a hawk.

Kenny's experience with models gave him a better-than-average grasp of elapsed time; ten seconds, he said, was about right between the emergence and disappearance of the flying critter. In Kenny's judgment it hadn't changed its course, or speed, or altitude. Between the trees lining the sides of the lake were eight hundred feet of lake and open sky. If the critter had been at treetop height, it had been moving some eighty feet per second; something like fifty-five miles per hour. That was very fast for a buzzard, not too fast for a hawk.

"Take another scenario. What if you just misjudged it, and it was a plane, a lot higher than you thought?" Rob asked. "Would it have been moving slower or faster?"

After a moment, Kenny nodded. "Faster. But I know that anyhow, because real planes fly a lot faster than fifty."

"Most of 'em do. And that's a kind of double-check on your guess. Doesn't remove all doubt, but it would tell you which way to bet, if you were a betting man. Now then, do you recall it flapping its wings?"

"Uh—no, but so what? Some birds don't, much."

"And real planes don't do it at all. Think about what you see all the time. The bigger birds are, the less they flap," said Rob. "That has to do with its weight and its breastbone, which is what anchors the flapping muscles. To flap wings hard enough to lift his own weight, a man's breastbone would have to stick out beyond his arm's reach. That was a problem I remember from OSU, a million years ago. Which reminds me: You know I was picked for grad school at Stratford."

Kenny took the cue; he'd been wondering when this particular hammer would drop. "I know you let Mom boot you out over it." Bursting out now: "Sometimes she really sucks!"

As a matter of fact, she hasn't for a long time, Rob's perverse imp replied silently. "Hey, buddy, come on," he said, knowing he trod a narrow line in the overlap of mutual openness and role-modeling. "That's the lady I married."

Kenny grumped, in an undertone: "Yeah, well—you sure seemed pretty willing to go, if you ask me. And nobody's telling me anything, Dad! Mom just tells me we'll be okay, and that I'm too big to cry."

Rob's peripheral vision told him the boy was suddenly close to that very thing. "Let me tell you something, buddy, that you don't have to say to your mom, so long as you never forget it," he said. "Nobody ever gets too big to cry."

Kenny digested this for a moment before saying, "You?"

A nod. "The night I realized that my wife and the university had both told me to get lost. Then pretty soon I started thinking maybe it was time I dried out and got over my self-pity. The trouble with self-pity is, it keeps you wasting time, blaming other folks for the pit you're in, when you could be figuring how to climb out."

When Kenny murmured, Rob almost missed it. "Hamlet," Kenny said.

"What?"

"English class; Shakespeare. We had to memorize that 'To be or not to be' stuff. There's this prince who's screwed six ways from Saturday and he says a lot of stuff nobody understood till Miz Penn explained it. She said he's saying, So what do I do, drink Lysol? And which choice will give me more self-respect, to stand at attention and let these assholes dump on me, or climb in the ring and beat the hell out of 'em? . . . Hamlet's solila-thingy."

"Ms. Penn said that?"

"Schoolteacher version," said the boy. "I may have cleared it up a little more."

"I'd say you did," Rob admitted fervently. "Where were you when I was trying to read *Ulysses*?"

Kenny lay back, hands clasped under his head on the sun-warmed stone. "You mean President Grant? I dunno. I don't even know whether you're like that Hamlet guy."

"I don't know, either, Kenny." But it sounded embarrassingly close to the facts: a man who dithered while home burned.

"According to Miz Penn, Hamlet couldn't figure out whether he was a guy who thought about things, or a guy who *did* things," the boy said dreamily, his eyes closed. "I don't see why it had to be either or. Seems to me he could a been a thinker *and* a doer. Who's that astronaut who's a Marine and a doctor and a poet, and, jeez, I don't know what else? Um, Musgrave. Yeah, now there's a real guywho."

"Come again?"

"A guywho. Somebody that does stuff for us to remember him for, 'the guy who' this, or 'the guy who' that. A guywho," Kenny explained patiently.

They both fell silent, eyes closed, the boy half asleep, the man fully alert. Presently: "Kenny?" Answered by a grunt, Rob went on. "If I decided to move out of town for a couple of years, long enough to get a master's degree from a different school, you'd have to work a lot more at home—fix things, clean things, learn to do careful shopping, be responsible."

"Would we see you?"

"A couple of weekends a month at least. Maybe more."

A long pause, so long he thought perhaps his son was dozing. Then Kenny said, "And you want me to decide."

With thunderclap abruptness, Rob knew that was exactly what he wanted, no matter how it might be phrased. The unerring clarity of Kenny's understanding was that of an adult. Further, the youth was probably willing to make that decision for him, if Rob were indecisive enough to ask. "No, that's a done deal," said his father, as if he had known it all along. His voice was firm with resolve now. "I'm going to climb in the ring and beat the hell out of everybody in sight, buddy. I just want you to hold my coat while I do it."

CHAPTER 8

AFTER ONLY ONE NIGHT ON LAKE LIZA SHARING A SINGLE trout with their noodles, Kenny wanted to move on. They made a game of striking camp, burning all their burnable trash, using Rob's trenching tool to bury the rest, then searching for any sign that would betray the fact that anyone had been there recently. Even the leftover firewood, with its fresh hatchet marks, was cached under humus fifty feet away.

"Our bootprints are still a dead giveaway," Kenny said, as they paused before heading down the trail.

"I don't think the next campers will mind," Rob replied. "Trail etiquette has its limits."

At the larger of the Heavenly Twin Lakes, they found hungrier fish. Rob chose a campsite there with better protection from the breezes that tended to stop stroking and begin cutting at sundown. Now that Rob's agenda had managed to fulfill itself sooner than he'd expected, he relaxed and accompanied the boy, saying little as Kenny improved his casting technique, with occasional murmurs of, "Try using a big gray hackle," or, "Good move," as Kenny studied a hemlock that might capture his dry fly, repositioning himself for a cast. Then, through midafternoon, Rob napped in his hammock and read a paperback mystery while Kenny toured the shallow lake alone.

Kenny was not exactly alone when he returned late in the day. His companions were smallish rainbow and brook trout, three of each, and he basked in his father's praise as they cleaned his catch. Neither of them needed to comment on the fact that, as this was a learning experience, Rob left most of the campfire chores to his son with only a tip here, a demonstration there.

As Kenny sliced curls of wood on a small dead fir branch

with his sheath knife, preparing one of several "fuzz sticks" for kindling, he said, "Did you see our whatever bird today?"

"Never even thought about it. Did you?"

Headshake. Kenny placed the fuzz stick among others to complete a V in the shallow firepit; arranged slightly larger branches to suit himself. "But I thought I heard it a couple of times. Coulda been my imagination."

Rob nodded as he broke open a cardboard cylinder of biscuit dough and mimed smacking his lips. And that was the last he thought about Kenny's whatever bird until much later. Long after dinner, Kenny dug his monocular nightscope from his pack and they spent a half hour peering through the stubby little instrument, the size and heft of a pound of butter. Its range was only a hundred yards or so, perhaps in part because a month previous, Kenny had removed its tiny infrared spotlight for a science project. Though the infrared feature illuminated nearby objects quite well, its advantage dwindled at longer range. The boy lamented having forgotten to replace it, though; the one creature that he spied was an owl that glided from the trees to make sweeping passes in rank grass, a stone's throw away. It was only when he happened to glance skyward, and saw the firmament crowded with many times more stars than ordinary vision permits, that Kenny snuggled down in his mummy bag and scanned the heavens until sleep overtook him.

THE NEXT MORNING, KENNY WANTED TO MOVE THEIR CAMPSITE again and Rob agreed. He had nothing else to do, and it was good practice for the boy. This time, just for fun, Kenny made a broom of a fir branch and swept away their footprints before they moved down the trail.

Kenny selected a site on little Lake Elizabeth, not far from Natasha, where the trail curved back down toward the Bronco. Rob was pleased; he intended to return to the trailhead late the following day, perhaps find a motel in Medford. It was uncanny, he thought, how easily he had come to an important decision—and how impatient he was, now, to get on with his trip to San Luis Obispo. The small pessimist in his head asked,

And what if I can't get into Cal Poly after all? Well, he decided, borrowing a phrase from Gus, he would just have to burn that bridge when he came to it. . . .

The fish weren't biting at Elizabeth but, by going their separate ways until noon, they fished other lakes with some success. Swilling soup with pretzels for lunch, Kenny proudly announced that he had seen signs of bear. "There's this rotten stump at the east end of Natasha and something's torn the crap out of it," he said. "And there's all these big ants still crawling all over the wreckage, and you can see pawprints in the, uh, punky wood stuff. Not as big as my hand, but good-sized. Maybe a little grizzly, Dad?"

"They say there aren't any griz in Oregon anymore, but there are plenty of the other kind. Regular little black bear, and their pawprints aren't all that big, either," Rob said. "They love ants, too. For a bear, ants are just candy with legs."

"Yum," said Kenny with palpable sarcasm. And, after a measured pause, "Did we bring a gun?"

"Uh-unh, but no sweat, buddy. They're not big enough, and they know it. All the same, if you run across a sow, a mother, with her cub, you climb a tree or something right away. Mama would make a run at you just on general principle. I'm not kidding about that."

"Boy, I'd like to see one," said Kenny.

"Keep an eye peeled. But they usually forage at night," Rob replied. Soon after that, they separated again. This time, it was Rob who walked to Natasha and, in time, found the savaged tree stump. He judged the prints to be those of a smallish adult, and no smaller prints to suggest a cub. Evidently, this bear wasn't concerned about leaving prints. Once he determined to look for signs, Rob found several places in the Natasha area where stumps had been shredded, holes dug for roots and grubs, and in one place, the stink of feces. It hadn't buried its scat as a backpacker would. This bear had staked out Natasha as its larder, and might even be sleeping nearby during the daylight hours. Rob returned to camp with a reflective smile, and a plan for the evening.

———

MORE EFFICIENT WITH EACH MEAL, THEY FINISHED PREPARA-
tions for dinner with an hour to spare, Kenny chattering like
a squirrel after Rob shared his notions of nighttime entertain-
ment. They smiled at each other often as the shadows length-
ened. "What do we do if he charges us?" Kenny asked, as they
sipped peach brandy slushies using remnants of gritty snow.

"I'd say offer him a credit card, but you've probably heard
that one. Don't worry, we don't want to threaten him," said
Rob. "Chances are we won't see him at all, and if we do, we'll
want to keep our distance."

"But what *if*?" Kenny persisted.

"Mmm, you get behind me and be ready to take a swim in
the dark, I guess. I'll be standing as tall as I can, yelling my
head off. Any bear with that size paws would be nuts to carry
through with a charge against something my size."

"But—"

Exasperated, amused: "Kenny, cork it off, will you? Or, if
you don't want to check him out after all, just say so. It's okay,
really. I just thought you might want to."

But Kenny insisted that he did want to. They made a small
fire and took their time pan-frying Kenny's trout, which they
placed on beds of the succulent medallions of ground cover
known as "miner's lettuce." It was wonderful, Rob mused,
how a teenager would wolf down strange vegetables in the high
country when, at home, he had to be dragooned into picking
at his salad.

They let the fire burn down, and shared sweetened instant
coffee with crumbles that had not survived the journey as
cookies. Finally, when their fire was reduced to embers and
the last of the western afterglow still offered them a bit of help
on the trail, Rob suggested that they head for the vantage spot
he'd chosen.

It soon grew too dark to navigate the trail back to Natasha
without their little Mag-Lites. Rob had discovered that the
nightscope would not focus nearer than ten yards, so that if
the user tried to use it to guide him on the trail, he would
stumble helplessly. Whoever was second in line, without the
scope or a flashlight, would fare even worse. They knew many

of the trail's little traps by now, and with his Mag-Lite Rob found his chosen stone promontory without trouble.

The next hour might have been filled with boredom, had they not handed the nightscope back and forth in virtual silence while sitting together on their small granite dome. As before, again and again they would turn the scope upward to marvel at the incredible profusion of stars visible only with a nightscope.

Rob had zipped his windbreaker and was wondering when the boy would tire of their vigil when he felt Kenny stiffen beside him. "Whoa, dude," the boy said softly, twisting his upper body. After a moment he continued, almost in a whisper. "Something pushing those ferns around."

Rob, his mouth near his son's ear: "How far?"

"Fifty, sixty yards. Too far to hear us."

"Don't count on that," Rob warned.

And then Kenny trembled. "Yes," he whispered, and, "yes!"

Anxious as any thirteen-year-old, Rob nudged his son. "Come on, give me a look," he pleaded.

"Near the trail," Kenny advised as he surrendered the scope. "The way he bumbles along, I wonder why we don't hear him."

After a disorienting moment of dark greens against lighter greens in the eyepiece, the monochrome circle resolved itself into trees, trail, boulders, and, yes, the big rounded backside of a bear, ambling near the trail. It had the rolling gait of a sailor on all fours until, crossing the trail they had traversed earlier, it stopped abruptly to thrust its nose about like a questing hound. Rob decided it was studying the man-scent their boots had made. Then it continued away from them, now moving in eerie silence parallel to the trail in the direction of their camp, leaving a series of ferns bobbing in its wake.

When it disappeared near the descending trail, Rob eased down to the turf and helped Kenny down to maintain silence. "I wouldn't do this," he said softly, "but he's heading for our camp. Without one of us there to keep him honest, he could rip our packs to pieces. Better let me go ahead, son." With that, he set off in the lead down the trail, infected with boyish

excitement and opting not to use the Mag-Lite again. He
viewed through the scope every few seconds, half expecting to
see the bear doubling back on them. Theirs was a half-blind,
clumsy procession, but it brought them to the downslope in
time to see ferns waving in the distance below.

Kenny demanded his gadget again and, after a moment,
whispered, "Oh, yeah," chuckling, leaning against his father.
Then, "Real bright light, like we left a lamp on in camp, but
can't see it at all without the scope. Hey, it's the heat from our
fire, I think. I dunno."

Rob took the scope, swept its view around to get his bearings, and saw the light Kenny had seen, a hard, bright yellow-
green dot that gleamed unmoving near the next lake.
Eventually he saw the bear as well, moving farther from the
trail but circling that point of light.

Rob's left eye, adapting better to darkness because he did
not use it with the monocular, gave him enough night vision
to pick his way down the trail. Kenny followed on his heels
finally to within a hundred yards of their campsite. It was
obvious now that the infrared glow of their campfire embers
was the source of that hard dot of light in the scope—and that
the bear, elevating its muzzle now and then to test the air, was
growing bolder in its approach to their camp. Bolder, that is,
until it stopped, frozen with one paw uplifted, muzzle pointed
campward.

Then, with a burst of fluid grace the little bear half arose
on its hind legs, pivoting and dropping on all fours to double
back on its tracks in an astonishing lope that could have been
comical. It failed to be funny to Rob because, near the edge of
the green tableau, a bright, almost white line swept their
campsite from somewhere off to the left.

"What's it doing?" Kenny pulled at his father's arm, impatient.

Rob shook off the imploring hand, gooseflesh marching up
his arms because his left eye did *not* register a flashbeam at
the campsite.

"C'mon," the boy insisted.

"Kenny, be absolutely still; something's wrong," said Rob,

very quietly, without turning. By now the bear was forgotten, probably still on the run, but something was scanning their camp. Something with a powerful infrared signature, and no visible flashbeam. And in the scope, it was now a spotlight throwing details into fuzzy relief.

A human figure stepped carefully from behind a tree, the light emanating from its head, and again the beam swept from mummy bag to hammock as the figure approached their camp. Rob realized that the stranger was using expensive night-vision goggles with a good IR illuminator, and for a moment he considered shouting at this man who was reaching to point toward his hammock.

He reconsidered abruptly as a brilliant flash erupted from that outstretched hand, and another; a third; a fourth. Rob's left eye registered those flashes as well, though no sound carried to him.

Kenny had seen the muzzle flashes, too. His alarmed "Dad!" was not very loud, but the gunman may have heard it across the slender arm of lake water.

"Not a sound, Kenny," Rob ordered in a gruff undertone, still watching. He squatted, pulling the boy down with him, thinking furiously. Without an IR illuminator of their own, Rob and Kenny would be hard to spot; still-harder targets from a hundred yards by a man with a handgun.

But this fellow was not scanning the distance. The IR beam playing back and forth between beddings, he thrust a hand into the hammock, saw how easily it swung without a man's bulk, and knelt quickly at Kenny's mummy bag. Finding it empty as well, he stood up and snatched at the nearest back-pack, which happened to be Rob's, still half-filled. After a brief moment of apparent indecision he dropped the pack and snatched up Kenny's—not only smaller, but practically empty, now that the boy had consumed most of the junk food he'd brought.

The next instant, the gunman wheeled with the stolen pack and trotted off, stumbling, locating the trail, his IR illuminator showing the way. Night-vision goggles could be very, very spendy, but some of them could focus within a few feet.

Some twenty yards down the trail from camp was a declivity that might one day develop into a ravine, and here the gunman paused again, the IR beam permitting Rob to see his next move. He swung the pack by its straps, a full two circles, then let it arc over and out of sight. That done, the gunman set off again at a slow trot, presumably to the distant trailhead.

Rob waited until the last fleeting, bobbing hint of that illuminator disappeared before he stood up, handed the scope back to Kenny, and dropped an arm over the boy's shoulder. "I know you didn't see much of that, son, but some dirty son of a bitch just stole your backpack."

"He was *shooting*, Dad," said the boy. "I don't think he'd care if he hit somebody!"

"He cared," said Rob. "And he might be back with friends."

CHAPTER 9

"THAT WAS A SILENCED PISTOL HE USED," SAID ROB, AS THEY moved down the declivity among breast-high ferns near their camp. Told that the thief had tossed his pack away nearby, Kenny argued that it shouldn't be hard to find using the scope.

They found it after only a few minutes. "I doubt he'll be back," said Rob, "but I'd hate to be wrong about that. I don't like the idea of heading for the car right now, either. He might even sit down and wait for us."

Kenny stood so near, Rob could feel the boy's full-body tremors. He put an arm about his son's shoulders. "I don't wanta go down that mountain in the dark," Kenny said, his voice unsteady.

"We're going to be okay, Kenny. Take it easy and zip up your jacket. You're shivering."

"So are you," the boy said, slinging the pack over one shoulder.

Rob realized that it was true, and made light of it. "No, *you're* shivering—I'm trembling like a dog shitting peach seeds. There's a difference," he said as they trudged back to the trail.

Kenny snickered; patted his father's back. "You'd ground me if I said that." Then, as afterthought: "I really love you, Dad."

Rob kissed the top of his son's head in reply, standing irresolute on the trail. "Look, it just doesn't make sense that some high-tech thief would be up here trying to kill somebody for an old backpack or two. This guy is nutty as a squirrel's nest. I think we should pack up and wait awhile, and then ease down the trail in an hour, crank up the Bronco and get out, tell the cops."

"I'd rather move our bags somewhere near and wait till morning," Kenny said.

"That was my first thought, but we'll have a better chance of spotting that guy tonight than in the morning."

"How d'you figure— Oh," said Kenny.

"Right. He can't know we've got a scope because yours doesn't give us away with an illuminator, but he's using his. And with your scope, we can see it from blocks away. If he's down there, we'll see him before he can see us."

"Boy, I hope you're right," said Kenny, as they began to scuffle about their campsite half-blindly.

"If I'm not, I should be in front," Rob mused, aware that he was no expert on the newer versions of night-vision equipment. The goosedown in his bag had provided little resistance to bullets, and the bag had lost little of its stuffing. He fumbled with his hammock before realizing that something, probably a bullet, had severed one of the two major cords supporting it at the head end.

On another level he tried to imagine the thought processes of a man who would ambush sleeping backpackers for such paltry goods while equipped with costly goggles and a silenced pistol that was not only expensive, but illegal in fifty states. *And take the small empty pack and ditch it right away. Crazy,* he thought.

Or maybe not. Suppose the guy wasn't insane. Why deprive a boy of his pack after killing his father? No, before taking the pack he had discovered he hadn't killed anyone; he hadn't taken the pack until after realizing no one was in camp. In that case, a thief should've taken the big pack, or both, one inside the other.

That's assuming he wanted the packs. Dump your assumption; why take it if he didn't want it? The answer buzzed around him like a deerfly, just out of reach, and he swatted it just as he finished casting around in the dark for dirty mess kits. *He knew we'd be back but he didn't know when, and he fired several shots that lit up the place, and he didn't know what risks he would be taking if he waited. He needed me to think he was just a thief; but an ordinary thief would've taken*

our stuff and hightailed it without shooting anyone. He had
something else to do, and he did it first. Or thought he had,
for a moment.

The sensation that coursed along Rob Tarrant's spine was
not cold, but hot and enervating. There must be plenty of other
explanations, but a very neat one was attempted deliberate
murder, with a quick effort to make it look like theft was the
motive, after the attempt was botched. And it wouldn't have
been botched if they'd been in camp, asleep.

I owe my life to a scruffy little bear, he thought.

They sat for a time near the confluence of trails below Lake
Natasha, Rob steadily holding the scope to his eye as they
spoke quietly together. Kenny, a devotee of TV plots, had to
be drawn away from the notion that a serial killer was loose
in the area. It wasn't so much that the idea itself was so unlikely, but that Kenny invested serial killers with superhuman
abilities: the stealth of a cat, the resources of a genius, the
strength of Rambo.

To set the boy's mind at ease, Rob downplayed the image.
"We know he wasn't quiet enough to fool the bear," he reasoned. "Little Bruin was spooked from fifty yards away. And
if he'd been all that smart, the guy would've checked my sleeping bag before he drilled holes in it. Plus, he was such a wimp
he didn't want to carry your pack twenty yards. No, we aren't
dealing with some superdude, Kenny."

But it was a scenario Rob himself could not dismiss for several hours. When they began their downhill trek, sometime
after midnight, Rob stayed in front and used the scope liber-
ally. The darkness slowed them and they stumbled badly more
than once, but the gentle downward slope prevented exhaus-
tion. Nearing the Bronco, Rob skirted the trailhead area alone
before returning to Kenny. No other cars were present. Rob
ordered the boy to stay among the trees until the Bronco had
been warmed and started to roll. Only then should he run to
the Bronco.

With no experience in such deadly games, Rob made nu-
merous little tactical errors: leaving the door open and the
interior light burning too long as he swung into the seat, taking

too long to stow his pack behind him, gunning the engine too loudly, forgetting to unlock Kenny's door until the poor kid was wrenching at it in dismay. But shortly after three in the morning, the two of them were headed down the access road, Kenny huddled out of sight while Rob drove defiantly with lights ablaze.

After all, the unknown gunman couldn't be certain who was driving the Bronco—could he? An answer to that would soon suggest itself. Meanwhile, Rob drove with such near-abandon that he left the trail and high-centered the tough old Bronco several times. Confirming his fears, he retained the sound of a new scrape, sounding like a broom beneath the chassis, after they reached the two-lane blacktop. He wasn't about to stop until they reached help of some kind.

They had come through Medford, but the events of the evening made Rob wary enough to return by a more easterly route, through the high-plains township of Klamath Falls an hour away. He recalled an all-night service station on the highway but, in the past fifteen years, the place had gone out of business. They had to listen to that swirling scrape all the way into town, and they found only one station open with a hydraulic lift at four-thirty in the morning.

Kenny pored over a road map in the office, charting their route back to the interstate after voting crossly for a motel room, before Rob helped the night attendant pull at the green fir branch wedged firmly between a suspension forging and the chassis. They finally cut it apart with a hacksaw.

The night man seemed unsurprised by anything a Bronco driver might have done. "You want my personal opinion," he said as if conferring a pearl of homespun wisdom, "all you Bronco riders are wacko."

Rob had told Kenny to say nothing about the gunman until they contacted the state police but, tired as he was, Rob forgot as he gazed along the frame rails. "If you think *I'm* nuts, you should've—" He stopped.

Perched on the rear differential casing was a gray rectangle the size of a cigarette lighter, a thin antenna rod protruding from one end. Given the way a Bronco stood high on its sus-

pension, that bastard with the gun could have emplaced it in
a moment. The night man raised his eyebrow, waiting for Rob
to continue. "Oh, well, maybe you're right," Rob finished,
smiling. He knew before he touched it that he was looking at
a transmitter affixed by magnets.

"Listen, would you mind giving my boy some of that coffee
while I check out the goodies under here? I'd rather do it myself, you know how us Bronc riders are." It was chilly in that
maintenance bay, and the night man was more than willing.

Rob pulled the transmitter loose, turning it over in his
hands, seeing a pair of miniature dials and switches. He
glanced into the half-lit street as a car passed, realizing that
he could be found wherever he went, and resisted the impulse
to dash the transmitter bug against the concrete floor. Instead,
he replaced it exactly where he had found it and began a closer
inspection. In the sudden blossoming of paranoia he half expected to find a bundle of dynamite in the guts of his Bronco.
He no longer thought of himself as a target of casual opportunity. This was personal; someone, he thought numbly,
wanted him dead.

He found the second bug when brushing dried mud from a
chassis rail nearer the front wheels. They had splashed
through mud on the trail going in, days ago, but the region
had dried since. The wire attaching that second and larger bug
had been emplaced before they ever left Medford—maybe before they left the motel in Redding. Maybe before they left
Sunnyvale. As he finished searching fruitlessly for more evidence, Rob knew that as long as the transmitters stayed in
place, his unknown pursuer would not know his hardware was
compromised.

And Rob knew that, whatever else happened, Kenny must
not remain with his father.

CONVINCING THE BOY WAS NOT EASY, AS HE FOUND WHILE
waiting at dawn for the Greyhound station's six A.M. opening.
He studied each car that passed with dark suspicion. "You're
asking questions I can't answer, son," he said, losing patience
at last, aware that the boy was fighting manfully against tears

as he insisted they stick together. "If I'm a wanted man, I won't have you caught in the middle. I've been hit pretty hard, several ways, in the past week or so. Maybe it's tied up with— Well, the less I say, the better. Whoever asks, you're free to tell what's happened so far; you have nothing to hide and you'll be safe at home."

Now the hazel eyes brimmed with tears. "And where will you be? How do I know I'll ever see you again?"

"I wish I knew, buddy," said Rob, and shook the boy's shoulder gently. "But I'll get in touch when I know more. Look, now that I've been warned, I'll be okay. In Oregon I can live on trout if I have to!"

"We've gotta go to the cops, Dad," Kenny pleaded.

"Unless it's some kind of cop who's running around with high-end goggles and a silenced pistol," Rob reminded him. He saw Kenny's eyes widen and pressed on: "I'm not saying it's a cop; it doesn't seem likely, but I don't know. Oh—I've still got your nightscope. Mind if I keep it awhile?"

" 'Course not," said Kenny, licking at the corner of his mouth. "Dad, I hate to ask this but I have to."

"Shoot," said Rob.

"That's not even funny," said the boy. "What I've gotta know is, um—you haven't done anything, uh, bad, have you?"

Rob couldn't help a brief grin at this, a perfectly natural question under the circumstances. "Not that I can think of."

"Well, you've pissed somebody off, big-time," said the boy.

Rob nodded, thinking about the GenStan security man he had slugged so recently. Security men probably had access to high-tech hardware, but it was an outrageous idea that the big fellow would take a grudge this far. Still, if you had to have an enemy, GenStan was not the one you'd pick.

"Look, they're unlocking the doors," Kenny said suddenly.

His paranoia in full bloom, Rob insisted he go alone to see about fares to San Jose. The bad news: Only one bus a day left for San Jose. The worse news: It left at midnight.

With so many citizens crowding into cafes now, Rob felt safe enough to stoke his and Kenny's inner fires with omelets while he considered other options.

A waitress gave them directions to Amtrak, only a few blocks distant. The station was opening as they parked, and the news there was almost as bad: Train number 11, once a day, leaving for San Jose at ten-thirty P.M. Rob used a credit card, his mind awhirl with what-ifs, balancing the risks to his son being alone in an unfamiliar town against the risks if they stayed together until the Amtrak arrived.

And every time a stranger glanced his way, Rob stiffened. As long as he left those tracer bugs in place, togetherness meant the greater risk to Kenny. In a central parking lot he handed the Amtrak ticket and three twenty-dollar bills to his son. "Take in a movie, find a museum or the library, you can probably snooze there, and call your mom collect to tell her when you get home. No point in filling you up with detailed instructions."

Now dry-eyed and sulky, the boy said, "Because you don't know what to tell me."

"If that was meant to hurt, give yourself a point. But it's also because I trust you to be levelheaded, Kenny. I'm treating you as a man."

To this, the boy had no reply. Rob's last image of his son was impeded by his own angry tears, glimpsed through his rearview: a slender youth dressed for hiking, hands thrust into his pockets, staring at his own feet and in dire need of a comb for his hair. *By God*, Rob told himself, *somebody's going to pay dearly for this.*

HIGHWAY 97 FED BACK INTO THE INTERSTATE AFTER AN HOUR or so, with many lonely open stretches that gave Rob plenty of opportunities to study following traffic. He stopped in one hamlet to let a car pass, and resolved to remember the gray Toyota sedan. He wondered how Kenny would have reacted if he'd known his dad was heading straight back to Silicon Valley, and concluded he'd done the right thing to leave the boy in Klamath Falls.

He gassed up in Redding, still watchful, his eyes gritty from lack of sleep. Then he took his own advice and, after locating the city library, parked several blocks from it. He chose several periodicals as props and slumped down with a copy of *Money* magazine open in his hands. Most engineers knew how to sleep in that position.

He was waked once by a whiskery geezer who wanted the copy of *Newsweek* near him, and again, early in the afternoon, by the heavy throat-clearings of a formidable lady with her glasses perched in her gray hair and an ASK ME placard on her frilly blouse. He took the hint and walked back to the Bronco wishing he'd had more than three hours of sleep before nosing the Bronco back onto the interstate. Gus would have said he felt shot at and missed, and shit at and hit. Gus would have been right.

CHAPTER 10

BY THE TIME ROB PULLED INTO THE LONG-TERM PARKING AREA near San Jose's airport, he had done several more hours of thinking, and had stopped three times at automatic teller machines for cash. People with the resources of GenStan security, he felt, might follow his credit-card trail but could hardly cancel a card. Had some law agency been after him, his cards probably wouldn't have worked. Whoever emplaced those bugs could trace the Bronco as far as that fenced, open-air parking area in San Jose. A panicky Rob Tarrant might just scurry back to his apartment, perhaps to call the police. A more savvy Rob would ditch the Bronco before fleeing back to Oregon, as he had hinted to his son, and as he intended to do.

But the Rob Tarrant he hoped the gunman wouldn't outguess was the Rob who would take an extra step; in fact, several extra steps, including linkage to someone who might confirm or deny hostile actions by the company. Rob used a credit card again at the airport, taking the day's last Alaska Airlines flight to Portland, Oregon, with his backpack as carry-on luggage.

His catnap aloft, and another at Portland's Old Town Greyhound station where he bought his next ticket with a false name and cash, left him with a sense of suspended disbelief in the events of his own life. Hadn't he told his father-in-law where he was going? He couldn't remember and didn't know whether it mattered, but at this point he was not absolutely sure of Gus. When he boarded the big highway cruiser at one o'clock in the morning, it was with a feeling of some relief; until after six o'clock the next evening he would be as anonymous as a hitchhiker and could hibernate if he chose.

Rob had not reached a firm conclusion about these next

moves until parking the Bronco in San Jose. The thing that had decided him was a memory from childhood, when seven-year-old Rob had developed a near certainty that something hostile, furry, and fang-y crept under his bed every night. After one plea to his scornful father, little Rob settled on a tactic: he secretly collected a mayonnaise jar full of wet sand from the family cat's sandbox, added water, and shook briskly. Then he poured the standing fluid into an old thumb-pumped plastic spray bottle which he hid among his toys.

Thereafter for some weeks, whenever little Rob's suspicions got the best of him he would fumble to his booger-zapper in the dark and let fly under his bed with a cat-piss cocktail potent enough to have sent any self-respecting booger lurching toward some other kid's bed. Eventually Rob decided the booger had given up his lair—but only after his dad had given away the cat. The central fact of that experience, for Rob, was not the sacrifice of the innocent, but that a powerful unknown nemesis would never expect a direct attack on its own turf. And Rob, officially on extended leave, still had his GenStan gate pass.

THE MAN WITH THE FIVE-DAY BEARD AND HIKING BOOTS WHO walked in line through GenStan's main gate shortly before midnight touched thumb and forefinger to his clip-on gate pass in approved fashion. Night-shift people were chiefly blue-collar workers, protected by union contracts, permitted to wear whatever clothing might be appropriate for welders, electricians, sanitary workers. Presently he angled off toward a distant parking area as though he knew exactly where he was going. In truth, he hadn't a clue where that camper stood but he knew it represented an unofficial kind of diplomatic immunity.

The vehicle he sought was the property of one Fred McGrath, an occasional lunch companion for Rob, and a Boston Irishman with a distinguished leonine head of graying hair. With his gift for blarney, McGrath had risen to prominence in industry a decade before. That was before the high-living McGrath discovered that his tastes ran—even galloped—to the spectacular and, where women were concerned, the kinky. McGrath was blindsided first by a private detective, then by his wife's attorney in a divorce he dared not contest. It would not have been good for a corporate vice president in proper Boston to be revealed in courtroom melodrama as a man who liked rough sex, even with commercially willing partners, when his first wife described his sex life as "the rapes of McGrath."

For a man as intelligent and charming as Fred McGrath, he learned too slowly: Another marriage, this one brief, and another set of alimony payments. Eventually Fred realized that as long as he wasn't going to be good, he must be very, very careful. Through the old-boy network he shifted loyalties to GenStan's Cambridge offices as a staff blarney specialist, better known as a proposals writer. And then McGrath abruptly disappeared.

Process servers failed to unravel McGrath's three moves within GenStan to Atlanta, then Los Angeles, then Sunnyvale—all with the help of executives who found in Fred a man of great talent in proposals work, and a greater talent for holding his liquor in a poker game. Fred McGrath was now a very senior proposals specialist who spent half of his time in Sunnyvale and the rest on temporary duties elsewhere. When away, he was impossible to locate. And when in Sunnyvale he lived in a longbed pickup with a spiffy camper conversion, complete with shower, in a GenStan parking lot.

Now and then, sometimes with Rob on a long lunch hour, Fred would fire up the Chevy pickup and drive off-site, dumping the camper's effluents, blowing out the cobwebs from the engine. Fred had explained his strategy to Rob Tarrant during a boozy Saturday lunch after they'd finished the engineering portion of a proposal together. On GenStan property Fred was immune to process servers. He had never made it clear whether this was with the help of some GenStan executive, but it was clear that McGrath had taken a shine to the young engineer.

Rob was hard-pressed to justify his end of this odd friendship, but finally admitted the truth to himself. While most of Rob's friends were decent and dull, Fred McGrath yielded an inexhaustible supply of tacky stories. An hour with Fred was like a weekend with a dirty joke.

On one occasion after working late, Rob had noticed the camper parked alone, and stopped to say hello. He never got as far as a knock; from inside the darkened vehicle came sounds of merry, vigorous activity and the camper was rocking on its springs like a rowboat. Evidently plant Security had orders to ignore McGrath's vehicle unless it was actually burning down. Rob had driven home laughing and reflecting that, in a paraphrase of George Orwell, some employees were more equal than others. This was especially true, at GenStan, for any employee who did the work of a vice president on the pay of a staff specialist.

For the past few weeks Fred had been cloistered with the company branch in San Diego, massaging a pile of GenStan pipe dreams into a proposal. Rob had only the vaguest notion what he might say if Fred had returned but he need not have worried; his chief problem was in finding where the improper Bostonian had hidden his spare keys. He located them beneath a small pile of rusty tire chains jammed between pickup bed and camper body, and moments later Rob sat inside his own upholstered asylum. It smelled of wine and old bedding. It was scarcely large enough to turn around in. Until he adjusted the window blinds it was as dark as three miles down a coal seam. It was also the first time Rob had felt safe enough to relax in a thousand miles of travel.

Fearful of showing any lights, unfamiliar with the camper's interior details, he eased down on the bed and wondered what might have happened if the camper had been equipped with an alarm system. He had a hundred little details to ponder, but they would wait for dawn. He did not even know how McGrath would react upon learning how his camper was being used. *He'll probably say it's a great joke on the system. If not, he ought to.*

All this, Rob mused, because another man had made a firm decision not to subsidize two ex-wives. Whatever the rakehell McGrath might deserve, in some ways his life was better than that of most working stiffs. He commanded his own little private office in the unclassified Tech Publications branch, from which an enterprising friend might send e-mail and make telephone calls. He had his own brand of protection backed by a corporation powerful enough to make its own rules. And with the infamous McGrath charm, good old Fred had a place to take various attractive GenStan ladies. What he did not have was a teenager willing to say, "I really love you, Dad."

As Rob relaxed atop the rumpled bedding, he knew he would not have traded places with Fred McGrath for anything on earth. He could not entirely trust Corrine, though he would contact Kenny as soon as possible, if only to exchange "All is well" messages. But first of all, he would contact his good friend, Ethan Lodge.

CHAPTER 11

A FEW HOURS AFTER ROB AND KENNY SEPARATED IN KLAMATH
Falls, Ethan Lodge canceled appointments and cleared his
desk for an appointment he dreaded. Edwina Doyle ushered
the trio of undesirables into Ethan's corner office, pretending
not to notice the approving glances of their central figure, the
Defense Intelligence Agency's Lieutenant Commander David
Sachs. The sleek, darkly attractive Sachs wore civilian clothes
and Ed could not help noting to herself that he wore them very
well. Sachs carried himself as if, unlike most men, he might
look just as good in nothing at all.

Ed knew better than to count too much on first impressions,
but they did set a tone. The man who hoped to begin well with
her would register an ego somewhere between self-acceptance
and self-thrilled, and she thought this military intelligence
man seemed a little too satisfied with what he saw in mirrors.

Ethan blinked as the three stepped in, using handshakes to
quickly recover an aplomb that had been briefly shaken. In
Ethan's limited experience, Defense Intelligence Agency people did not commonly meet appointments in threes. The
woman, Marie Vallejo, was an additional surprise, and Ethan
wondered how she had risen to such a position. He quickly
guessed that this team had been picked more for finesse than
rough-and-ready operations. Vallejo seemed as fit as Sachs,
wearing her short curls like a helmet, and in a suit as finely
tailored as any of Ethan's own. The third member, Frank
Carnes, had the look of a chess-playing stevedore with his
open shirt and sport jacket, and his hand, when Ethan shook
it, might have been sculpted of bronze.

Ethan confided that his coffee was a cut above the usual
and passed their orders out to Ed Doyle: cream and sugar for

Sachs, Navy black for Vallejo, water on the rocks for Carnes. Then he asked, "Anything else?"

Sachs's delivery was lazily alert. "One thing: Do you record?"

"If you like, I could."

"Please don't. We won't. This may be a topic of some nuance," Sachs added, as if that explained anything. "We understand that one of your engineers has disappeared from a micro-UAV program."

As Ethan frowned in confusion, the woman spoke. "A Mr. Robert Tarrant. Scheduled for graduate work at Stratford. He never enrolled," she prompted.

Ethan's smile was for them all. "I think I can clear up some misconceptions," he sighed. He went on to explain that though he knew this engineer slightly, Robert Tarrant was not under his direct supervision. Furthermore, General Standards had no Unpiloted Aerial Vehicle programs in any stage of development. This man Tarrant had put himself in danger of dismissal while trying to bring a tiny flying toy into the plant, and Ethan himself had appeared on the security memo after interceding on behalf of the overwrought engineer.

"Just between us, I thought Tarrant might be happier in academia. Helping him into a graduate program might not have been to GenStan's benefit, but we aren't all bloodless bureaucrats. One does what one can," Ethan finished, with a self-deprecating smile. He saw no advantage in volunteering the reason why Rob Tarrant had tried to bring that little gadget into the plant.

Sachs jotted notes in shorthand during the explanation. "But after a routine inquiry, your company security records flagged the fact that this man is not shown on Stratford's enrollment lists," he said.

At this point Ed Doyle followed her discreet knock with a serving tray, and the conversation ceased until, obeying a gesture by Ethan, she had shut the door behind her. For one thing, Ethan Lodge knew it would have been impolite to interrupt the admiring glances that followed Edwina Doyle out. It was not that she curried attention with a bumptious sway of the hip or a fashion model's glide. It was . . . it was—for Ethan, no outdoors enthusiast—it was indefinable.

The coffee, said Sachs, was outstanding. After Ed's departure he went on: "The fact is, we've spoken with Tarrant's estranged wife and she doesn't know where he is, either, except that their young son went with him."

Ethan took his time sipping. *Give every appearance of aid, but don't lead them anywhere they can't go by themselves,* he reminded himself. *These people are spycatchers.* "Have you spoken with Stratford about Tarrant?"

"Not yet, and I'd rather not. The fewer waves we make, the fewer ripples reach the media," Sachs replied.

"I gather the man has had some personal setbacks, Commander," Ethan said gently. "Isn't this much ado about very little?"

"The Department of Defense—*your* Department of Defense," Sachs stressed, naming the body responsible for much of GenStan's profits, "hopes so. It must be obvious, since we're here, that the sudden disappearance and possible defection of a man involved in micro-UAVs is a matter of considerable interest. You say you're a friend of Tarrant's."

"Well—an acquaintance. We don't move in the same circles but his wife and mine are friendly. Call it a halo effect," said Ethan.

"Do you like him well enough to protect him, Mr. Lodge?"

Sachs might as well have slapped him. Ethan drew a steadying breath, hoping to stop the flush he felt on his cheeks. "I don't know anyone quite that well," he said. "Nor do I believe Tarrant would expect me to. He will probably confirm that when you find him."

"*If* we find him—if he's not running to the cover of some other flag. I've already shown you a face card here, Mr. Lodge, because of your clearance: The DOD considers micros as the infancy of a vital technology."

"That's a bit out of my field," said Ethan. "I'll take your word for it, though I think Tarrant's gadget was in the nature of a hobby."

When the sturdy Carnes laughed, Sachs shared a fraternal

glance with him. "Bull was a hobbyist," Carnes said, in the soft rumble of a friendly lion.

When Sachs nodded, so did Vallejo. Ethan, mystified, said, "I don't . . ." and Sachs made a democratic take-it-away gesture to his burly companion.

Carnes: "Gerald Bull's hobby was guns. Great big guns. I mean, cannons with huge shells you could damn near put in orbit."

Ethan: "Isn't that impossible?"

"Probably, but not impossible to send an artillery shell the size of a phone booth several hundred miles. Mr. Bull's hobby was also his career, and he was a world-class consultant. It's just not a very popular idea, though it has a few fans in the Pentagon," Carnes admitted.

"Frank," said Sachs, in gentle restraint.

Carnes waved a hand as if to erase what he had just said. "Okay, but it's old news, David; the media had a field day with it. Anyway, Mr. Bull couldn't understand why our DOD wasn't showering him with money, so he put out some feelers, first to Canada, which was acceptable, because we knew the Canadians wouldn't bite. Then some more feelers we didn't know about. Finally, someone passed us the word that a nice fellow in the Mossad had offered Mr. Bull a suggestion about ways to remain in good health."

At the word "Mossad," Ethan's sphincter tightened with an abrupt fear that this conversation was taking a sinister turn. Inside him a small boy was blubbering, *I didn't mean any harm*—because the slightest mention of Israeli intelligence, from the mouths of American counterspies, was a nightmare revisited for Ethan.

Outwardly he showed only polite interest. "I'm guessing they weren't interested, either."

"Guess again," said Carnes. "They were *very* interested, not because they wanted such a weapon, but because they knew Mr. Bull was dickering with Saddam Hussein. They gave him fair warning, I'll say that."

"Bull was a hobbyist and he knew his stuff, apparently like your Mr. Tarrant," Sachs put in. "The worst kind of loose cannon—pardon the pun. He wanted to see his big guns in action, even if it was the devil himself who fired them. If several agencies hadn't intercepted some incredibly large steel forgings on their way to Iraq, Saddam might've had a gun that would shoot into Tel Aviv."

"Not that our Mr. Bull would've lived to see it," Carnes added. "He was told to lay off. He didn't listen. It got him seriously killed. Officially, we don't know who aced him, but if you know who Saddam Hussein's most likely targets were, you can guess. Mossad plays rough when it feels threatened."

Ethan let the silence last for three beats before he replied. "You actually think that an ordinary GenStan senior engineer like Robert Tarrant could sell what's basically a high-tech toy to Iraq?"

Now it was Vallejo who spoke, crisp and cool as shaved ice. "Or North Korea, or Libya, or—some others. It's our charter to worry about little people at a crucial point who want to become big at all costs. We would prefer that he didn't act on that desire."

"Very much prefer," said David Sachs, who then shifted gears with a sigh. "That's a pretty dark scenario, but it's looking more plausible by the hour. Tarrant hasn't left the country unless he's better at it, or getting more help, than I think. Yes, our tax dollars are at work on it as of this morning, at sites of exit and embarkation," he said, reacting to Ethan's raised brows. "But even if we intercept him, at this point it's still not too late. We're hoping he'll listen to reason."

His blood pressure now under control, Ethan placed elbows on his desk and interlaced his fingers so that they would not shake. Leaning forward with a smile, he said, "And you'd like GenStan to do—what?"

"Not so much the corporation as you, personally, Mr. Lodge," said Sachs. "We hope you might be a voice of reason for us, assuming you have any way of contacting him. I know," he added quickly. "You've said you haven't been close. I'm not challenging that. But if by some chance you should think of any conduit to Robert Tarrant, you might save a patch on several hides before it's too late."

"Give him up, you mean," said Ethan.

"I wouldn't put it quite that way, but essentially . . ." He shrugged and sipped his coffee. "Or at least convince him to contact me. I can be reached." He offered a business card to Ethan. "Phone or fax or e-mail. In this case, we might even find Tarrant a research position somewhere."

This ploy was not very different from Ethan's own tactic in aiming Rob Tarrant toward Stratford. He studied the card and essayed the barest of smiles. "An offer he can't refuse?"

"We aren't the Mafia," said Sachs. "You wouldn't be turning the man over to a death squad, for God's sake."

I wonder if you're sure about that, Ethan thought. He said, "No, of course not. Rest assured, if I'm in a position to help, I will. I'll be out of the area for the next day or so but if he turns up, I'll do my duty."

"I believe we understand each other," Sachs said with a nod, "and I'm sure you're familiar with SAPs."

"If you mean special-access programs, yes." It was obvious, thought Ethan, why some phrases got shortened to acronyms. At his invoking of the phrase "special-access programs," each of these counterspooks squirmed in a special way: the woman, Vallejo, recrossed her legs; the husky Carnes reached to straighten a tie he was not wearing; and even Sachs found it necessary to shift his buttocks in a very comfortable chair. Only a handful of people at the top of Washington's food chain could impose absolute secrecy on a short list of programs, and people like Sachs spent their lives genuflecting to that bible. It was as though the full utterance of that phrase, for them, was equivalent to a Jew's unutterable Name of God.

Ethan simply couldn't resist a trial of his ability to make them squirm, and he saw no danger in it. "I assume that micro-UAVs are part of a special-access program," he said.

"If they were, I couldn't comment on it," said Sachs, adjusting a shirt cuff. "But I recall the military language verbatim. In an SAP, the information is exceptionally vulnerable, and the normal criteria for need-to-know simply won't work. I know we can count on your discretion."

"I'm always discreet with a special-access program," said

Ethan, watching different tics appear, wondering if they were aware of their Pavlovian responses. *If they are, I'm teasing a five-hundred-pound gorilla*, he decided. Enough was enough. "It's possible my wife could hear something about Tarrant from the man's wife, and not realize it was important. Should I—?"

Sachs's interruption was immediate. "Mrs. Lodge is on our interview list. You needn't say a thing; best if you don't. I brought Vallejo and Carnes today so we'll all be in step, and you may consider a message or a visit from one of them as being from me." With that, the commander stood to slide his empty cup onto Ethan's desk and remained standing, a signal the others responded to.

As the trio filed out, Ethan made efforts to repeat eye contact with each of them, showing them his best three-quarter profile, every inch the patriotic executive. When they had gone, he gripped his office door with one hand. "Ed, will you see what's holding up my tickets to San Diego?" She nodded, picking up her phone, and Ethan closed the door very carefully. For the next few moments he simply stood and gazed out past the parking lot, and waited for his tremors to pass.

CHAPTER 12

ROB WAS WAKENED BY THE RAPID FILLING OF PARKING SPACES for the day shift. Fred McGrath's electric shaver neatened-up his beard to a point where he did not look downright shabby, and McGrath's tan slacks were only two inches too large at the waist, his sports jackets sleeves an inch too short. The hell with it; they'd have to do. The wingtip oxfords, however, fitted like horseshoes. If forced to break into a run, Rob would most likely sprint right out of the damned things, but if he was going to pass in the Tech Publications wing he couldn't deviate very far from GenStan practice. Rob waited until moments before ten A.M., when many union employees took their breaks outside, and strolled off toward Tech Publications as if he weren't tingling all over with apprehension.

The door to McGrath's windowless office, in accord with Security directives, remained unlocked but could be locked from inside during classified discussions. Rob lingered at a water fountain until the corridor was empty, then slipped inside, locked the door, and took several long breaths. This wasn't going to work if he continued to feel like barfing on an empty stomach, merely from a stroll to Tech Publications. *If anyone recognizes me, so what? I'm supposed to be here*, he reasoned. *Now all I need is to find that Fred's terminal has a special password.*

At the desk he pulled McGrath's keyboard to him, waited for the screen to respond, and relaxed another notch: it used the standard internal GS coding, no special password for normal memos, and the management menu quickly led him to Ethan Lodge.

After mulling his message over he typed furiously for a few

minutes and paused to study his composition. He made a minor change, then took the risk and hit ENTER.

To: E. Lodge
From: F. McGrath
SUBJECT: Personal

No better way to say this, Ethan: On fishing trip, someone tried to shoot me at night, close range, with silenced pistol. No mistaking his intent. What have I done? Anything to do with GenStan? Stratford? Hate to impose & won't show up @ your door but can't overstate my case of nerves. RSVP ASAP? Will stay on the move. R. Tarrant.

And what if Lodge plays it safe and turns that e-mail rocket over to GenStan Security? Suddenly picturing a phalanx of security men on the march toward McGrath's office, Rob left the terminal and walked to a row of vending machines near the stairwell. If he heard all those flat feet pounding up the stairs, the beard might give him a slender chance to disappear.

He bought a cup of wretched decaf and munched a Payday bar, turning away as a brace of young women hurried by. The coffee was too hot to take more than an experimental sip. *Better than no weapon at all,* flashed into his mind and he gently carried it back to McGrath's refuge; a refuge that, without a second exit, could become a prison.

His heart leaped when he saw that Lodge's reply had arrived almost immediately.

To: F. McGrath
From: E. Lodge
SUBJECT: Personal

Attack probably not connected to company or school. Yesterday DOD team under a David Sachs visited regarding you and device, claiming they only needed to talk. I believe you, outraged to learn of their attempt & you are crazy to be in-plant. Don't know how I can be of further help.

GROUND RULES: No e-mails after today. Never refer to this reply in any way by memo or in person. I will say it didn't happen. I can delete msgs from mainframe but you must delete from yr terminal. Acknowledge ASAP, then delete. Good luck. EL.

Department of Defense? My God, what do they think I'm up to? At least he had one friend left, and one with enough clout to dump messages from the mainframe's memory. He had been hopelessly naive to forget about message storage in GenStan's mainframe computer system. Rob sent one truncated word—"ack"—before he deleted the messages from McGrath's terminal. Then, wondering when his unwitting host would return to kick him out of the camper, he checked the GenStan list of employees on temporary duty outside the plant.

The TDY list was a long one, with each name functioning as a subfile. "McGrath, F." was still in San Diego and not scheduled to return for a week. Rob was sipping that bad coffee, reaching to snap off the terminal, when his gaze was arrested.

Lerner, T.
Lippert, M.
Lodge, E.
Lohle, A.
McGrath, F.
Moore, L.
Nissen, R.

Then, with a thrill of gooseflesh, he moved the cursor to the second name above McGrath's and clicked on it; there might be two E. Lodges in GenStan, but not two Ethan *R.* Lodges. Ethan was in San Diego for three days. And whoever sent that e-mail knew too much for comfort. Rob's mind worked feverishly as he hurried from the building.

With its GenStan windshield logo, the camper could be driven in and out at will by anyone showing a gate pass. Rob feared the battery was too weak to start the engine but at last it rumbled into a stammering idle that presently steadied.

Rob kept it idling until, a few minutes before noon, other vehicles began to exit the parking lot. He became part of the caravan, juggling thoughts about shopping while spending as little money as possible, calling Kenny, and perhaps contacting Gus.

The Salvation Army operated a thrift store on El Camino, the oldest arterial in the Bay Area. Rob spent over an hour there, reflecting that here in Silicon Valley, where anyone who could fog a mirror could make a living wage, a man might dress as well as he liked from used clothing racks. He stopped next at Safeway and stocked the camper's refrigerator before returning to GenStan in midafternoon, decked out in a conservative gray suit and tie. He knew that security men daily checked each office for vulnerable classified materials left out after close of business, but the tech library remained staffed until midnight, and its unclassified room needed no security check. Another advantage: Its terminals were anonymous.

No one disturbed him there. After an hour seeking information on federal agencies he concluded that anything the government had a secretary of, it had a million cops for. Departments of State, Treasury, Transportation, Justice, Defense, with special charters for teams devoted to the Army, Navy, Air Force—the whole interlocking matrix became incomprehensible to an ordinary taxpayer who had somehow landed on someone's "shoot on sight" list.

In his turbulent state, Rob had been waiting for four-thirty P.M., the time when Kenny habitually returned from school. It was almost four when he remembered with a start that school was out. Kenny might have been at home all day; worse, he might have failed to get there.

Thirty seconds later Rob was fumbling for change at a payphone kiosk in the library's hall, cursing his muddled thinking, praying that his son had arrived home safely.

When a voice said hello, Rob thought, *There is a God*.

He wanted to gush out his relief. Instead, he said, "I see you got home okay," a bit gruffly.

"Dad! Jeez, I've been going flaky; where are you staying?"

"In a camper. Wish I could tell you more, son. If you don't know, you won't have to lie to anybody. I'm okay. You have any trouble? How's your mom?"

"I was fine till I got home," the boy said grimly. "There was this guy named Sachs here asking about you today."

"Who's he?"

"God's gift to women, but he spells it 'DIA,' whatever that is. He wants me to—"

"I'll call you again soon," Rob blurted, and broke the connection. If the DIA had already infiltrated his home, they could be tapping his call without Kenny's knowledge. A hundred TV plots had insisted that, to backtrack a call, even the omnipotent feds needed something like a minute for a pinpoint location. Feeling cold sweat on his scalp, Rob strode briskly away from the library and hurried toward Mahogany Row. Given a phone tap, even if he'd hung up in time, they almost certainly would know he had returned to the San Jose vicinity after doubling back. He knew Ethan Lodge would not be in his office, but Ethan was not the one he was anxious to confront.

WHILE ROB HAD SURFED THE INTERNET, A THOUGHT HAD nagged repeatedly: *Who could it be but Edwina Doyle?* No one else would have such constant access to Ethan's e-mail. And Rob's own son had just confirmed that the DIA was involved, which made that warning from Ethan's office seem still more credible. He needed to face Ed as soon as possible, preferably away from the plant site.

The immediate problem was that, while he found Lodge's outer office open, Ed's terminal screen was shut down; a sure sign that with Lodge away, she had taken off early.

Her desk was properly locked; so was her file cabinet. He knew that employee residences and phone numbers were accessible through Security, but otherwise unpublished by GenStan. His gaze roamed over her telephone, desk calendar, a supposedly obsolete Rolodex, and three telephone books including GenStan's booklet. The five o'clock buzzer was ten

minutes away but occasional footsteps scuffed along the hallway. It seemed highly unlikely that she would have her own
address and number in that Rolodex but he checked anyway,
and fruitlessly. If anyone stopped now to ask why this bearded
stranger was hovering at Ed Doyle's desk, Rob feared he might
just stand at attention and start reciting the Pledge of Alle-
giance. He took the telephone books and hunkered down in
the desk footwell. Thank God she had forestalled gawkers with
a matte-painted metal shield. With legs like Ed's, gawking
could be a real hazard to foot traffic.

He found a column of Doyles in the San Jose directory, only
one of which might be Ed's. He tore a strip from a Customer
Guide page and copied the number and address, then checked
the Sunnyvale directory, finding a half-column of Doyles,
three of which were possibles. He copied them, then pulled the
telephone down with him beneath the desk and called the San
Jose number.

The man who answered disclaimed any knowledge of an
Edwina Doyle, and chafed at being disturbed. Rob's next try,
to a Menlo Park prefix, was more pleasant but just as negative.
His last was to a Mountain View number, to a woman who
seemed disposed to learn more about a local Doyle she hadn't
known existed. Rob stopped talking because he heard footsteps pause outside, then the plant buzzer, then many more
footsteps. Silently he broke the connection, thinking, *Okay,
she's unlisted, but she's got a phone. Everybody has a phone.
Don't they?*

He had become so accustomed to cold sweat, it surprised
him to note that his scalp had become dry, his palms barely
moist, by the time people stopped trooping past. He pulled
Ed's little two-ring desk calendar down and, feeling like the
voyeur he was, began to study her notations. He passed telephone numbers with notations such as *hair, Jem*, and *Tempo
oil*, and paused, trying to force an old memory of Ed leaving
one of Ethan's parties. Wasn't her car a Ford Escort? But
maybe a Tempo. The "*Tempo oil*" number had a 968 prefix,
suggesting the nearby suburb of Mountain View. He called the
number and was rewarded on the first ring.

"Performance," said a young male.

"You do oil changes on Edwina Doyle's Tempo, I believe," said Rob, copying the young man's quick pace.

"Uh—who?"

Rob repeated the name.

After a brief pause: "Yeah. Last one in April." A one-bark laugh. "Four stars. Lenny ranks 'em. She must be hot."

"I've got some aftermarket parts to deliver direct to her but I've, um, lost her address. Get me out of a hole, will you? I need her address and phone number."

He knew he'd earned a D-minus in "glib" when the reply came: "Oh, I dunno, man—I could get reamed for that. Four stars, remember?"

"Come on, this could cost me my job, buddy."

"Better yours than mine. Sorry," said the youth, and the line went dead.

And that is why Rob drove to Mountain View and waited until he could see, through the plate glass of the office, that all three employees at Performance Auto were busy servicing cars.

The listings, on four-by-six index cards grayed by too many grease-stained thumbs, lay in a shoebox in plain sight near the phone. No one could have stopped him in time even if they'd noticed him and, in ten seconds, a dead calm Rob Tarrant had his information. Ed's Middlefield Road address was there in Mountain View, near the NASA complex at Moffett Field.

Emboldened by success, he ignored the pay phone and used the old rotary-dial instrument before him.

Corrine must have had the cordless phone with her; she answered during the first ring. "Rob?" She sounded breathless, or excited.

"How'd you guess," he said calmly.

"Kenny said you'd called and hung up right away and said you'd call again and, my God, that was two hours ago," she began in a rush. "I've been beside myself, Robbie. Are you in some kind of trouble?" Evidently she was truly concerned; she hadn't called him "Robbie" since their Virgin Islands vacation for two, a decade before.

"I got shot at, a few nights ago. He missed, but even an engineer can take a hint as broad as that. I figured Kenny would've told you."

"It sounded—well, fanciful to me. I'm not doubting you," she added quickly. "The connection's really good if you're calling from Seattle or something."

And you've been talking with someone who's filled you with bullshit about my flight north, he decided. But he had honeymooned with this woman, created a home with her, lived with her for fifteen years. He replied with thoughtless honesty: "No, I'm right here in Mountain View. Did you think I was skipping the goddamn country?"

"I—I didn't know what to think," she said in a small contrite voice that shifted subtly as she continued. "I just know I've been worried out of my mind. After all that I've been through recently, I mean." Not offering sympathy; asking for it.

"I'm really, really sorry, Corrie. I'm trying to find out what I'm supposed to have done to have pissed somebody off that badly, and meanwhile I'm just holding on to my butt with both hands."

"That used to be my job," she said, her meaning unmistakable.

Half disbelieving, half amused: "Jesus, Corrie, are you hitting on me at a time like this?" They'd talked for more than a minute now, but if somebody pinpointed Performance Auto, so what? He'd be gone before they could arrive.

"I suppose, um, well, now that you mention it—Robbie, this is a different you." She was all but whispering now. "You're my randy husband but we haven't been sleeping together, and in some kinky way it's different. Sort of like when I used to put on my classic pink Spring-o-lator heels in the bedroom and call you Mr. Tarrant, in a commercial sort of way. Does that make sense?"

When she reminded him of those weird and wonderful playlets of theirs, when they both gave free rein to their imaginations and worried only about waking the baby, he didn't care

whether it made sense or not. "More sense than our separation," he said.

"I'm starting to think the same thing," she said, all but
purring. "Listen, Kenny's been asking permission to go to a
baseball game with some friends this evening. If you waited
till about nine, you and I could be alone awhile before he got
back. Later we could all make popcorn or something."

He saw a Camaro hood slam down outside and had no wish
to make explanations. "Got to run now. I'll come at nine," he
said.

"I'll see that you do, Mr. Tarrant," she promised softly.

He had parked a block away, and hurried to the camper,
mindful of an erection he could have hung his hat on. If this
was the way Corrine reacted to his apparent status as outlaw,
maybe he should've been robbing banks for a living.

Thoughts of this sort, and a growing disposition to take
action on the spur of the moment, fought against years of his
regimentation as a solid citizen. The responsible parent in him
argued that he should drive home immediately and see Kenny
before the game. However, in that case Kenny might not go
at all, and his parents would miss their own lusty game. The
bulge in his slacks won that little debate easily and he forestalled guilt by reminding himself that, before nine o'clock, he
had an urgent appointment on Middlefield Road.

CHAPTER 13

HE FOUND ED DOYLE'S LITTLE MAROON FORD SEDAN PARKED
beneath the lacy umbrella of an acacia tree. The car had been
virtually hidden by a newish VW Vanagon at one side of an
unassuming duplex of 1960s vintage. Rob parked around the
corner, a long block away, and walked back, rehearsing what
he would say.

His rehearsal was for nothing. The man who answered the
chimes did it in style, calling from inside before he opened the
door. "On my way. Keep your pants on—or not," he sang out
merrily, and Rob's first impression was of a cheery smile. He
was tall, slender and barefoot, in close-fitting jeans and T-
shirt, with swarthy features and a strongly chiseled nose. He
held a pair of water-pump pliers big enough to brain a horse.
"Help you?"

"Guess I got the wrong— Ah, I'm looking for Edwina
Doyle," Rob stammered.

"Within. Follow me. Jem Kasabian," said the tall man,
with a smile and a quick handshake, motioning Rob inside,
hurrying off toward the kitchen. "I'm Ed's roomie. We're
changing a faucet gasket, if you can wait."

Unbidden, Rob's mind matched Ed with this thirtyish up-
tempo gent and concluded they would make an attractive couple. Rob hadn't known about this arrangement; perhaps not
even Ethan did.

He saw long jeans-clad legs protruding from beneath the
kitchen sink. "Whoever it is, we'll be through in a minute—I
hope," Ed's voice echoed pleasantly.

Kasabian had the faucet valve out already and, after choosing one wrong gasket from a packet, secured the right one
using long strong fingers, adept as a cardsharp. When the un-

used gaskets fell into the sink, Rob slapped one hand over the drain hole and used the other to collect the errant washers. Now the men were chuckling and shifting their feet as Ed banged into them with her calves.

Kasabian urged her to turn the cutoff faucet again; cranked the replaced handle several times. "We're in business, luv," he crowed. "Come out of durance vile and and take your rightful place in society."

A dull *thonk* from below. "Damn," Ed said gently. Another thump. "Well, shit," she said, now with full sincerity, rolling over, backing out, rubbing hard against the back of her head as she did so. "Ow, ow, ow," she went on as if to herself, but raised both arms in an obvious bid for help in rising, still facing downward.

Rob stepped behind her and lifted from her armpits, and she levitated with a squeal. Kasabian had both hands full of hardware when she found her footing and turned to face Rob, their noses a handspan apart. "Oh! Oh my God," she gasped, shrinking from his grasp, her back against the sink.

"What? What!" Jem Kasabian's friendly smile had become something else in an instant, his glance darting from her to this stranger. He swiveled to wedge his shoulder between them, his back to the woman, face-to-face with Rob, and now those dark eyes glittered. "Talk to me, Edwina," he demanded. He held the water-pump pliers very close to Rob's chin.

"No, Jem, he's not— I mean, it's okay."

"You're sure," Kasabian prompted, beginning to relax, sliding away but still warily alert.

"Bad start," said Rob. "I'm Rob Tarrant."

"That doesn't explain a lot," said Kasabian. "Ed?"

She rubbed her upper arms with her hands and tried a laugh that didn't quite work. "Really, Jem. Rob's a good guy—I think. And I have an idea why he's here but I'm not sure you should," she went on, moving away from the sink, patting her hair.

Kasabian sighed and rolled his eyes to heaven. "Oh, dear sweet goddy, it's going to be like that, is it?"

"It's GenStan business, kind of," she told him, then motioned Rob to a chair as she washed her hands. "Now, Mr. Rob Tarrant: an explanation, if you please."

"Isn't that my line?" He decided she was playing for time, hoping to settle her nerves. "I'm grateful for that e-mail you sent, but I have to know more before I risk my neck in public again."

"E-mail? I don't know what you're talking about," she said crisply. "And how did you find my address? It's not published."

"Oh ho," said Kasabian with deceptive softness, folding his arms as he leaned against the cupboard. And he would *not* put down those whopping pliers. "I wondered if you'd reviewed your decision about dating within the company, Ed. Curiouser and curiouser," he said.

"I haven't changed my mind. This isn't about relationships, Jem."

"The hell it isn't," Rob snorted. "Not for you, maybe." He turned his gaze to Kasabian. "Don't get the wrong idea, I'm no stalker. I'm an engineer whose life has been turned upside down—and at risk, by the way, and I still don't know why—and I'm sure Ed can clear up some things for me."

"I really don't know," she shrugged, pulling a basket of fruit to her, making a great show of choosing a bowl and a paring knife. "I have enough to do without e-mailing people under false pretenses and—" She fell silent.

"Who said anything about false pretenses?" Rob asked softly, letting his gaze slide toward the suspicious Kasabian, whose brow lift signified that he was paying close attention. "You said you had an idea why I'm here, Ed, but it scared the pudding out of you when I showed up. You think your, um, significant other here shouldn't know about it. And you know that e-mail was sent with a false name but when you said as much, you clammed up."

" 'Clammed up,' " Kasabian sighed and put down the tools. "I can't believe you said that; I feel like I've wandered into a bad Bogart movie, if there were any such thing. Ed, if you don't quit womanhandling that banana, I swear to God I'll stab someone with it. Myself, maybe. Rob Tarrant, I may yet throw your svelte butt out of here but in the meantime, have you had supper? It's only fruit salad."

"It would be," said Ed wryly, receiving only a jaded, "*I caught that*" glance from Kasabian.

"I'm okay," said Rob.

Kasabian: "Don't make me repeat myself. Two portions or three? It's the same trouble either way."

"Three, then," said Rob. "Give me something to peel."

"Straight lines, straight lines," murmured Kasabian, tossing an orange to him. Whether playing to Rob or to himself, at least he seemed willing to advance an ounce of camaraderie. "Edwina, my cabbage, the gentleman makes some salient points. I think I may believe him. Mango, anybody?"

She sat down and covered her face with her hands. "That's exactly what I said," was her muffled admission.

Kasabian, tentatively: "You offered the man a mango."

Ed, laughing despite herself: "Jem Kasabian, you can be the most exasperating poof on this planet," she said. "All right! Yes, I e-mailed Rob that I believed him, under my manager's name. Rob had sent him a message claiming he'd been shot at, but Ethan Lodge is out of town. Even if he'd been in-plant, I don't think he would've warned this poor guy. Wouldn't fit with company policy, y'know. I said I believed Rob because a guilty person wouldn't have been where he was, clueless and begging for a hint. I paid attention when a tough-looking little crew of federal agents came to the office, and I'm not supposed to listen but I did. No one said Rob was in immediate danger, but if they're shooting at him, he needed to know who it was. I hoped he'd take my reply as being from Lodge, and warned him to never mention it again." She pursed her lips, shook her head. "Right; the master plan from Miss Naïveté. See if I ever play the Good Samaritan again, huh?"

Kasabian paused in peeling the Technicolor mango. "You don't look like a man people should be shooting at, but then, neither did Ted Bundy," he said. "Maybe I shouldn't be a party to this. Naturally, thanks to my hopeless in-fucking-satiable curiosity, now I am. And even if gays are above the salt these days, I have no need to waste my life as a cog in some big industrial machine, tugging at my forelock to some vapid cipher like Mr. Lodge. As your escort, Ed, I once met the man—remember? A drone, mated to a knickknack. If his wife were any more hollow she'd have a clock in her navel.

"I do multimedia graphics, by the way," he went on, to Rob. "I sculpt, really, but there's not much money in it so I earn a passable salary in commercial art; coaxing it out of fractals by computer, and so on. I'm not afraid of my government, which doesn't mean I trust it. When I start being afraid of it, I'll begin looking toward France or Canada or some such. Meanwhile, I do know how to keep my mouth shut, Rob Tarrant."

"I wouldn't ask for more," said Rob. "I wish I could just go to the police with this, but they'd probably call in the very people who tried to put some holes in me the other night."

Kasabian paused in his work. "You weren't exaggerating, then? I mean, real gunfire?"

"I was afraid this would happen," said Ed. "Look at your hands, Jem."

He did, set down his knife, and took a chair. "Diabetic," he said to Rob, with a sorrowful smile, and showed how his hands trembled. "On top of some emotional stress I've had with a friend—ex-friend—just what I needed was to get all macho with you. Not good for me," he sighed, "but I can still listen."

Ed brought a glass of orange juice from the refrigerator, demanded that Kasabian drink it all, then took Rob's peeled orange. While she finished concocting the salad, Rob described his fishing trip with Kenny for them, now and then fielding a question from one or the other. Finally Ed slid bowls of fruit salad onto the table, with tall glasses of iced water, and took a seat. "I didn't hear everything they said in the office," she confessed, "but this fashion plate, Commander Sachs, repeated a phrase I've never heard before. Are you working on something called a 'micro-UAV'? If it's classified, I don't want to know," she added quickly.

"Mine sure aren't," Rob grinned. "It's a hobby." He tried to be brief, skimming over such details as carbon-fiber wing ribs and special batteries. "I'd hoped to interest GenStan in some killer applications, through Ethan Lodge," he finished.

"Seems you found one, all right," said Kasabian. " 'Killer application'—unfunny. *Baaad* Jem," he said, and slapped his wrist lightly. "Is this anything like those little models they used to fly in the old Moffett blimp hangar? Cellophane coverings, propellers that move so slowly you could count the revolutions?"

"Based on some of the same technology, but smaller; radio-controlled, stronger materials, especially different morphology. You can fly mine outdoors if the wind isn't blowing up a storm. Of course, you need to work out the right combinations: wing shapes, materials, actuators, Reynolds numbers you can count on your fingers," he said, saw Ed's eyes begin to glaze over, and shrugged. "Anyway, it took me years of playing around to get it right. Lots of that was luck," he admitted. "I thought I could pass it on."

"That's exactly what those people in the office were worried about," said Ed. "They're watching airports and borders for you, Rob. Pretty serious about it."

"They think I intend to sell a hobby project overseas?" In his disbelief, Rob's voice went close to falsetto. "Loony-tunes. If they think that, they're capable of anything."

"But they swore to Lodge that they didn't want you hurt," Ed protested.

"After they'd already had a go at it," Rob reminded her, and vented a mirthless snort. "Why am I not convinced of their goodwill, I wonder?"

"Rob, I hate to say it, but this scares me. If they would kill you on such flimsy grounds, they could do it to Ethan Lodge, or me, or . . . or anybody."

"Sorry you sent that e-mail?"

She shrugged. "Not yet, but ask me again after I've been shot at. It also makes me pretty damned mad."

"That's our Edwina. Couldn't mind your own business," said Kasabian; but his smile was tender.

"It was so—so unfair," she burst out. "Reading that message from Rob, I kept thinking that, of all the men I danced with at those parties, Rob Tarrant was the only young one who never tried to put a move on me."

"Well, hell, I was married," Rob muttered, stealing a glance at his wristwatch at the thought of Corrine tricked out for a friendly tussle at home.

Ed's glance was acute. "So were most of the others. You're not, now?"

He made a flip-flop motion with one hand. "Legally, yes. We're just not living together. For Corrine, it's probably for the best right now. Christ, I shouldn't be sleeping next to anybody until this is cleared up!"

"That's why I wouldn't suggest you crash on the living-room couch," said Kasabian. "I'm sorry, Robert, but there's this old phrase I keep hearing in the news: 'collateral damage'. I would dearly loathe to be seen as collateral—in any sense of the word."

"No problem. I'm staying in a camp—"

"I don't want to hear it," Ed interrupted. "What I don't know won't hurt me."

"—said the frog on the freeway," Kasabian murmured. "What I'd like to know is, how you hope to calm these nice people down without getting yourself killed."

"This is just off the top of my head, but I think I need to face one of them when they least expect it, convince him I'm not a threat to national security. I'd do it in public if possible," said Rob. "Identify them, make sure I have an escape worked out . . . Hell, I haven't worked it out," he admitted.

"But I'd bet they can identify you on sight," said Ed, "though you gave me a start with that beard. It might fool them."

"Little dye job would help," Kasabian suggested. "I could do it in a half-hour. No, don't look at my roomie like that, Robert; I'm the one in this house who knows how to do hair."

"True," said Ed, abashed. "And he's done one of my girl-friends, as well. So to speak," she added, cutting a sly glance at her friend.

"Bite your tongue. Well?"

"If you'll quit calling me Robert, you've got a deal," said Rob.

Kasabian's bedroom was nearest to the living room, with Ed's at the end of the short hallway. The bathroom was between the two, and it was here that Rob got his "do." The result, he decided, made him look like a stranger—and, with his darkened beard, a slightly piratical one at that. "Your own wife won't know you now," said Kasabian, admiring his own work.

"She'll love it," said Rob, but didn't explain why. If Corrine wanted to play "strangers when we meet," he was up for it in more ways than one, and, in his present mood, more focused on that promising encounter than caution would dictate. He thanked his hosts profusely and left feeling more confident than ever. The detached Ed Doyle he knew at GenStan was turning out to be like pie à la mode: cool outside, warm and spicy beneath.

CHAPTER 14

BECAUSE MOUNTAIN VIEW AND SUNNYVALE ARE ADJOINING suburbs, Rob found himself cruising past his own home twenty minutes before nine in the evening, his erection pounding with memories of that telephone call. The only cars he saw in the neighborhood were familiar, including the black Porsche, but around the block directly opposite the Tarrant bungalow sat a house vacated the month before, and Rob drove around to park in its driveway. Residential space had been at such a premium for thirty years, local developments had no alleys, and only a wooden fence separated the vacated property from Rob's own backyard. In his present mood, he had no trouble scaling that fence.

He had not expected the sense of not–quite–déjà vu that washed over him as he moved past a swing set that Kenny never used anymore, under the foliage of the tangerine tree he and Corrine had planted together, to the bin that neatly hid garbage cans next to the back door. He'd been in that shadowy backyard at dusk a thousand times, yet it seemed not the same. He realized the irony of this introspection with a sad smile: Yes, the fondly remembered backyard was exactly the same. It was Rob himself who had changed, no longer the lord of his familiar three-bedroom manor; stealing through suburban yards to a tryst like some lust-maddened teenager. But he refused to knock on his own screen door and allowed it to bang shut behind him as he stepped into the kitchen.

Evidently Corrine had been standing in the bathroom; she clip-clopped into the kitchen wearing a frown and not a whole lot more—vintage spike-heeled sandals, negligee, and plainly visible through the gauzy fabric, a garter belt to hold up the long dark stockings. A vagrant thought by Rob: *Good think-*

*ing, Corrie. I'd love to get my hands on the silly son of a bitch
who designed pantyhose.*

Corrine's expression of concern lasted only a second, to be
replaced by the faintest of smoky glances. "Come to read my
meter, stranger?"

"Service with a smile," he said, and swallowed hard. "It
was service you had in mind, I believe."

She sashayed to him, her eyes roving about his face. "You
look amazingly like my husband," she murmured, "if he had
a beard. I wonder if it scratches."

He had his coat off before he replied. "What's a little friction
between strangers?"

The coat fell to the floor as Corrine met him halfway, her
fingers in his hair, one thigh insinuated between his. They
kissed like famished gluttons, hands roaming, bodies finding
remembered accommodations.

He realized that she had unzipped him only when he felt a
coolness and then a warm thrilling squeeze, and the next moment she had grasped his shoulders and hopped aboard for a
ride that was merciless, and more brief than he'd intended. By
the time they uncoupled, Corrine lay across the breakfast table, teeth bared in ferocious eagerness, though Rob remained
standing, and somehow her ankles had migrated to his hands.
Her gaze was fixed to the slick wetness of him, bared to view;
and this time his insertion was as slow, as deliberate, as he
could manage. She moved against him more carefully now,
sometimes pausing, sometimes thrusting, but always watching
the process. He concentrated on her face, hoping to discern
what she wanted most. If Corrine had ever shown him this
much frank lust, he decided, it had been before they married.

She left no doubt when she climaxed, gripping his upper
arms, her head twisting from side to side. When she lay back
again, he released her ankles, caressing her calves and smiling.

She needed time to recover her breath. "Wonderful. You?"

"A quick wonderful. I'm saving up for my third," he
grinned.

"Oh my God," she said, and sat up quickly. "Kenny may
be home early but he never has a key." She slipped to her feet,

clip-clopping across linoleum toward the living room. "You clean up and we'll start over," she called over her shoulder.

He slung his coat over a kitchen stool and hurried to the bathroom as bidden, not wanting to hurry at all, cleaning himself with a warmed washtowel. He heard her call him from their bedroom, and found the lights on. "No, leave it on," she pouted as he reached for the wall switch. Noting that his trousers were zipped again, she sat on the bed, legs apart, and murmured, "Come here and let me do you. See how long you can save it this time."

"An offer I can't refuse," he said, striding to stand before her, meeting her gaze as she began to prepare him again. He gasped as he felt her tongue at the very tip of him, their eyes still locked. He began to massage her scalp as she nibbled and kissed in ways she had not chosen in . . . in . . . perhaps not ever. In time, Corrine had become more fastidious in her bedroom behavior—until now. "Been watching porn videos, ma'am?"

"Maybe. Or maybe just watching the news. You like having your own Monica?" And now she fell silent, her mouth otherwise occupied. After a few moments he pulled back, feverish but still with shreds of self-control. She looked up. "Hurt you?"

"No," he smiled, "but I want this to last. In more ways than one, Corrie. This is, uh, great, but right now I really need to lie down and hold you, do it with you the way—"

In the dusk, he saw headlight beams through the bedroom window as they swerved to a curb somewhere nearby. The beams went out and, in that instant, his sex drive winked out as if a spell had broken. "Then do it," she insisted, lying back on the bed. "Do me, do me, Robbie."

"Honey, that could be Kenny's ride," he said, darting to the hall, then to the living room, making himself presentable. Through a front window and past their shrubbery he could barely make out a dark sedan parked two houses away. Three figures hurried along the sidewalk, none of them Kenny, and now the bulkiest of the three slipped toward the side of the Tarrant shrubbery.

Corrine was still begging him aloud when Rob bounded to the kitchen, grabbed his coat in passing, and kicked the screen door open. He clearly heard the front door open as he raced through their unkempt grass. Whatever Corrine had done in the living room, she hadn't locked that front door. He flung his Salvation Army coat over the back fence and followed it, all but vaulting the fence, and risked one glance back through the gloom. If those bastards had used a night scope before, they might see him yet. The high shrubs lit by the kitchen window shook with someone's rapid passage. Now, every sound he made was magnified in his mind as he sought the camper's ignition key, but from his own home he could hear voices, male and female, raised in stridence. Somehow he knew that his wife of fifteen years was in no danger, and when the back door's familiar slam told him a second person had gone inside, he dared to start the engine. It started quietly enough and he kept his wits enough to avoid using his head-lights until he was a block down the street. Though crestfallen at Corrine's defection, he was encouraged by the idea that those junketeering gumshoes still did not know what vehicle he drove.

ON FIRST REFLECTION HE FELT THE ANGER OF BETRAYAL AND, he admitted honestly, of sexual frustration. *Sure as hell, she drew me over there to be caught. Those assholes have co-opted my own wife into playing Mata Hari, and she really took to the role, goddamn her.*

On the other hand, he *had* got some of what he'd come for, and this mysterious Sachs, if that's who it was, had not. Rob's was a paltry, even pathetic, little victory but it was better than none. He laughed softly to himself as he neared Gus Kallas's little home. This would be a hoot to old Gus; not many men had to worry about getting caught in flagrante delicto with their own wives by federal cops.

His amusement drained away as suspicion took center stage in his thoughts. Yes, Gus was a close friend, but if Corrine could be turned against him so quickly, why not her father? Other solid American families had disavowed a member accused of . . . what? Terrorism, treason, and any number of lesser crimes.

Seen in this light, Rob could even find a glimmer of sympathy for Corrine and Gus, but not enough to risk seeing Gus this time. He drove past, seeing a light in Gus's little trailer. He would be working on some big RC model no doubt, readying it to show off for the June meeting of the RC Rogues on— he worked the date out silently—the following night.

Rob astonished himself, thinking about his hobby at a time like this. He had found more than he expected while in the GenStan tech library, searching the Internet for micro-UAV work. Perhaps somewhere in all that data lay the reason why federal agents thought Rob was worth a summary execution. At this time of night, however, there would be few drudges courting eyestrain in that library and he'd taken all the risks he could stand for one day.

He drove to a mall parking lot and changed to jeans and jogging sneakers in the camper. A double scoop of lime sherbet in the mall and a few brisk laps around its sea of parked cars should set him up nicely for a night's sleep in GenStan's parking lot. He could enter at the main gate among the night-shift traffic.

THE FOLLOWING MORNING, ROB VISITED FRED MCGRATH'S office twice. His first visit told him that Lodge was again in the plant, and that there was no change in McGrath's scheduled absence. He took a GenStan notepad with him to the library and worked his way through more of the recent work on UAVs. Something kept pestering him, something about the newly proposed UAV studies, but he could not force it to the surface. Researchers at MIT had done some interesting studies on paper; too bad he hadn't been working in Boston where a lot of the science was being done: Engineers figured out how, and then scientists figured out why. The Romans had made many tons of cement centuries before scientists figured out why it worked, and how it might work better.

En route to Fred McGrath's office again, he saw people he knew slightly, and not one gave him a glance of recognition.

His remembrance of Ethan Lodge's calm, friendly manner tempted him again to contact the man, and he went as far as booting up McGrath's terminal. As it happened, McGrath had a message from Lodge . . . or so it seemed.

To: F. McGrath
From: E. Lodge
SUBJECT: Doing Lunch Today

. . . here in cafeteria with familiar trio. Understand you have urgent work elsewhere. Ack only & delete.

No need for a signature. He felt gooseflesh crawl near the nape of his neck, realizing that the courageous Edwina Doyle was probably sitting within twenty feet of Lodge when she had sent this bulletin. He transmitted only "ack," deleted the correspondence, and checked the time. The company cafeteria opened at eleven-thirty, but at that time it was chiefly management who sauntered in for unhurried service before the main crush of diners at noon. He had ten minutes to make himself scarce.

Or longer, if he chose to stroll into the jaws of danger. Management had their own alcove in the cafeteria, visible but separate from the common herd, and if he chose the right vantage point Rob could inspect those three visitors. Corrine would have told Sachs and his people about the beard and dye job, but GenStan employed a lot of computer programmers who made a fetish of distinctive appearance. They wore everything from beards to blond afros; T-shirts to jumpsuits. The programmers' chaotic dress code was practically part of their special little subculture in California's Silicon Valley. Programmers were the same folks who tended to wander in early like managers. The implication of this behavior was clear: *"Fire me if you like, I can be working for your competition by this afternoon."*

There might be no better way, and no better time, to get a good look at this murderous little bunch of hunters, and even if he was recognized, he did not think anyone would begin shooting in such a public place. Until now, by necessity, he had been reacting, and reactive steps implied the spur of the moment. Shadowing his pursuers would be proactive, a chance to level the playing field—or for disaster.

When Rob entered the dining area, two dozen people were seated, another ten serving themselves. The man in tweeds speaking to the cashier was erect, blow-dried perfection: Ethan Lodge. Behind him stood a swarthy woman with strong, moderately attractive features, in business suit and sensible shoes, and behind her moved a solidly-built gent, his suit coat tight around a heavy torso, his dark hair cut too short to be parted. He was speaking with the woman, mulling a choice of iced drinks. Next in line was a man of Lodge's height, slim-hipped, wide shoulders, ruggedly good-looking, and he paid less attention to the slice of apple pie he chose than to the woman behind him: Ed Doyle, with a perfunctory smile for what the man was saying. The fourth person behind Ed was Rob himself, sidling along, already beginning to repent of this madness.

With his vision impeded by the line and his averted face, Rob had no opportunity to indulge in a harmless male pursuit—watching Ed Doyle walk. Besides, that walk of hers was not at its best when she moved slowly along, encumbered by a lunch tray and taking small steps. Rob had never discussed this particular woman's gait with anyone; he did not need to. A runner and hiker of long experience, he knew a distance-swallowing stride on sight, and if pressed on the subject, might have gauged her normal stride at a remarkable thirty-four inches.

Ambulation like that readily separated a population of alert males into two categories: the physically active and the physically passive. To an Ethan Lodge, a man of strict diet and sagacious tailoring, Ed's walk was neither attractive nor unattractive; just an oddity and a mystery, nothing more. To a Rob Tarrant, it suggested an athlete with stamina.

Ed's wasn't a walk calculated to draw admiration. Quite to the contrary, it was not calculated at all. Ed's walk was simply the result of a young girl's matching her father's hiking stride, then growing to the height of an average man. The long, strong legs added to the effect that they were loose-jointed. Other women, mincing along with twenty-inch strides, thought Ed's walk must look foolish to men, and most women were damned glad of it.

Switching his attention, Rob identified David Sachs and his charismatic confidence without a second of doubt. And loathed him. Recapturing the moment on the previous evening when he had stared from his window at three figures hurrying toward his home, Rob concluded this trio fitted those silhouettes. The heavyset guy, no doubt, had been the one fighting through the shrubbery to the back door.

Lodge's group left in file following the manager toward a nearby alcove, and Rob, his stomach suddenly turned gymnastic, selected a chicken salad as the item least likely to become a Vesuvius in his belly. By the time he carried his tray to a table near a structural pillar, Lodge's quintet had seated themselves.

Almost the first thing he saw was Ed's iced tea as she upset it onto the sleeve of Mr. Prettyboy seated beside her. "Good work," he muttered, meaning it, deciding she had done it deliberately. Sachs seemed to be taking it in good humor. Rob was no lip-reader, but now he could catalog the features of these three who had torn his life apart.

ED WAS SO STARTLED TO RECOGNIZE ROB TARRANT IN THE distance, she dumped her iced tea onto Sachs's tray. At least the gaffe might explain her sudden case of nerves, and David—the first-name business, like her presence here, was his idea—was not put off by it. "I probably ought to be fed intravenously," she said, donating her paper napkins. Across the table, Lodge was listening to Frank Carnes describe a close encounter with their fugitive engineer.

"I'll see if they offer intravenous cioppino at Fisherman's Wharf," Sachs murmured, mopping carefully.

The opening was obvious. The famed complex of San Francisco eateries was an hour north of Sunnyvale, and if nothing else, a dinner there would remove David Sachs from the field of play for an evening. There was also no denying that Sachs was an attentive escort whose attentions flattered her. "I suppose your team eats there often," said Ed. Marie Vallejo, quietly taking everything in, hid a faint smile at that. It wasn't the sort of smile, Ed judged, that suggested a strained relationship.

"I wasn't thinking business, Edwina, I hardly know the place. But if you'd care to show me the Wharf sometime, I'd be more than honored."

"Sometime, perhaps," she said, refocusing on the middle distance. Rob Tarrant, the audacious lunatic, was now half-hidden by a pillar as he toyed with his lunch and stared in her direction. Unconsciously she gave a disapproving shake of her head.

Sachs, misunderstanding, parodied an old song. " 'Your words say yes-yes, but there's no-no in your—' "

"Yes, Mr. Lodge?" The manager had been trying to get her attention.

"Mr. Carnes asked about GenStan hobby groups, and I must say I haven't a glimmer," said Lodge. "A modelers' club? People who may be intimates of Tarrant?"

"I don't know of any, but I could check this afternoon," Ed offered.

"Most fugitives don't abandon their old ways, Edwina," Sachs put in, as if she needed him to connect the dots. "Take our man Tarrant: We almost caught him last night at his own home, right here in Sunnyvale." She'd heard about that, too, ten minutes ago. Did they imagine she was deaf in the outer office?

"I saw the bait," said Carnes, with a deep chuckle. "Can't blame the guy. For a hausfrau who shops at Victoria's Secret, Miz Tarrant's a long way from a bowwow—" He saw Sachs's glance and shrugged. "Anyhow, you were right, Commander. And he's found a pickup camper somewhere. We thought maybe from his father-in-law."

"That's a negative," said Vallejo, her first words at the table. "I pulled a records check; the old fellow owns a small house trailer. No camper."

"Wasn't a house trailer I spotted over that damn fence," Carnes insisted. "Only a glimpse, and I couldn't make the plates, but I know what I saw. Back East, now, that alone would be a good lead."

Ed recalled Rob's admission that he was staying in a camper, and felt suddenly weak inside. All innocence and misdirection, she said, "Really? There must be a hundred thousand of them in the Bay Area."

"True." Lodge wiped the corner of his mouth with a napkin and cleared his throat, a sure sign to Ed that he was setting sail toward an anecdote. "We have hundreds of the ungainly things in our parking lots. The fact is, we have one proposals specialist who literally lives in his camper."

"I'm surprised you'd allow that," said Sachs, though his antennae were still chiefly waving toward Ed.

"We don't, officially," Lodge continued. He had the full attention of both Carnes and Vallejo now. "It's expressly forbidden, but this is a special case; one of those flawed experts who'd have an office next to mine if not for his, ah, unsavory past. Ex-wives, process servers—a messy life. We look the other way for McGrath, but for anyone else it would be a termination offense."

Vallejo, as if to herself: " 'Gypsy rigs,' they're called. People like that all seem to know one another." -

"Two minds, one thought," Carnes said with a smile, miming a playful trigger-pull at Vallejo with thumb and forefinger. "Might not hurt to pay him a call, Commander. Especially if he knows Tarrant."

Lodge grunted; shook his head. "Unlikely. He's a fierce poker hand, much in demand along the second floor."

"They don't move in the same circles, then," said Vallejo.

"Hardly," said Lodge, with the beginnings of a smirk. Ed was gratified that she had spilled her iced tea; she would have had to resist the impulse to toss it in her manager's face.

"You never know," Sachs sighed, and glanced at his wrist. "It's a good idea, Frank. Do a peripheral interview with this McGrath today."

"You can't do that," Ed said quickly. Ethan Lodge and

David Sachs wore identical openmouthed expressions, and it was time for some rapid fence-mending. "Well, I'm sure you could, but you'd have to drive to— Where was it? San Diego, San Somewhere. He's off-site, I'm quite sure of it."

"This woman is magic," smiled Lodge, as if congratulating himself.

Ed gave her manager a heavy-lidded smile, then slowly turned its full wattage on Sachs. "If it's magic to check everything twice," she replied. "I maintain your off-plant company listing, Mr. Lodge, and I check to make certain the computer gets it right. I always see Mr. McGrath's listing below yours when he's off-site, and it's been the same since May. I saw it again this morning, so I imagine he and his camper are still in San Diego." She spread her hands and smiled. "I really should pretend I'm clairvoyant, but it's only attention to detail. Mr. McGrath should be back in-plant in a few weeks, as I recall."

"Doesn't matter," Carnes said in dismissal. "It was just a thought."

Having achieved his "Sometime, perhaps" from Ed, David Sachs turned his attention to Lodge again, recapping their office conversation of an hour before. He finished with, "So there's a good chance he'll contact you after all, Mr. Lodge, and you know what to do when he does. We don't know why, but we know he's here."

Ed, in a small voice: "Here?"

Because Sachs laughed, Lodge laughed, too. "Here in the Valley," said Sachs, waving a negligent hand around. "Don't be afraid, I didn't mean here inside GenStan."

"Wouldn't last a minute," Lodge said with conviction.

"From the profile we have, he's unpredictable enough to be interesting, but the man isn't crazy," Vallejo put in, sliding her chair back because Sachs was already rising.

From the edge of her vision, Ed saw a well-built, bearded figure in the distance stand up quickly, carrying his tray toward the exit. *Getting a ten-second jump on the hounds,* she guessed, remembering to smile at Sachs as he stole a glance toward her cleavage. *But they're only half-right about you, Rob Tarrant. You're the most interesting man I've met in years, but my God, you're crazy. . . .*

CHAPTER 15

THE SURGE OF INCOMING TRAFFIC AFTER LUNCH MADE ROB'S surveillance more difficult but, peering through the camper's windshield, he was slightly elevated over other parked vehicles. When his trio of hunters left the building sometime later, they climbed into a dark blue Pontiac sedan, the woman driving. Rob hurried to the camper's cab only to find that they'd driven into employee parking, evidently to a second car. He waited until he saw what looked like a black Chevy pulling out to accompany the Pontiac. Parked nearer the main gate, Rob was able to exit the plant well ahead of them. He had already determined to follow them but was now faced with an unexpected choice.

Two sets of eyes were more likely to spot him than one, and two hunters more likely to box him in somehow. What clinched his decision was this: He did not want to shadow two people who might face him with drawn guns. He drove a long block from GenStan property, then into a parking lot, where he was outmaneuvered in a momentary gridlock mess.

Two minutes later the blue Pontiac cruised past, much too distant for him to get its license number. After a wait so long he despaired, the black Chevy sedan appeared. The guy now wore a baseball cap and was speaking into a cellular phone, oblivious to Rob who bluffed a lady in a tiny Geo and, a moment later, eased into traffic a half a block behind.

Even had he wanted to follow more closely, the ungainly camper kept him so far in the rear he briefly lost sight of the Chevy. He saw it again as it turned toward the Bayshore Freeway, and tried to keep up. Ten minutes later he saw one of two black dots far ahead as it scooted onto an off-ramp. To his right was the San Jose air terminal and he briefly entertained the idea that Mr. Fed had scheduled a flight.

But only for a moment. His Bronco was still in long-term parking nearby, and it wouldn't take a genius to backtrack him from his own flight to Portland, especially when they had emplaced those transmitter bugs. Now he lost the Chevy completely but, with a sense of foreknowledge and no hesitation, drove to short-term parking. From there he walked along the periphery of the open area. He did not see the Chevy, nor need to. From several hundred yards away, afoot, he saw a figure wearing a baseball cap submerge among the cars near where he knew the Bronco was parked. *I'll bet he's servicing the stuff they put under my chassis,* he thought. *Or maybe exchanging it for . . . what, video? Wish I knew, but damned if I'm going to check on it anytime soon. A digital readout might tell them when I pulled my little inspection, which would also tell them I was right on Mr. Fed's heels. Wouldn't do to let the hunters know the quarry is stalking them. Maybe I'm starting to get the hang of this.*

His sense of satisfaction popped like a soap bubble with another thought: What if, while he stalked this guy, the others were stalking *him*? He stretched elaborately with a slow swivel of his neck that took in most of his surroundings. The fact that he saw nothing suspicious did nothing to lessen that suspicion, and he found it difficult to walk, not run, the quarter-mile back to the camper. There he waited and watched from that high window inside the camper, fuming at his inability to get any closer than this without taking insane risks.

His need wasn't just for physical proximity—it was for . . . what was that jargon term? *Teleproximity,* "close-up" in effect, but from a safe distance. What he really needed was sensors like the feds had. If only he could plant an audio bug of his own in one of their cars! *They might be ready for that. Shit, it's what they do. Okay, drop that idea before they drop you. But wouldn't it be nice to bug Lodge's office?* Another bad idea; not impossible, but equally dangerous in there. When he thought how easy it might be for Ed to do it for him, he cursed himself aloud and and flatly refused to consider it further. Even if he got inside and planted it himself, and it was discovered, poor Ed would come under suspicion. No, the "insider" approach was a minefield of risks.

Outsider. The word sent a familiar chill down his back; a welcome signal in Rob's case, one of those subtle alerts his subconscious provided whenever a new approach took root in his mind. Much of his engineering career had been spent studying unconventional solutions to GenStan's problems. Sometimes, when balked by a problem, it was necessary only to restate that problem before he could begin solving it. Yes, by God, using an *outside* solution he could avoid going into Lodge's office or implicating Ed. Couldn't he?

He hustled around inside the camper in search of decent sketch materials, juggling old ideas and new ones, finally standing with a stubby pencil poised as he stared vacantly from the window. His gaze refocused sharply as he realized that the car moving through the long-term lot toward the distant exit booth was the black Chevy he'd been waiting for. He scrambled back to take the wheel, with every intention of following Mr. Fed again. It would be exceptionally nice to find out where these people spent their nights, worth a small risk of exposure if he stayed far enough behind.

It was a good try, he decided when the Chevy disappeared in a long burst of acceleration, but he'd been lucky to follow this far. *And what if he's spotted this big wallowing turd I'm driving? Won't help to underestimate him; he'd probably turn it around on me, use that cell phone, bring his pals while he tails me.* The way he had sped off, he might be doing it now.

Rob reversed direction at his next opportunity, watching every mirror available to him and suspicious of every dark sedan, finally turning on the Alameda, a familiar arterial older than the twentieth century. It was a very public boulevard and, better still, led straight to the stately cluster of Santa Clara University campus buildings. He knew from years of experience that a few faculty and staff parking slots were always empty. He could abandon the camper for a time, watch for signs that the hunters were closing in. If the camper got a ticket in the meantime—well, Fred McGrath would doubtless know some way to avoid paying for it.

WITHIN AN HOUR ROB DECIDED HE HADN'T BEEN FOLLOWED. By early evening, he had sketched his way through half a notepad. He drove past the home of Gus Kallas and, seeing Gus's old Chrysler still parked in front of the trailer, continued to a nearby playground where he parked. Because Gus was dependable in his club meetings, Rob relaxed at the wheel and resumed his purposeful doodling. He intended to make another pass within a few minutes but, when he next looked at his watch, a half-hour of his life had fled by. On his next pass, the Chrysler was gone. Rob parked two blocks away and hurried back. The trailer door was, as always, unlocked, and Rob soon immersed himself in the process of laying out the flight surfaces of a new mantis with carbon fiber, catalyzed cement, and modeler's jigs. This tiny UAV would waste no bulk on a chemchip and, in his sketches, resembled its insect namesake with slender wings. Its only payload would be a short-range audio relay and he would stick to a proven design.

Though much of his work could be done in the camper, the first intricate bits required strong light, magnifying goggles, and patience. He knew better than to ignore the passage of time, but his first hint of his own stupidity was when the door swung open. "You dumb, dumb, dumb shit," said Gus; "don't you know that lamp is a dead giveaway?"

Rob froze in place, poised halfway out of his chair. "Just give me time to take my sketches and I'll be out of your hair," he pleaded, flushing.

"Stand up or siddown," said the old man, climbing the steps, letting the door shut behind him. "Just don't squat there like an undecided toad, f'God's sake." Rob reseated himself; rubbed trembling hands across his face. Gus watched him closely. "And what's this about begging for time? If I wanted you outta what little hair I have left, Ro-bo, I coulda snuck in the house and made a phone call when I saw this light on instead of parking out front. I dunno why, but you're on a major shitlist."

Shakily: "You probably know more about all this than I do," said Rob.

"If I do, you don't know diddly about anything—which seems pretty likely if you're scared of *me*. Look, Kenny told me stuff that sounded like so much eyewash, but just tell me one thing: You do anything to sic a coupla steely-eyed assholes on you? They were here yesterday."

Staring into the face of his father-in-law, Rob gave a firm shake of his head. "But if Kenny told you someone tried to bag me anyway—with a silenced handgun, no less—believe it. They did. They've also got Corrine on their side. Christ knows what they told her."

"Prob'ly the same crap they told me, so I parked out front when I saw the light on. Since even I could figger out it wasn't me in here, I thought it'd be you or Kenny, and I'm not up to chasing you. But what the hell makes you think Corrie's against you?"

The phrase "against you" made Rob laugh helplessly. "I may have to clean it up a little for you, Gus, but you're the only one I'd want to tell."

"Do it over hot chocolate in the house, then. I can nuke it in the dark." With that, Rob snapped off the high-intensity lamp and followed Gus into his house.

The living room's big TV set shed a faint diffuse glow into the kitchen, where Gus prepared the chocolate and set out a package of Double Stuff Oreos—Kenny's favorites. "I really miss my kid," Rob sighed, after recounting their Sky Lakes trip with a bare-bones outline of his entrapment by Corrine. He made no mention of Ed Doyle or his use of that camper. "If Corrie decides to give up on me, well, I guess I can take that. But I lie awake worrying that my son might wonder about me. Or . . ." he faltered in the gloom, waving a hand vaguely in the direction of Gus.

"I'm not very good at this kinda talk," Gus rumbled, "so gimme time to say it right." A long pause. "Some guys with badges say my young buddy, who also happens to be my daughter's husband, may be a major security risk. I think about that. I try and match it with what I goddamn *know* about him, and it won't—fuckin'—fit. For one thing, if you're squirreling around Silicon Valley, you must not have anyplace else to go.

"Corrie calls and bends my ear about you, dead sure you're suddenly a spy for Germany, or Russia, or Mars. But I know my daughter, and ever since she was a little kid she tends to believe whoever gets to her first with his story. She even uses some of their jargon shit she prob'ly never heard until an hour before. If I argue, we'll only get mad, and who needs it? I know what she wants—she wants me to agree with her. I even know why she druther call me than come over; she's ashamed to look me in the eye while she says a lotta stuff."

Gus paused, sipped from his mug, and resumed. "Okay, Corrie can tell me I have to decide between the two of you, but she can't make me do it. I love my little girl, Ro-bo, and it—it spears my gut when she tells me blood is thicker than water. Because she's never learned that integrity is thicker than blood. If it isn't, there's no hope for us all. Maybe I'm just a shitty father." Another pause, another sip, and then a growled, "Well, goddamnit, tell me I'm not! What the fuck are friends for?"

"I thought it goes without saying."

"Nothin' goes without saying," Gus insisted. "You don't know that by now?"

Rob laughed softly. "Never thought of it like that, but you're right. Okay then, I'll say what I thought you knew. You're a great father; grandfather, too. And, uh—I love you, Gus, but I don't want to know whether you're a great kisser."

The massive shoulders shook with suppressed mirth. "Aw shit, now you made me spill it," said the old man. "All I can say is, if you're a spy, you're *my* spy, and I'll do what I can. And you better not be— What's so funny?"

"Sorry, Gus, but it just occurred to me that I *am* a spy, in a way." Rob's grin faded as he went on. "Not for anybody else, but for myself. I've managed to get a look at these people who want me on ice. That's a start, at least. Someone else I thought was a friend may not be. What I need most, right now, is to listen in on their conversations, and I think there might be a way. You said you'd do what you can for me. Are you up to putting a superlight contact audio sensor on a mantis?"

"You don't mean bugging a phone," said Gus.

"Nope. All it has to do is touch a window firmly enough for contact adhesive to work. But if it's found—it'd be best if you wore latex gloves putting it together. Then the whole rig stays my responsibility," Rob explained.

The old man's silhouette delivered a shrug. "No problem; shouldn't take more than a few hours if that's all it is. Just show me some schematics. Hell, I thought you'd need money, a place to stay, borrow the Chrysler maybe," he said.

"Only if I have to. Right now I don't have to; I hit some ATMs pretty hard and I don't want to involve you more than necessary. It'd be best if everyone thought you were pissed at me, too. Except Kenny. And I don't know if he's mature enough to deal with all this."

"Don't underestimate my grandson, Ro-bo. I'll talk with him anyhow. Trust him like you trust me, okay?"

Rob reached across and placed a hand on the old man's wrist. "Thanks. You want to see those sketches now? I'll need to take off in an hour." He did not explain his need to enter GenStan during the night-shift rush. Gus might've decided he was crazy after all.

CHAPTER 16

IF THE GENIUSES WHO RAN PIZZZAJOINT, INC., HADN'T BEEN SO
hot to use every possible wrinkle to beat the competition, they
wouldn't have promised a free pizza anytime the delivery
wasn't complete inside of thirty minutes. And because, as
someone once observed, there ain't no such thing as a free
lunch, that free pizza wasn't free to the poor harried bastard
delivering it a minute and a half late, who not only still had
to deliver it, but also got to pay for it himself even though the
traffic tie-up or whatever made him late wasn't his fault. And
it wasn't as if the Yugo delivery car getting thrashed to make
those deliveries actually belonged to Pizzzajoint. They were
too smart for that, and they knew that there was a never-
ending supply of Timmie Crumps who weren't too smart.

The car Timmie Crump drove was his own, or rather, his
and his roomie's and the finance company's, because the only
way you got to drive for Pizzzajoint was if you had your own
wheels, or somebody's you could borrow. And Pizzzajoint had
this nifty deal that made you a private subcontractor for deliveries, and if you're nineteen and flogging hard just to stay
afloat in Bonehead English, you don't always understand the
reasoning behind the fine points in that contract you signed,
so you might not think it all the way through.

You might not realize, for example, that Pizzzajoint didn't
want to foot the insurance tab on deliveries made at breakneck
pace by nineteen-year-olds. And with guys like Timmie, and at
least one girl who'd taken a few shifts before she stressed out
with a case of the boo-hoos, the subcontractor was responsible
for all expenses to the car, the insurance, the gas and oil and
tires and, oh yes, the traffic fines.

Jesus, the fines! Just one was all it took to get you so far

behind, you had to start scamming to stay in business, and
Timmie had managed to accumulate two tickets in one month.
Also, because Timmie's roomie was the only one named on the
insurance policy, strictly speaking, Timmie was a rolling tort
on wheels. There were cool operators who dealt dimebags
among fellow junior college students to make their jones or
their car payments, but Timmie had *some* standards.

In times when he was being a sober citizen, Timmie's old
man had filled him with horror stories about what happened
to dropouts and what kind of business the addict business was,
and his old man had known about both, all right. Timmie was
all of twelve when it occurred to him that his old man's vodka–
and–clear-spirits habit was as hard an addiction as anybody
needed. A couple of years later, 190-proof spirits fueled the
old man up for one domestic blowout too many, and he swung
on Timmie's mom a little harder than he intended. And when
she got out of the hospital, she didn't come home again.

Timmie eventually came to realize he should've left with his
mom, but he had stayed, after a fashion. Home was hell, but
it was a hell he knew. And from then until graduation from
high school at eighteen, Timmie had been smart enough to
crash in the garages of friends when the old man was juiced,
which was roughly half the time. Though Timmie had grown
as tall as the old man and could have laid him out the next
time a fist was cocked, you didn't hang one on your father. It
was just one of those things, a standard you accepted.

The funny thing was, between the old man's sober reflections on a man making something of himself, and his drunken
wallowing in what he had made of *him*self, Timmie developed
a whole set of standards. He would get that two-year associate
degree somehow, even if something called mild dyslexia made
reading a real chore, and he wouldn't so much as nod at pot
or 'ludes or anything heavier than a Miller Lite, and he had
definite scruples about ripping off anybody he had a relationship with.

Which said nothing at all about the 260 million people in
the country that Timmie *didn't* know. He didn't know the
managers at Safeway or Lucky, so they were fair game to the

extent of a pocketed can of tuna and a Baby Ruth or some such, two or three times a week. He didn't know anybody with a nice car, and he'd learned which ones had filler-neck covers that were easiest to pop so that he could siphon a gallon of fuel into a plastic milk jug for the Yugo.

Timmie even tried to remember which cars he sucked off, so he'd never hit the same one twice. Standards, standards! And then, three nights back, he'd been delivering two Pizza-joint Giant Mediterranean Everythings after midnight, time getting down to the nubbin, Timmie rechecking his Cupertino map at a dark intersection once too often while driving at his limit—and he'd looked up to see this goddamn jogger dead ahead in the street, face pale, eyes wide, mouth open and hor-rified, but no more so than Timmie himself.

Timmie did have good reflexes, and time for a decision, and he made it. He wrenched the steering wheel away from his almost-victim and hit the curb so hard the Yugo bounced over it before stopping in deep ruts in somebody's front yard, the fool jogger in dark sweats coming over to cuss Timmie out before he trotted out of Timmie's life again, curses doppler-ing down to silence.

And all Timmie Crump could think of was, *I'm gonna get stuck with a pair of Giant Med Everythings*; though the real capper was that after the homeowner came outside and saw this Yugo squatting in his lawn, trailing little bitty fence pick-ets from the flowerbed, he asked if this was the Pizzzajoint, Inc., delivery, and Timmie realized he'd crashed the right party with a minute to spare.

"Yes," said Timmie, beginning to tremble for several rea-sons, and added that he thought maybe the pizzas were okay.

"Well," said the guy, who was as foozled as Timmie's old man as he studied the wreckage of his lawn, "that's what you call true dedication." And he ponied up a fifty and said, "Keep the change." Which Timmie did, easing back to the street, wondering why the Yugo was now steering like a dump truck.

It was steering that way because a Yugo's steering arms weren't intended to take on a concrete curb. Timmie got back to Pizzzajoint having worn off about five thousand miles of rubber from front wheels that now toed in like they were eye-ing each other in mutual suspicion.

Timmie agreed with his roomie that he must fix the car, which would be ready in another few days. Meanwhile, if he wanted to keep his job he had to have wheels. He didn't know anyone who would lend him a set. Therefore it was up to those 260 million strangers to furnish him a car, one each night, which he would return as good as new so not even the strangers would have any justifiable complaints about Timmie Crump's standards.

And that's when Timmie had his brainstorm. Cars parked at the San Jose airport's long-term parking lot usually kept the stub on the dashboard. Timmie had learned to pop a latch and hot-wire a car back when his mom had needed the old man's panel truck, so all he had to do was hitch a ride down near the airport, slip into the open-air lot, and choose some-thing that had fuel and didn't look too rich for Timmie to be driving it.

In Timmie's mind, not as easy as it might seem. The first night, he rejected fifty vehicles before he realized that folks who could afford to buy airline tickets didn't drive beaters like Timmie Crump drove. He finally picked a small Chevy be-cause it wasn't locked, and the parking fee was modest enough that he might even come out a few bucks ahead for the night, and it had a crumpled right front fender. Yep, if it was among the walking wounded it might look just about Timmie's speed.

Timmie drove it that night, and returned it to the very same slot, separating the ignition wires and shoving them back un-der the dash so the owner might never realize how he had helped put a kid through junior college.

He picked another car the next night, but had to return it to a slot some distance from where he'd borrowed it. Well, maybe the guy would figure he'd forgotten where he parked, and if he didn't, it would just have to remain a permanent mystery.

And on the third night, Timmie's search ended when he came across a vehicle that might have had BORN TO BE TIM-MIE'S stenciled on the window. Even in the dark he could see the old Ford Bronco must've carried a bucket of dirt on it, and there was a mound of stuff in the back which didn't interest Timmie because if you ripped off a stranger by borrowing his wheels you didn't add insult to injury by glomming his shit.

There was something else about a Bronco, too, something that Timmie had learned to appreciate in his coursework. He had taken a course, Appliance Repair 151, because his forty-year-old fridge was acting up and he'd thought how neat it would be if he learned to fix it—at long last, something practical he could get out of school. And damn if it didn't work that way, with Timmie learning all about freezers and top-loader washers, and disposals and trash mashers and . . . Jeez, you name it, or just point to it, and Timmie would fix it or find out why it couldn't be fixed.

What he liked about that Bronco was, it looked like it had been cast out of granite. It reminded him of some of the industrial machines he was now into in the next course, Appliance Repair 152, heavy-duty hardware that you could roll off a cliff and expect to work afterward. If he'd been driving a Bronco the other night when he'd plowed furrows through the picket fence, there probably wouldn't have been any need to get a steering arm fixed, though the city of Cupertino might've had to pour a new curb.

So Timmie was already beginning to realize he'd found himself a career, something he wouldn't mind getting up to do every morning for the next thirty years. Two weeks before, he'd already found out what it was like to have a client cooing in surprise and pleasure, when he fixed a Sears dryer for the cosmetics clerk next door. He'd thought she was just shining him on so he'd fix her microwave, too, but after he'd done that, she had nothing more for him to fix and yet he was still invited over for the next Sunday's brunch.

She'd said she liked it that he was shy and smart, too. Timmie had hopes about where this was going, guiding him toward a life where he could do honest jobs people appreciated and rewarded him for, a life that might have a girl in it, and maybe a Ford Bronco he could wash and polish in his own driveway.

Timmie got the driver's door open, thinking what a kick it would be if he ran this old Sherman tank through a car wash before he returned it, and, with the kind of suspension springs a Bronco has, it didn't even lean as he climbed in, not even when he swung down under the dash with his pocketknife and flashlight, shaving off a bit of insulation so he could apply a big alligator clip—and the last thing he ever intended to do was screw up a vehicle he respected that much.

CHAPTER 17

THE SHOEBOX THAT ROB CARRIED TO THE CAMPER WEIGHED more than the materials it held. After returning to GenStan for a night of protected sleep, he spent the next morning inside the camper. With inadequate light, he had to struggle against eyestrain as he nudged delicate subassemblies together. He joined noon foot traffic in a migration toward the GenStan cafeteria, alert for faces to avoid. While his pursuers must know about the beard by now, it still had its uses inside the company.

Waiting in line, shying from eye contact, he was struck by the subdued atmosphere in the place. Several diners had copies of the *San Jose Mercury-News* folded open, some discussing it as they ate. He assumed it was some new crisis or an airline disaster until he was seated, listening for some cue to the news.

Rob had not the least shred of a suspicion that the news might involve him directly until he heard a passing diner say to the woman with him, ". . . think he worked for Halloran. It's always those quiet friendly types that go postal . . ." He saw no copies of the newspaper that he could secure for himself. Moments later Rob was striding outside, his stomach a hard knot, half of his sandwich tucked into a pocket.

After another ten minutes he sat at the wheel in a Safeway parking lot and finished that sandwich. To his immense relief, the news piece was not on the front page, which told him at first glance that it wasn't a widespread disaster. It only took up a few column inches.

FUGITIVE'S CAR BOMB IN SJ

A San Jose engineer was critically injured late last night when his SUV was destroyed by explosives in a long-term parking lot in San Jose. Robert Tarrant, a disgruntled former employee of General Standards, had been sought by federal authorities on charges that remain unspecified. Earlier, Tarrant had been thought to have fled the country. Several vehicles were destroyed in the midnight blast. Sources theorized that Tarrant may have intended suicide.

"Good God," Rob muttered. Whoever the victim was, he'd been so thoroughly maimed the cops thought he was Rob. Could it have been one of those bastards hunting him? If so, they knew damn well it wasn't Rob who'd been injured, though they might have claimed it was, for reasons of their own. They might even have brought the car bomb themselves. He had a flash of cruel satisfaction, hoping one of his pursuers had paid the price. Perhaps that was what the fed had been doing at his Bronco, but he'd seen the guy leave, so probably the victim had been someone else.

So much for my old Bronc, he thought. Then, *Oh shit, Kenny will be devastated; probably Gus as well, and maybe even Corrie. I wonder what Ed Doyle will say*. It was possible that if she thought he'd been badly injured she might lose her cool and somehow implicate herself in his troubles. And hard on the heels of this thought came another: All this misinformation might have been leaked deliberately, to smoke him or his friends out. Was there really an injured man? Had his Bronco really been scattered? He no longer believed anything a federal authority might say. They had obviously known where the Bronco was, and he thought it suspicious that no specific location had been given for that long-term parking lot. Maybe it was all a pack of lies.

And Rob could verify the basic claim himself. He eased the camper into traffic and drove to San Jose Municipal's short-term parking. Then he strolled along the perimeter of the long-term parking area, hands in pockets, and had no difficulty spotting a big van near the line of fluttering yellow tape that covered an area fifty yards wide.

Somewhere, a fire extinguisher chuffed a brief rebuke at smoldering upholstery. Men with plastic bags were retrieving debris within the area. As he watched, a crane-equipped truck lurched off, towing a flatbed trailer, and with some difficulty Rob recognized the topless, hoodless remains of his Bronco on the trailer. The injured man had been incredibly lucky to survive. Anybody inside that thing should have been torn to pieces, he decided as he approached the buxom young woman who sat in her kiosk at the exit gate, gazing toward the damage area.

For a long moment Rob watched with her. The extinguisher snarled again. With feigned ignorance he murmured, "Jeez. You have a fire over there?"

A headshake. "Car bomb. Killed a guy."

"No kidding. You see it?"

Another headshake as she turned toward him with a grimace. "Happened before my shift, but Ernie told me it was the loudest thing he ever heard. Broke this," she said, tapping a cracked windowpane beside her.

"How'd he know it killed anybody? I wonder," Rob mused, in hopes he wasn't overplaying his ignoramus card.

" 'Cause he saw the guy. It was Ernie called it in," she explained. "Said his pants were blown off. The guy, I mean. Part of his head and an arm, too. *Gaaah.* And when the paramedics were on the way out, they told him—Ernie, I mean," she added for this bearded stranger.

This earned her a silent nod from Rob, who shook his head and sighed. "I guess this is no place to park now," he said, and turned away.

"BATF says they'll be done this evening," she called after him. The Bureau of Alcohol, Tobacco and Firearms was a federal arm, too, but paramedics were local. Whatever else he might doubt, his Bronco and a dead man were real casualties.

DRIVING BACK TOWARD SUNNYVALE, HE DETERMINED TO SPIKE the rumors as carefully as possible. Outside the CalTrans Rapid Transit station in Santa Clara were several hinge-top boxes full of throwaway newspapers, and Rob stopped long enough to take an armload of them. It might be easy to tap Ed Doyle's phone, but more labor-intensive to have someone

watching every house he might visit. He invested a bit of time
in this newspaper ploy to explain his presence in the event
someone was staked out near Ed's. If it felt right, he'd do the
same thing at Gus's house.

When he parked a block from Ed's duplex he scribbled a
note on his scratch pad, then placed it among a stack of the
papers. At every front door on the way he rolled one of the
little fliers and stuck it where it would be noticed. He had only
three of them left when he reached Ed's front door, rolled his
note around the flier, and inserted it into the ornate metal
screen of the door. Anyone who got close enough to touch it
would see the large block letters—JEM—another layer of dis-
simulation.

He had written, in much smaller cursive below:

3 PM: Don't believe everything you read.

He'd signed it *Bogart.* It seemed foolish to leave any broader
hint than that.

Before driving to Gus's place he toyed with the camper's
radio, alert for any late news. The local broadcasts evidently
had more important items to report, so Rob wrote another
note, for Gus.

4 PM: The old horse is dead but
I remain,
Yours truly.

It had been Gus who, with his weakness for nicknames, had
dubbed the Bronco "the old horse."

Again Rob parked two blocks away and began distrib-
uting papers. But halfway down Gus's block he saw two
unidentified cars in the driveway behind the Chrysler. A bit
nearer he saw, with a feeling of fresh dread, more crime-
scene tape stretched from Gus's porch to the house trailer.
Resisting an urge to sprint away, he simply crossed the
street and distributed more fliers. He saw no damage to
Gus's place and no debris suggesting an explosion. Could

they be dusting the place for prints? He and Gus had tried to wipe down everything Rob had touched, including the kitchen chair and cups.

He scarcely noticed the figure riding a bicycle when he unlocked the camper, until the bike squealed to a stop beside him as he started the engine. A pair of familiar soccer shoes were clamped to the cargo rack. "Can I hitch a ride, mister?"

"Kenny!" He rolled down the window, looking around wildly, then at the grinning face of his son.

"You kept the chin fuzz. Gross; I like it," said Kenny, one foot on the camper's step. "But I wouldn't've known that black hair if Mom hadn't—"

"Let's go somewhere else. Stick your bike inside the camper."

Soon Kenny had hopped into the passenger's side, his happiness at finding his father quickly abating as Rob said, "Son, you've got to tell me how you knew where to find me."

"Granddad told me you'd need stuff at his place, and I heard Mr. Hotshot—James Bond—Sachs brag to Mom that you had a camper. And so this one I never saw before shows up parked in the neighborhood with a GenStan decal. I wasn't sure, but gimme some credit, Dad. I just hung around cruising the streets. Granddad said you'd be back sooner or later for your stuff."

"Great. I'm so *damn* glad to see you, Kenny—but I can't believe you could find me when Sachs and his bunch couldn't, if they're so anxious to blow me away like they did my car."

"Oh, the Bronco. I was hoping that was BS, and I didn't believe that crap about you blowing yourself up for a second. For one thing, Sachs seemed really browned-off that he couldn't talk to you. I don't think he wants to hurt you. I mean, yeah, I worried a little, but not like I let on. My dad isn't a mad bomber. I'm a lot more worried about Granddad."

"I was on my way to let him know I'm okay but you can . . ." Rob had reached a suburban park and, pulling to the curb, shot a sudden glance at the youth. "Wait a minute. What about Gus?"

"He got shot, is what." Seeing Rob's openmouthed gaze, Kenny elaborated. "Just before noon today. Twice. Little fire-cracker *pop-pop*s when he was coming out of the trailer. I was with him, helping strip wire and stuff for your project. We hear a car pull up behind the Chrysler and Granddad gets up and opens our door. I see him miss a step, and then those shots, and Granddad fell on the grass and I shouted, and then an-other shot comes through the door right next to my hand, and I realize somebody else is pretty close but he can't see me through the door any more than I can see him, and I yelled like hell and slammed the door. And kept yelling until I heard the car—"

"Kenny. Stop. How—is—Gus?"

"Oh. I called 911, and the paramedics came. They said he's gonna be okay. The hole through the door was just a .22, the cops told me. You know that baseball cap Granddad fixed to hold his magnifying goggles?" Kenny got the nod he sought, and went on. "Well, it doesn't anymore. One bullet glanced off that big rivet on the swivel, you know, right over his ear? It bled like crazy and made a big groove behind his ear. The other one went along his butt—I think they're taking it out. Granddad was mad as I've ever seen him."

"Conscious, then." Rob began to relax.

"Yeah, but partly he was mad because he didn't get a look at the guy. He fell, and I guess he passed out for a minute 'cause he was just sitting up when I peeked out the door again, cussing himself a streak. What's a 'morphidite'?"

"Doesn't matter. Make Gus tell you; might put a leash on his tongue," Rob said with a wink.

"Not," Kenny replied. "Hey, if you want the stuff we were working on, I could get it easy. It's cool."

"I've got to have it but I don't want you in this, Kenny. Good Christ, you could've been shot in there! Lots of people get killed with a .22, son."

"Gonna just walk in and get it yourself, huh?" Before Rob

could reply, the boy added, "Sure, with the trailer full of big cops trying to chugalug coffee out of a thermos without making noise. I already asked if I could get some toy stuff I have here and they said okay, if I didn't get in the way, but I thought it'd be better to patrol the camper instead."

"It is absolutely uncanny," Rob marveled, "how little imagination the authorities show if they're really trying to grab me."

"Mr. Bigshot Sachs spends more time at our house than he does looking for you, and I know the police aren't trying— they think you got blown up. There's one cop in the trailer and one in the house. They think maybe the guy with the .22 might come back if he's after Granddad."

"And Corrie lets you hang around there?"

"Not exactly." To Rob's piercing glance, the boy shrugged. "When they said Mom and Sachs were on the way, I told those cops I was gonna play soccer." A one-beat pause. "I lied," he added with perfect equanimity.

"So Sachs was at Gus's after the shooting. I wonder if he knows it wasn't me at the Bronco."

Kenny thought that over. "I bet he does. He was on the phone at our house early this morning, and they're still looking for somebody."

Rob's tone was elaborately casual. "How early?"

"Mom fixed him breakfast." Kenny said it grudgingly, almost guiltily. "I really don't like that guy, Dad."

"Because Corrie does?"

A long pause, and a sigh. "Yeah. Granddad says the guy will pass like diarrhea but meanwhile he's at our house late, and early. Not all night, though," he added hurriedly.

Rob could not resist asking, "How would you know?"

"Because I set my alarm for four A.M., and I check your bedroom!" Angry now, loath to discuss it further, Kenny stared out toward the park.

"Kenny, your mom thinks I'm a bad guy at the moment. She's having a rough time, too, and she needs an authority figure to lean on, so try not to make it tougher on her."

"You don't care how hard she's leaning?"

"I don't know what she's doing. Nothing I could do about it, in any case."

"You could buy a .22," said the boy.

"That's enough, Kenny." Fearing he had spoken too sharply, Rob softened his tone. "You watch too much TV. I don't own your mom—and vice versa. Does all this put knots in my stomach? Of course it does. I hope she'll realize she's being a—um . . ." he trailed off.

"Bimbo," the boy supplied.

Caught between a flash of anger and heartfelt agreement, Rob could only chuckle. "I'll get back to you on that. But don't say it again, okay?"

For a moment they sat in silence, watching a boy with a Frisbee and a gymnastic terrier in the park. At last Kenny said, "I'll ask again. You want your stuff or don't you?"

"Yes, it may help me. But for all we know, someone could follow you back here. You need to go home first, hang around awhile. Look, those parts have gotta fit in one of those soccer shoes. Take it all home and stash it till you can make another excuse to get out. You'd make the delivery in Mountain View, so be careful of traffic and go down a few alleys if you can find any—you know, whatever a bike can do that'd be hard for someone in a car. If you think someone's following, just go home. Now, can you remember an address?"

"Write it down. Wait, that'd be dumb, wouldn't it?"

" 'Fraid so. But there's a man I once met, name's Jem, who'd probably hold something for you. If he won't, put it in a baggie in the flowerbed next to his porch. He's—an okay guy." *I was about to say "gay." Why? What I did say was a hell of a lot more important.*

"Jim. So where is he?"

Rob told him twice, but wasn't entirely forthcoming to his son with respect to his female friend. "Jem lives with someone from GenStan named Ed, who might hold the contraband, or maybe not. Now, what was that address?"

Kenny gave him a faintly pitying look and repeated the

address exactly, then pointed in delight toward the Frisbee dog. Before Kenny left on his bike, they spent another ten minutes as spectators, laughing together at the terrier's spectacular leaps. All the while Rob was thinking, *Before the shitstorm broke, I never realized that moments like this with my kid are more precious than fame or diamonds. I wonder if this guy Sachs knows that. . . .*

CHAPTER 18

"I CAN'T WATCH EVERYONE AS A SINGLETON," SAID MIKE, speaking into the latex-enclosed device that seemed half doughnut, half condom, snugged over the telephone speaker. A similar gadget fitted closely around the receiver opening. At the other end of that connection, in Hyattsville, Maryland, a matched audio scrambler reassembled every word. "A capacitance tap on Lodge's office phone is out of the question, and the only recordings I get from his home phone are endless, maddening chatter from his socialite wife. If you're so sure the man is handling Tarrant, send me some backup."

"Not an option, Michael." The Hyattsville spymaster had both a tradecraft name, "Jonathan," and a title: *katsa*. Very few *katsa*s operated in the U.S. Yonnie had a limited budget, and his assets were already thinly spread. His accent was almost imperceptible unless his patience was tried, and at the moment it told Mike the man was growing irritable. "And as I have said before, I am not sure about Lodge. I have never been sure about him, if you take my meaning."

"Only too well. As my recruit, he is my responsibility. I will remind you that he has been very useful, and for the record, I remain confident about Lodge. It was you who insisted I run closer checks on him. That takes time. I do have a day-job." The phrase, borrowed from the theatrical profession, referred to a cover identity, and Mike's, combined with a handler role, left little time for sleep or irksome contacts with Hyattsville.

"I am wondering why you didn't use a surveillance kite over Tarrant's vehicle." A "kite," in European English, could mean a toy device or a hawklike predator that soared like an American buzzard—or, as in this case, something much more sophisticated: an Israeli kite fitted into an attaché case and which used an almost silent ducted fan, battery-powered, to send it aloft for extended surveillance, its tiny video monitor transmitting the scene to a distant operator. From twenty meters away, a kite was indistinguishable from a live creature.

"I didn't because I'd be out of its range much of the time and it does have limited battery life. It's a good tool in its place—open forest and countryside, for example—but check a map of this area sometime, Yonnie. It's huge."

"But you would have seen who planted that plastique," said Yonnie. "A damnable complication. It destroyed a bait that might have drawn Tarrant back at any time."

It would have been fruitless to point out that the same explosive could have just as easily solved the Tarrant problem. Instead: "Tarrant is a technical man. He could have planted that bomb himself," Mike replied, avoiding an outright lie.

"Even if he did, it's one more casualty to draw attention, and the only one we want is Tarrant. The Office doesn't like collateral casualties and now, today, we're dealing with another one," said Yonnie. No one in Yonnie's business ever said "Mossad," even on a scrambler phone; to its active members it was always "the Office."

The less said about that, Mike decided, the better. The victim of that car bomb was a safer topic. "The BATF used some influence on the local emergency team, so officially it is Tarrant in intensive care, not a dead car thief in the morgue. Tarrant might still nibble at that press release, but I don't like it. If he goes to the San Jose police I'm not sure I can get to him fast enough. I'm not trying to drop this assignment, understand," Mike added quickly, "but just because I've put my butt on the line doesn't make me a specialist."

"So it would seem," said Yonnie dryly.

"So call in the *kidon*, be done with it." *Kidon* was an Israeli term for a small team of specialists; *kidon* means "bayonet." The *kidon*'s work is up close and very, very personal.

Yonnie made a small, scornful noise deep in his throat. "They do what *they* decide, not what I decide: But if you continue to fail in this, the *kidon* may come in on it. Someone in the Office would make that decision. It would not redound to your credit, Michael. They worry that your Mr. Tarrant is one of those TLAR wizards."

"I've been away too long," Mike complained. "I can't even keep up with the jargon."

"It's American, actually. Intuitive design that eliminates years of paperwork, trial and error; it simply means 'That looks about right.' A gentleman named Rutan is the archetype of TLAR design. You recall the aircraft he designed, that flew nonstop and un-refueled around the globe? He admitted that much of its design was intuitive, some constructed without even a blueprint to follow. To Mr. Rutan it looked about right. And it was. The Russian, Mikoyan, was a man of that stripe. Robert Tarrant, it would appear, has the TLAR gift with respect to extremely small aircraft. It is simply his misfortune that his gift is one we cannot afford for him to give. I lie awake worrying that your man Lancer will confer with him for even an hour."

"We share a nightmare," said Mike. "If Lancer puts too much together, I'll be cooling my heels in Montreal."

"You may not see Montreal if that old man saw more than you think. I wish I had your confidence, Michael."

"It's me that's hanging out in the breeze here. And I'm still here. Is that confidence enough for you?"

"It will have to serve," said Yonnie with resignation. "Meanwhile, Lodge is your most likely channel of choice. Unless Tarrant's wife or son can be co-opted."

"The wife is a possibility. The boy is only a boy, and it is summertime," Mike said in dismissal. "He goes charging off here and there on his bicycle, sometimes hanging around with the old man." With faint sarcasm: "Would you rather have me following that kid?"

"I won't dignify that with a reply. A wonder you did not shoot him as well," said Yonnie.

"I'd never mistake him for his father. The old man and Tarrant are of a size; I thought I had finally nailed our man, but all right, you want to hear me say it? I blew it. An error of enthusiasm, Yonnie."

"See if you can enthuse your Mr. Lodge. I take it you have

a tactic in mind if Tarrant and Lancer should meet."

"Several. After all this, it will be a real pleasure," said Mike with feeling, and moments later Yonnie broke the connection.

DAVID SACHS, UNAWARE THAT HE HAD BEEN GIVEN THE CODE name "Lancer," checked the digital clock in the Tarrant living room as he sat alone and finished tapping notes into his palmtop computer. Much of the time, he kept current on his team's progress by cell phone. With Vallejo making plausible explanations to a San Jose medical examiner, and Carnes switching audio tapes on phone taps, David might have had time for a brief boff with Corrine Tarrant. As luck would have it, however, she was shopping for groceries, and it was probably just as well. That damned kid of hers was always popping in and out at inopportune moments.

With the house key Corrine had lent him, David felt like a kid himself, loose in a candy store. It wasn't often that an operation afforded him so many genteel opportunities. Unlike Frank Carnes and most of his other colleagues, David had never enjoyed practicing his pickup lines with divorcées in metropolitan gin mills. The noise, the pace, the air of subdued mutual desperation—all of it put him off his game and, with AIDS a corollary of anonymous coupling, David had long ago realized the advantages of married women.

They were often bored with whatever they had. They were far less promiscuous than nightclub habitués, and usually discreet by necessity. Generally, even the prime specimens were pathetically pleased to be noticed by a man with David's élan, and with the sense of mystery that he managed to convey with that knowing, devil-may-care smile he had perfected.

In matters of the loins, if not the heart, he operated with tried-and-true principles. You never plonked anyone who had less to lose than you did, or who obviously had lots more emotional problems than yours. You let them know you were interested, but you waited for them to pull you down on the couch. And at some point past the couch, you always hinted that, as a dedicated cog in a Very Important Machine, you never knew when implacable Fate might whirl you away on the winds of risk. It was wonderfully romantic claptrap, and by now he could give his soliloquy by rote.

For a day or so he had thought he'd stumbled into three candidates. In the Tarrant file alone, he had dossiers on what would have been two keepers, if Deirdre Lodge had passed muster. But with recordings he'd heard from a recorded telephone tap she had flunked entry-level Discretion, which left Corrine Tarrant—perhaps not quite the supermodel look-alike that Deirdre was, but more tautly assembled and, he knew now, an ardent lay. After a half-dozen bouts of rutting, a woman like Corrine usually began to show those subtle signs of inattention suggesting that generic novelty, not sex itself, was what she really sought without realizing it; that her boredom was, in fact, essentially built in. David understood and secretly sympathized. It was the precise mirror image of his own view.

The third candidate for his sexual excursions had no dossier, but only because Edwina Doyle did not seem to have any real personal connections in the Tarrant case. When you requested a dossier, also known as a "profile," you had to justify it. Many executive assistants developed relationships, sometimes extending to the executive's family, but that was always a risky habit. The supple and succulent Edwina had clearly avoided that risk, and it was equally clear that Lodge depended on her competence more than she depended on his.

David knew that this Doyle chick had been favorably impressed with him. Trouble was, with looks like hers she could afford to wait him out, and waiting, as long as his own looks held up, was *his* game. Still, you never knew what cards the other player held until you anted up. She just might be waiting for that expensive dinner in the City before hurling herself on his bones. It had happened before.

But when could he steal that evening away from what was becoming an endless round of stakeouts and recorded phone calls? The case wasn't stagnating only because this wily son of a bitch Tarrant was hovering close at hand. Eventually he'd show up; they always did, especially the ones steeped in domesticity who were suddenly thrust out in the cold.

If David's outlook on personal relationships barely exceeded the depth of an oil slick, he had developed an uncanny ability to pigeonhole the subjects of his investigations into broad categories. Tarrant did not fit any of the classic profiles. Studying the wife, the boy, Tarrant's own profile, and the family albums, he was almost certain by now that Robert Tarrant had not been turned by some foreign power. He was not a Gerald Bull, who had left his government aerospace job in despair when officials lacked interest in his work. Tarrant had stayed loyally in place for years with a corporation that, from its own personnel files, recognized him as an intuitive rarity while it rewarded him with crumbs.

He was no Aldrich Ames, who had enlisted his own wife in espionage while he soaked the Russians for a bundle and spent wildly on luxuries he could not afford on his middle-class salary. Tarrant's bank balance was so meager his wife wore hand-me-downs donated by a statuesque mannequin, and his second car was—or had been—a bad joke his wife refused to drive.

Nor was he an Ed Howard, who knew exactly how to flee the country when the FBI gave chase, and who promptly resurfaced in Moscow. Tarrant remained floundering around on his home turf, probably without the means or motive to stray far from it. Nor yet a Jonathan Pollard, a poor schlemiel who'd embarrassed David's own U.S. Naval Intelligence by wholesaling American secrets for ideological reasons. Tarrant was no political activist. The only secrets he held were special, intuitive design talents he openly enjoyed as a hobby.

In David's opinion, Robert Tarrant's was a unique case that might have begun with an Intelligence error, and could have ended with the man transferring to one of the U.S. National Labs; Sandia, or Lawrence Livermore, perhaps. The case would not even have qualified as criminal until Tarrant's old Bronco blew up. If Tarrant had booby-trapped it, the silly schmuck would probably face a charge of murder one. The less said about that, the better, until Tarrant had been caught.

Marie Vallejo had already called in the findings on the victim, a positive make based on dentition and prints. The subject had been a small-time scuffler with a two-page list of priors featuring burglary and GTA, grand theft auto. He might not be mourned, but misidentifying him had failed to smoke Tarrant out, and David had told Marie it was time to make an apology for their error to the San Jose police. They would love it; metro cops had a definite inferiority complex about feds.

David heard the screen-door springs and said "Corrie?" too soon. He hadn't heard her car.

"It's me," said the boy, none too friendly, either. He came in holding a pair of sport shoes, rummaging under the kitchen sink, coming up with a used plastic bag. He thrust the shoes into the bag with an almost defiant, "Where's my mom?"

"She didn't say. I'm just the hired help, Ken." Usually David had no trouble with kids, and by putting himself down a bit he might yet get chummy with this one. "She did ask if I wanted dinner here, something better than McDonald's."

"Again." Not a question. The kid continued on to his room, avoiding eye contact.

If he suspects a game of footsie, I can't blame him, David thought.

"Tell her I'll catch a pizza with some friends," the boy's voice echoed from down the hall.

David followed the kid, amused at his own concern at failing Basic Charm with a thirteen-year-old. The kid's door was closed. David knocked.

"Yeah."

"Mind if I come in?"

"What for?"

David thought about it. What indeed? "Just talk, I guess. If your room's like mine used to be, it's full of neat shit."

Apparently this was the right tack. "It's not locked."

David opened it and stood in the doorway, looking around, smiling at what was, to all appearances, the aftermath of a tornado. Posters of soccer jocks, comics, clothes, the balsa-and-tissue model of a sailplane. The boy sat on his unmade bed and still wouldn't look at him. "I used to build models like that," David tried, nodding at the sailplane.

Finally, a spark: "How'd they fly?"

"Like rocks. Plastic's heavy."

"My dad says why build it if you know it isn't gonna fly," said the boy.

"Look, Ken—"

"It's Kenny."

"Kenny, then. It's a terrible thing to lose your father, but there's something I just learned that I want to share." No response. David said, "We don't think it was your father after all. At the Bronco, you know."

The boy's face went through a set of subtle and cryptic changes, including suspicion and hope, and perhaps fear. "How do you know that?"

"Forensics, dental records. We think it was a car thief, but we know it wasn't Bob."

"*Rob*. He hates 'Bob.' But he's still a spy, right?"

David hesitated. "That's what we call an allegation: remains to be proved. In this country a man is still innocent until proven guilty." A guarded look from the kid, but no answer. "I don't suppose you've seen him around here," David added cautiously.

Real surprise in the boy's face now; he glanced around as if his father were pinned to the wall like a poster. "Here? Why would he, a spy and all? He and my mom aren't—" The boy trailed off with an all-encompassing shrug.

So he didn't know how close we came to bagging his dad. "To talk to you or your mother, maybe. It was just an idea," David said. "I'm trying to do a job, that's all."

"I wish you'd do it someplace else," said the boy.

"I can take a hint," said David, trying that lopsided smile as he backed out and closed the door, hearing a car in the driveway.

If I were this kid, thought David, *I'd be a lot happier to learn my father wasn't spread all over some parking lot. But he still thinks the man is a spy, and he's protective of Corrine, so maybe he just doesn't care that much.* Yeah, that would account for it.

CHAPTER 19

ROB DID NOT NEED TO CHECK THE FLOWERBED AT ED DOYLE'S front porch when he saw a familiar scarred yellow bike leaning against the railing. Originally it had been too big for Kenny, but they had raised the seat and handlebars twice. The front door swung open while Rob was smiling down at the bike, before he could knock. "I wasn't sure you'd—" he began.

"Get in here," said Jem Kasabian in a mock-scolding tone. "Your pizza's almost cold." He shut the door behind Rob, who could see Kenny and Ed stuffing themselves in the dining room. When he saw faint parentheses of tomato sauce flanking Ed's mouth, something long-dormant in him groveled like a puppy.

"Your emissary is a glutton," Jem observed, with a nod toward the boy.

"I heard that," Kenny called. "Dad, you never said Ed was *this* kind of Ed." Across the table from the boy, Edwina Doyle favored his father with a grin that said, *Bless this youngster*, and *Maybe I impress you more than you admit*, in quick succession. Rob did what any father would do in his son's presence: He blushed and changed the subject.

Though he claimed he wasn't hungry, Rob accounted for two slices of vegetarian Pizzarama. He discovered in the process that Kenny had heard from Gus, already filibustering about hospital food and promising to be home soon.

It seemed that Kenny had also obtained permission to use the kitchen table afterward. "This young man said you two were putting together one of those ersatz insects of yours," Jem said, "and I'd love to watch, if it's allowed. Don't tell me you've got the parts hidden on you."

"Left them in the wheels I borrowed. I wasn't expecting

this," Rob admitted. "If I can use the pizza box I can carry it here in a few— Oh hell. Listen, I'll need to buy a soldering pencil at Radio Shack, and— Kenny, if I drop you off near home, could you borrow another bike from one of your buddies and say nothing about it to anyone?"

"I guess. But I've already got my bike. And I brought Granddad's soldering pencil."

"You don't have the bike if you don't mind that I steal it for a while. And I'll have to buy some spraypaint. It'll be green."

Kenny was agreeable but mystified—and more so when he realized that Ed was laughing. "That went right over my head, you guys," he complained. Jem, glancing from Ed to Rob, could only shrug agreement to the boy.

"GenStan green," said Ed. "People go grunting all over the site on green bikes the company supplies, and you're going to bring your own. Tell me I'm wrong," she challenged Rob.

"You want me to admit it?" He shook his head silently.

Jem: "And what shade of green might that be?"

"Generic," said Ed.

"I'm a graphics person," said Jem. "There's sea green, lime green, verdigris, emerald green, olive green—"

"Bile green," said Ed. "God's truth, Jem, it doesn't matter at GenStan, they just use whatever shade is on hand. Olive is a stretch, but—"

"If I don't have to match something, you're home free. I must have fifty spray cans in the garage," said Jem, his lank frame already in motion.

Rob licked his fingers and helped Ed clear the table, then left with the pizza box to retrieve his unassembled mantis from the camper. It would have been much easier to drive the camper nearer to the duplex, but Rob had given a lot of thought to unhappy scenarios. If his future worked out badly, his use of that camper might become news. The least he could do was to keep some inquisitive neighbor from a damning connection.

Evening shadows crept across the sidewalk as he returned, the radio control transmitter protruding from his jacket pocket, to find the bike gone. Ed was extracting a breadboard from its slot above the kitchen drawers. "I thought you'd need a cutting board. The boys are in the garage with masking tape," she said, handing him the broad wooden slab. "I will not have my kitchen smelling of spraypaint, Mr. Fix-It. Spraypaint and anchovies are two things I consider above and beyond the call."

He sat at the table, laid the transmitter aside, and opened the pizza box while she stood leaning on his chair-back to watch, her breathing soft and regular, very near, and somehow almost a benison. Corrine had never shown this much interest in his pastime, even when the first tiny craft had whispered around their living room. He murmured, "I've got one smart kid," as he unwrapped the electric cord from Gus's slender soldering pencil.

"A good kid," Ed replied, pawing quickly through a drawer full of kitchen oddments, pulling out an extension cord unbidden. It was obvious that Ed Doyle was thinking ahead like a surgical nurse to assist him, and her willing subordination in the interests of a wanted man made him acutely aware of her nearness. When she handed him the end of the extension cord, their fingers touched. Why did he feel culpable at that blameless contact? He knew the answer. *If guilt were electricity she would've jumped like a gazelle*, he thought, and bent to his task with a focus that was fierce.

He went to the garage when Jem called. The place had been given over to storage but had enough floor space for the bike, a flattened cardboard shipping box arranged to catch the overspray, the bike's moving parts now protected with buff-tinted tape. "Your choice, sire," said Jem, handing him a pair of spray cans.

Rob tried both and chose the duller shade. "Forest green," said Jem, and nodded happily. "You're not Bogart, you're Robin Hood. You know what I like most about this?" At Rob's headshake, he said, "The paint will cover my fingerprints. I'm starting to enjoy this kind of thinking."

"Uh, Dad? I talked to that Sachs guy at the house this afternoon before Granddad called," said Kenny. "Haven't had a chance to tell you. He says he knows it wasn't you that got blown up, after all."

"That must've ruined his whole day," Rob said.

"He was trying to buddy-buddy me, but—"

"Okay, I've got work to do," Jem interrupted, fluttering the backs of his hands toward them. "I've got only one mask, so *shoo!* Out with you," he said, before slipping a molded felt-paper mask over his nose and mouth.

Rob let Kenny describe his brief conversation, as they sat in the kitchen, their heads virtually touching, Kenny holding parts steady when directed, utterly unconcerned about the smoking tip of the soldering pencil that now and then came within an inch of his fingers.

"You're a trusting soul," Ed murmured to the boy.

"Nah. We have an agreement," Kenny replied calmly. "Whoever gets a blister gets to use the pencil next."

Her nearly silent "hee-hee" drew a warning glance from Rob, who nevertheless was smiling as he sweated an infinitesimal joint together.

Soon after, Jem returned from the garage, followed by a faint, sweetish waft of spraypaint, showing them a circled thumb and forefinger. He hopped onto the sink counter to watch, legs swinging with nervous energy.

As they finished each major connection, Rob would reach for the transmitter. As he manipulated its tiny joysticks, a wisp of carbon fiber would extend or retract, or the two-inch propeller would become a blur and then stop. And each time, the device looked a little less like a disassembled toy, a little more like something that stood on spidery legs preparing to fly. "This is bigger than some," he said at one point. "More mass means more power, means more torque, means the little bugger wants to corkscrew in flight. And so on."

AN HOUR LATER: "THIS IS THE DAMNEDEST THING," ED MUT-tered as Rob began to assemble a skeletal structure that looked vaguely like the much-fattened wing of an insect. "But why our government would care is a mystery to me."

"I can figure that one myself. Rob mentioned chemical sensors," said Jem. "Some pundit on TV the other night said Iraq and North Korea have thousands of tons of chemical weapons we haven't found. Couldn't a fleet of robots from Lilliput like this one sniff them out?"

"Oh, I suppose so. I can see problems with the idea, but—" Rob stopped, frowning, considering. "Well, yeah, with a bus, a carrier for dispersal. Interesting. But I was thinking more along the lines of agribiz, industry. Peaceful uses."

"Like Alfred Nobel thought about his high explosives," Jem replied. "I think it was the Discovery Channel—they said Nobel endowed the prizes because he was bummed over what the military did with his work."

"Just a little ray of sunshine, aren't you?" said Ed, giving her housemate a sharp look.

Jem's reply was arch. "We kill the messenger now, do we?"

"Maybe we do," Kenny said suddenly. "Not him, Dad. You."

Rob looked up crossly. "Will the Mountain View Paranoid Liberal Debating Society kindly table this discussion before my hands start shaking? Jeez," he finished with an eyeroll.

"Soreee" Jem sang, letting it trail off with a demiquaver.

"I can't spank *him*," said Rob, now eyeing his son, "but *you're* another matter."

"Gotta catch me first," the boy said.

"And as it happens, I've got your bike," said Rob. By now Ed was studying father and son with some uneasiness.

"Oh crap." Kenny tossed a pleading look at Ed. "Then he really can catch me. Just gimme another year," he begged of Rob, and as the two grinned at each other, Ed exhaled with relief.

Still later, Rob and Kenny created the cellophanelike cover material for the mantis wings, a handcraft process Kenny understood quite well. Into a large flat pan of warm water they inserted a wire coat hanger, bent so that its triangle became roughly rectangular. Then they poured a clear concoction, smelling rather like nail polish, onto the water's surface. After

waiting for a moment of carefully-judged duration, Rob lifted
the coat hanger vertically to the surface, then slid it up at an
acute angle into the air.

Both Ed and Jem offered astonished, admiring "Oooh" 's to
see the glistening sheet of clear material covering the space
within the coat hanger's rude rectangle, an apparent soap bubble, but a bubble with a tough hide that remained temporarily
sticky.

Kenny smiled at them, though Rob remained too focused
for that. "Let's try for two-in-one," he said, picking up one of
the gossamer wing skeletons, gesturing for Kenny to follow
suit. "Go for the thickest part; this is for outdoors. Ready? You
first."

The boy nodded, then squinted at the clear sheeting and,
with some variable of judgment only his father understood,
his fingers trembling with intent, Kenny placed the wing skel-
eton flat on the sheeting. He quickly pulled his hand away and
Rob, with a surer hand, followed his own squinting assessment
with a quick emplacement of another wing structure. He
puffed out his cheeks, gave an exaggerated exhalation, and
began to wave the coat hanger languidly about. When he
smiled, the others did, too.

The clear sheet created by the solidifying plastic skin was
of varying thickness, yet everywhere so thin, Rob explained,
you could judge its localized thickness by the oily rainbow
sheen. They cut the covered wings from the coat hanger frame
with a razor blade. The plastic had by now cemented itself to
the carbon-fiber wing skeletons and even followed contours of
wing ribs that swept back like tiny reflexed longbows. Jem
claimed it made the gadget look even more like a true insect.

Because the mantis had two sets of wings instead of conventional tail surfaces, they repeated the covering process. Ed
offered to make coffee. Rob said that with work of this sort, it
would have to be decaf unless they wanted his nerves strung
like a tennis racket. He began to assemble the wings onto the
minuscule device, eyeing his work from every angle, making
almost invisible adjustments.

Jem disappeared into the garage, where they soon heard the

sounds of tape being stripped from the bike. At last, sighing with fatigue, swiveling his head back and forth to accommodate aching neck muscles, Rob pushed the mantis aside and offered his palm for a high five with Kenny.

"Nobody does that worth a lick by himself," said Ed, as the coffee began to trickle noisily into its carafe.

Rob was starting to ask what she meant when she stepped behind him, and, with the first firm urgings of her fingers at the juncture of his head and neck, he felt floodgates of tension give way. He groaned softly, his forehead sinking to touch the tabletop, and luxuriated in relief that was, if not sexual, perhaps equally satisfying. Only half aware of it, he began to chuckle at a new thought: If Corrie had done this back at the house, he thought, he might be a dead man now.

Ed, still kneading with those strong fingers: "Doesn't she do this?"

He jerked, realizing he had mumbled those thoughts aloud. "Oh, yeah. Yeah, sure," he lied, "but not lately." He realized that Kenny was a spectator to this, and sat up with a profound sigh and a stretch of both arms. "Thanks, Ed." She moved away toward the coffeemaker, putting physical distance between them, and he saw in Kenny's gaze a speculation both judgmental and friendly. "Boy. That almost put me to sleep," he said to his son.

He had never been more astonished than when Kenny, his back to Ed, silently mouthed "*bullshit*," and grinned at him.

ON ITS FIRST TEST FLIGHT, THE MANTIS SHUDDERED ON ITS skids as the propeller pushed it across the tabletop, and it virtually leaped aloft only to drop nose-first onto the carpet. Into a chorus of "Awwww" 's, Rob scoffed, "No problem, just a trim adjustment. Let me retrieve it. A little bonk like that shouldn't hurt it, but I'll need to shift the battery forward, adjust the CG, maybe lower the angle of incidence."

"Exactly what I would've said," Jem said, voice dripping with bogus wisdom.

Kenny was laughing at this. "Sure you would," he said.

"Prayer might help," Jem drawled. "You don't actually

know these things ahead of time, then," he guessed.

"Not exactly. You can make a pretty close guess, but one test is worth— Finish it, Kenny," he said.

" '—a thousand expert opinions,' " Kenny quoted proudly.

As Rob repositioned the battery, Jem clucked his tongue. "Already brainwashing this innocent into an engineer," he said.

"He had to, my brain was dirty," Kenny rejoined, loyal to the core. "Aw, I didn't mean it that way," he added, as the adults laughed.

"He's your son, all right," Ed observed. "He has your blush."

"Mark Twain said that man is the only animal that blushes, or needs to," Jem put in. "By the way, what's that little whisker for?—the one that curls out in front of your bug."

"I, uh . . . Jem, the day may come when you have to face a polygraph. So: No comment. Trust me, it isn't a hypodermic needle."

Jem shook his head. "God knows, that wouldn't scare me; my bedroom fridge is full of them. I've been poking myself with needles so long I'm used to it." Seeing Kenny's sudden glance of surmise he quickly added, "Not what you think, Kenny. Diabetes. You learn to live with it," he said. "One of these days, they tell me, I'll be able to take insulin orally, but not yet."

Now Rob placed his mantis on the table again and picked up the transmitter. As he moved the joysticks, the wings canted very slightly this way and that, provoking a giggle from Ed. "Contact," she intoned. Then: "*Udnn, udnnnn,* and Snoopy is off in his trusty Mustang in search of the Red Baron."

"His Sopwith Camel," Kenny corrected. "Wrong war, Ed."

"It knows what I mean—well, it needs a cheering section," she said to Rob's bemused glance.

Evidently it enjoyed cheers. The six-inch mantis skated across the tabletop, airborne in two feet, and hummed across the dining area, then toward the right-hand wall of the living room, banking around steeply to reverse direction at a pace that seemed brisk though Kenny could have raced forward to catch it. When it began a sidelong slide toward the carpet, Rob cut power and made it swoop up sharply before it encountered the carpet again, bouncing slightly on its spidery legs. "The Red Baron is toast," said Rob, and then they had coffee.

Shortly after eleven P.M., Jem supplied a different cardboard box from the garage and claimed that the evening had been more fun than any TV channel. "Sure you don't want me to run you to your car? My Vanagon's right outside. It'll take you two, the bike, and a troupe of performing Chinese acrobats. I'm saying 'roomy.' "

"But you don't know what I'm driving. Let's keep it that way," Rob told him, patting his shoulder, pocketing Gus's bulky little transmitter as he walked toward the door.

With the briefest glance toward Kenny, Ed stayed in the kitchen. "I don't want you to tell me where you're going, but—" she said, and paused. "You're probably no less crazy now than you were yesterday or the day before."

"Probably," Rob agreed.

"Then e-mail can still find you, I suppose—you lunatic. In case there's more about the Lodge connection."

"I wouldn't be surpri—" Rob began.

"Miz Lodge? Mom's friend?" Kenny perked up. "Before I left home, this Sachs guy was talking on his cell phone about her."

Rob: "Or *him*?"

Kenny: "Whatever. He was saying maybe they needed . . . Uh, he said another Lodge meeting, but not tonight. He repeated 'Lodge meeting' and laughed, like he was so cool. Like I can't add two and two," he finished in disgust.

Rob nodded. "He say when?"

"Nunh-uh," said Kenny.

"Might help to know," said Rob, and helped Kenny steer the bike outside.

Walking with his son through a night filled with arias of Wagnerian crickets, the two spoke softly. "I gather you like those two back there," said Rob.

"If you're wondering that I know Jem's kinda swishy, don't worry about it," said the boy.

Rob chuckled at that easy dismissal. "The very least of my worries. You didn't answer my question, though."

"What's not to like? I prob'ly oughta be asking you how you like Ed, but maybe I'm not ready to hear it," said the boy.

"I danced with her at a party, once. Your mom was there, and that's all there is to me and Ed."

"Ed," said Kenny, and laughed. "She's an 'Ed' like Sophia Loren's an old lady."

"You're growing up entirely too fast for my own good. Okay, can I help it if she's a looker?"

"Coulda warned me," the boy said, teasing.

"I'm warning you now, kid: If you let slip anything about them helping me in any way, the very least that'll happen is that Ed will lose her job; probably a blacklisting of some kind; which means she might go on welfare for being a good guy. We weren't there tonight."

"Gotcha. I don't know any Jem or any Ed, and I haven't been with you, either."

Rob sighed. "Now I'm coaching my son in lying to the authorities. I hope you never have to find out how much that bothers me. You know, I doubt anyone will give you too hard a time about the help you're giving me, but you don't have to testify against yourself, and I don't want to find out Ed's duplex has been scattered from hell to breakfast by a bomb."

"That's crazy," said the boy, obviously troubled by the idea.

"It sure is. Just as crazy as someone tracking us down and shooting my bedroll, not to mention what happened to poor Gus. There's been one bomb already, so it probably could happen to Ed or Jem—just like it happened to someone else."

"Oh: The guy who blew up the Bronco. You think he could've been the one after us in Oregon?"

"No, I think he leaned on the wrong car while he was walking through a parking lot."

Kenny only grunted, and for a moment they walked in silence. Then Rob worried aloud that by now, Corrine would be concerned at Kenny's absence.

"I hope so," Kenny replied cryptically. "Dad, I wish there was some way you could talk to David. Without taking chances."

"We're on first-name terms now, are we?"

"Sorry."

"It's okay," Rob insisted gamely, though it wasn't.

Now Kenny's voice was a growl. "I really, really—no-shit *really*—don't like him around, but he doesn't act like a guy who's out to shoot you. If we could get him alone, maybe I could be your backup."

" 'Backup.' Do you hear yourself, Kenny? With what, a silenced pistol and an infrared scope? And he has backup of his own. This isn't like TV, son. I'm trying to figure out whether I can isolate one of those people so I can safely talk, make my case; go to the San Jose police maybe. I just don't want to do it facing whoever it is that shot Gus and marmaladed some poor devil along with the Bronco. If that was on David Sachs's orders, I have to know."

They reached the camper and put the bike inside before climbing into the cab. Then Rob said, "Have I mentioned recently, how absolutely proud I am of my son?"

"Every time I see you looking at me," said Kenny, and hugged his dad before he buckled up.

CHAPTER 20

IT WOULD HAVE BEEN UNTHINKABLY BAD JUDGMENT FOR DAVID
Sachs to confer with his team in the presence of Corrine Tarrant, so they convened in her driveway, the Pontiac's windows
rolled halfway down to catch the night breeze. Frank Carnes
held a device the size of a small brick on his knee, its screen
lit softly in the darkness, lending a pallid glow to the men's
faces. "Let's see; I wanted you to check on the old Kallas fellow
again, Vallejo," David said to the woman sitting behind them.
"Did you see him?"

"Per orders. Not for long," she said dryly. "The staff felt he
was . . . I believe 'agitated' was the term." The faintest of
smiles. "A poor substitute for 'monumentally pissed-off.' "

"Was he any help?"

"You mean beyond insisting it couldn't have been Tarrant
that tried to pop him? No help at all, and it made him mad
enough to chew nails. Could be wishful thinking," she added.
"When I suggested Tarrant's motive could've been revenge if
he thought Kallas might've been involved in the Bronco thing,
Kallas hit the ceiling again. He just wasn't buying anything
we were selling." She sighed.

David craned his neck to face her. "Would you buy it, in
his place?"

After a silence: "Probably not. I'd have said 'absolutely not'
until Tarrant—well, somebody, anyway—scattered that car.
You realize how the San Jose police see us right now?"

"Sure I do: egg on our chins," David grumbled. "But now
that the locals are interested in Tarrant, he's less interesting
to me."

"Because they are?"

"No, because I think he could clear himself, except for that car bomb. That makes him a very dangerous man, but I suspect nobody's running him. If they were, he'd be long gone. Carnes, you keeping an eye on the tracer bugs?"

"Watching my screen for a reason. You realize if either one of the Lodge vehicles starts to move tonight I'll have to hightail it, Commander. The bugs on their cars have been nothing but a pain."

Vallejo: "When were they anything else but? You have an agenda here, Frank?"

Carnes replied only with a grunt.

"Let's hear it," David prompted.

"I just don't think this is taking us where we want to go," said Carnes. "If Lodge and his wife are helping Tarrant, they've gotta know better than to drive their cars to see him. A whole lot more likely that Tarrant would go to them. No tracking, no phone contacts that way, which is exactly what's happening: nothing. And when I'm on stakeout I don't see any of the usual signs of a rendezvous. Goddamn it, I don't think Tarrant is in contact, and watching Lodge is a waste of time!"

David was patient. "And your recommendation?"

Carnes hesitated, but when he began to answer it was like the first leak of the breach in a dike, a trickle becoming a flood: "I think we ought to wrap this, officially. Clear out, let the locals do their thing about the car bomb, take it as likely that Tarrant has some way of knowing where we are—especially you, Commander. You assume Mrs. Tarrant is an asset, but whose asset is she, really? Maybe if she thought we'd closed up shop and caught the red-eye back East, Tarrant would come out of the woodwork. And because we'd be out of the overt picture, that's when he'd be vulnerable. You thought much about that?"

Vallejo was laughing softly. "Well, Commander, you asked."

"I know what you think; both of you. If I'm wrong I could be bucking for a reprimand, but I'm convinced Corrine Tarrant is not abetting her husband. We know he wants to see her, though, for whatever reason."

"Oh, come *on*." Vallejo drawled it softly. "I should have to tell you, of all people, the handiest reason?"

Though Marie Vallejo had not proven immune to David's charm, she had never betrayed a trace of jealousy. He let the provocation pass without comment. "All right, so let's say I'm wrong. We know Tarrant's not telephoning here, or the Kallas place or the Lodges'. If he's coming here in person somehow, for his wife to brief him, I think I'd spot any attempt she'd make to flag him off; and she doesn't have a schedule for my comings and goings—and stop that snickering, Vallejo, you know what I meant. As for the boy, he isn't a factor. He isn't even here much, because, if you want the truth, I think he's uncomfortable here.

"So if Tarrant is in contact with his wife, what better way to confront him than by my being here late at night with this car parked out of sight?"

"Plus a few motion detectors," Carnes put in. "Are you setting them up correctly?"

"You're the bug man on this team," David reminded him. "Check them out for me, you have my permission." Hearing a grunt of assent, he went on. "Are you saying we should just admit defeat here, and hope the man turns up someday?"

"I thought I was clear. No, I'm not saying we should leave; but yes, I'm saying we should appear to," Carnes corrected.

From the backseat: "Ahh. Particularly to Corrine Tarrant."

Carnes turned to face David. "Yeah," he said. "Maybe have someone rent that vacant house across the fence from this one, fill it with remote surveillance gear. Then we move in at night, sit back, and wait."

"I should've thought of that," David admitted.

Carnes cleared his throat. "And one more thing, Commander. About the kid."

"What about him?"

"He's not a factor, you say, but what if he is? Say he's a whole lot slicker than you think. Like, it's nearly midnight and where d'you suppose he is right now?"

Marie Vallejo had been gazing out her window, lifting her

chin to catch stray breezes, and now she sat up straight. "Well, I'm damned," she said softly. "Speak of the devil, and check the sidewalk on your port beam. But doesn't the boy have a bike?"

Limned by a distant street light, a slender figure was trotting along the sidewalk toward them, still nearly a block away.

David slid from the car and eased the door shut fast. "An interesting point. I'll be back shortly," he said, and slipped through the shrubs toward the back door.

The runner proved to be the Tarrant boy, who took no obvious note of the silhouettes in the car but disappeared along the same path through the shrubs. Hearing a bass chuckle, Vallejo said, "I could use a laugh about now."

Carnes said, "Just thinking: Seems like almost nobody uses the front door here. Shit, Marie, it's almost like a signal that nobody's on the up-and-up. Goddamn Keystone Kops comedy."

"Back-door diplomacy, domestic version," she replied. "You know, renting that house is a nice touch. If our glorious leader weren't thinking with his crotch, he would've thought of it himself."

"A fifth of Bushmill's says it'll be his idea before long," Carnes grumped.

Their wait was not as long as it seemed, marked only by a light going on in the living room. David Sachs emerged from the front door presently, and swung into the driver's seat. "I watched from the hall where it's dark," he told them. "Exhibit A: Our delinquent tried to sneak to his room while Corrine was dozing at the TV. She heard him and called him in to bitch him out for being so late. He couldn't know I was there, and the only message he brought her was, 'Guess what, Mom, it's not a school night.' Exhibit B: She tore a strip off him, not knowing where he'd been—seems he blew a tire on his bike and had to walk the rest of the way—and even if she'd known I was in the house, she's not that good an actress. Listen to me, you two: Corrine Tarrant didn't send her kid off on some family rendezvous. She sent him to bed. I flushed the toilet for a cover action, and that surprised them both. When I came out of the john I thought I might have to put a headlock on him. Not a happy camper," David finished.

"So they aren't co-conspirators," said Vallejo. "But Frank could be right; we've pretty much ignored the boy."

"And I'm definitely right about the other thing," said Carnes.

"Go undercover, you mean," David said.

"You got it," said Carnes. "That, and focus more on the boy."

David drummed his fingers on the steering wheel long enough to irritate the others. "It can't be more frustrating than the past week. We'll try it your way, Frank. We've already got a sit-down scheduled with Lodge; I'll just change the agenda from bearing down on him, to no pressure at all. *Wham, whirr*, 'Thank you, sir, we're out of here,' or words to that effect." A long exhalation. Then, "But for tonight, check the recorders one more time and turn in at the motel."

"You coming, too?"

He thought there might be a hint of teasing in Vallejo's question, so he tried to sound resigned. "I'll be here late. Business as usual." As he swung out of the car, Carnes was singing an old ditty. "And the name of that tune is 'Insubordination,' Frank. Don't make me say it again."

Carnes and Vallejo both laughed. The real name of the tune Carnes had sung was "Nice Work If You Can Get It."

ROB HAD DROPPED KENNY OFF A HALF-MILE FROM HOME BE-cause the boy had insisted. Watching his son set off beneath streetlights with the tireless lope of a soccer jock, Rob had grown misty-eyed with pride. Kenny hadn't even asked how this particular mantis was to be used, though he had to be curious. Perhaps Gus had already told him.

During the ensuing ten minutes Rob had the camper tee-tering around corners in his hurry to queue up before mid-night, one more anonymous vehicle in the line of nightly GenStan traffic. Normally he would have looked forward to outdoor flight tests with optimism, but he had a hell of a lot of testing to do in darkness, alone, with a gadget that needed exactly one tiny subsystem failure to become a totally wasted effort.

He drove past a bored gate guard, yawning for effect, before parking within sight of Ethan Lodge's office, some three hundred yards distant from the building. He'd had Kenny remove the dome light from its socket in the cab after determining that the lamp in the glovebox would shed enough light for his needs. For the next fifteen minutes, then, he prepared for testing.

He'd never even tried the dash-mounted radio, but to his relief it began to play salsa music almost instantly. He donned a featherlight audio headset, tucked the transmitter under one arm, and brought the mantis outside, stopping to wait until some latecomer finished parking and hurried off to work. Rob moved off to another line of cars nearby and set the propeller-driven mite down on the still-warm hood of someone's Buick. He gently touched the end of the wispy forward-jutting proboscis, cursed, made an adjustment at the headset, and tried again; no problem. It had been only a matter of adjusting the volume, although it was one thing to get an audio signal when you were literally touching the audio pickup, and quite another to get a clear signal when the tiny probe rested against a windowpane several blocks away.

He could have simply placed the mantis's probe against the camper windshield for the audio test, yet this would not have been a rigorous test. He moved around until he had the most advantageous view, with only GenStan's yellow vapor lights to help, because mounting even the smallest light-emitting diode on the mantis itself would have meant a weight penalty. Then, with a prayer to the gods of chance, he energized the propeller. The mantis scrabbled across the Buick's hood and began to climb.

And disappeared whispering into the night.

Muttering an unbroken string of "ohshitohshitohshit," he strode in front of the car and manipulated the controls for a climbing turn to the left. For a moment he saw only the sodium-yellow glow of a distant light, and during that moment his confidence died a dozen times. Then he saw something glisten against the light fifteen feet above him, crossing and turning, and he cut power instantly. He squatted to keep that faint gleam in view as it descended at the pace of a child's toy parachute, and he thought it was sinking toward him as he went down on all fours.

When it struck him lightly on the forehead and dropped to the macadam he was in no mood to enjoy the irony. Of all the things that might have halted the tests of his mantis, losing the damned thing in a parking lot had been among the least of his fears.

After that, he decided rigor could go to hell. He merely moved to the front of the camper itself and let the mantis take off from its hood, impacting directly against the windshield only a few feet away. It wasn't much of a test. It also didn't give him any recognizable audio, possibly because the mantis slid down the windshield slope, its probe resting lightly against the glass.

He'd hoped to avoid anything as risky as quick-drying cement on the tip of the probe, but clearly it was either that, or no real expectation of success. The nice thing about cyanoacrylate cement was that it solidified literally in a matter of seconds. The trouble with the stuff was—it solidified in a matter of seconds. Well, he could sever the tiny daub of cement with a razor blade if necessary. After applying cement to the probe and trying again, he saw the mantis slide down the windshield again. He actually heard the faint unintelligible sounds in his headset become something like music, then distinct chords from guitars as the cement polymerized from a viscous liquid, through a gel, to a hornlike solid in a matter of half a minute. Some of the more expensive formulations were still more unforgiving: they hardened so fast, a user could see an instantaneous flicker as the stuff solidified.

In the end he had to shorten the probe, leaving its very tip cemented near the bottom of the windshield. No matter. It flew, and it transmitted sound through a big pane of glass. He moved off again to a point fifty yards distant, and still heard salsa music. He kept going back another fifty yards before he reached the limit of reception. It would have to do. At dawn, when he could see to control the mantis, he would have to move much nearer the building for its emplacement against a second-floor window; in fact, dangerously near. In some ways the final placement of the mantis would be simpler than against a sloping windshield, and in other ways, more problematic. He would have several hours to wait before dawn. Feeling the scrape of eyelids like emery boards across his eyes, he knew he'd need every wink of sleep he could cram into that time. He trudged around to the camper's rear entrance and, edging past the green bicycle that occupied most of the floor space, set Fred McGrath's alarm clock for four forty-five.

THE GRAVEYARD SHIFT WAS AN HOUR SHORTER THAN THE DAY shift, and Rob was heartened when, at earliest light, he saw a cyclist pedaling briskly across the macadam between the shops. He never had had occasion to wonder whether couriers were needed at such times; whether, in fact, he would need to skulk as he moved through the ranks of vehicles with a big shoebox clamped to the bike's rack.

Getting Kenny's bike out of that camper was a little like detaching a treble fishhook from a smallmouth bass, and with bells on the damned thing when he needed to avoid extraneous noises in the early morning's utter silence. At one point, with the bike half in and half out of the camper and the handlebars hooked firmly between plywood partitions, he realized how this would look to any security man who happened to be roving the area. Bringing a personal bike, freshly painted GenStan green, onto the site might take a lot of explaining but it wouldn't take a nuclear physicist to figure out why a man might be trying to squeeze a GenStan bike, worth perhaps a hundred dollars, *into* a camper. That would earn him a trip to the Security office, and that was one trip he did not want to think about. He finally dislodged the handlebars using brute strength.

His first pass by his goal with the bike began with a circuitous route among rows of vehicles. Roughly seventy yards from the building he found one of several sloping depressions in the macadam where the runoff from heavy rains was directed through a grating. He located that spot slightly west of a line between Lodge's office window and the fifth light standard from the main gate. The drainage slope was steep enough that he could lay the bike on its side, beyond any casual notice, between a car and a high-clearance pickup truck.

Pedaling on toward the main building, he confirmed what he recalled of that window and its ledge, and he continued on to circle one of the shop buildings before returning. The transmitter and headset were both impediments in his jacket, but infinitely better than the alternative. To place either gadget in that box with the mantis would be a risk equivalent to shipping a mouse with a bowling ball. Even so, he rode very, very carefully.

It was nearly six A.M. before Rob lowered his bike near the storm drain and gave the mantis a careful pre-flight examination. Its controls operated well, but a few drops of cyanoacrylate cement had leaked from its soapy plastic applicator, and he inadvertently managed to glue Jem Kasabian's donated box to the macadam.

At last he decided he was ready. He was perhaps two hundred feet from that second-story window. The occasional languid motion of the decorative plumes of pampas grass near the building said that the prevailing breeze was faint and unpredictable. For the mantis it would be effectively a tailwind when it came.

Okay, if I don't want the cement to harden too soon, I'll have to launch the very second after I apply cement to the probe, he coached himself. *The stuff will begin thickening in flight, so I've gotta get it there ASAP. My V Max is, say, twenty feet per second without the breeze, call it ten seconds to impact, plus maybe two or minus one if the breeze puffs on it.*

Complicating this further was the fact that, assuming the second-floor window ledge setback was identical to that of the lower floor, that ledge was exactly as deep as the thickness of a standard cement block—eight inches. Rob could not fly his tiny craft toward the window at an angle with any hope of adhesion. He would have to guide it to impact headlong, and very near the bottom of the window. Inside the office, that window ledge was at shoulder height to a standing man. To gaze out the window one must stand up, which must have pleased the efficiency expert who set those window specifications. A seated man would not be able to see over the interior lip of the window; therefore he could not see a gossamer electromechanical insect with its proboscis pressed against the glass. If Ethan Lodge happened to glance at the window ledge when he walked into his office—well, he was one of a very select few who would know what he was looking at.

And who had put it there.

And every minute that Rob sat on his knees considering all these variables it became more likely that the early-morning breeze would freshen in response to sunlight. With what he'd intended as a final glance he realized, absolutely, he was simply too damned far away to make exact visual judgments. He snatched up the transmitter and the mantis and, bent at the waist, went scudding past two more rows of cars. The last row was still thirty yards from the building. It would have to do.

He squatted and tried the transmitter again, flexed his fingers, applied a daub of cement to the probe with one hand, and manipulated the transmitter with the other. The mantis whispered its faint good-bye, shuddered across the macadam, and quickly climbed away.

He knelt clutching the transmitter controls with both hands now. With the motion of that pampas grass he had an instant's warning of the errant breeze that met the mantis head-on. *"The principles of physics don't give a damn what you want,"* ran the old engineering truism, and he knew the mantis must leap vertically as that breeze was translated into extra lift. He could only hope that the breeze was a mere puff as he guided the mantis up and over on its back, continuing its loop, then proceeding as before, but now with another six feet of altitude. Dry-mouthed, he stared and urged the device slightly to the left, a half-subliminal clock tallying numbers. Three to four seconds thrown away in that goddamn loop, but he'd gained something like five seconds by darting this far forward. *Still in the ballpark*, his mental clock told him.

When the mantis looked as though it wanted to climb over

the building, Rob remembered how architecture affects air-flow, and directed his tiny craft downward. He was too late with the correction and knew that the point of impact was going to be against the blank wall above the window.

"No you don't, by God, get your butt around there," he muttered aloud, his transmitter calling for a steep right-hand bank. The springlike legs of the mantis kissed the wall above the window in its sharp turn, rebounded like a live thing, and completed its circle. The steeper the bank, the more speed is needed to maintain enough lift to hold a given altitude. But the mantis needed to lose altitude, and in some way that he had never fully experienced before, Rob *was* the mantis. He finished his turn, saw his new impact point rushing toward him, and cut power a second before his probe encountered the window glass.

The mantis bounced back slightly, dropped to the window ledge, and hung for a moment in danger of falling backward, nose tilted up. Rob fed one more burst of power to the propeller and saw the gossamer thing leap against the window. He kept the propeller running for another ten seconds.

Then he stood up. The sun was warm on his face but the hair on his forearms stood erect, and he was grinning.

CHAPTER 21

ETHAN'S EARLY MEETING WITH MCADAMS, ONE OF RESEARCH and Development's top people, did not go well. The root of the problem, as Ethan saw it, was a cultural clash between Neanderthals rigidly adhering to the muck of realism, and modern humans who could free themselves to fly above dirty, objective little facts. The case in point: Ethan could not see why engineers should resist a few slight marketing exaggerations in a media release about GenStan's next generation of chemchips. McAdams, a plain spoken sort, could not understand why R&D should be held hostage to wild marketeering claims which Mac almost certainly would have to deny to their own board of directors in a few months.

Mac, who would have looked right at home on the deck of a New England whaler, saw fit to put it succinctly: "It'd be my ass in the sling, not yours. That's why I can't sign off on it."

"We'll take another cut at the release, massage it for you," said the marketeer, always willing to try for a fresh nuance. "But a little poetic license never did any harm. People expect us to put our best foot forward, gild the lily a bit. We're trying to build some excitement about the product, Mac."

"A product that doesn't exist the way you described it, Ethan. In the lab we have a word for that kind of product: 'unobtainium.' Infinite strength, but cut it with a butter knife. Weightless, odorless, colorless, tasteless, and improves the flavor of tossed green salad. The unreachable dream for us lab rats, so when you announce some version of unobtainium, we tend to snicker. And speaking of things that don't exist, what's this rumor about some poor schlub in your tent going off his nut and car-bombing a Security man?"

Ethan crafted one of those knowing smiles of his, the sort that said, *I know more than I'm telling*. Often, that was a pose, but in this case it was genuine. "Wasn't Marketing's man. I guess Security hasn't anything better to do than invent rumors. You must've missed the piece in the paper, then."

"I know better than to believe everything I read, thanks to Marketing," McAdams said with a wry smile, as he started to rise. And he did not deny that Security was involved in the rumor, at some level. Ethan decided he should have a talk with Security.

At that moment, Ethan saw the flasher on his telephone and put up a silent finger. A moment after he answered, his face went through a series of changes that made Mac wish he had time to waste listening to other people's phone calls. Because he didn't have that time, and because the interruption allowed him to leave on cordial terms after refusing to endorse more Marketing goofiness, the R&D man waved a casual two-fingered salute—one more than he might have used in the lab—in Ethan's direction and strode out past Edwina Doyle. She wore one of those gimmicky little headsets over her ears, and jumped in surprise as his shadow flickered across her workstation.

That headset was both blessing and curse to Ed, who could listen to any number of things unheard by others, but when focused she tended to ignore nearby footfalls. As he passed, McAdams could not know she was listening to the call from David Sachs to Ethan Lodge.

Two minutes afterward, Ethan replaced the phone and stood up. If Security people let these rumors multiply, sooner or later they would include the very thing that Mike hoped to avoid: a tight focus on tiny UAVs equipped with chemchips. Security was a tiger you didn't want to grab by the tail, but a brief face-to-face objection might work. The back of Ethan's head came within two feet of a tiny UAV cemented to the outside of his window as he moved toward the doorway.

Ed let the headset drop to her throat before the manager swept past her on his way out.

"Route only priority calls to Security; I should be back in

half an hour," Ethan said hurriedly, then turned with an afterthought. "Oh: Clear my decks for a two o'clock with the
Navy today. Could last an hour."

"Yes, sir," she said, and brought up his calendar on her
computer screen. When his steps had faded down the hall, her
fingers began to fairly fly over that keyboard. In another three
minutes she had erased all trace of her most recent in-house
message, to an office that was usually untenanted.

TWO COPIES OF THE MORNING PAPER HAD BEEN DISCARDED IN
GenStan's tech library, and Rob took one of them to the men's
room down the hall. A follow-up story claimed that Robert
Tarrant had been misidentified as the car-bomb victim, who
was now known to be a younger man, one Timothy Crump,
deceased. Tarrant was now sought for questioning, though
sources would not categorically state that he was a prime suspect in the bombing.

Rob allowed several old scenarios to plod past his awareness
and still did not like any of them. Essential to them all was
his coming in from the cold, facing his tormentors. He might
just walk up to GenStan's head of Security and ask for an
interview with this man Sachs, trusting Security to keep his
skin unperforated. Or he could go to the San Jose police, or
even to the FBI's little Palo Alto office.

The flaw in each of these notions was that he no longer
trusted any of those official bodies. *If a conservative is a liberal
who's been mugged, maybe a paranoid is a trusting citizen
who's been chased and shot at,* he thought. Yet sooner or later,
he feared, he'd inevitably run out of help, or out of luck. Most
likely sooner.

It never occurred to Rob that those who wanted him dead
might fear exactly the same thing.

What did occur to him now, for the first time, was that other
innocent fugitives had succeeded by throwing throwing themselves in front of another kind of judge: the media. Should he
walk into one of the network TV stations with the promise of
a scoop? How about the newspapers? This was something he
should have thought of sooner, but what did he have to say,

really? Without some insight into the motives of his pursuers he had only half a story. Maybe his little mantis, its audio probe against a window fifty yards away from where he sat, would furnish that motive.

Rob visited a coffee machine and carried one of those steaming cups of caustic brew to McGrath's office, then locked the door behind him. As a precaution, he checked the status of Fred McGrath and was instantly glad he had. Evidently Fred had finished his work off-site; the old blarney specialist was now scheduled to return by close of the workday. This was a complication Rob had not worried much about until now, but he realized that he needed to do a fast cleanup in the camper before finding another place to sleep.

But there was more on the computer screen: in-house mail, ostensibly from Ethan Lodge.

To: F.McGrath
From: E. Lodge
SUBJECT: Personal

Welcome back to Sunnyvale, Fred; noticed your new return schedule. FYI, will not be available this date after 2 P.M. Unavoidable meeting that time my office with Navy personnel. Ack & delete. EL.

Rob shook his head in awe. This little piece of e-mail might actually have been an innocent greeting to McGrath, and moreover, one that Ed Doyle could have sent like a Get Well card without mentioning it to Lodge. Yet the "acknowledge and delete" phrase said otherwise. Rob made a fast acknowledgment, deleted everything, and sat drumming his fingers on the desktop for a long moment, mentally lost in his effort to sort priorities. It was still very important that he come in from the cold on his own, but equally crucial that he must never have to reveal how Ed had been helping him inside GenStan's facilities.

Then he went to work. After shutting off the computer he took a coffee-dampened Kleenex to the keyboard, then the

back and seat lip of McGrath's chair. Hadn't he used the
phone? It got the same attention, and by the time he had wiped
his prints from everything he'd touched, the coffee was gone
and so were most of the tissues. He felt a tinge of smugness as
he wiped down the doorknob and its lock, using tissues to hold
the knob as he opened the door, the empty cup in his other
hand.

He closed the door carefully, again holding the exterior
knob, turned and started down the hall. Only then did he notice the two young women who'd been standing quietly at the
coffee machine, fifteen yards away; and he was already walking in their direction.

"Oh, Mr. McGrath's back," one of them said, which caused
the other to glance his way. *Turn around and walk the other
way?* That would prevent them from a closer look, but it would
be a move so obvious as to demand reporting. He chose to
continue his brazen approach.

"That's not him," said the second young woman under her
breath, half laughing. As Rob approached, he vaguely recognized the second speaker, who was now regarding him closely.
A tech editor, publications writer, one of that ilk he'd seen
long before he got that beard. With any luck, she wouldn't see
past it.

Now Rob was very near, stuffing damp tissues into his cup.
He dropped the cup into the nearby trash receptacle, nodded
and forced himself to make eye contact, said, " 'Morning," and
continued past them.

He made it to the stairwell, straining to make sense of the
furious whispers in his wake, before the two women fell silent.

But only for a moment. When he heard one very clearly say,
in a small voice, "Oh my *Gohhhd*, are you sure?" it took all
his presence of mind to keep from breaking into a headlong
sprint.

ETHAN HAD NOT BEEN IN THE OFFICE OF THE SECURITY SER-
vices Director more than ten minutes. In fact, Ethan was well
within his rights in pointing out that the top Security man, of
all people, should not be making casual references about sen-

sitive events to a man he carpooled with. Not even a lab manager. "I suppose mentioning my name gave McAdams the idea
one of my people was involved," he was saying, when a light
appeared on the telephone of the ex-FBI man.

Ethan paused, though he disliked any interruption just as
he was pressing home his point.

The director answered, listened for a moment, then glanced
quickly at Ethan as if he had just drawn the right card to fill
an inside straight. "Bring them both down ASAP. No, wait.
Where are you calling from? . . . Good, keep them there. And
for God's sweet sake, keep smiling, George, I want them relaxed for the interviews."

Ethan knew that in Security parlance, "interview" meant
"interrogation." Evidently this was to be a gentle one. When
the telephone was cradled again, Ethan remarked, "Don't tell
me you've caught some media people sneaking in to chase
another rumor." His grin said he was joking.

"No, I won't tell you that," said the director, standing up,
seeming very pleased with himself on short notice. "Someone
has reminded me very recently that I, of all people, shouldn't
be talking out-of-turn. Remember that I said so, Ethan, for
future reference. And now, I'm awfully sorry, but there's a
little matter I must attend to."

Ethan shook the proffered hand by reflex. Ordinarily he
would have chafed at being dismissed in this fashion but, in
this case, he felt that he had won a small battle. The two men
separated in the hall, the director fumbling for the powerful
little radio unit on his belt. Ethan smiled to hear the director
humming a sprightly tune as he hurried off; it was hard to
figure these security people.

THE DIRECTOR SPOKE TO HIS GATE CHIEF BY RADIO. FROM THAT
moment on, everyone trying to leave GenStan would not do
so until matched by a photo ID, and bearded men would get
specially cautious treatment. He made himself slow down before he walked into Technical Publications, smiling, setting
the two young women at ease as they moved to a cloistered
corner table. His little Nagra recorder, an expensive reminder

of earlier times, would have made them nervous, had he taken it from his coat pocket. He sent the guard off for three hot chocolates—some things, even a vending machine couldn't ruin.

"Now then: First, let me assure you that our conversations will be considered both company proprietary and confidential," he said gently. "We won't discuss it with anyone. As long as we all do this, you have nothing to worry about." He paused and got their nods. "So: What makes you think you've just seen Robert Tarrant?"

Both women tried to talk at once but the director calmed them, nodding judiciously in the right places, raising his brows in surprise when he learned that the bearded man had absolutely, positively emerged from the office of Fred McGrath before going past them and downstairs. Excusing himself, the director walked into the hall and made another radio call, this time for his forensics team. In very short order, McGrath's office would be the site of some very close company scrutiny.

It wasn't exactly a crime simply to enter someone else's empty office, but if Tarrant had been doing it, the director wanted to know. And he did not want anyone else to know if his vaunted GenStan Security system had proven, after all, as porous as cheesecloth.

The technical writer, at this point, was chewing her lower lip and fidgeting. "I can't be certain it was Rob Tarrant," she said. "But I've got a thing about eyes."

"You mean flirty, evasive, direct, or something else?"

"Well, that, too, but I meant how you see them in a snapshot. Black like volcanic glass, or yellowish, or deep-set, or round Betty Boops or whatnot. When this guy passed us he was as close to me as you are, and he just flicked me a glance as he was fooling with a paper cup he tossed, and I thought: *Tarrant*. Rob Tarrant helped on a proposal about a year ago, and it bugged me the way he looked at you when he was thinking about a problem. Like he was seeing right through you, to something beyond you."

"Unfocused, as if he was nearsighted?"

"No, more like he was flying a jet and looking way ahead.

A visionary look, maybe. I don't know," she shrugged. "But when he looked at me today it was like that, same intensity. Same big brown eyes, too," she said, coloring. "But it could've been someone else, I suppose. I've heard the talk, and I'd hate to start some dumb rumor."

"Too much of that going around," said the director, his nuance lost to the writer. "By the way, do either of you have more than a nodding acquaintance with Mr. Tarrant? Your answers will go no farther than this," he said, "but you must be perfectly candid."

One of the young women only shrugged and shook her head. The writer smiled and said, "I get your drift and no, I barely knew the guy. I called a guard, didn't I?"

The director nodded, studied the young women; decided against brandishing any threat, however oblique. "Tell you what," he said at last. "I'd like us to go back where you were—right down the hall, wasn't it? Try and recall everything the subject did."

As they neared the coffee machine, two men carrying leather satchels were entering the office of Fred McGrath. Both wore latex gloves, and the one holding the doorknob did so with great care. The director nodded to the men, then turned his attention to his companions.

CHAPTER 22

KENNY'S BIKE GAVE ROB AN OUTLET FOR A BUNDLE OF NERVOUS energy, and by the time he arrived at the camper he had almost convinced himself that he had panicked over nothing; those young women undoubtedly had been gossiping about something else. *The guys in the huddle aren't talking about you*, he chided himself. Still, he had good reason for fleeing to the camper. Old McGrath couldn't help but realize someone had been using his little bagnio-on-wheels. The least Rob could do was drive outside the plant, fill the fuel tank, replace some cans of junk food, maybe get the camper washed before returning after lunch.

It was only decent, too, to leave McGrath a note which, among other things, would absolve the old rake of complicity. And while Rob was at it, he should try his jury-rigged audio link from outside the chain-link fence. You never knew about the range of those things from various directions, and it would be nice to listen in on that two o'clock meeting from neutral turf.

Rob stowed his transceiver in the passenger's seat but left the bike chained against a light standard, unwilling to try horsing it aboard in broad daylight. The camper was already in motion, moving toward the main gate, when he realized that someone's Dodge had braked, plugging the exit of his row. As he continued, rolling almost to a stop, the Dodge turned right and eased into a queue leading toward the exit.

A queue? To get in, some mornings, assuredly. To get *out* before noon? *Probably a fender-bender at the gate*, he told himself, but while engaging in that internal dialogue, he stopped the camper and used its height to gaze over the tops of other vehicles.

Ordinarily there would have been a solitary gate guard standing outside the gate kiosk, waving vehicles on. Now Rob could see three of the uniformed men, leaning down, reaching through windows, interacting closely not only with each driver but with passengers. They were checking ID badges.

They're looking for someone who's inside—me, that's who. That damn sharp-eyed tech writer had blown the whistle on him after all.

He'd passed the slot the Dodge had vacated, but there was no car waiting behind him. Rob backed up very slowly, then eased into the slot and turned off the engine. If Security had been alerted to his presence inside GenStan, it was already too late to get out by any of the usual exits.

A prickly-heat sensation on the back of his neck accompanied his regret that he hadn't already run to the media: *Mercury-News*, KNTV . . . hell, almost any media forum. Maybe he could get to a pay phone inside, call a reporter. But as he left the camper's cab he realized the futility of his idea. Say he got a reporter on the phone; he couldn't get outside to make his case in person, and GenStan had never been keen on letting the media roam around inside without a compellingly good reason, and with someone—someone like Ethan Lodge— riding herd on them. And if Rob admitted he was stuck inside, that smacked of guilt or paranoia, maybe both. What now?

Now, pal, you're screwed, he decided.

Or maybe depantsed, but not quite screwed yet. His intent to set down the facts on paper, often considered, but always put off in favor of something more pressing, now presented itself in big letters etched in acid. He couldn't get outside, didn't dare show himself inside a building, and desperately needed to stay hidden until two o'clock. Shaving the beard now would be pointless. What better way to spend his last free moments than writing down the facts?

Rob was an indifferent typist but that was quicker than longhand, and he'd moved McGrath's Royal portable, a manual typewriter older than Rob himself, out of the way half a dozen times. He climbed into the camper and arranged the typewriter on Fred's pull-down table. *Jesus, a red-inked rib-*

bon? At least the thing worked, if your fingers were made of stone.

He used pages peeled from a yellow pad, the only stationery he could find; rolled a sheet around the platen. He almost addressed it "To Whom It May Concern," changed his mind in favor of Kenny, then reconsidered once more. Of all the things Fred McGrath was, a cowering company yesman wasn't one of them.

Dear Fred, he began,

when you're through consigning me to hell for using your goodies without asking, please see copies of this get to my son Kenny, & to unbiased media. DOD? Up to you. I'd do it myself if I could, should've done it sooner. Hindsight. Still don't know who wants me dead or why.

Again he mentally reprised the possible reasons for his predicament, and could not decide which of those reasons was most unlikely to give anyone reason to kill him. Maybe, if he didn't make it past this alive, someone else could assign probabilities. An engineer to his core, he denied he had any good reason for the order of his listing.

Possibilities, in no special order: Chemchip microvortex generators, but Halloran's my group leader on it. Why me instead of him or the R&D guys?

Mistaken ID; Stratford dumped me for bum reasons but I'm not the only Tarrant in the world. Just seems that way.

My little mantis micro-UAV hobby fliers? But I was TRYING to show my demonstrator to GenStan! Lodge knows that. Several labs doing paper studies, some on Internet. But maybe worth mentioning if there's a patent in it, down the line.

Personal reasons? Can't imagine who: I'm not romancing anybody's wife, don't gamble, & haven't even touched pot since student daze. Worst thing I've done is hang a right on the Security man who trashed my hobby project—UAV demo—I brought to show Ethan Lodge, week or so back.

And living inside GenStan isn't a crime; I'm still on extended leave last time I heard.

After shrugging off even more fanciful possibilities he recounted his astonishment at the last-minute rejection from Stratford, and his estrangement from Corrine, in a few phrases. The fishing trip with his son got a few more lines, chiefly because of the nocturnal shooting, which Kenny himself could verify. The tracer bugs, his decision to stash his Bronco, and his movements thereafter, all were briefly mentioned though he wrote nothing at all about Ed Doyle or Jem Kasabian. He couldn't believe he'd typed this much in less than an hour at the old portable when reports usually took him hours.

His third page began,

Who was Timmie Crump? Have no idea, I didn't blow up my own car. Ask a Fed named David Sachs, I saw his team visit my Bronco. Listened to them @ GenStan lunch w/ Lodge. Helps when you don't shave for a week!

The little piece of disinformation about listening might derail suspicions toward Ed.

He checked his watch before noting the current time on the page, careful to avoid an implication that he knew an exact time when he should be monitoring Lodge's office.

And that hobby of mine? May help me hear what I'm supposed to have done. I figure Lodge must know. Someone NOT GenStan should check his window ledge before next local storm if I'm not around to do it.

All this has to make sense on some level, Fred, but it's put my life in the dumper, & if Feds behind it, who could I go to? I'm tired, going broke, wife helping the hounds. If I'm running loose when I see the media report my side in the news, I might come in. If I don't call SOMEbody in next few days, I could be in a hole somewhere & I'm not the suicidal type. Sorry for all the trouble.

Counting on you to do right thing. Wish I knew what
THAT was. Only good thing is, my son knows I've done the
best I could.

He withdrew the page and reread it all carefully. He signed
it in longhand, stuffed the folded yellow sheets flat between
McGrath's pillow and pillowcase where others might not look,
and checked his watch again.

The time was 1:28 P.M.

IN THE OFFICE OF GENSTAN SECURITY, A BALDING FORENSICS
man studied forms on his clipboard before replying to his director. "No sir, not really, except for McGrath, F.—plenty of
his prints in that office, as you'd expect. If it's germane, I'd
say somebody's probably done some wipedowns in that
room."

"You did the Dustbuster routine, of course," the director
prodded.

A nod. "Filled some baggies, yessir; results take awhile, as
you know." A bleak smile: "We came up empty so far, but
maybe our cup will be half-full when we hear—"

" 'Cup!' " The director sat up straight, grabbed the audio
recorder from his desk. As he pushed buttons, brief phrases,
then gibberish, then more discernible speech filled the office:
the director and two young women.

He raised a forefinger at one woman's voice: ". . . fooling
with a paper cup he tossed, and I thought . . ." and stopped
the Nagra with one hand while he snatched at his phone with
the other.

Moments later he had the technical writer on the line, and
the forced nature of his casual tone brought a grin to the forensics man's face. "I was just wondering what you meant
about this fellow tossing a paper cup. An actual playful toss,
or what?" He nodded into the air, eyes narrowing, then said,
"Would you mind meeting me at the coffee machine right
away? Yes, now."

He was standing, motioning for the forensics man's kit, before he cradled the phone. "Your wipedown may have been

with hand tissues stuffed into a coffee cup in a trash bin. Let's see if we can break some records lifting a few prints off that cup, shall we? And if someone's emptied that bin I'm going to give myself two weeks off without pay."

THOUGH IT WAS STILL A QUARTER HOUR BEFORE THAT SCHEDuled meeting and Rob needed a place to hide, he knew that with every minute, Fred McGrath was more likely to show up in a taxi from San Jose Municipal. After all, the man *lived* in his damned camper and it wasn't where he had left it. When McGrath discovered it was missing he might put it down to forgetfulness. Or he might be bitching about it within minutes to Security, and two women could already place Rob in McGrath's office earlier in the day.

When someone finally did spot that tall, top-heavy vehicle lurking in the lot, it might not be ol' Fred who came to check it out. With this thought, Rob abandoned the camper ten minutes earlier than he had intended. The audio receiver was bulky in his jacket as he walked between rows of cars to Kenny's repainted bike, unchained it, and began to pedal to the rearmost row of cars that might furnish cover for him. A spot between his shoulder blades itched as if someone had painted a bull's-eye there. Why would a courier be pedaling that far from any building? *Stop it, you have no choice, and panic isn't that far away,* he commanded himself. It didn't matter why a courier would be doing what he was doing, so long as no one searching for him happened to notice and asked the same question.

He was in luck because, he reflected, some asshole with a forty-thousand-dollar sport-utility leviathan, about as sporty as a stretch limo and as utilitarian as a cement condom, had parked away from everyone else, perhaps to be sure this immense machine never risked a scratch to its bumper. All but its front windows were so heavily tinted he couldn't see inside, and it was almost seven feet to the roof rack.

For Rob, it was perfect. He blessed the owner for his foibles and leaned the bike against the rear fender of the four-ton monster.

His heart leaped when he arranged his headset; he could identify the voices of Ethan Lodge and Ed Doyle clearly. For a year, GenStan had been bragging about its high-tech windows with inaudible white-noise generators that would defeat a laser audio pickup. The inside joke among GenStan engineers was that the company was so intent on producing its own randomized white-noise modules, it hadn't quite got around to actually installing these paragons of security. The tag line among the cognoscenti was, "Any day now . . ."

The signal was not very loud, and the frequency range wasn't as wide as that of an ordinary telephone, but if that smarmy cocksman Sachs showed up there would be one more auditor of the meeting than anyone else knew. Rob switched off the receiver to save the batteries and peeked around this freeway boulder to check the area. He was still alone, but now, angry little horn bleats in the distance signaled that the main gate had its own little traffic jam going.

Rob was hoping to see Sachs and his team arrive, but incoming traffic was masked by the outgoing bottleneck. When he switched his receiver on at three minutes before two, he knew he'd failed to see Sachs coming in.

CHAPTER 23

WHEN ROB SWITCHED HIS HEADSET ON AGAIN, THE VOICES were tinny, but quite clear.

Lodge: ". . . others be arriving?"

As Sachs's voice grew louder, Rob pictured him moving nearer the window to sit down. "No, they're winding up some details. I wish they were here now, though. I dropped in on your Director of Security on my way up here. He didn't have much time for me at the moment, but he changed my mind about some things." A two-beat pause, and a shift to a faintly threatening tone. "Guess who was seen coming out of an unused office in this building, shortly before noon? It shouldn't be hard, Mr. Lodge. There are only so many people who could hide right here in plain sight. The question now is, where in the plant you're hiding him. By the way: He's no longer in the office he was occupying. Fairly crowded in there, I imagine."

Lodge, aghast: "You can't actually think— It's Tarrant, isn't it? Here?"

"I was ready to wrap this thing up. Couldn't see any way that Tarrant could be in contact with you. Except that suddenly I find, with Tarrant living right here inside the plant, you've had the perfect opportunity here every damn day. Both of you must've been laughing about that, and that makes it personal." The voice in Rob's headset did not sound heated, but coldly angry.

"But how could— I haven't even—" Ethan Lodge stammered, and then fought to steady himself. "I swear to you," he said, "I had no idea. Listen, the sooner you catch that man, the sooner you'll learn I'm telling the truth! This is insane, let me just call—"

"Security? They're pretty busy at the moment, verifying

some prints. I've asked the Director to call me here when they're certain, which should be any minute now. Tell me: Are you familiar with Section 1001, Title Eighteen, of the U.S. Code?"

"I'm not certain, but I'm sure you'll clarify it for me," said Lodge grimly.

"It states that lying to a federal officer in a criminal investigation is a felony. I suggest you give that a lot of thought."

When Lodge did not reply, Sachs plowed ahead. "You know, for a while I thought Tarrant might have discovered what brought on his original problem with Security. If so, it's likely that he might have some unfinished and very unpleasant business with you. But," Sachs said with a bitter little laugh, "living right in your lap, he'd have all the chances in the world. Maybe that Security trouble was something you cooked up together. You're not on a slab, and you would be if he wanted you there."

Almost wailing: "I befriended the man," said Lodge.

"Oh, I believe it, and I'm working on that one. You had to have a motive. If you were such a friend, Tarrant might have known you set the wheels in motion when you had that little UAV of his confiscated by Security. And I can't see why he'd want that."

"Son of a bitch," Rob breathed, two hundred yards away.

"I've spoken with your Security people about it," Sachs went on. "I never saw his little gadget but I gather its chemchip could be removed only by tearing the UAV to pieces."

"I wasn't there," said Lodge, with a touch of hauteur.

"Of course not, you're too careful for anything so obvious. You just set up the dominoes and gave one of them a nudge. But if that thing actually flew under control, when labs all over this country are having fits trying to make them do a Wilbur-and-Orville at such a size, in some circles you and that Security thug both may be seen as saboteurs."

Two hundred yards away: "Son of a *bitch*," said Rob.

Lodge's usual mellow tones had tightened and thinned. Rob got the impression of an inner struggle, with a light veneer of urbanity covering a roil of panic as Lodge said, "Even admitting a certain compassion for a dreamer like Tarrant, I have a higher duty to the company. What they did with his toy was not on my orders!"

"But predictable, given the circumstances. And you've been on GenStan's short list for DOD's vital technology topics for a long time. I checked that out. Why would you sic your dogs like that on a man you befriended, I wonder?"

"I don't recall what I was thinking at the time, Commander. Certainly I'd be right to apply caution with regard to, well, a special-access program, you said."

"No; *you* said," Sachs reminded him.

"But you didn't correct me."

"I gave you credit for being able to draw an inference," said Sachs.

And far away, in the parking lot: "Goddamn son of a bitch," Rob muttered. From time to time, he had been involved briefly in programs that required a higher security clearance; in one case, something called an SAP.

At the SAP level, need-to-know constraints gave rise to outright comic failures of communication; as an in-joke went, *sap* was exactly the right word for it. A newspaper article or an Internet discussion might be common gossip in any coffeehouse, yet anyone involved in the program was absolutely forbidden to take part in such talk. So his hobby was deeply enmeshed in an SAP, yet no one had told him so. *Damn you, Ethan! Your fucking "caution" has ruined me*, Rob thought furiously.

Sachs, meanwhile, was trying to assemble his puzzle aloud, perhaps to rattle Lodge into some admission. "I'm taking it as probable that you could have saved at least one life, and a great deal of trouble on everyone's part, by simply acting as an intermediary between us and Tarrant. What I can't decide yet is why you didn't."

"Because you're full of—," Ethan Lodge burst out, then caught himself. "Because your premise is wrong. Whatever you may think, I'm stunned to hear that a mad bomber has been lurking here on the premises. I'm still not sure I believe—"

The telephone's ring stopped him. A second later Lodge

said, "Ethan Lodge here. . . . Yes, just a moment. Uh, hold on, I need to hear it from you firsthand. Can it be true that Rob Tarrant has been seen here in-plant? . . . Oh my God; could he be involved with McGrath somehow? Yes, well, I'm beginning to think I may need a guard posted outside my office, if— All right. Here he is. It's for you," he finished.

Rob, squinting toward that distant window, said it aloud: "You know something, Ethan, old chum? I'm starting to think you'll need a bodyguard, too, if I ever get close enough to you." As much as he longed to put a boot squarely up the backside of this wife-romancing shithead Sachs, he had to smile. Whatever reason Ethan might have had for seeing that the micro-UAV was destroyed, he truly could not have led Rob to the Intelligence team because he hadn't known that, much of the time, Rob was virtually underfoot.

By now Rob had no doubt that the call was, as Sachs had predicted, from Security. ". . . Very quick work, but you'd have employee prints on file, of course. . . . Inside the cup? They always forget something, don't they? . . . At least there's not a shred of doubt now."

"Shit," said Rob. He had been so careful, and then let everything go into the dumper at once. He'd been seen coming from the office, left his fingerprints on that stupid cardboard cup, and capped his idiocy by discarding the cup in front of those women.

Rob was shaking his head at his own foolishness as Sachs completed the call before resuming his talk with Ethan, evidently still in the hope that Lodge would confess something, anything. "All the gate guards are alerted now," Sachs informed the manager. "He's going to be found, Lodge. And when he is, and we show him the list of crimes hanging over his head, beginning with illegal entry to this site, sooner or later he'll sing like Placido Domingo. Whatever scheme you two have cooked up, we'll know. It'd be very much in your own best interests if you told me now."

Perhaps it was simply having a few minutes to gather his wits that let Lodge speak with something like his old self-assurance. "Commander, when all this is done, I'm going to have an abject apology from you. I don't know why Tarrant is here; maybe he's just out of control and had nowhere else to go. I certainly haven't conspired with him in any way. That being so, whatever your findings, I have nothing to fear from you and your damned hectoring attitude. I'm not so sure about Tarrant because, to be perfectly frank, I've always thought he was a bit too unpredictable. What was it your people called him? A loose cannon. And we know he can turn violent over a trifle."

"He might not have considered a fully-developed, functional micro-UAV to be a trifle," Sachs replied. "I'd have to agree. As you very well know, it's the reason we're here."

"I'm not sure I care much anymore, Commander. You've been here in my office longer than I like, apparently on a fishing expedition for evidence that doesn't exist. You said once your people aren't the Mafia, but you're starting to behave as if you were. You wanted to give me food for thought? Let me turn that around. Think about this very carefully: When you learn that I am not engaged in some conspiracy with Robert Tarrant, you'll have reason to hope I don't forward a report on your actions up the line. Not to your immediate superior, but to *his* superior. When that time comes, I'd like to see you back in my office for a retraction. Not before then. Are we on the same page?"

"I'll see you in hell, Lodge."

"You may eventually have good reason to think this is hell, Sachs." Rob heard nothing more for a moment. Then: "Oh, one more thing. You knew that my wife and Tarrant's are close? Perhaps it hadn't occurred to you that Corrine Tarrant tells my wife Deirdre all of her little secrets. Or that Deirdre tells me. You might reflect that your soiled laundry will be hung out to dry in the report I may decide to write. Have a good day, Sachs, but have it somewhere else."

Rob was so filled with conflicting ideas at these revelations that he could not decipher what David Sachs muttered, and he wasn't certain Sachs had left until he heard Lodge raise his voice. "Edwina! No more calls. In fact, I'm giving you the rest of the day off as of now."

Ed's reply was too faint for Rob, who nevertheless continued to listen. He heard a drawer slam; a muffled male curse; and after perhaps a minute, Lodge again: "Just leave it, Edwina, I'll lock up the files for you."

"If you're sure," Ed called back.

"I'm sure I need a little solitude," Lodge shot back.

That was their last exchange. Rob suddenly realized that Ed Doyle would be hurrying out to her little Ford very soon, and that he might intercept her. He started to remove his headset when Lodge spoke again, in tones urgent and quick: "Mike, what did you call this, a rainy-day contact? It's raining hard. Pick up if you can."

Whoever "Mike" was, Ethan Lodge had not wanted his assistant to overhear this call to him. Rob was formulating an idea for getting outside the plant, but suddenly he felt it absolutely essential to hear what was happening in Lodge's inner office. *Priority one: Get the hell out of here*, he decided, and, *Also priority one: Don't miss this call.*

Dilemma. *No, not until I see Ed coming out of the building.* Still wearing the tiny headset, Rob secured the transciever in his jacket and groped for the bike, unwilling to turn away for fear that his own movements might somehow interfere with the reception.

As he continued, Lodge sounded resigned, gloomy: "It's now two twenty-five P.M. GenStan Security says the missing pawn has been living inside the plant all this time. Lancer was just here in my office, accusing me of helping the man hide. After talking with Security, he's figured out that I'm the reason that damn toy was destroyed."

A pause, then a resumption. "I may be watched closely after this, and I don't rule out an office phone tap. I never thought I'd ask for a takeout, but if there's any way you can reach the pawn inside the plant, you should. Don't ask me to, I don't know where he is and I wouldn't know how to do it barehanded. Jesus Christ, Mike, I'm afraid to leave my office and don't try to call me, I—"

In the silence that followed that rushing outburst, Rob saw a lithe blonde leave the building and recognized her from afar, more from that loose-limbed stride of hers than anything else. He began to pedal away, hurrying to keep Ed in view, and as he lost sight of her among the parked cars he heard a final entreaty from Mr. Refinement: "Jesus God, just leave me alone," whined Ethan Lodge.

Rob decided to do exactly that, though he had a brief impulse to rush up to Lodge's office and kick his slats out. When the wires to his transceiver unit pulled the headset awry, he stuffed the headset into his jacket and pedaled hard, aiming for the spot where he last saw Ed Doyle.

On the way, he had to swerve abruptly to avoid slamming into the open rear door of a parked camper. He caught only a few words from the occupant, but they were zingers: ". . . devious son of a dirty hoore . . ." In a rage, too. Rob was so mentally focused on his search for Ed Doyle, it was ten seconds before he realized that the camper was Fred McGrath's, and that Fred tended to lapse into South Boston argot when he was truly exercised over something.

Before he could pursue that train of thought, Rob spotted Ed as she bent at the door of her little Ford. When she looked up, Rob was leaning the bike against another car.

CHAPTER 24

ED'S HAIR NEEDED A BRUSH AND HER EYES GLISTENED AS SHE stabbed her key, squinting, at the car door. Seeing Rob, she relaxed the set of her jaw and tried the key again.

"You look a little frazzled," he said as the door opened.

"I'm absolutely furi—" she began, and then her eyes widened. "Oh Lordy, Rob, get in this car!" She dived into its hot interior, unlocking the opposite door.

He obeyed, his right hand thrust into his jacket, and told himself, *You're armed and dangerous. Make her believe it.* "I've got a gun here, Ed," he said.

"I wish I'd had one ten minutes ago," she said, with a slap-dash attempt at a smile. "Not really, but that man is a— Rob, they know you're inside! How are we going to get you out of here?"

He narrowed his eyes to maintain his ruse. "You're going to take me out in the trunk of this car, Miss Doyle."

A quizzical V appeared between her brows, then disappeared. "Yes! Why didn't I think of that?"

"Because you wouldn't help me if you didn't know I have armor-piercing rounds that will go completely through this car," he said evenly. "You're going to do it because you know I'm a man who doesn't have anything to lose."

Now she unleashed a peal of giggly laughter that took him by surprise. "No; uh-unh; wrong answer. I'm going to do it because I don't want to leave you boxed up in here like a fox in a zoo." Her eyes were bright and, he thought, perhaps a bit excited.

He could not have explained why this made him angry. "God *damn* it, Ed, I'm a dangerous escapee. It's going to be known how I got out, and you *have* to believe I'm ready to shoot you, and—and I will if I have to," he insisted, poking his finger hard into the fabric of his jacket.

She leaned sideways, placed her right forefinger on the exact tip of his nose, said, "Bullshit, my dangerous escapee." Then her left hand grasped that stiffened finger of his through the jacket. She made an exaggerated face, eyes comically wide, mouth a small O of bogus awe, only inches from his own face. "What was the old Mae West joke: ' . . . a pistol in your pocket or are you just glad to see me?' "

"Don't do this," he groaned, slumping into the seat.

"It just wouldn't work, Rob. I know, you're thinking about lie detectors, but so am I. There is no way in this world I'd believe you'd hurt me—there's a joke about that, too, but this is hardly the time," she said.

"Christ. You're one of *those*," he said. "Adrenaline addicts, risk junkies. This is bloody goddamn fun for you."

More suddenly than it began, her amusement snapped off. She was already leaning so near he could see flecks of yellow in her eyes, smell the faint flowery essence of her perfume. "Not if you're caught. But men can be awfully funny to their women without intending to be, you know." And with that, she kissed him full on the lips, her mouth meltingly warm and full of promise. Then she moved back and started the engine. "I shouldn't have done that without the air conditioner on," she murmured.

At that moment, Rob's peripheral vision identified a vehicle he know all too well as it was passing slowly behind them. He had made a complete botch of his attempt to use Ed, but he was still determined that it would never be necessary for her to admit she had sneaked him out of GenStan. "Go, go," he urged. "Back out and get behind that camper!"

She did it with only a questioning look. "I'll have to stop so you can get into the trunk before someone pulls in behind us," she reminded him as her Ford nosed near the camper.

"Don't worry, I have an idea. Let me see how long it's taking them at the gate," he replied, craning his neck for a better view. As ideas go, he reflected, it wouldn't win any prizes. But it was the only one he could think of that wouldn't put Edwina Doyle at further risk.

The gate check was taking slightly more than half a minute for each vehicle, he found, and the four guards were all concentrating on each car as it stopped. To forestall more questions from Ed, he said, "I gather my old pal Ethan is on a toot today."

"Your old pal isn't your pal, but he may be in trouble," Ed began, with grim satisfaction.

As she described what little she had gleaned from the office confrontation, Rob put in an occasional monosyllable to imply that he was listening. The line ahead dwindled to eight, then finally to five as Ed unburdened herself, leaving Rob time to consider more than one move ahead. Finally in midsentence she paused, to resume with, "Rob? You're cutting it awfully close."

"You're right," he said. "You know that little park, five or six blocks down the boulevard from here and two to the right? Hell, I don't even know its name."

"Um, I think so."

"If I make it, you might cruise by there a time or two," he said, and slid from his seat.

"But I thought," she began.

"Can't let you do it," he said, closing the door quietly. Then he strode ahead, slipped between the camper and Ed's Ford, and reached for the camper's rear door.

The thought came to him much too late: *If McGrath has locked it, I'm toast.* But the door opened, and Rob stepped up into the camper, transferring his weight slowly.

The small forward-facing window had drapes. Pulling one aside a few inches revealed the inside of the cab. The irascible McGrath was intent on the guards as he leaned from his own open window, now moving ahead a car-length, now pulling back inside with exasperated shakes of his head. He was talking to himself, but Rob could not make out the words. Obviously McGrath did not yet realize he had a passenger. This was something that needed a remedy, but its timing would be critical. Or possibly fatal.

The car ahead of McGrath had two occupants. Rob waited until their IDs had been returned, waited an endless few more seconds while McGrath started to ease the camper forward, then rapped smartly on the window a foot behind the head of Fred McGrath.

Fred jumped. The camper jumped, too, then bucked and stopped. Rob heard a bellowed, "*Jasus!*" and saw the beleaguered Bostonian's head swivel to face him. Rob tossed him a fast thumbs-up gesture, then let the drape slide back in place.

From inside the cab: pandemonium.

Rob went out the back of the camper like a ferret, latching the door again as quietly as he could, and dropped to the warm macadam before squirming forward. He knew he must avoid that drive shaft above him but the camper had far more road clearance than a standard automobile. He also knew he must be making some noise as he scuttled forward in a desperate crawl, but it was nothing compared to the litany of curses coming from that cab.

The camper engine stopped. Rob saw polished brogans under creased, dark green uniform pants shuffling around, a foot or so away to each side. He saw a pair of wingtip oxfords alight below black trousers, the camper rocking faintly, and heard McGrath's voice added to several others, all shouting at cross-purposes now.

"Just need your ID—"

"Stay in your vehicle—"

"This is the one, boys—"

"When I get my hands on the omadhaun inside here—"

And now, as McGrath made them understand he had discovered an unwanted passenger hidden in the camper, there seemed to be a primitive parade massing toward the rear of the camper, complete with shouting. Rob scrabbled hard to avoid the oil pan of an engine well-warmed from idling on a sunny day. He ducked below the steering rods, and to his astonishment the front bumper actually rose slightly. Several men were evidently standing on the rear bumper, trying to crowd into the camper box like circus clowns in reverse. The weight shift was all Rob needed to speed his exit from under the front of the camper. He was on his feet, past the gate, and sprinting almost to the boulevard intersection a handful of seconds before anyone realized his strategem. And in California traffic, even against the light, a pedestrian hurtling through a crosswalk is not fair game for motorists.

IT WAS SHEEREST COINCIDENCE THAT MIKE HAD BEEN DRIVING the vehicle with the special attaché case, within a mile of GenStan, when David Sachs had alerted his team. The Israeli agent had explained to Yonnie that a surveillance kite was not well-suited to a sprawling American city, yet the *katsa* had complained bitterly. So be it; Mike would follow orders.

Certainly there was a good case to be made for a kite circling over the GenStan plant if Tarrant was on the run, perhaps even forced into the open. The kite's remote operator must simply monitor its video and feed in occasional control inputs while driving a car. A half-mile from the GenStan gate, Mike had pulled into a loading zone long enough to deploy the little device at roughly the same moment when an astonished Rob Tarrant was discovering Lodge's duplicity.

Passing motorists did not see how cleverly the kite's wings unfolded, nor how a set of tiny glowing diodes between the wings signaled that the little drone was ready for service. One woman blinked to see a motorist hauling what appeared to be a stuffed hawk from a parked car, and blinked again when the bird was hurled into the air. Its wings did not flap, yet it climbed steadily into a spiral turn and was soon a dark wisp in the sky.

Not a live animal, but an expensive toy! Before the woman could get her window rolled down to ask where such gadgets might be purchased, the determined-looking driver had sped away.

As the synthetic predator circled higher, a courageous smaller bird gave chase, daring a grisly death—or so it assumed—to protect its nestlings. It managed to gain an ideal attack position above and behind the kite but broke off its attack after one terrifying view from above. The kite's designers had learned how to deal with this counterattack phenomenon: the kite had a second beak and a second pair of eyes, facing upward, an avian Janus discernible only from above. Even the most daring of small birds knew the folly of attacking into the face of a hawk, eagle, or whatever this softly humming beast might be.

Mike found the traffic too distracting and soon claimed a supermarket parking space down the boulevard from Gen-Stan's main gate. So long as the video showed a clear view below the kite, it was not necessary to keep the kite itself in sight as it soared to a lofty thousand feet above the plant.

The kite video was crystal-clear, though it rocked slightly in vagrant gusts; art imitating life. At the portals of major GenStan buildings, men in pairs detained workers who entered or exited. All gates were double-manned. When a tiny, fore-shortened figure discarded a bicycle in favor of a small sedan, Mike saw the event but was more interested in a worker who engaged a portal guard in arm-waving discussion. And when all four tiny figures at the main gate were joined by the driver of a camper as they swarmed like ants to the rear of the vehicle, Mike toggled the kite to swing nearer.

The sudden emergence of a single trousered figure from under the camper's front bumper caused Mike to grunt aloud. It seemed that no one at the gate noticed this sudden development for ten seconds or so, and by this time the runner was fleet enough to dodge boulevard cross-traffic almost a block away.

Mike toggled the kite controls again; fed maximum power to its ducted fan; let it nose over in a shallow dive, both to overtake the runner and to gain a much closer view of him. "Dark hair and beard," the agent muttered, as the runner turned a corner into a private parking area. "Clever bastard, or just a lucky one? Doesn't matter, I've got you now."

Tarrant had appeared from beneath that camper as if he had been hiding there. If he had somehow strapped himself below the camper's chassis, as seemed likely, he might very soon duck beneath another vehicle to wait out hot pursuit. Mike, parked near that supermarket, glanced about to take

necessary bearings, while hoping to see Tarrant himself go to
ground half a mile distant.

For Tarrant, it wouldn't be a good tactic under the best of
conditions, and with Mike watching it would almost certainly
prove fatal in short order. Seeing the fugitive move swiftly to
an alleyway and then, in a fast purposeful walk, toward the
next street, Mike urged, "Go on, find a hole. Oh shit, don't do
that," as Tarrant trotted into the next block.

From time to time, Tarrant disappeared beneath an awning
or a marquee, never for more than a few seconds. Mike kept
hoping the man would duck into a shop, but after a few
minutes the agent began to suspect that Tarrant had a distinct
goal in mind. When Tarrant turned down a street with tree-
shaded bungalows, it seemed obvious he had no intention of
hiding as a shopper among shopkeepers.

Mike set the kite for a slightly climbing spiral, pulled the car
away from its parking slot with brio, and almost collided with
a white-haired woman with a shopping cart full of groceries.

"Are you crazy?" demanded the old woman, glowering and
shaken.

"Screw you, granny," Mike said with a tight smile, tires
chirping. A quick glance at the kite's video monitor revealed
that Tarrant was still afoot, still making good time. But once
on the street, Mike made far better time. When the fugitive
reached the verdant little residential park, Mike was only three
blocks from it, but in the time it took for the driver to steer
around a double-parked delivery van, Tarrant hurried into the
shade of a mimosa thicket.

To Mike's next glance at the monitor it seemed as if the
quarry had blinked from existence, at least temporarily.

It was time to park again. " 'Softly, softly, catchee monkey,' " said Mike, fighting agitation with forced good humor.

ROB SAT, THEN LAY DOWN ON RECENTLY MOWED GRASS, HIS
heart still hammering in the way of hunted animals. Though
anxious and hyperalert, he did not feel particularly winded,
and the nearest park patrons, a young woman with a pair of

preschoolers, paid no attention to this newcomer who had flopped down in shade.

He propped himself up on his elbows and watched residential street traffic as it passed a hundred feet away. There wasn't much of it, and he swept his gaze around. A hawk ghosted high above on unmoving wings, visible for only a moment through tree branches. Rob sent a wish after it: *Wish I could soar away like that.*

Two minutes later, he scrambled to his feet and began a fast jog, angling across the grass. Ed Doyle's Ford moved slowly along the street and a quick glance told him that no other car was following. The instant she saw him, Ed pulled over, and seconds later, she was under way again as he slumped down in the front passenger seat. "Let's go to your place—or someplace," he said.

"A-*mazing*," was her reply, half laughing. "You actually got away with it."

She was wrong. That transfer into Ed's car had not gone unnoticed from above.

CHAPTER 25

ED'S ACCOUNT OF THE GENSTAN GATE FIASCO PROMPTED HER to dissolve in giggle fits more than once as she drove home. "I thought they'd get stuck in that little doorway, and they'd begun to throw the camper's bedding out onto the hood of my car, looking for you, I suppose, before one that couldn't squeeze inside started jumping up and down, pointing toward the boulevard and shouting, and I couldn't see you from my car but I had a good idea what was happening.

"And I'll never forget the look on Mr. McGrath's face," she added. "Nobody else could leave until they tossed everything back and moved the camper to one side. When I drove through, the poor man was holding a pillow under one arm and staring at some papers. You could've stuck a tennis ball in his mouth."

Rob had been only half listening but now he brightened. "Yellow papers," he guessed.

"How could you have seen that?"

"I put 'em in that pillow. I meant for him to find them, but not so soon. Now I wish I'd had the gadgets to tape everything that I heard in Lodge's office."

She gave him a sidelong glance. "You almost scare me, Rob; you weren't even there."

"In a way I was. You watched me put my flying audio bug together, Ed. It was on Ethan's window ledge, probably still is." He gnawed his lip in thought. "Listen: Could you get a record of his telephone calls very soon, without putting yourself at risk?"

"Probably; they keep tabs on everything. Why?"

"That's right, you wouldn't know—he told you to clear out," Rob mused. "But right after you left, he made a call to someone; I forget who. Hell, in all this Chinese fire drill, so much has happened I'm starting to lose some of the details. I really need to get this stuff down on a tape recorder before I forget everything. You have one at home?"

She nodded abstractedly, judging the traffic around her as they passed the expressway near Mountain View. "Well, actually, it's Jem's stuff. In his work he uses more recording gadgets than George Lucas. There's a little video camera in the closet; he lets me use it sometimes."

"It'll do. Guess I should shave off this face-fuzz before I sit down in front of a video camera. That way no one can say it wasn't me just in case I, uh, you know."

"I have a good idea, and that frightens me more than a little. Rob, listen to me: There has to be someone you can give yourself up to, someone who'll protect you."

He folded his arms and nodded toward her. "You mean someone who won't bow and scrape before a federal agent while the bastard draws a bead on me. Like who—network TV people, but with burp guns? If you know of any, Ed, trot 'em out. I got the crap scared out of me when Ethan Lodge was making that phone call, that's why I need to be able to trace it. He called for—and this I remember exactly—a 'takeout,' and he didn't mean chop suey, he meant me. Said he wasn't up to it himself. He was practically crying at the time."

For a moment she remained silent, steering carefully toward her neighborhood. "So he's scared, too, as well as angry," she murmured. "I might've guessed, the way he was acting." She fell silent again until she nosed her little Ford into its parking space. Then: "You know what he's probably most scared of? *You.*"

Rob considered this as they hurried into the duplex. "Oh, I'd like to beat the L. L. Bean goosedown stuffing out of him, but I can't get to him," he said as Ed locked the door behind them. "Besides, too many people already think I'm a nutcase."

Hands on her hips, she gave him a firm headshake. "That's not what I meant. I think he's afraid you and Mr. Wonderful might compare notes. If he wanted Sachs to have you . . . disappeared or something, why didn't he say so?"

He watched her rummage in closet shelves, ruminating on the question. As she handed him the little video camera, Rob said, "He did say so, after you'd left."

"But not to David Sachs," she said, measuring each word slowly as if Rob weren't the brightest bulb on the string. "Rob, there's someone else in Ethan Lodge's loop who doesn't answer to Sachs."

A dead silence preceded Rob's almost inaudible, "I'm an idiot, Ed. You're right, and I missed it." He began to look the camera over, shaking his head and repeating, "Stupid, stupid . . ."

"Here, let me see that," she said, and took the camera back from him. As she checked function lights and video cassette tape she murmured, "My God, if I'd gone through what you have for only the past hour I'd be in a coma. It's ready, by the way," she added more brightly, displaying the camera with a smile. "Weren't you going to shave?"

He slapped his forehead with the palm of his hand. "As soon as my brain catches up with my body," he assured her. "I'm too caught up in trying to make some sense of what was going on in that office, I guess."

Familiar with the bathroom and its contents, he was soon standing before a sink with a throwaway razor, smearing lather over his jaw, voice raised over the swirl and burble of hot water. "At least I know one thing for sure: My damn hobby is mixed up with something called an SAP. You know what that is?"

"I forget what it stands for, but I know SAPs are fast-track programs, very hush-hush," Ed replied, leaning in the doorway in an unconscious intimacy.

"Sachs admits that's why his team is here, so maybe he really wants to talk more than he wants to disappear me," Rob said.

"He said that to Lodge?"

"That's right."

"He could've been lying," she pointed out.

"True. He said he thinks Ethan and I are in cahoots, but he knows Ethan had my demo destroyed on purpose. More lies,

maybe, but I don't think so." For some moments he concentrated on shaving below his chin. Then: "Damn if I'm not half
convinced that Sachs wants me healthy. He's trying to make
everything fit, just like I am. Oh yeah—in that call he made,
Ethan used a code name for Sachs. It's 'Lancer.' "

"It would be," Ed replied, with a faint snort of derision.
"He's probably off right now, lancing some— Um, never
mind. Sorry."

"Somebody's wife," he supplied for her. "Yeah. I don't
know why that doesn't bother me more than it does, Ed. Not
anymore. Sure, it hurts, but I guess it's like a kick in the stomach; puts you down for a while, but you do get over it. Corrie
cut me loose before Sachs came on the scene, you know." He
studied his reflection; caught her glance in the mirror. "And
I've seen the guy. Look at him, and look at me," he said.

"I have," she said evenly. "I will bet a dollar that David
Sachs was beautiful in grade school, a heartthrob in high
school. He was probably pretty when he was a larva. And I'll
bet two dollars you were awkward into your teens."

"You win two bucks. I wouldn't know about him."

"Bet on it. And you know what? I prefer what I see right
now. You missed a spot under your jawline," she added.
"Here, gimme." And with that, standing almost as tall as Rob,
she took the razor. After a few careful passes at the offending
stubble she set the razor down, dampened a face towel, and
used it to wipe away a few remaining flecks of lather, holding
his chin with one hand, her face temptingly close. Very softly,
she muttered, "And stop frowning. It makes wrinkles."

"Imagine that. You don't suppose I have a few things on
my mind," he said.

"So do I. Not the same things, I guess." Now she was gravely
smiling again.

"We've got some stuff to work out," he said, and, without
any move toward an embrace, he kissed her gently. "But later;
if there is a later."

She nodded agreement and led him back to the dining room
where he was soon seated across the table from the video camera. "I hope the audio pickup is a good one," he said.

"If I don't make too much noise. It's not a directional mike."

" 'Mike'! Jesus, that's the guy's name," Rob exclaimed. "The one Ethan called after you left."

"The one Sachs may or may not know about," Ed reminded him, and glanced at the wall clock. "There's no reason why I couldn't go back to the office right now, on any of several pretexts, and check on that call. I can be back in an hour. And there's every reason why I should leave you alone so you can concentrate." Her wink was provocative.

"Pretty sure of yourself," he murmured, grinning.

"No false modesty," she agreed, retrieving her keys. At the first ring of her telephone, she pirouetted gracefully to reach for it, cutting off its summons in midwarble. "Kasabian and Doyle." Her glance quickly darted to Rob. "Where are you calling from? . . . Ah. Sure thing, I'll put him on." She held out the receiver. "It's Kenny, from some Safeway. Smart boy."

"You bet," said Rob, taking the receiver to make sure his son heard him, "but don't ever tell him I said so. We've got to keep these whippersnappers off-balance." Then, "Hi there. . . . No kidding; that's great! Did your mom drive him home? . . . I'd love to, but his phone could be tapped, so I don't—" Now the pause was longer, and his smile became broader as he listened. "Where'd you get it?" Now Rob was grinning. "No, I think it's a terrific idea. Want to give me the number?" He made a scribbling motion. Ed quickly pointed toward a Bic pen and a scratch pad lying near the phone cradle.

"Okay, go ahead. . . . By the way, where does Corrie think you are? . . . Uh-huh. . . . No, I can't pick you up and your bike is, uh, well, you know you've been hinting around for an eighteen-speed? Maybe it's time we got you one. . . . Yes, that's exactly what I mean. Sorry. Look, maybe you really should crash with Jerry after all, in case your mom should check up—and besides, I'm not comfortable with helping you tell her one thing while you do another. . . . I know you will, son. . . . Right; sure I will. 'Bye," he said, and shook his head in wonderment as he set the phone down.

Ed didn't ask, but her eyebrows did. "Gus released himself from the hospital," said Rob. "Kenny put two and two together and realized that Gus's phone probably isn't secure, so he borrowed a cell phone from one of his buddies and lent it to Gus." Another brief headshake: "Kid named Jerry Feisler. His parents, so far as I can tell, deny him nothing."

"And what's wrong with that?"

"Don't deny your kids the gift of struggle," Rob replied, wagging a finger playfully. "Gus once told me they forgot that with Corrie, and now he's sorry."

"I'll remember that, in case I ever have any kids," Ed told him. She tossed her keys and caught them. "Where were we?"

"Ah, you were denying you had any false modesty, and I was about to take violent umbrage," he said, smirking.

"Hey, I paid for the privilege, buddy."

"Sure you did."

"I most certainly did. In high school they called me 'Beanpole' and 'Stringy,' for good reason, and a few things not that friendly. The summer after I graduated, I started filling out here and there, and no one was more surprised than me. I'm glad I turned out looking like this, but it's just icing. I had to get along without it for a long time, and someday I'll have to, again."

"Go on, get out of here, Ed. I'm a sucker for icing."

"But not an utter idiot, and most men are," she replied, heading for the door.

"Most women, too," he called after her.

"Not so many, but too many for our own good," she said, waggled her fingers, and left.

SEVERAL HUNDRED FEET ABOVE ED'S NEIGHBORHOOD, THE birdlike UAV spiraled slowly downward. On one pass it had dipped almost to treetop height, close enough that Ed Doyle's rear license plate showed plainly on the video monitor. Its energy cells were now depleted to the point where it might respond to control inputs for another five minutes. In this situation, parked several blocks from the duplex, Mike was forced to choose some open area where the device could be retrieved, and during much of its descent the kite was not positioned to show the little Ford's image.

A housing development with newly-poured foundations, now devoid of workers in late afternoon, was to be the kite's landing site, and the kite made one last arc.

The Israeli agent cursed. "Oh fuck, there they go." The Ford sedan, once more in the monitor's frame, sizzled away toward the south. Well, that was no great loss, they'd be back. The location of that duplex was now a dot on a street map, and though the kite had an incendiary self-destruct timer in case of loss, it might be useful again. Yonnie, damn his eyes, would wallow in self-congratulation for insisting that it be used.

The newly-strung power line did not show on the monitor until the kite had settled within ten meters of the ground, and Mike's last-second toggling of the controls kept the little structure from the worst-case scenario, in which the UAV would have been snagged there, to hang in plain sight until the train of incendiary material set it spectacularly alight.

What happened was this: The boron-filament leading edge of one wing struck the bottom wire sharply as the kite flew beneath, causing the kite to pivot, though its inertia kept it moving forward—but now spinning like a boomerang. In Mike's car, the video image spun dizzily for a moment and then—nothing.

Mike already had the car moving, and reached the housing development in less than two minutes. But it took another frantic quarter of an hour to locate the kite, pancaked on a concrete slab, one wing pathetically snapped at an unlikely angle.

With the little UAV folded into the sedan's footwell, Mike ran a quick function assessment. The wing might be repaired in the field, but the video monitor no longer received an image. There were a hundred ways that a heavy jolt against concrete could cause that: a cracked circuit board, a broken wire, a transistor for video transmission. None of those failures was field-repairable.

"Looks like a dead bird to me," the agent sighed, then reached down quickly to disable the self-destruct timer, muttering, "Procedures; follow the fucking procedures!" It would be the end of a perfect day if that damn kite torched off inside the car simply because a harried double agent, thinking along three tracks at once, forgot to press a microswitch.

Wherever those two had gone in the little Ford, Mike could find them here later. It would take only a few minutes to get a name to match that license plate and, if the address was also a match, this whole mess was as good as laundered. It might take another day, surely no more. Okay, so Tarrant had led everyone on a nice little chase, but to judge from recent experiences he couldn't be driven out of Silicon Valley with a bullwhip. He'd probably been staying in that little house in Mountain View most nights. But *whose* house? Was it possible that this McGrath character was renting the place as an aerospace gypsy's pied-à-terre? But it couldn't have been McGrath who picked Tarrant up on the fly. Mike needed a name, and needed it *now*.

By the time Mike fought the traffic to Sunnyvale and Tarrant's old neighborhood, the California State Police had provided a name and address that had Mike laughing aloud. No wonder that knockout blonde was so attentive to Lancer; Edwina Doyle had to be sleeping with the guy they were trying to catch! And of course, Ethan Lodge would want to cut Tarrant's legs out from under him, if he knew or suspected his own assistant shared pillow talk with Tarrant! Was Lodge jealous? If he was, who could blame him?

So: Edwina Doyle's direct involvement provided at least two revelations and possibly more, and Sachs hadn't shown the faintest suspicion of any of it. Was this Doyle chick pumping Tarrant for information while she stroked his fevered brow? If so, for which flag? Maybe it didn't matter. She was just as expendable as Tarrant, and probably an easier mark.

Until now, Mike would have had reservations about a hit on a woman. Now it was different, and in this impatient mood Mike suspected that more than one woman might have to go. Edwina Doyle was up to her curvaceous butt in Rob Tarrant's activities—probably had been from the first—and there was no telling how much she had learned that would set Yonnie's teeth on edge. Under these circumstances, if Doyle were taken down with Tarrant, it would surely be endorsed from above.

The DIA cell phone's chirps interrupted this reverie. It was Sachs, with an account of the past two hours, and an excitement that was palpable. With their rental of the house behind Corrine Tarrant's, Sachs was sure they'd have their missing man very soon.

Mike made all the right responses and agreed to meet at the rental after a quick dinner—"unless you need us sooner."

"No, no," Sachs said quickly. "Good idea, I'll catch something myself and see you both later. I think this thing is finally breaking," he added, and rang off.

CHAPTER 26

AFTER DINNER, FRANK CARNES PULLED INTO THE DRIVEWAY OF
the bungalow Vallejo had rented for surveillance. He saw Vallejo's car already parked near the garage on a concrete pad,
one of those West Coast status symbols meant to accommodate—or merely to imply—a recreational vehicle. Carnes carried a trio of air mattresses to the door, though he would have
preferred to let Vallejo do her own carrying. It would be like
her to already have her luggage plopped down in the center
of whichever room she liked best. Among Marie Vallejo's principles, "First come, first served" was paramount, and Carnes
promised himself that this would be her last case with him.
There were ways, and other ways. . . .

She had locked the back door after her, of course, and he
rapped against it with his foot, begrudging the time it took her
to open the door.

She let him in with, "What took you so long, Frank?"

"Scut work," he said, shouldering his way in with his arms
full. "Try it sometime." She made no reply but relieved him
of part of his burden, including the little electric air pump,
carrying it to the bedroom of her choice.

"Pick a room. There are two more, but you might want the
living room," she called, friendly enough. And why not, when
she'd already made her choice? "I'll bring in a load, if it's such
a bother."

"No, I'd just as soon—" But she had already deposited her
small load and he heard her exit through the kitchen alcove. He
shrugged and chose the rearmost bedroom, with windows
from which he could see the rear of the Tarrant place. He
began to empty his pockets, which were full of toilet articles,
in the adjoining bathroom. Vallejo had already placed her toi-

letries with military precision in shelves behind the mirror. *Typical*, he thought, then smiled to himself. It was just as typical of him that he'd pile his stuff on any flat surface, more or less randomly.

When she returned, he was taking a leak, glad of an excuse to let her lug a load by herself. Damned women, always clamoring to prove they could do men's work, while expecting courtesies due a protected group. He heard her go out again. She was bringing everything in, then. That was something he didn't want.

He washed up, ran wet fingers through his hair, and emerged in the hallway as she was arranging their folding chairs around the card table she'd just set up. At dusk, and echoing with vacancy, the place was gloomy until she plugged in one of those little high-intensity lamps and set it on the card table.

"David's bringing the coffeemaker," she said brightly. "Said he would, anyway."

"About midnight, I expect, after he's paid his disrespects next door," Carnes grumbled.

She studied him for a moment. "You're getting tired of fieldwork, I take it," she said at last.

"When it goes balls-up and stays there, yes."

"Is that why you've been out of range so much? Hard to reach, at any rate."

"Maybe." He didn't like justifying himself to Vallejo, and didn't like where this could lead. A bit defensively, he added, "I've been available when I was needed."

She didn't reply until he glanced directly at her. "Mind telling me what you were doing the rest of the time?"

"Yeah, I think I do, Vallejo. Inasmuch as I'm senior to you, why should I? Take it up with Sachs." He slumped into one of the folding chairs across from her, deliberately untidy and, by extension, unmilitary, a reminder that she was not above him in the chain of command.

She did not miss it. "Just curious, Frank." She plopped her big shoulder bag on a corner of the table and rummaged for a cigarette pack and lighter. Exhaling a fumarole of smoke, she said, "You must've heard how Tarrant exfiltrated the plant, I suppose."

"You're kidding." He didn't like the way she was watching him as he continued. "Last I heard, their nine-to-fivers were doing a room to room search. I figured they'd nail him and then this rental business would turn out to be an exercise in futility."

She took another drag. "Is that what you figured? Why doesn't that convince me, Frank? Why am I starting to think you're playing games with the rest of us?"

"And I think you must be smoking something stronger than tobacco. What the hell are you getting at, Vallejo?" He had heard her play at cat-and-mouse interrogation before, and it was only too obvious that she already had answers, or thought she did, before she asked the questions. But this time, he decided, she was on what shysters called a fishing expedition. "Say what you mean."

"Well, for example, you've had all kinds of chances to confer with that Ivy Leaguer, Ethan Lodge, all by yourself. You're pretty cute with electronics and such, too. You wouldn't just happen to have a second cell phone, would you?" Her smile was teasing, which made it all the more infuriating.

"I don't even have one in decent working order," he snarled, "as Sachs knows full well. And I've about had it with you and your fantasies. What the fuck would I be cooking up with Lodge, and, more to the point, why would I?"

"My question exactly. But I suspect it has to do with what I found in your car. Maybe you'd like to explain that to David."

He met her stare with mounting anger. "This is your scenario. Maybe you'd etter just tell me."

"I popped your trunk latch, too. Now can you guess what I found?" Her voice dripped with poisoned honey as she placed her cigarettes back in her bag.

He burst out with, "I don't give a good shit what—"

"Don't do it!" Her shout cut him off. And the next sound was a muffled cough from inside her shoulder bag, the leather expanding like a bladder for an instant, and Carnes was slammed back hard enough to tumble him from the chair.

The tremendous shock of a medium-caliber slug into the breast of Frank Carnes was so sudden, it short-circuited what might have been pain. Thrown onto his side, he rolled onto his back to find her standing, her eyes wide, holding the suppressor-equipped automatic pistol on him with both hands.

He wanted to ask her not to fire again, but: "Don't make me, Frank," she cried, as his mouth worked silently, the pain beginning to build until it replaced the shock and, as he relaxed, he voided his bowel. His eyes flickered but remained open. She did not fire a second time.

For perhaps five seconds Marie Vallejo held her frozen stance with growing tremors before she hurried to kneel at his side, feeling the artery at his throat, shaking her head in dismay. Then she flipped the front of his jacket open and verified that he'd been carrying his own Beretta on his belt, starting to sob as she stood erect. "Why, goddamn it, why? Oh, Frank, I'm sorry," she crooned, crying aloud now.

Moments later, Vallejo found her cell phone and got David Sachs on the line. She had never watched a man die at her hand before and found herself, unaccountably, hiccuping as she spoke. "David, lis—listen to me. Carnes has be—been playing false—flag games. . . . I don't know! Just listen—he's dead. Started to draw on me . . . Yes, hic-cups, damnit. David, I had to, it was self—defense— Oh God. . . . no choice."

She listened for a long moment, forcing herself to draw long inhalations, experiencing the abyss between imagining a crucial event and actually going through that event. Then: "No pulse—for one thing. Look, it was him or me. . . . So I'm pretty shaky and I'm not hand-handling this very well. Never had a briefing on some—thing like this."

She listened, snuffling, silently cursing those hiccups, then responded. "Of course not, we're alone here. There's not much blood. Should I call in civilians?"

Another pause. Then, "Why aren't you on the way? If you ever—heard a Mayday, you're hearing one now. . . . No, I'm all right. . . . I thought he might, and he never got it out of the holster. . . . I'll be waiting. With proof," she added, then terminated the call.

After drying her eyes she detached a shower curtain and brought it back, rolling the body of Frank Carnes partially over, then back, tucking the plastic around him. In life the man had weighed perhaps two hundred pounds, but in his present state he seemed to bulk half a ton. She tried to avoid looking directly into those open eyes although, by now, his expression was that of mild surprise.

One lucky break: The slug hadn't gone through. If Sachs intended to keep this entirely an agency matter as he had implied, it would be essential to keep from contaminating the scene with any evidence of violence. Sachs would keep the evidence that really counted: That second cell phone she had taken from the car, holding it by its stubby antenna to minimize her prints.

SACHS ARRIVED WITH A TRENDY LITTLE OLYMPUS DIGITAL CAMera slung over one shoulder. He found the side door unlocked. Vallejo was sitting in the same folding chair, virtually in a fugue state in a roomful of her cigarette smoke, four butts mashed out before her on the surface of the card table. Time was, when he would have held her close, but "time was" is rarely "time is." "You all right?" He asked a second time before she nodded assent. "Not going comatose on me," he said, stepping nearer. This time her headshake was immediate.

"Have to do this, Marie. Jesus Christ," he went on, repelled at the sight of the lifeless colleague he had so recently supervised, shared lewd jokes with, considered above suspicion. He hurried over to the body to check for vital signs, sighed when he failed to find them, then prepared the camera's flash attachment, closing every door into the rest of the house and pulling down shades. Hell of a note, he muttered to Vallejo, if someone called the local law over camera flashes in a vacant house. He took several photographs, one of them from over the shoulder of the listless Marie Vallejo. After each photograph he studied the result on the Olympus's tiny integrated monitor to make certain the camera now stored a digital image suitable for forensic analysis.

Next, he carefully studied the site of the entry wound but did not find any sign of singes or powder residue. "You must've fired from clear across the table," he said.

He got an abstracted nod from Vallejo. "From inside my big bag. No time," she said in a monotone.

He grunted to himself as he searched fruitlessly for exit-wound bloodstains; made a face at the odor that was strongest near the body. "You did something right, Marie. Even crap stains on the floor could have people wondering," he said at last. Then he stood erect, set Carnes's fallen chair on its feet, and lowered himself into it as if expecting it to be hot. "Moment of truth now: What made you so sure Frank was doubling on us?"

"I wasn't certain even after I found this," she said, and pushed the cell phone toward him with the nail of one finger. "The look on his face when I showed it to him—that's when I was sure. I don't know if it'll have a couple of my prints but it's bound to have his, too. I was taking stuff from his car trunk and it fell down from the liner. Not one of ours." She remained silent for only a moment, then turned a tortured look on Sachs. "If you'd seen the way he looked at me . . . He wanted to put me down, David."

His reply was deceptively soft: "So you fucking shot him dead. Jesus H. effing Christ, Marie."

"Not like that at all," she gulped. "I can prove that, too."

Sachs spread his hands out and looked at her expectantly.

"I taped it all," she explained. "I can't recall everything we said, but I started recording when he came out of the head." Now she pulled her little audio recorder from her bag; set it on the table near blackened parallel stripes, char marks of several cigarettes. "I'm sure he didn't know I was taping. I know, I know: Should have waited for you."

Sachs listened to the taped exchange, beginning with, "David's bringing the coffeemaker," and flinched at the muffled explosion. He sat looking around him as he heard Vallejo speak to the man she had just shot, then sobbing, hiccuping as she reached Sachs on her own cell phone. Finally he shut off the machine and said, "So he went for his sidearm first?"

She nodded, biting her lower lip. "He wasn't well-positioned for it, though. I believe he just blew his stack. And I was putting my cigs away, I— It as just luck; I ruined a perfectly good bag; and why am I worrying about that at a time like this?" She looked down at the shrouded body, fighting tears again, shaking her head. "Oh, Frank, Frank . . ."

"All right," Sachs said crisply. "We keep this internal." He took his own cell phone and a palmtop organizer from inside his jacket and began pressing keys.

In a voice that lacked self-assurance, Vallejo asked, "Should I have called Alameda?"

"Pull yourself together, Marie, Alameda NAS was sold off to the feather merchants. It's an industrial site now; electric-car manufacturing, movie soundstages, everything but military." Then, to further separate himself from personal regret over the loss of a man he had trusted: "Unless you intend to film a reenactment," he added wryly.

"Don't, David, please. Next you'll have me signing a register." She brightened a bit with, "How about Detachment Concord, then? That's Bay Area."

"Yeah, but it's ordnance. We need a MedEvac unit we can meet at the nearest secure heliport, so I'm calling NAS Lemoore." Meanwhile he was pressing keys on the phone as he spoke. "Lemoore's got Search-and-Rescue helos, and they can get him from here into their cooler without civilian media attention. We've got to think about the debriefings, board of inquiry, all that shit. Not to mention whatever Carnes was trying to do."

"It's your call," she shrugged, and fell silent as Sachs began to identify himself, coolly, professionally. Before he had finished, her confidence in his quick mind was largely renewed. The transfer of Frank Carnes's body would be made to a helipad inside the GenStan perimeter which was only twenty minutes away by car, and GenStan Security had ample reason to give Sachs anything he asked for without questions. With any luck, no civilian would realize they were moving a corpse into that helicopter.

Though Vallejo tried to help carry the body outside in darkness to the trunk of Sachs's car, it proved simpler for Sachs to make the transfer using a fireman's carry. "Lemoore is just south of Fresno, so they should be on the GenStan pad in . . . call it forty-five minutes. I should be back by twenty-three hundred hours."

"You don't need me along?"

"I need you right here. We still have a man running around loose who's been doing it under our noses, Marie. Maybe with Frank's help. Shit. This is turning into a basketful of cobras and no flute." He toyed with his car keys, making judgments. Finally: "The question is, are you up to tending the surveillance here? Nothing prejudicial if you're not," he amended quickly.

But she knew that was a lie. "I'll be okay," she promised.

Then he did give her the comradely hug she needed. "Just try not to shoot anybody else tonight, okay?"

She told him what to do with his suggestion and watched him back out without headlights, before she returned to the empty house.

CHAPTER 27

THE VOICE WAS CARAMEL-MELLOW WITH CAREFUL ENUNCIA-
tion, the kind that Gus loved to berate on his TV set. "Mr.
Theodore Kallas?"

"Yeah."

"Also known as Mr. Gus Kallas?"

"Who is this?"

"*The* Gus Kallas, star of stage, screen, and shooting galler-
ies?"

No more Mr. Nice Guy. "Who the fuck is this?" Gus bellowed.

"This," said the voice, with extreme unction, "is your
conscience speaking."

The ensuing few seconds were filled with a silence as deep
as parental regret. Then, in utter calm, the old boy said, "Ro-
bo, one of these days I *am* gonna kick your ass." But now he
was chuckling too. "Had me going there for a second."

"A second? I could've sold you a load of aluminum siding
before you caught on," Rob gibed, dropping the pose.
"Though who else could it be, calling you on some kid's cell
phone you haven't had two hours? I think some of your brains
must've leaked out of the hole they put in you." Rob had not
doubted for an instant that a call full of gentle concern was
the last thing Gus would have wanted.

"Nah, the one on my head was just a graze."

"Not that one; the one in your rump. Where your brains
are," Rob persisted.

"Who taught you about bedside manner—Dracula? Well,
I'm glad you called, anyhow. That kid of yours is off somewhere doing I-dunno-what, and I need somebody to help
spraypaint a fuselage."

"I only wish I could," Rob said. "In case you've been out of the solar system, I'm still the guy people were aiming for when you got in the way. They're still looking, but that little audio bug . . . ? It worked like a champ. Now I'm thinking about coming in from the cold. Gus, from what I've managed to overhear, this is all about military uses of my goddamn mantis designs! You'd think they might've just asked me," he said.

Gus vented a long, reflective "Mmmm," then: "Makes sense, Ro-bo, I mean, it's already a spymike. . . . Whoa, and I helped. Does this mean they'll be after me for real?"

"Why? It's my little bird, they don't know you had anything to do with it. Hey, take down this number, but keep it to yourself; don't leave it around for some asshole to find. It's where I am, from time to time, and you and Kenny should keep this to yourselves." Rob recited the number twice. Then he added, "In fact, might be a good idea not to call unless it's important."

"Gotcha. But what's this about coming in? You mean like giving yourself up, I take it." His tone was rich with uncertainty about the wisdom of that idea.

"Yes, but I think I should be able to do it without putting my neck in a noose."

"Wanna tell me how?"

"I'd be happy to, if I knew. I'll figure it out," Rob promised.

"I hope you've figured out once and for all that government is as likely as anybody to dump on you: Promise one thing and deliver another. They promised me Social Security, but they delivered a matched set of lead spitwads."

"It may have been them, Gus. But somehow, a .22 pistol doesn't seem like Uncle Whiskers's style." Rob recalled Ed Doyle's canny observation, but did not elaborate beyond, "I've been thinking maybe there's somebody else involved besides the feds."

"You mean like Jack Ruby, some weirdo who thinks he's doing the country a favor by offing a citizen or two?"

"Maybe. For all I know, Ethan Lodge may have put out a contract on me but—I just don't know: Another branch of government?"

"How 'bout another government entirely? If there's a military use, why not the Chinese, or Iraq?"

Rob's thinking had been focused so tightly that this broadening of the field of suspects was like strolling from a thicket into a broad plain. "I suppose, if they found out about it. So much for military secrecy, huh?" After a moment he went on: "Gus, are you sure you were physically ready to leave the hospital? It's not as if you have anyone there to help if you have a relapse, start leaking your hydraulic fluid . . . hell, I don't know, whatever."

"Now you're second-guessing me like Corrie. Don't," the old fellow growled. "I'm okay. When I'm not, I'll get help."

"How's she taking all this?"

"Like it's a humongous plot by everybody to intrude on her valuable time. In short, business as usual. Much as I love my kid, I wonder why you give a shit, Rob."

"I worry about her, that's all."

"So does she. In case I didn't mention it, she dropped me off here but she didn't stay. Why not? Big star on her social calendar? I didn't need her to, but it'd be nice if she asked me, like Kenny does. You know what I mean."

Rob let his sigh carry. " 'Fraid I do, Gus."

Grudgingly: "Oh yeah, and she's concerned about Kenny, when she thinks about it—ah, shit—and to be fair, about me when I call and ask for something like a ride home. I could let all this drive me nuts, trying to keep my loyalties straight, but it's really pretty simple: If everbody knew what you're doing, would you embarrass yourself? If I didn't teach her that, I deserve what I get. But I don't think you do."

"I don't need an apology," Rob said gently.

"Well, it's as close to one as anybody oughta expect from me," said Gus.

Rob glanced up as headlight beams swung across the parking area outside. Attuned to machinery by long habit, Rob thought he recognized the rasp of Ed's little four-banger. "I've got to go. But mark my words, they broke the mold before they made you, Gus."

"Uh-huh. I got it, and up yours very much," Gus replied.

Rob was still grinning in the afterglow of his call when Ed Doyle unlocked her front door. She tossed him a responding smile as she relocked the door.

He spread his hands. "Well?"

"Wasted effort," she said, shrugging. "No record of any calls by Lodge after I left." Seeing his frown, she underlined her report with, "None at all. I wonder . . ." Her expression shifted abruptly.

He was shaking his head now. "Me, too. Is it possible that Ethan would pretend he was phoning, for— Nah, no way, he couldn't have known I was listening. But who else might have been?"

"I have no idea. But I do have a perfectly obvious answer," she said, leaning one cheek of her backside on the table where he sat. She swung a long leg and winked. "Give you ten seconds to figure it out."

After five, Rob said, "He was taping himself, for some reason."

Headshake. "Uh-unh. He was using a cell phone."

"Hell! Of course," Rob exclaimed. "Why didn't I . . ."

"Because you don't have a cell phone," Ed said, tapping a forefinger on his nose.

"Neither do you."

"True," she said, getting up, smoothing her skirt, "but I'm reasonably bright. Ah-ah, no fanny flips," she laughed, avoiding his backhanded swat. "Tell you what: I'll make it up to you with pie à la mode, if Jem left any."

As she prowled the refrigerator shelves, Rob said, "I thought he was diabetic."

"Type One. Doesn't mean he can't have a little of stuff he especially likes, but he has to adjust his medication. He's pretty good about it. I have to nag him now and then. Ah, we're in luck," she added, showing him part of a cherry pie. "Want melted cheddar on it and peach yogurt ice?"

"God, you'll spoil me," he said fervently.

"Maybe I will," she said. It had the sound of a promise.

He felt a familiar tumescence but did not move from his chair. Somehow this did not seem the moment to put a move on a woman who had become a sort of comrade-in-arms. *Even when she hints that it might be welcome. Besides, I'm enjoying her too much this way at the moment,* he told himself. *And I don't know how Jem Kasabian would react. A lot of stuff about all this that I haven't scoped out.* "Ed? About your roomie: Mind if I ask about your setup here?"

She was cutting a slice of cheddar at the time but turned to him with Victorian hauteur; struck a pose. "The nerve of this man. The gall. The, uh, whatzit—*cupidity*."

"The envy," he supplied. "Does Jem mind that we're getting along pretty well?"

She slipped the slice of pie into the microwave oven, magicked its controls expertly. "If he thought there was anything remotely false about you, he would. And you wouldn't have to ask, either, and I trust his instincts about people. I've known the guy since high school. He's always been—like he is, and up front with it. It certainly cost him some friends, of course. But our school annual and the proms would've been total flops without him, and it was Jem who got people to start calling me Ed instead of things like 'Stringbean,' which I mentioned, and worse."

"What could be worse to a teenaged girl?"

"Try 'Anorexia.' "

"Ouch."

"Try 'Bulemia,' " she expanded.

"Jeez, I'd have opened a can of whup-ass for that," said Rob.

"Jem did, too. Even though he was more likely to take the whipping himself. You backed your friends if they were blameless, and if they backed you, they *were* friends." The oven pinged. She took the hot saucer out with an insulated mitten and carved a big crescent of yogurt ice from its container with a spoon. "It worked then; it works now."

She slid the confection across to Rob, leaning on the table as she did. "And in case you want to know what you almost certainly do want to know without actually asking: Yes. We tried, once, a couple of years back when I was bawling over a software genius who dumped me for a job in Jakarta. It was my idea. He gave it his best shot, but we ended up laughing and cussing and then we went out for fudge sundaes which should've killed him. The way Jem put it, he couldn't make himself want to enough. Do me, I mean."

Her face was inches from Rob's. "Now, three people know that; Jem and I, and you. In a peculiar way, it underlines how true a pal he is."

Rob nodded as if his understanding was complete. "Ed, I'm not good at putting things just right, but—I don't want to be *that* good a pal to you."

"Ditto," she said, and went back to assemble her own pie à la mode. "I expect him back anytime now. And I half expected Kenny to drop in. I think I still do." Her sidelong glance said, *Otherwise I might be acting with less decorum.*

"He's sleeping over with a buddy. By the way, I called Gus while you were gone."

"Poor old fellow," Ed said. "This family crisis must be pulling him every which way. Is he mending?"

"Says he is. He also wondered whether it was a Chinese or Iraqi bullet he took for me. I suspect the list could be a hell of a lot longer than that, but I wasn't about to say that to Gus."

"From what you say, he must be a hoot. I'd like to meet him," she added, a bit hesitant.

"You wanta look out for those old guys; Gus is a widower," Rob cracked.

"You're kidding," she replied, uncertain.

"Yeah, I am. Even if I wasn't, he's a guy I want you to meet."

"One more item on our growing list of unfinished business," she smiled, seating herself with her own sliver of cherry pie. "Speaking of which: Where did you plan on sleeping tonight?"

"Oh—I thought I'd see if McGrath has room in the camper," Rob said, deadpan, and didn't laugh until she did.

"You deliberately waited till I had a mouthful of pie," she accused, wiping her lips. "I'll get you for that." She took another bite.

"It's a deal. Am I going to sleep on your living-room couch?"

"Possibly, if it seems like Jem's going to be a grump about it. Or if you're chicken," she replied with a challenging glance. "Mm-mm. Delicious."

"The pie, or the sexual tension?"

"Yes, and yes. Well," she said, looking up as footsteps scuffed on the porch.

Jem Kasabian let himself in, took in the scene at the table. He grinned when Ed said, "You caught us."

"Yeah? And not even touching. I've been expecting this, but I must say you're both too easily pleased," said Jem.

"I was speaking of your cherry pie," she rejoined, "but a lot has happened today and Rob does need a place to sleep."

Jem looked at the ceiling as though addressing some invisible auditor as he strolled past them toward his room. "Almost anything I say will be dancing into a minefield," he observed, but couldn't resist adding to Rob, "And thanks, but I'm getting a headache."

"Besides which, I saw him first," said Ed, her chin held up in bogus pugnacity.

Rob shook his head and chuckled, aware that he was blushing. "Do you two make up this stuff as you go along, or steal it from a bad porn flick?"

Jem paused at his bedroom door, enjoying the moment. "I always say there are three things that betray a lack of imagination: hospital white, vodka on the rocks, and pornography." Now he waggled his brows. "And I am a man of considerable imagination. I'll probably let it entertain me for the next hour or so. Toodle-oo," he finished, smiling, and slipped into his room.

Sharing a grin with the woman across from him, Rob used his fork to corral a final bite of pie, then realized that his system was in no mood for further detours. He could not have swallowed that bite for any inducement, but if he arose suddenly at this moment his erection might topple the table.

Ed sighed with satisfaction; put down her fork, then took their unfinished portions to the sink. "I think," she said in a near whisper, "we can consider that as Jem's benediction."

Rob stood up, hands strategically placed. "Now there's a

metaphor to unsettle a guy, under the circumstances," he said.

Her laugh was nearly soundless as she put a hand out to be taken. "Whoops. Well, if it had been a bullfight, you'd have won both ears and the tail."

He took her hand as they moved down the hall to her room. "I don't care about the ears," he said.

"Why, *Mis*ter *Tar*rant," she murmured, batting her eyes outrageously, leading him into her room. "If you're going to talk like that, you just come right in here with me."

But when they stood with both hands entwined, both fell silent, solemn, sharing an unspoken commitment too profound to require words. For a time they sat on her bed, side by side, with faint smiles that said, *I like that*, or *Do you like this?*

And neither of them could have said how or when their clothes happened to migrate, and they did not need, after all, to engage in further banter, nor to count climaxes.

CHAPTER 28

IT HAD TAKEN LONGER THAN DAVID EXPECTED TO GET FRANK Carnes's body secured in that MedEvac helicopter with Navy regulars who weren't too charmed over the idea. While driving back, David spent some of his time reflecting on periods during the past days when Carnes had had opportunities to fulfill an agenda of his own. That car bomb, for example: it made a lot of sense for a man whose free time was limited and who was determined to see Tarrant on a slab—or several slabs.

In such times as this, David's essentially cold-blooded nature became one of his virtues. He could partition off his anger at the defection of a trusted subordinate, the better to deduce overt action by his opponents. He could even smile over the plight of Tarrant, thinking how this desperate, fugitive engineer they sought must be dealing with some of the same questions.

Almost everything Tarrant had done could be forgiven, assuming that Carnes and not Tarrant had rigged those explosives. On the other hand, an increasingly rash Tarrant might well be packing an arsenal by now, and equipped with the audacity to use it. Had Tarrant shot his own father-in-law by mistake? Or perhaps he'd done it deliberately; something to do with his wife's estrangement. That was an unexplored idea, and one that David would pursue very carefully with Corrine later that night.

With every passing hour it was becoming more important to face Robert Tarrant calmly. Barring a rational face-to-face with Tarrant, many of those questions might never be resolved.

En route back to Marie Vallejo, David called her twice and Corrine Tarrant once from his car, making the last call only minutes before he arrived. In Vallejo's present state of mind, it could be worth his life to startle her, as Carnes had found out too late. If Vallejo failed to settle down during the next twenty-four hours he definitely would have her replaced as a priority matter.

As it was, David would have to do some nifty footwork to avoid, at the least, ugly notations in his own personnel file. A mission commander who failed to spot defectors in his team— had not, in fact, even suspected one—would not command many more missions.

He shelved these worries as he doused his headlights and, a moment later, pulled into the driveway of the rental. Vallejo let him into the darkened house, and he could tell she'd been crying again. He patted her shoulder and asked, "Pick up anything new from the sensors?"

"Not since you called the first time. Could've been some damn dog running loose," she said.

"More likely the Tarrant boy; the timing would've been right. I spoke with his mother around dark and he'd already left to sleep over with some other kid." He paused. "On the other hand, we don't know who else Carnes might've been working with."

"My thoughts exactly, David. What Frank knew, someone else probably knows. If we had any spare motion sensors I'd be using them around this rental."

"I pity anyone who approaches you without warning," said David, with a lightness he didn't really feel. "So I'll call again before I drive back from the Tarrant place."

"Oh God. I don't even want to hear what reason you'd give me for going over there again. But knowing you, it would be more appropriate if you just vaulted the fence."

"And have Corrine Tarrant wonder how come I'm walking, and where I must've walked from? I don't think so. And it's just a few wrap-up questions," he said, pulling her near enough to nuzzle her cheek, a dirt-cheap reminder of intimacies past.

She thrust him away. "Don't. Go on, hump your groupie," she spat. "But don't forget to call on your way back."

"Phones work both ways, and I'm as near as this," he said, patting the cell phone in his pocket. With that, he left her and drove into the street before turning on his lights for the short drive. The likelihood of Tarrant or some unknown perp casing the neighborhood seemed very low to David, but it was reason enough to keep Vallejo in place. Meanwhile, David could tie up some loose ends by—he smiled to himself at his own phrase—pumping Corrine. Frank Carnes had been right: It *was* nice work if you could get it. . . .

He called Corrine from the car, saying he was moments away and needed to clear up a few points with her, and with the boy. He smiled again when she reminded him that Kenny was away. "As if I thought you'd forgotten," she added. "We'll be alone."

"Hold that thought," he purred, and pulled over to the curb near the Tarrant driveway. He smirked, recalling the riddle:

What is a cinch: a strap that passes under a horse's belly?
   No. When you park next to a drugstore, and your date asks you why, and you tell her you're going in for condoms, if she's still there when you return, *that's* a cinch.

The front door opened as he crossed the darkened porch and David, suddenly alert, stepped to one side. Corrine Tarrant took a step outside, no longer in complete blackness. "Because of neighbors, David. Did you think I'd bite?"

"One can hope," he said, and let her draw him inside.

This time, and probably conscious of the role, she was the stereotype of the hot suburban bitch of legend, all over him, one knee thrust gently against his groin. He played the part expected of him, hoping she wasn't smearing lipstick on his collar, but what the hell, that's what the extra shirt was doing in the trunk of his car.

Presently, after a perfunctory grope under her skirt, he said something cute about the charm of native welcomes, and she murmured something about Tondelayo, and he chuckled as if he got it. "You know, I really could use a cup of something about now."

"Martini, scotch, whatever you like," she said.

"Not on duty," he said, and asked for tea, following her to the kitchen.

As she was heating cups with tea bags in the microwave, already somewhat disheveled in the oven's faint light, she said, "I wasn't sure I'd see you again, Mr. Bond."

Oh fuck, another one of those, he thought. "Her Majesty's Service comes first," he said, with what he hoped was a faint Scots burr.

"But you found time to service me? Charmed," she said, and actually curtsied.

When she served the tea, he said, "There really is something that's been puzzling me. About Mr. Kallas."

"Daddy? He made me drive him home today; said if I didn't he'd call a taxi."

"Not very wise of him, Corrine."

"*You* try and stop him. Bring a bunch of Marines," she said with feeling.

"Wouldn't surprise me if he'd had Robert pick him up," said David. "That is, if they're still friends."

"Nothing surprises me about Daddy and Rob."

"Meaning . . . ?"

"Just the way they get along."

He saw her shrug in silhouette.

"As in, hot and cold, off and on, that kind of thing?"

"Not off and on. On and on," she replied. "Jesus, they wear each other's clothes, swap sexist jokes—I know Daddy offered to let Rob stay with him after we, um, agreed to disagree."

"Why didn't he?"

With some heat: "I wouldn't hear of it. Drive a wedge between me and my own father? I beg your pardon," she said in dismissal of the notion.

"So they remained close? No coolness developing between them, I mean."

"Kenny would've noticed, and I'd have heard." She paused. "Why do you ask?"

His turn to shrug. "Just curious. Wondering if they're getting together somehow right under our noses. If they are, it might work to everyone's advantage. Your father would be smart to . . . let's call it, broker a meeting. Some public place, if it would help. I'd be willing to give him guarantees, even let the old fella pat me down. He could help Robert avoid a great deal of trouble, you know. He may be in real danger, but not from me."

"I'll pass it on," she said. "Daddy might even do it." Begrudging the idea: "Sometimes my father seems more like Rob's father. You wouldn't catch a woman acting like that."

Privately, David thought she might be wrong. But that wasn't what she wanted to hear, so he said something women generally do want to hear: "I'll never understand women."

She chortled deep in her throat. "So long as you understand what I need before you leave forever."

"I'm getting a faint glimmer," he said, rising, taking her hand. The tea had been only a credible delay while he pursued the idea of hostility between Tarrant and the old man. Now his goal was the living-room couch.

But Corrine was more inventive than that, and the old-fashioned living-room window was fully open. She perched her rump on the sill, legs apart, and pulled him to her.

For David it was not a coupling to remember but he was a reliable performer. Trousers at his ankles, her little bleats of pleasure urgent on the night breezes, he proved to himself once again that he was a man to be desired and envied.

His leave-taking might have seemed ludicrous to anyone watching after Corrine misunderstood his intentions when he stooped to retrieve his pants. They spoke their good-byes awkwardly. David promised that he would never forget, though he suspected that her tears had been squeezed from some internal script borrowed from films. His cruelties were rarely deliberate, more like the willfulness of a thoughtless, pretty child, and he swore that they would meet again someday.

"You have my cell-phone number," he told her from the doorway. "Tell your father what I said. If he really wants to help Tarrant, I can be reached." And with that, he walked quickly out to his sedan.

Had David stopped on the walk to make his call to Vallejo,

he would have given the watcher enough time for an easy head shot. Instead, he continued another thirty yards to the car. He swung into the car and because he was perspiring from recent exertion, rolled down both front windows and set the small glass wind-wing nearest him. He reached Marie Vallejo on the second ring and announced his departure, which took all of ten seconds. After twelve seconds he was pulling away from the curb, and one second later an explosive *cr-aack* kicked the wind-wing fully open.

David's first, instantaneous fear was that Corrine Tarrant had fired at him but, by the time he had swung back to the curb and opened the driver's door, he knew better. The car's interior light revealed a narrow silvery streak of lead proceeding from the point where a slug had struck the wind-wing a glancing blow from inside the car, breaking but not puncturing the glass, then continuing God-knew-where.

If David tended to focus too tightly on a favorite theory, he could think very quickly under pressure. In seconds he had concluded that the width and modest impact of the slug implied .22 caliber, possibly a .25, and not from a high-velocity weapon. He also realized that he would have heard the report from a deer rifle. He reasoned that someone had fired from a long-barreled pistol with a silencer. The slug had passed through the open window on the passenger side before the car had moved to a position where Corrine could have fired that round.

Was it remotely possible that Vallejo . . . ? No, and for the same reason; the narrow aperture between trees and structures from house to house would not have permitted that shot. The Tarrant garage was a more likely source.

As he was thinking these things, David was calling Vallejo again, rolling out of the car, letting its door shut gently, drawing his 9-millimeter sidearm. Light from a distant streetlight would have revealed anyone running from the Tarrant place toward him or the street. And no matter which way the shooter ran, their sensors would tell Vallejo— "It's me. What do the sensors say? My car just took a small caliber hit meant for me," he said without preamble.

"After your first call?"

"Yes! If he's on the run, you should get a reading"—he paused, seeing a light go on in the house they had rented—"after you turn the damn light off, that is." But if he'd had the faintest remaining notion that the shot *had* come from Vallejo, it died with the fact that she was still inside a rental with clerestory windows.

"Sorry. Nothing moving. The only recent sensor activity was in front of the Tarrant house, which I gather was you leaving. Nothing else."

"Then he's staying put, and we can find him," David said between his teeth.

"I'm calling for backup," Vallejo said suddenly.

"No! I'm thinking it's Tarrant himself, and he knows this turf well enough to melt away before backup arrives. Get the night scanner."

"You just don't want civilians mucking around in this, isn't that right?" she said.

His silent reply was, *Damn straight,* but he said, "Wait," and took a few seconds to work out a new ploy. "Look, Tarrant probably thinks he has good reason to squeeze off on me."

"Probably several," she replied.

"Shut up and listen. I want you to take your scope to the back fence as a stakeout. Don't shoot unless you have to, and if you do, shoot for the legs."

"What are you going to do, David?"

"This may be our last best chance. He's in cover somewhere around here with a small-caliber weapon, and I'm going to try and talk with him while he feels secure. Secure enough to take a potshot at me, anyhow."

"And you're in the open? Are you insane?"

"I'm going through the house. If he can't get a clear view of me, he may be willing to talk. If he responds, you'll hear us. You're my sleeve ace, Marie. If I convince him you could've nailed him and didn't—enough. Just try and follow orders, Vallejo." And with that, he pocketed his cell phone.

He ran to the Tarrant house and knocked a quick tattoo. Corrine opened the door enough to ask, "David?"

He pushed in quickly, brushing past her in the darkness, his way dimly lit by the TV she had turned on. "I think your ex may be around the house somewhere," he said in passing. "Garage, maybe. Where's the remote opener?"

"We don't have one," she said, as though admitting a misdemeanor.

"Doesn't it have a side door?"

"Yes. I never lock it."

"Turn off the TV and lie down on the floor."

"You won't shoot him," she said in a small voice.

"I hope it won't come to that," he said, now in the kitchen, seeing the open back door and the screen door in outline. He lay prone, shoving the screen door open slightly. Far off, he heard the faint *skrinnnch* of another screen door; almost certainly, Vallejo easing outside, fifty yards away.

In a seldom-visited corner of his mind, David's imagination quavered warnings. It wasn't likely, but it was just possible that Tarrant had some kind of weapon with a night sight. That would make David's position, once he began to speak, terribly vulnerable. One error in his judgment, or one excellent guess by Tarrant, and Lieutenant Commander David Sachs might take a small slug through the forehead. He was not the sort of man who relished such action, and cursed his situation as he recalled an old line about ignorant armies clashing by night.

Yet David had honestly taken the vows of his profession— bought the package, as he put it. This was one of those pucker-factor moments that challenged his manhood more than any number of beddable women. *Forget you're scared of that little piece of lead*, he told himself as his imagination began to push from its shadowy corner. *Remember the job at hand.*

"Tarrant?" His voice lacked conviction and volume, and he tried again: "Rob Tarrant! My name is David." The trainers always said it was vital, in situations like this, to get on personal terms immediately. Sometimes it helped to identify yourself as a federal, even to flash your tin. David's intuition told him this was not one of those times. With his goddamn imagination now capering center-stage in his mind, he could feel that next little leaden slug boring into his brain.

The trainers had also advised to keep telling as much of the truth as you could afford, because a besieged man can be almost supernaturally attuned to lies. "If no one fires again, Tarrant, there's probably no need for you to spend even a single night behind bars. We need to talk. Do you understand me?"

Silence. Maybe the guy was shit-shorts scared and needed to commit himself a bit at a time. David could understand that, for sure. "I don't blame you, I probably wouldn't answer, either. Just toss something that'll make a noise somewhere away from you. Let me know you're there."

More silence. Then a scraping sound somewhere, faint but protracted. "Okay, you're listening. Tarrant, you're surrounded and yes, we're armed: Defense Intelligence Agency. We don't want to hurt you in any way. We know you've got a weapon, and you're pretty good with it. You're very lucky because—" *Another scrape? Maybe he's coming out. Best to keep talking.* "Because you haven't shot a federal officer. Yet. And we'd like to keep it that way," he went on, his laugh not as firm as he'd have liked.

"Tarrant, we've known you feared someone was trying to hurt you, maybe kill you. Now we're convinced you were right. It isn't us, Tarrant! Your country needs your expertise. Our mission is to keep you healthy, and you're not making it easy."

David could feel a presence at his back, and turned his head to find Corrine Tarrant kneeling behind him, her breathing quick and shallow. If the silly bitch couldn't follow orders, best to ignore her. "Listen to me, Tarrant: It was a mistake for them to destroy that little device of yours. They didn't realize it was highly advanced, with vital national-security applications. Tarrant, do you know what it means to lead a development team as a staff scientist at some national lab like Sandia, or Lawrence Livermore? That could be you, very soon. But not if you shoot a federal operative—and we will defend ourselves. Please don't make it necessary."

He strained to hear any response whatever. Nothing. "All right, Robert, I'm coming out now. I'm taking a chance on you. We can sit and talk at a distance if that's what you want."

As he came to his feet, Corrine whispered, "Do you mean

that? A national lab scientist? Oh my *gohhhd . . .*"

David forestalled her with, "It's where he belongs. Now will you kindly shut the fuck up?" He heard her gasp.

Then, taking a deep breath, he pushed past the screen door and sat down on the cold cement steps. A moment later: "Tarrant? David again, and I'm outside now. I have people located around you, but no one fires unless you do." Raising his voice: "Confirm that, Vallejo."

The single word, "Confirm," floated back.

David waited for an eternal thirty seconds. "Your move, sir," he said, hoping the "sir" would carry an implication of respect. After another thirty seconds, David said, a bit unsteadily, "I'm going to walk to the garage now, so that we can meet face-to-face. Please understand that I don't have any choice; it's what I have to do, and I'm depending on your good judgment."

His imagination was now clamoring for him to make an additional statement, something along the lines of, . . . *And if you shoot, you lucky, sneaky amateur feather-merchant son of a bitch, I hope to see that you spend the rest of your life in a fucking wheelchair*—but David managed to avoid any such outburst.

His steps quickened as he neared the faint outline of a side door, and he swallowed hard when he grasped the doorknob. "It's locked," he said aloud.

From the house: "If you hurt my husband, goddamn you, I'll sue you for everything you're worth! I'll make you as famous as Slobodan Milos–what's-his-name."

And that staff-scientist thing has nothing to do with it, I suppose, he thought. Aloud he said, "Vallejo? Take up a position behind the garage. Mrs. Tarrant: There's no other door, is there?"

"No. Only a window on the other side. It doesn't open."

After repeated patient assurances to the suddenly overprotective Corrine, David broke a small pane in the side door and let himself in. He squatted cautiously before he flicked on the interior light.

Eventually he discovered, with Vallejo's help, that if the

garage had contained Rob Tarrant, it no longer did. Corrine was wrong: The window on the other side did open after all, because it was open now.

Had Vallejo been inside, monitoring those motion sensors, she would have known when their quarry slipped from the window. She mentioned the fact no fewer than five times during the next hour.

AND IN HYATTSVILLE, MICHAEL'S *KATSA* JONATHAN LAY AWAKE and frowned at his ceiling. He had not received the scheduled call from Michael earlier in the evening, and Michael was extraordinarily punctual. It might mean a simple role conflict, in which case the Israeli agent would be calling later with a perfectly acceptable explanation.

But it could mean Michael was no longer in place. Jonathan enumerated the possibilities until dawn. . . .

CHAPTER 29

ROB BARELY STIRRED WHEN HIS BEDMATE SHUT OFF HER ALARM, and he was not entirely awake when, after regarding him tenderly for some minutes, she slipped from bed. She returned moments later, closing the door like a conspirator, wearing only the skimpiest of housecoats and a smile that brought him fully alert.

She made a production of letting the coat fall, sliding back into bed. "Guess what I've got for you," she said, showing him a fist.

"You're gonna hit me? Boy, talk about rejection. . . ."

"Idiot." She opened her hand, revealing a condom in its wrap. "You didn't have any, and we used both of the ones I've had forever, so I borrowed one from Jem."

He took it; peeled the metallic wrap away; watched as she took the little disc, still smiling, her hands busy beneath the light summer sheet. "I hope you're feeling up to— Well, well, we *are* up, aren't we?"

He clasped his hands together under his head and waggled his eyebrows. "We are now, Betty Bombshell. You sure you have time?"

"After you fell asleep— There we are, safe and snug in our little raincoat," she said, giving him a grasp that widened his eyes and brought a portion of him to rigid, quivering attention. "—I set the clock for an early wakeup. No," she said, as he started to roll over, "don't even move. This one's on me, as it were. My treat." And with that, she wriggled astride him, sitting up, fluffing her loose blonde hair with both hands as the sheet fell away.

As she closed her eyes and began the classic sinuous motion of the wanton, he let his gaze linger over the marvelously tapered rib cage, her breasts full and small-aureoled, nipples erect with her desire. As he reached to cup them in his hands: "Not yet," she murmured without opening her eyes. "Leave a little something for the finale."

And now her motion shifted to a stronger, more voluptuous undulation, that languorous, *Gioconda* smile of hers suggesting that it was all effortless, and when she finally chose to open her eyes her pupils were enormous, the smile gone, her mouth an O of total abandon, and then a faint smile returned as she nodded to him, and his hands caressed her as her climax produced his own.

For a long while then, she lay nuzzling his cheek, her breath warm, her kisses savory with—he made a guess: "Juicy Fruit?"

"Quicker than brushing," she giggled, "and I was in a hurry. Wanna share it?"

He nodded, and she let him suck the chewing gum from her lips before she rolled away. She lay beside him as he chewed dutifully. "When I was in high school, this meant you were steadies," he said.

"And boffing each other's brains out didn't?"

"Depended on your brains, I think. Or your opportunities."

"Same here. I'm glad I got a late start. And I'm *very* glad we, uh, fit so well." They lay quietly for a time, sharing a single smile between them, until she sighed and made a wry face. "I suppose I'd better be up and about. Unless you'd prefer I call in sick," she added wistfully.

"God, I wish," he said. "Whatever small part of you Ethan Lodge shares, he doesn't deserve. But what I need now is a certain telephone number."

"TV reporters? They should be in the book," she said.

"Nope. Sachs. Unless you've already got it."

She kissed his cheek and rolled out of bed with a knowing laugh. "Oh, I've had his number from day one, but not so that I could call him. Or would want to." She paused, no longer quite so lighthearted. "You're sure that's how you want to proceed? No TV or press people?"

With an effort, he kept his gaze on her face. "Tempting,

but no. It's obvious that if national security is an issue, my calling in the media at this point would be a real Mr. Fumducker. And with so many people knowing my side of this by now, zapping yours truly would be just as dumb on Sachs's part and I think he knows it. Yeah, facing Sachs is the best tactic." He showed her a pair of crossed fingers.

"Right. We hope," she nodded.

He watched her moving about in her naked glory, gathering her scanties, shoes, and a severely tailored suit, laying them out on the bed before she shrugged more or less into that housecoat again. He wondered briefly how the devil she managed daily to hide such plentiful charms within a trim facade, and gave thanks that Jem Kasabian's tastes ran in another direction. "Got to do my duties and doodahs," she said brightly.

"You have a GenStan phone book here?"

"In the hall alcove. You don't intend to call there from here?" He shook his head and she left the room, satisfied.

When he heard her adjusting the shower he forced himself to think about other things. He needed to make several calls, preferably from widely-spaced public telephones. If he could get anything more than Gaelic curses from Fred McGrath, he would know whether his typed account might yet be an asset.

He wanted to call Gus, too. And while he had avoided the slightest hint of his intention to Ed, he wanted to resign from GenStan before facing the DIA. He owed it to them; he particularly owed it to Ethan Lodge, and the resignation ceremony he had in mind would not take long.

Ed did not dress immediately. Still in her housecoat, she busied herself in the kitchen while Rob showered. As she called him in to breakfast he could hear Jem Kasabian's VW van starting up, and Rob was relieved. Facing Jem on this particular morning would have been awkward for a half-dozen reasons.

He pored through the company directory and jotted down numbers while Ed busied herself at some strange concoction at the stove. Once seated, he eyed the strange dark mass on his plate with misgivings, noting that she had a smaller portion of the same stuff for herself. Though its aroma was tempting, it looked like a gift buzzards had left. Greenish black, with gray lumps and brown lumps, it defied any guesses. "I give up," he said at last, trying the coffee first. It was strong and fresh.

"Never had an O-Joe's special? It's the dish that made San Jose famous," she said. "Lean ground beef, diced mushrooms, cut spinach, and eggs. Think of it as an omelet for the fight crowd."

"No wonder they fight," he said, but he took up a fork and marveled at the things men do for love. A little salt, a dollop of catsup, and after the second bite he was Hoovering through it like a famished middleweight.

She left him to dress, returning in less time than he thought possible. Lingering over her coffee, checking her wristwatch now and then, Ed fairly glowed with satiation. "I really do have to run," she said finally, "but you can drive me if you need the car. I can walk a couple of blocks to the gate. But if you call, for God's sake make yourself sound like someone else. You never know when Himself will pick up the phone."

" 'T's all *right*," he said, making it guttural, rolling the *r*, and she laughed.

HE DROVE HER WITHIN SIGHT OF THE GENSTAN GATE, UNABLE to keep his gaze from her body as she whisked herself out of the car. "One thing," she said, running her hand along the windowframe. "This is the only car I've got, Rob. Okay?"

"And here I've been thinking your Ferrari was in the shop," he replied. "I'll be careful not to dent it, I'm no NASCAR hot-shot anyhow."

"Don't get yourself dented, that's the main thing," she said, and turned away after another smile. Momentarily double-parked, he watched her stride until someone honked. He was reminded suddenly of a secret weapon the Brits had used on the high seas during World War Two. What was it called? "Q-ship," he recalled aloud. An enemy raider would approach the innocent-looking little freighter only to find its trim exterior hid torpedo tubes and big guns of awesome potency. *The woman's a bloody Q-ship*, he thought happily.

His first call, from the Donut Stop, was to Fred McGrath, and he began by using his gutteral accent. "Mr. McGrath, do you have a minute?" He heard a guarded yes and went on. "Can you talk freely?" Another yes. Now Rob dropped the pretense. "What did you do with the pages I typed yesterday and left in the camper?"

McGrath had a light tenor voice, and it went into virtual falsetto. "You typed . . . You? Jasus, I know who— You wee bastid, you put me in the chowder!" In quick succession, Rob discovered that he was a pig-fookin' hooremaster, a thankless ingrate, and a man who could expect fuck-all from his poor oul long-suffering friend.

"I admit it, Fred. Everything you said, and more." This left McGrath nonplussed long enough for Rob to add, "But you were my ace in the hole."

To which McGrath said, "Thanks to you I felt like an ace-hole, and no mistake, boy-o."

Chuckling, Rob went on. "Enough with the professional Boston blarney, pal. I hope to make it up to you; honestly I do. Meanwhile, people really have been gunning for me. What'd you do with those pages? It's important."

"I'm not through," McGrath protested.

It occurred to Rob that the old boy could not help himself— venting his spleen was one of the few exercises McGrath could perform while vertical, and he hoped to go on loading and firing until his verbal ammunition was spent. "I can't spare the time, Fred. Love to hear everything you can call me, it's a real education, but later. Someone may be tracing this call. I just need to know—"

"I heard you," said McGrath, in more resigned tones. "I read it. Later I turned it over to GenStan's Finest."

"Shit. Did you make a copy first?"

"Was I born yesterday? At least it took me off the hook! Do I know how to protect my backside in case someone claims I invented that bizarre drivel myself?"

"Better than anyone I know, Fred. Just make sure, in case everything goes wrong for me, that those pages get to, hell, I don't know. FBI, maybe."

"Yeah." After a long pause, a guarded, "I'm still pissed at you, me boy."

"Here's a kiss on that backside you protect so well," said Rob, and produced a loud smack before disconnecting.

He drove to the Donut Field and ordered decaf, reminding himself not to call from a third doughnut shop . . . just in case. *If someone's tracing me somehow, they may waste resources trying to cover the wrong places,* he decided. He did not want to risk Lodge penetrating his vocal sham, but there was another way, one that might just work because it *was* so far out in left field. It wasn't yet nine in the morning, however, and he'd once heard Corrine mention how some ladies of leisure rise at the crack of noon.

So he called Gus, who apparently had the borrowed cell phone in his hand awaiting that call. "It's me, Gus. I'll make it short. Still think you were right to go home so soon?"

"Man can't dick around eating hospital food when he has airplanes to build," said Gus. "Goddamn pills make me sleepy, so I druther have the headache. I'll mend."

"Heard from Kenny?"

"Young fart woke me up. Still at his buddy's: Jerry Nislar, Feisler, whatever. Wanted to know where you were."

"He probably called where he expected me to be but I won't be there for a while. Let him know I'm okay. Maybe he can help you on the model. I'll call you both later."

"You better. You got the sound of a man touching bases," said Gus with gruff concern.

"Well, I am, those that matter."

"I mean," Gus persisted, "a man setting his affairs in order, Rob." Gus only called him Rob on the most serious occasions. "Anything I can do?"

"See if you can build a fuselage with your fingers crossed. Can't hurt," Rob said. "And Gus?"

"Yeah."

"Don't worry."

"Oh, right. I bet that's what Yeager told his wife before he climbed into that little orange bullet plane."

"Yeager made history that day."

"Yeah, but you're no fuckin' astronaut, Rob. Be careful what kinda history you want to make."

"Will do," Rob agreed. He broke the connection and hurried out to Ed's little Ford.

He had intended at first to choose one of the big industrial parks as a meeting place for his resignation, but on sober reflection he realized that he didn't know the layouts and exits of any of them well enough for his purpose. Maybe he was doing something a little unorthodox—*maybe, hell*—but with a little forethought he could do it without serious consequences. And that required a setting that would seem innocent, but could lose its innocence in a hurry.

He was driving past the Santa Clara railroad depot when the impulse struck. A landmark in the Bay Area, the Santa Clara passenger depot was over a century old before it was moved bodily across the tracks to its present location. The original building was no longer open to the public, but its freight annex still functioned as a museum, and CalTrain commuter trains still made regular stops at the site. Something about the building's classic square lines and broad overhangs said "familiar and safe," and while its parking lot was not large by local standards, it was big enough to handle the cars of scores of commuters. Rob drove around the area twice, then left the Ford in a temporary parking slot and strolled to the CalTrain schedule postings.

The early-morning and late-afternoon stops, he knew, would find dozens of commuters hurrying about. Knowing how quickly the few passengers usually left the depot, Rob decided his timing: a half-hour after a midday stop. A bright, sunny day in a public place in Santa Clara—how innocuous can you get? He returned to the car and then drove around the site, locating likely parking spots beyond the commuter lot.

In a mini-mall near San Tomas Expressway he found a series of pay phones where the background noise was acceptable, and unfolded the notes he had made. If Deirdre Lodge was still snoring, tough luck, lady. He was fairly sure the woman wouldn't recognize his voice—but if she let an answering machine or a maid do her job? Not a good option for him. He'd have to say something to make her want to pick up the phone. Something along the lines of: *If your shit-eating husband doesn't get this message before noon, his dickless little career is toast and you'll be clerking at K-Mart next year.* Well, maybe not quite that direct. . . .

Wonder of wonders, on the fourth ring: "Lodge residence," said a well-modulated contralto.

Because he recognized her voice, he suddenly decided that she might recall his. "Mrs. Lodge?" Rob said, affecting what he hoped was a generic European accent.

"This is she."

"My call is more important to your husband's future than I can possibly say, *madame*. I must not call Mr. Lodge directly. I will explain why to him. You must call him immediately at General Standards. Do you understand?"

"I— He's not here. . . . Who is this? If it's about that stupid AmEx card business, I—"

"Mrs. Lodge!" At least he had her attention. "It is not about a stupid charge card. Write this down."

"Write *what* down?"

"That a call to Michael would *not* be secure. But Michael must see him today without fail, at the Santa Clara railroad depot." He had to repeat it twice, and repeated the exact time as well, and got her to recite it back. "Also tell him that if he fails to appear, Lancer may make the connection," Rob added, for the hell of it. For the further hell of it, he let a peremptory headmaster's tone creep into his, "Repeat, please."

She did, breathless, stumbling over it. *She's bought it,* he told himself. Then she said, "Which is the important part?"

Oh, for God's sake. "Every word is crucial to his career," he said icily.

A gasp. Then: "So why can't *you* call him, Mr. Michael?"

"I have not given my name, *madame*. Call him. Call him *now*." And with that, he terminated the call. He stood there, staring at nothing, replaying it in his head. Okay, he'd sounded like a cross between Jeeves and a Transylvanian Nazi, but at least she had the words down. And the bit about

"Lancer" ought to dispel any notion Ethan might have as to the call's validity.

He began to walk, faux-shopping, wishing he could know whether he could depend on Deirdre Lodge to deliver the message. He smiled when he recalled that Lodge's office had several lines. He hurried to another pay phone, and this was a number he knew by heart.

" 'T's all right," he said in a gutteral when she answered. "I think it is, anyhow."

"Yes; he's on another line," said Ed.

"I hope he's gibbering like a monkey," said Rob. "It should be his wife. When he hangs up, I've got to know whether he makes a call to this Michael guy on his cell phone."

"Wait one," she said. He could hear her breathing; it reminded him how that soft susurrus had felt against his cheek, and: "You're giving me an erection," he said softly.

"Will you shush?" It would've sounded sterner without the delighted giggle. Then, "He's telling her it isn't what she thinks. There's a flash: She can think—wants to know how Michael sounded; hurried or worried. Now he's whispering."

"I'll call you back."

"Could I call you instead? Bear in mind that I might not be able to."

"For the next five minutes," he said, and recited the pay phone's number. She broke the connection without another word.

He walked away, scanning reflections in a shop window, suspicious of other shoppers but staying within earshot of the telephone. When the ring came, he hurried back to answer.

Ed's first words were, "Are you in cahoots with Deirdre, luv? I know that was her voice when I put her through."

"Not my type, but you're welcome to speculate," he teased. "Is he calling anyone now?"

"If he is, he's doing it on the run," she replied.

"He's gone?"

"You must've built a fire in his drawers, sweetie. He told me to call Sachs and then canceled. I heard him call and ask for the director of Security but he hung up before it went through. And then a minute ago he lurched out of here like that gold robot—C-3PO, you know? But he wasn't gold, he was white as a bedsheet."

"*Bedsheet*. You're doing it again," he crooned. "Uh, did he say where he was going?"

"Didn't seem to notice me. He was carrying an old-fashioned leather satchel that I've seen in his secure cabinet."

Rob had an instant's fear that he had misjudged the time, but the second hand of his watch was still sweeping its dial. "Maybe he has a train to catch," he said.

"My boss," she said darkly, "is not a 'train' kind of guy. He's a 'company jet' kind of guy."

Another thought shouldered into place. If Lodge was panicky enough, he might not want to meet "Michael" or anyone else. "I never thought of him as a pilot. Does he fly?"

"Only first-class. And you have to go through procedures to use the company jet, and he didn't. No, I was just characterizing him. Do you think he'd actually leave town?"

"If he's ducking out from feds and company Security people, he might try and leave the solar system. But I don't think so. I think— Jesus, honey, I don't know what I think, except that I've pushed a domino over and now I've got to run and see how many others will fall. Thanks a bunch; catch you later."

"I won't run fast," she said, putting a world of insinuation into it.

CHAPTER 30

WHEN HE NOTICED THE SPORTSWEAR STORE IN THE MALL, ROB hurried in for some protective coloration. He was already wearing his jogging shoes. The shapeless, pre-ruined twill fisherman's hat had a circular turned-down brim that hid most of his features like a wilted halo. He chose a long-sleeved sweatshirt not because its lettering said STREET PIZZA, but because its pattern was a wild montage of pizza slices in realistic colors, chiefly yellows and reds, and it fit like a tent.

The trousers were cutoffs from a sale rack, and apparently they weren't supposed to fit any human specimen. He had always wondered where teenaged skateboarders got those high-water pants with the crotches sagging halfway down to their knees, but had never realized they could be bought that way, until now. It was still over an hour before he was slated to meet Lodge; time enough for a change of clothes.

He felt like an outright buffoon when he walked out of the store carrying his regular pants in a bag while showing the world a set of hairy calves, the clerk's bemused stare at this thirty-something throwback burned into his memory. But no one else gave him a second glance, and by the time he reached Ed's car he walked with a bounce in his step.

He still had time to burn, and grinned as he recalled the skateboards he'd seen while stocking his apartment from secondhand stores. None of the scarred and swoopy plywood boards had looked usable—but they wouldn't cost a bundle, either. Besides, Rob had once tried to ride one of Kenny's and knew he could no more ride a skateboard than he could walk a slackwire. He found only one board at the Salvation Army store, and its wheels were shot. For two dollars, he left with the thing over his shoulder, and another clerk wearing a pensive look.

To keep from letting himself grow a case of nerves, he thought about ways to contact Sachs, and about places for the meeting.

He wondered what Ethan Lodge was carrying in that satchel.

He wondered whether Ethan was going somewhere to fill the satchel first, and what he'd fill it with besides French-cuff shirts and manly cologne.

And he wondered whether Ethan would think to arrive at the Santa Clara depot very early, so that he could observe the arrival of "Michael," or perhaps someone Ethan did not want to meet at all. That's when Rob put the hammer down in the little Ford.

ETHAN HAD A HALFHOUR'S LEEWAY WHEN HE ARRIVED AT THE old depot, just as he had planned. His safe-deposit box had been a cagey idea, but leaving a resealable plastic pack of athletic socks in it as slipcovers for the cash might have been cagier still. An hour before, with fingers that shook, he had separated the money into two equal piles; one he fed into socks, the other into rubber-banded envelopes. Whatever deal he might have to negotiate, he felt certain that half of his cash would be an adequate sweetener. After all, it had worked on him. . . .

The final item he'd kept in that safe-deposit box was the little pearl-handled .25 automatic he'd bought for Deirdre before he found she absolutely refused to touch it. He had always thought it was the height of folly to fear touching that thing. Until now.

Now, with his Taurus parked in a slot near the edge of the depot lot, every time Ethan moved, the pistol bumped like a sashweight in his pocket though it couldn't have weighed a pound. He moved the flimsy package of socks to the backseat, hiding his stash in plain sight—and the pistol bumped his ribs. He turned this way and that, searching for a sign of Mike— and the pistol reminded him it was there. For the first time, he actually followed a scenario through until, in his mind, he had a choice of wearing handcuffs or pulling that little trigger.

And at that point, his imagination balked.

He had no better luck trying to imagine what could have prompted Mike to call by way of Deirdre. He never doubted that the call was genuine because of the insider knowledge it contained. Could the problem have anything to do with Mike's cell phone? Could it have been Mike's superior—what was that word, *katsa*—who did the calling? In any case, Ethan felt that he had no more Israeli goodwill left in him.

The commuter train thrummed in, disgorged a few passengers, inhaled a few, and left again. Automobiles started up and moved off. The heavy woman with her brace of children were gone now. He assumed the big kid with the skateboard and the girl with the backpack had gone aboard as well. The place was just about as deserted as it was going to get, and Ethan decided he could watch for Michael from the doorway of the museum. He emerged from the Taurus, felt the little weapon nudge his kidney, then sensed a presence immediately behind him.

He turned to find that his companion was the youngster carrying the grungy skateboard—only it wasn't, exactly. "I quit, Ethan," said the newcomer, in a voice of unearthly calm.

"I beg your—" Ethan began, before the words and the face all impacted him in the same instant. Beneath that floppy hat brim, familiar eyes bored into his with a certain intensity; a familiar lopsided smile suggested a private joke that Ethan himself might not find a compelling amusement. "Tarrant?"

For, nightmarishly, the youth he had seen slouching near the trackside telephones twenty minutes before, had become the last man on earth he wanted to see this close, with such a look on his face. "That's right," said Tarrant mildly. "I know this isn't the usual formal memo with two weeks' notice, but you and I went past formalities some time back, didn't we?"

Perhaps, Ethan thought wildly, this was all an accidental meeting of two old acquaintances in passing, a one-in-a-million circumstance that happened to people every day. Judging by that outlandish getup, he wondered if Tarrant had lost his mind, and looked around, hoping to see Mike within hailing distance. "Really sorry to hear you're leaving us, Rob," Ethan croaked, and stuck out his hand for a friendly shake. "But good luck to you."

Tarrant looked at the proffered hand as if it were roadkill, still smiling. "That's not what I came for, Ethan. I came to get some answers. Oh, yes; and to spit on your shoes." As he said this, he let the old skateboard drop against the Taurus with a prolonged scrape. Ethan winced, glancing at this insult to his property.

And felt a stunning backhanded slap across his cheek that spun him halfway around.

Oddly, it did not register as pain, but as a second insult. Facing this madman again, Ethan blinked and drew himself up. "That's actionable," he said, realizing that his lower lip had split, reaching up to touch it—and that hurt, shockingly.

But if anything, the peculiar little smile of Tarrant's had broadened. "Your idea of action is a lawsuit," he said, nodding. "It figures. You'll forgive me—or not—for having more direct action in mind. Defend yourself, boss man." And with that, he sent Ethan reeling again, with an open-handed slap that came faster than Ethan would have thought possible. "Greetings from the little people," he added.

Ethan managed a single "*Helllp*," before he went down on his knees, arms protectively over his head, rocking back and forth as his arms intercepted a rain of slaps.

"I was your friend," Ethan protested, his voice muffled. "Why are you . . ."

"Shut the fuck up, I'll ask the questions now," said Tarrant. "And stand up like a man. When you grovel like that, it makes me itch to kick you." As Ethan pulled himself to his feet, hands before him as if to ward off more of those slaps, Tarrant went on, disgust flavoring each phrase: "I'd hoped you'd make it interesting, but you're not worth a clenched fist. I could stone you to death with a sofa pillow."

"I'm—not a violent man," Ethan said, seeking dignity.

"But God help the guy who turns his back on you," Tarrant rejoined. "With you, what I *don't* see is what I get. Okay,

question one." He growled it, in a furious snarl: "Why did you
have an invention scuttled when I was practically giving it to
GenStan?"

If Tarrant didn't know, the truth might still hide under a
smokescreen. "That's company-private information. The decision was made above my level."

" 'Just following orders,' in other words. *Whose* orders?
Give me a name. Whoever he is, he's fucking-over a special-
access program."

Ethan's mouth trembled as he shook his head. "I'm not
sure."

"I'll find out sooner or later anyhow. Is it Mike? That's question two: Who the hell is 'Mike'? Mike who, Mike what?"

Ethan considered lashing out with a foot; shouting again;
turning to run. But something told him that none of those
actions would do him much good, and meanwhile he was tast-
ing his own blood from cuts in his mouth, and his lips had
thickened to make his most elegant phrases sound like self-
parody. Forlorn hope made him play for time. "I know several
Mikes."

"But maybe only one you begged to take me out, asshole.
The one you called for help after that goddamn fed scared
puddles out of you in your office yesterday," Tarrant snarled.
"*That* Mike. Who is he?"

"Who is *he*?" Ethan straightened; thought quickly. "He's
very high up, higher than the DIA team. *They* can't even protect you from him," he said, staring his best two-pair bluff. It
was still possible, he thought, that he could make Tarrant melt
away and run for cover.

He saw a flicker of doubt in Tarrant's face, and upped the
ante. "Believe me," he said with confidence.

Tarrant called Ethan's hand with stiffened fingers that
prodded just below his breastbone. The jab did not travel more
than a few inches. Ethan's diaphragm had not been paralyzed
by a blow in forty years, and for a moment he feared that he
had been somehow broken inside.

While Ethan fought for breath, his interrogator stood
calmly before him. "All my years in GenStan and you don't

think I recognize a typical middle-management lie? Feel free to do it again. And so will I." But something in Tarrant's face said he was not enjoying this. All the same, he was doing it, and now Ethan feared for his life.

As he began to draw ragged breaths, Ethan stood more or less erect, put his hands on his hips, and said, "All right, then. You wanted to know—who Mike is. I can show you his—written charter." He reached inside his jacket as Tarrant watched suspiciously, then patted both breast pockets, feigning confusion, and at last reached into his left outer pocket, then his right, and found what he sought.

The ensuing *pop!* was no louder than a firecracker through the expensive houndstooth fabric, but it struck Tarrant somewhere along his left side.

Tarrant's reaction was a sidelong recoil so fast that the next round went into the door of a nearby Toyota. Before Ethan could pull the little weapon out to aim it properly, Tarrant took advantage of the fact that both of Ethan's hands were still in his pockets. As the men struggled, they twisted so that two more rounds discharged into the side of the Taurus before Ethan's head ricocheted off the bodywork.

Ethan heard, "Federal agent! Not another move," with genuine gratitude.

ROB HAD ONE ARM WRAPPED AROUND LODGE TO TRAP THE pocketed weapon, the fingers of his free hand gripping Lodge's hair with the intent to pound the man's head against his car, when the command caused him to look around.

"I mean it," said David Sachs, knees bent, an automatic of respectable caliber held in both hands. "Both of you hold it right there."

Because both men ceased struggling, Sachs came up from his crouch, his glance moving quickly between them. "Good God, it *is* Tarrant, isn't it? Well, let him go, man, looks like you've had a nice little piece of him in the time I gave you."

Rob moved back with a heavy sigh, feeling along his side, leaning against the neighboring Toyota, grunting with pain and watching intently as Lodge put both hands into view.

"Thank God," Lodge gasped. "He said he was going to kill me."

"Bullshit. I heard every goddamn word, Mr. Clean," said Sachs. "You were both too intent on your agendas to spot me, I guess. We've had a tracker on your car for over a week and I moved in as soon as I saw this—this apparition circling behind you." His glance moved to Rob and he shook his head, marveling. "Congratulations. I thought you were some punk trying to panhandle him. Nothing like a creative amateur to keep a man on his toes," he added to no one in particular. "And by the way: Did I hear shots fired?"

"Yeah, by this piece of shit," said Rob, gathering the folds of his STREET PIZZA shirt. "Look in his jacket."

"Watch the hands, Tarrant. So far, I don't think you've made any serious breaches. Don't start now."

"Okay if I find out why this stings so much?" Rob peeled up the shirt to find an angry two-inch horizontal welt, slowly leaking crimson for most of its length below his ribs. After a moment he found two small holes in the enveloping shirt. "What do you know," he said, letting the shirt drop, "I've actually been shot. Kind of." With a hard look at Lodge: "I'm starting to wonder if you can do *any*thing right, you pusillanimous pussy." He delivered another light backhand to the Lodge cheek and, as the manager raised his hands to his face, Rob tore at the jacket pocket.

Sachs stepped forward. "No you don't, Tarrant, not in your present frame of mind."

"Then you grab whatever that thing is in his pocket, before he empties it into some tourist by mistake," Rob demanded, still watching Lodge.

Sachs stepped forward, waving Rob a step farther away, and found the pearl-handled weapon after roughly turning Lodge around to face his car. "Jewelry that shoots," he said, with evident scorn, and pocketed the pistol. He finished patting Lodge down in workmanlike fashion without finding other weapons. "A 'Tootsie Toy,' maybe a .25. I hate to think this thing came so close to bagging me last night. About as accurate as a spitwad."

Rob ignored this soliloquy. "I was wondering how to get in touch with you safely, Sachs," he said. "I'd like to reach out and touch you in other ways, but never mind."

"I've done more professional work than this," Sachs admitted ruefully, shaking his head, "but it's never too late to follow procedures. Turn around, Tarrant, you could be carrying. And somehow I don't think you'd pop me with anything small."

"Eighty-millimeter fist, for starters," said Rob, but he turned and leaned both hands on the Toyota. "And don't tell me you don't know why."

"I know why. She's not your property, Tarrant." As he spoke, Sachs continued the pat-down. "She was looking. I was looking."

Rob jerked. "Ow, you son of a bitch."

Sachs: "What?"

Rob: "That's where he shot me, is what."

"Wups, sorry." Sachs lifted the shirt himself; studied the crease a moment. "It'll need cleansing but you got lucky. Christ, man, wearing that stupid shirt you could be leaking like a sieve and nobody would know it."

"I'd know it; that's enough for me," Rob grumbled.

"Relax," Sachs instructed him, "but don't think I won't drop you for cause." A wink and a brief smile: "I just realized something. It wasn't Lodge who's been feeding you our conversations, so it had to be his leggy office blonde, Edwina. Nice going," he added.

At this, Lodge took renewed interest. "That bitch! She's been recording my phone calls, hasn't she?"

Rob raised a hand, almost casually, but with its threat implicit, and the manager subsided. "I didn't need Ed Doyle to listen to you, Ethan. I flew one of my little micros to your window from outside. It may still be there," said Rob.

"You couldn't," said Sachs, awed.

"Should be sitting on the sill, cemented by cyanoacrylate, if the wind hasn't blown it off. When you two assholes were threatening each other I was in the parking lot, listening. It was great. Practically came in my pants," Rob informed him.

"You've got it that well-developed, then," said Sachs.

"I've also got my account of all this, on paper and videotape, and they're not all with the same person. I'm not really all that sure of you, Sachs. You or somebody like you has tried to kill me and my father-in-law—and there was that poor bozo who got blown up with my old Bronco. Your doing?"

"That was a glitch in my outfit. A big one, but now we know who it was," Sachs replied with a shrug. "He's been—taken out of the equation; you don't need to know any more about it than that. But someone tried to nail me late last night with a small-caliber weapon." A long searching look, and then a sigh. "Outside your wife's place. If it was you, I won't press charges."

"If it'd been me, you wouldn't be in any condition to press charges," Rob assured him.

"Brave talk from a man with bullet holes in his clown suit," Sachs observed. To this, Rob merely snorted and looked away. When Sachs gestured toward Lodge with his weapon, the manager shrank away. "As for you, Mr. Ethan Lodge—well, if you were to meet anyone here, he must be miles away by now. Why here? Waiting for a train in the other direction?"

"I've been so frightened by all this, I just wanted to get away," said Lodge. "That's all I wanted."

"So you took a satchel full of—what?—out of your office," Rob asked. "Classified documents?"

Lodge drew his teeth back, turning a sidelong glare at Rob without turning his head. "It *was* Ed Doyle, goddamn her. You couldn't have known that with some audio pickup."

Rob saw the brows of David Sachs elevate. The DIA man made a rolling *"Get on with it"* motion with the barrel of his pistol. Rob sighed. "All right—she told me what this flyspeck did after I sent a message to him. No crime in that."

As if speaking to a child, Sachs said, "She knows you're a wanted man, Tarrant. And she helped you. Can you say 'accomplice'?"

"Can you say, 'Unfuck you and the cockroach you rode in on'? A few minutes ago you said I haven't done anything wrong."

"I spoke too soon," Sachs said quickly.

"You did, but you were right," said Rob, just as quickly. "So don't try to toss some innocent lady in the dumper just because she won't fall for your all-American secret-agent horseshit and you think maybe you can use her as a bargaining chip. She hasn't committed any crimes."

"And you're protecting her just a little more than seems necessary," Sachs retorted, then grimaced. "Wait a minute. You sent the message that made Lodge scamper out here?"

"By way of his wife; she didn't know who I was. Ethan thought he was going to meet some guy named Mike. Same guy he called after you left his office yesterday," Rob explained. "And I still wonder what he was carrying in that satchel."

Sachs, to Lodge: "What satchel?"

Rob, gesturing toward the Taurus: "*That* satchel. Either something to give to Mike, or something to keep our mutual friend in margaritas south of the border, would be my guess."

"I can tell you one thing," Sachs replied glumly, "Mike isn't going to show up here."

Rob barked a joyless laugh. "Of course not, you jackass, that was just a ploy of mine to get *him* here."

Sachs adopted a pained expression. "Look, can we have a little respect here? I'm the one holding the convincer; focus on that."

"Focus on this," said Rob, jabbing a single digit upward. "Either you're going to blow me away, and you'd have done it already, or you need me healthy. I vote for healthy. With reservations," he amended.

"Oh shit," said Sachs, stuffing the automatic into his waistband. "Where was I?"

Rob folded his arms with a great show of abused patience. "What's—in—the fucking—satchel?"

"It can be yours," Lodge interjected quickly. "Go ahead, look, Commander."

"Here's a bulletin, Lodge: I intend to. I hope it's classified documents," Sachs rejoined with feeling.

"All you have to do is look the other way, let me drive off, give me just an hour," Lodge pleaded, raising his voice as Sachs shoved him roughly out of the way to reach into the front passenger seat of the Taurus. "Half an hour— Get away from me, Tarrant!"

But Rob only held the manager by his collar as Sachs emerged from the car. Rummaging inside the satchel, Sachs withdrew a nifty folder and one of several manila envelopes— opened the folder; snickered; looked up at Rob. "Would you believe," he said, "it's his résumé? Who's going to hire you, Lodge: Patagonia?" With an impatient shake of his head, he opened the envelope, then spoke calmly to Lodge. "How much is in here, and where'd you get it?"

"Savings, about a hundred thousand in cash."

Rob whistled at that, but made no comment.

"I swear it's all legitimate. I live simply," Lodge added, noting the disbelief in Sachs's face.

Rob redefined a term: "Like his wife's BMW is simple. Like his fifty-dollar haircuts are simple."

"Think of it," Lodge begged. "A BMW of your own, Sachs."

"Uh-huh. How thoughtful of you. And how do I keep him from talking?" Sachs nodded toward Rob.

To this, Ethan Lodge spread his hands in a broad shrug and smiled, until he saw the look that crossed the face of the DIA man. "But if I killed him, Lodge, how could he be my witness that you tried to bribe a federal agent? Let me clear up a misconception here, gentlemen. . . . I use the term loosely."

"Fuck you," Rob murmured it as a single word, bored by this.

"I'm not in this work for money," Sachs told them. "I love my country. Ever since I was a boy I wanted to do just what I'm doing; living my fantasy. That's a real job perk, for me. I cannot tell you just how much it pleases me to find, in the same case file, a victimized genius with well-developed new cutting-edge weapon technology and a scumbag sleeper agent. hiding in an aerospace company. Because those are the profiles you fit."

"And you swaggering around sweeping up all the stray nookie in sight—don't forget the profile you fit," Rob answered.

Though a muscle throbbed in Sachs's jaw, he refused the bait. "All right; time to wrap this thing up. Right now it's got more loose ends than a bad haircut. I'll have to bring Edwina Doyle into it, too, and Marie Vallejo. We could do it in any of several places, but if you're so antsy, Tarrant, you can pick a friendly place. You still think I want to put a hole in you?"

"After what I've been through, nothing would surprise me," Rob said, with utter conviction.

"I suppose not," Sachs agreed, with a nod. "But if I made a call to some civilian authority not in my outfit, and put you on the line, how would that be?"

"Hell, I don't know. What for?"

"Think about it. I've apprehended you alive and well, and I'll acknowledge that you're no longer my suspect," Sachs said, "though we have one with us. I'd say that, too," he assured Lodge. Fumbling his cell phone out, he went on. "I'd be pretty stupid to turn on you after that, Tarrant. So: San Jose metro police, or even GenStan's Security director, who was FBI at one time—anybody but the media. Name it."

"You're turning down the chance of a lifetime," Lodge said.

"Of *your* lifetime, maybe," Sachs replied. "How about it, Tarrant?"

"GenStan Security," Rob blurted. "I know his voice, and I can't wait for him to hear how ol' Ethan here has come up in the world."

"Then you call him yourself, and we'll take turns," Sachs told him, handing over the cell phone.

CHAPTER 31

ROB VETOED SACHS'S SUGGESTION THAT THEY CONVENE IN THE
Tarrant bungalow. "It's not my home anymore," he growled.

"I happen to know your wife—" Sachs began.

"Listen, you; gun or no gun . . ." Rob burst out, and was
interrupted in turn.

"Will you wait? Let me rephrase that: I feel reasonably sure
your wife has developed a new appreciation of you. She heard
some things I said," Sachs went on. "I thought you were listening, so—look, I'm dealing with what we call intervening
variables here."

"I'm an engineer, Sachs. I speak 'intervening variable,' "
said Rob. Lodge seemed happy to be ignored for the moment,
running his tongue along his teeth, licking blood from his lips.

"It won't be an admission of any crime if you tell me
whether you were somewhere around your home last night,"
Sachs insisted.

Rob gave him a blank stare, then let a smile accompany
memories of delight. "No, Commander, I was somewhere else.
I repeat: I no longer think of where my wife lives as my home."

"I think you might, eventually. I got the idea she'd be glad
to see you again." On the face of David Sachs was an ill-fitting
expression that might have passed for guilt in another man.

"Later, maybe. I'll feel a lot more comfortable, and I'm sure
Edwina Doyle will, too, if we thrash this out at her place. On
second thought, I'm not sure; but with that phone of yours I
can find out in a hurry."

Sachs surrendered the phone again and Rob climbed into
the rear seat of the Taurus to gain minimal privacy. Lodge
immediately began to plead to Sachs again, in a furious whisper. Much as he wanted to hear this, Rob wanted more to hear

Ed's voice. As he punched in the GenStan number, he pulled a lumpy package of socks from beneath one cheek of his rump.

Ed became by turns happily animated, uncertain, then decisive again as Rob explained the bare bones of their situation. "Do you mean I get to see Himself roll over and beg? I never realized how petty I can be," she said. "Just give me time to cancel his appointments and lock our confidential office files. You've got my car. Can you pick me up at the main gate?"

"I think we can manage that," he said, sliding from the car, tugging gingerly at that all-enveloping sweatshirt. By now the bleeding had stopped. He advised Sachs of his intention, got a nod, and ended the call before locking up the Taurus. Sachs, too, had parked beyond the lot and produced handcuffs for Lodge before marching him away.

TEN MINUTES LATER, CLOSELY TRAILED BY SACHS WITH HIS morose passenger, Rob met Ed Doyle outside the main gate and endured her amazed scrutiny as she buckled up. "One of these days," she said, gazing at his singular choice of clothing, "you're not going to surprise me, and that will *really* surprise me."

"Don't even ask," he said. "How else was I going to get within butt-kicking range of Lodge? Son of a bitch shot me, by the way."

"Ho ho," she said, unamused at what she imagined was his fit of whimsy. "At least take off that goofy sombrero." She whisked the hat off for him, then smoothed his hair possessively.

"Your constant admirer won't like that. He's right behind us, using his cell phone," Rob told her with a grin.

"As if I cared," said Ed, and reached her fingers up to claw gently at the back of his scalp. "Is he watching us?"

A glance at the rearview as he grunted with contentment. "Yep, and I could swear he's grinning."

"Maybe he's a better man than I thought," she murmured, but kept the massage going.

A few blocks before they reached Ed's duplex, a dark sedan fell in line behind Sachs. "I think that's the rest of the DIA team back there. Or the woman, at least," Rob commented. "I know Sachs was going to call her in on this."

"Lordy, we'll have a houseful," Ed replied. "I called Jem and asked him to come home. I hope he's there already."

"Because?"

"To turn on that video camera. For the rest of my life, whenever I'm feeling down I can plug in a cassette and watch Ethan Lodge munch ca-ca," she said with an evil chuckle.

Jem Kasabian's Vanagon, at least, was there. Rob's little convoy filled all the remaining spaces. As Lodge, propelled gently from behind by Sachs, passed Ed, he proved the bean-counter's typical devotion to detail with, "Did you cancel my appointments?"

"And rescheduled for the day you get out of prison," she replied, nodding pleasantly.

Jem met them at the door and introduced himself to the DIA pair. Rob saw him smile as Jem spotted the video camera slung from Vallejo's shoulder opposite her big leather bag. Jem did not point out that another camera was in operation.

"Good man," Rob said, last to enter, as he passed Jem.

"Three guesses who was—" Jem began, but stopped as he heard David Sachs call for their attention, and left the front door open to alleviate the afternoon heat.

"This can be short and sweet for some of you," Sachs said, "though we may ask you to repeat some statements later. Recording, Vallejo?"

"I am now," she said, and remained standing some distance from the others who crowded into chairs at the dining area. "Excuse me, Commander, but should this man Lodge hear the statements? I could cuff him to a steering wheel until we're ready for him."

"Ordinarily, but he's committed one attempted bribery felony within the hour and the sooner he sees his position is hopeless, the sooner he'll cooperate," Sachs replied, with a glance that might have carried a touch of reproof.

"Sorry. You're right, of course," Vallejo said, then turned her gaze on Lodge. "Whatever you've done, the sentence will be lessened if you—"

"Damnit, Marie!" This from Sachs, who wheeled toward her. "That's a protocol violation. We are not—repeat, *not*—empowered to make any such bargain." Turning back to Lodge: "That's for others to decide. For now, no promises. That's official."

"I'm feeling— I'm going to pass out," Lodge croaked, and staggered to his feet.

"We'll be here when you come to," said Sachs. "Someone get him a cold towel and—"

For a man about to faint, Ethan Lodge husbanded a lot of energy as he twisted, hands still manacled behind him, and bolted for the front door. "I won't be your sacrifice!" he screamed. He made it as far as the screen before Vallejo could draw her weapon with its short suppressor. It coughed heavily; coughed again, somewhat louder. The screen bowed outward but did not split as Ethan Lodge sagged into it, then fell back to the floor, quivering.

"He was getting away," Vallejo said to Sachs in the voice of a small child, her video camera now forgotten at her waist.

Sachs, now on his feet, leaped toward the fallen man, then knelt beside him. "Someone call 911!" At this, Jem moved to the telephone.

Then, his body shaking uncontrollably, Lodge focused on the woman who had shot him. "Mike—you said . . ." And the tremors, with his breathing, ceased.

Rob heard the words, too. "Mike? Her?"

David Sachs looked up at Vallejo for an eternity of three seconds. Then, "Whoever. She'd have a cover name. Yeah, it fits. A lot better than that sorrowful-little-girl shit she's been feeding me since last night."

"What are you— Keep your hands in view, David," said the woman, her tone suddenly, remarkably, steady and commanding now. She moved back to keep everyone in view, standing well behind Jem, taking the telephone from his hand.

Sachs stood up and sighed, his gaze on Vallejo. "Those char marks on the edge of the card table? Cigarettes lined up neatly, all burning at the same time. You were creating a pile of butts so I'd think you had spent your time smoking instead of producing evidence. Or removing some. Which was it?"

"I think you've gone crazy. Please don't make me do some-thing I'd be sorry for," Vallejo said. It didn't have a *"please"* tone; it sounded like *"or else."*

Sachs spoke slowly, as if mulling it over for himself alone: "You've been running Lodge yourself. But if I had let you handcuff him outside, you'd have killed him there with some cockamamie excuse, hoping I still wouldn't tumble, Marie."

"You really are nutso, David. Pure supposition."

"That audiotape you made was too clever, you know. It proves premeditation. And when you were conning me about why you killed poor Frank," Sachs continued steadily, "you said something about signing a register. That implies a major crime scene. Why, unless you'd just committed one? Guilty knowledge. Big mistake, Marie."

Something washed across the woman's face. "Small mis-take, David," she corrected, with a frosty half-smile. "I don't intend to make any more." With an instant's glance toward her hostages in the dining area: "And keep your hands down, Tarrant, a Beretta has several rounds for everybody." She moved a step farther away from Jem, nearer the hallway.

"I was only motioning for my friends not to panic," said Rob.

"I don't give a good goddamn what you were doing. Don't do it if you want to live," Vallejo barked. "This is going to be a little complicated, so anyone who breaks my concentration is not going to survive it." She considered them each in turn, then said, "You, Tarrant—stand up and come around here. I'll need a shield while I blow a few tires.

"David, I know you're heeled. Don't give me a reason. Just to be on the safe side, you turn around and lean against the wall. Go ahead, assume the position. Remember, I can't miss from this distance."

"But you can miss a man in a sleeping bag from six feet"— Rob said it before considering.

Marie Vallejo, watching Sachs face the living-room wall, did not bother redirecting her gaze. "Because you weren't in it. Don't jerk me around," she said scornfully. "Too bad you weren't in that mobile home, instead of the old man."

"He wasn't in the car you booby-trapped, either," Sachs accused.

"You think I'd cop to that, David? Let's just say Tarrant's been the little man who wasn't there, but now I'm through following him."

"And guess who was following you when you paid a visit to my Bronco?" Rob said. "I just assumed it was a man wearing that baseball cap."

"Baseball cap," said Sachs, with a nod. "That's our Vallejo, all right."

She made a peremptory motion with the barrel of her weapon and her tone was just as firm: "Both of you shut up! You're stalling, Tarrant. Get the hell over here or I'll waste your cutie-pie, for starters."

Rob had paused halfway out of his chair but now he swallowed and took a heavy breath to quell his tremors, his mouth dry. If this woman was going to start firing, it would be better if he weren't near Ed Doyle when the killing began. He looked into Ed's tortured expression and shook his head. "No choice," he told her in a choked voice, and pushed his chair away as he began to move back from the table.

And with Ed uttering little moans of, "My God . . . oh my God," no one clearly heard the single faint squeak of Jem Kasabian's bedroom door as it swung partially open behind Vallejo.

Only Rob was in a position to see half the torso and the face of his son, whose eyes blazed with an unholy light as Kenny raised his arm with something in his hand. It was ludicrous, beyond belief, that the youth intended to toss a paper dart at the woman. Yet that is exactly the nightmare Rob Tarrant saw unfolding.

Looking past Vallejo, Rob shook his head violently but continued to move.

With a bored "Really now, Tarrant," Vallejo motioned with her free hand.

"She'll kill you," Rob said, as Kenny flung the dart.

Because he knew what to expect, Rob flung himself toward

the living-room wall as Vallejo, her shoulder jerking, fired into
the wall. As she cried out—hardly more than a surprised
"Ah!"—the bedroom door slammed and locked.

If Rob had hoped for a window of opportunity, he was dis-
appointed. Kasabian, Ed Doyle, and Sachs had all turned toward the commotion. "Hold it," Vallejo demanded, teeth
bared, as she reached up past her neck and tore the arrow-
winged paper airplane from where, incredibly, it had stuck
into the back of her shoulder.

As she studied the fistful of wrinkled paper, Vallejo and Rob
both saw the slender hypodermic needle protruding from the
forward tip of the dart. Shouting now, but unwilling to turn
away from her hostages, one of whom carried at least two
weapons: "What the hell is this? I start shooting in five seconds!"

"Snake venom," shouted Kenny in a voice that must have
carried through the neighborhood. "How long does she have,
Jem?" It would have been impossible for them not to hear the
shattering of a window from Jem Kasabian's room. If Kenny
wasn't already outside, he could be within seconds.

Vallejo needed only one second to make her decision. Instead of wasting time in pursuit of Kenny, she stepped three
paces forward and jabbed the needle into Rob's forearm as he
raised his arms in an attempt at defense.

Rob plucked the thing out and hurled it away as Vallejo
whirled toward the astonished Jem. "You! What did he mean,
'venom'?"

An instant of silence. Then: "Snake venom. Bu-bushmaster,"
he said hoarsely. "Nastiest toxin in the Americas. My pets
aren't tame, but I make extra money milking them for anti-
venin. How could I have known the boy would—"

She cut him off, rubbing her shoulder, with a whispered
curse. "If I go down, he goes down," Vallejo said, indicating
Rob. "Antidote?"

"Not here. Emergency ward, but it'll be too late if you don't
call ahead. . . . I'm sorry, Rob," he said, now evidently at the
point of bursting into tears.

And now Ed Doyle was up, facing Vallejo, hands on her

hips. "Do you intend to die right here? You shoot anyone else now, and no one will help you!"

"Yes you will. God*damn*, it stings." Vallejo continued rubbing at the spot where the needle had penetrated her shoulder. To Jem: "What kind of maniac would keep—"

"Rubbing just works it in," Jem cautioned, and she jerked her hand down. "You want me to call?"

"Just do it," she husked, the whites of her eyes showing. She backed toward the bedroom door and tried the knob, to no avail. Now she was breathing fast, shrugging her shoulder repeatedly, the Beretta's suppressor shaking as she swept it across her field of view.

Jem reached the telephone, consulted a handwritten list inside the phone book's back cover, then punched in a set of numbers.

Vallejo and Sachs faced each other, silently glaring from across the room as Jem began to speak rapidly. After stating the problem he paused for a moment. "I said *bushmaster*. . . . Of course I'm sure, I'm a registered breeder—it'll be quicker if we drive. . . . No more than ten minutes . . . Well, we'll try for five," he said, and replaced the receiver. Turning to Vallejo: "You'll be unconscious by then, or in convulsions. Which is the fastest car, and who wants to play Formula One driver?"

"Not Sachs," said Vallejo. "He gets too cute. And not him," pointing a wavery finger toward Rob. "You and Doyle." She began to herd her two choices toward the front door.

Rob had been sucking furiously at his tiny wound but this got his attention. ". . . the fuck do you mean, not *me*?" he demanded, outraged.

"That's the deal," said Vallejo. And stumbled.

Because Ed was nearest to the weapon, it was she who moved first, and in a way no one could have expected. She pirouetted to face Vallejo, grasping the woman's throat with both hands while flinging one leg to shoulder height, then knifing it downward with balletic precision. Vallejo's gun hand, its forearm locked between Ed's legs, was forced vertically downward as Ed butted her repeatedly in the face.

As the two women reeled against a wall of shelving, Rob

leaped forward, heedless of the loud, spatting coughs that fired slugs into the floor. His right arm whipped around at full length, the heel of his hand connecting—more through luck than skill—with the slight hollow at Marie Vallejo's left temple. The blow sounded like a cantaloupe dropped onto concrete, and Vallejo was limp before her head snapped against the shelving.

Dropping to his knees, Rob shouted, "I got it, I got— Oh hell," he finished as the Beretta and its suppressor thudded against carpet. Rob kicked it away, spitting on the palm of his hand.

By this time David Sachs stood beside the women, his weapon in hand. "I'll take it from here. Damn nice work, but we're wasting time, Edwina," he said.

Ed moved back, releasing the unconscious Vallejo. Hands cradling her own cheeks, she turned toward Rob, rocking back and forth—laughing, sobbing. "I did that? Dear God, I can't believe I did that," she babbled, as Rob embraced her.

"Move! We can't let her die," Sachs thundered, picking up Vallejo's inert form. Then he turned, his face a mask of fury and concern, to see Jem Kasabian leaning against the dining table.

Laughing.

Rob looked past Ed's shoulder; caught Jem's eye. "It was bullshit," he guessed.

Jem nodded, still laughing. "But brilliant bullshit," he managed to say. "That lad will go far."

Sachs, with an expression none of them would ever forget: "The registered breeder business . . . ?"

"I have no idea if there is such a thing. I do my most creative work under pressure," said Jem.

Rob patted Ed's back with one hand and, again, spat on the other hand. "Jesus! You sold me." Then, to the woman in his arms: "Did you know?"

"Dear, dearest Rob," she said, disheveled and shining and gorgeous, and patted his cheek. "My roomie could not touch an earthworm without having a conniption fit. The very idea that he would keep poisonous snakes in this apartment, even if I'd let him . . ." And she buried her face against his neck.

At this point a youthful voice inquired from behind the locked bedroom door: "Dad? Okay, Dad?"

"Okay, kid. All-ee all-ee oxenfree," Rob called back, and heard the lock release. He released Ed Doyle and moved quickly to grab his son in a bear hug. He released the youth, blowing hard on his open palm. "That thing on the gun burned the shit out of my hand. And my arm stings, too."

"Not browned-off at me, then?" Kenny's question was muffled in his father's capacious sweatshirt.

"Chocolate-brown, Kenny. I didn't know what you had in mind," said Rob.

David Sachs, having deposited Vallejo across the table, was busily removing handcuffs from the body of Ethan Lodge. Jem said, "I tried to tell you when you came in, Rob. I had ordered Kenny to leave but he wouldn't go."

Rob kissed his son's forehead resoundingly. "You sure fold paper airplanes in a hurry."

"Naw," Kenny said, abashed. "Already made it and tossed it a few times in there, just something to do while I was waiting. Jem was pissed at me 'cause I wouldn't leave, and he said not to come out. We'd been talking about snakes and stuff the other day, and I knew about the supplies in his little fridge in there, and I thought maybe I could find something like alcohol to throw at the crazy woman, but when I saw the bottle of iodine . . ." He gave them a shy smile and shrugged.

Snapping the shiny little manacles on Vallejo's wrists, Sachs said, "One thing she's not, is crazy. Iodine, hmm? No wonder she bought the venom idea."

At this, Kenny's face hardened. "I wish she'd shot you. Somebody needs to." Only then did his gaze fall on the body of Ethan Lodge, who lay facedown near the front door. "Oh jeez, is that a dead guy? . . . Dad? Guh-*ross*," he announced.

"This doesn't seem to be my day for making friends," Sachs said ruefully.

"You stay away from my mom," Kenny burst out. "Even after Dad goes to a federal lab, just stay away!"

"National lab," Sachs corrected quietly. "What was it, Kenny: a .22 rifle?"

A long silence. "You don't have to answer him," Rob advised. To Sachs he said, "We don't even own a .22."

"Fortunately, or unfortunately from some points of view, there was no harm done. I guess I had a good scare coming."

"You had more than that coming," said Kenny. "I meant what I said. You stay away from my mom."

Sachs: "Or?"

Kenny: "Or next time it won't be a pellet gun."

Rob: "That's enough, Kenny! I've told you a hundred times, that damned old Benjamin pump could put somebody's eye out."

"Thank God," Sachs said, to no one in particular. To Rob he said, "That wraps it for me; as long as the midnight shooter was out there somewhere anonymously, I thought Vallejo might have had her own team trying to bag you. She asked for a lot of singleton work on this, and now I know why. If she'd located you alone, you wouldn't be here now."

Marie Vallejo stirred; moved her head and struggled for an instant against her bonds before she ceased to move.

"So which alphabet-soup agency does she work for, if not for you?" Rob demanded.

"I don't know yet. Not one of Uncle's, for God's sake, if that's what you're thinking," Sachs retorted with some heat. "We'll find out sooner or later, and it'll be someone—" Here, he prodded a finger against Vallejo's back. "I know you're listening, Marie. You've just about run out of roles to play for me, but unconscious works nicely."

"Go to hell," was Vallejo's terse comment.

Sachs chuckled, glancing to Rob. "Anyway, it'll be someone who had the most to gain if we lost you." Another finger against Vallejo's shoulder. "I won't even ask who, in front of these folks. Not that I expect you to tell. But we'll backtrack your movements." Shaking his head as he stuck his pistol in his belt, again looking toward Rob: "Like father, like son, I guess."

"You've lost me," said Rob.

Sachs: "The boy builds micro-UAVs, too. One of 'em just saved our collective bacon, so I guess our scores are settled."

Rob held up his left forefinger. "All but one. I still owe you." He brought a roundhouse right whistling around, catching Sachs flush on the side of his cheek. The DIA man reeled back, stumbled; sat down heavily. *"Now,"* said Rob, "I've paid it."

Sachs shook his head and blinked. "I'm going to give you that one, but I won't stand for it again. Satisfied?"

"Yeah, I guess I am."

"Well, don't stand between me and Vallejo—she's a resourceful bitch." Sachs got to his feet and, standing a pace away from the woman, fumbled his cell phone out. "We've got some housecleaning to do here," he sighed.

EPILOGUE

THE GRASSY FOOTHILLS NEAR SAN JOSE ARE DRY AND BUCKSKIN-tan with bright patches of California poppies in late July, and the slopes are subject to fitful breezes. The radio-control hobbyist who doesn't pay close attention to those unseen currents can easily lose his six-foot soaring glider above those slopes. "What'd I tell you about that, Kenny?" said his grandfather, making a circular gesture with his bottle of Anchor Steam as he lazed in a folding chair.

"I lose it, I build you another one," the youth recited dutifully, squinting upward. He toggled the transmitter on his knees; saw the model, obedient as a border collie, wheel and turn back toward them on wings as narrow as those of an albatross.

Rob swigged at his own beer and kept silent. In the few weeks of his new employment he had become familiar with wondrous new micro-devices, but not with a better teacher than Gus.

"Okay," Gus said, as Rob lay back on the slope to watch, "so when can you tell us where they're keeping you?"

"What was the old line? 'We can't go on meeting like this,' " Rob joked. "It's not up to me, but I can make day-trips home like this every few weeks. By Christmas I think I can resurface. The folks who wanted me out of the game are foreign, and I gather that they're finding out they were an hour late and a dollar short this time."

"When can you tell us which bunch of bastards it was?" Gus demanded, rubbing the scar behind his ear.

"Maybe not ever. They don't tell me everything. All I would have is a guess, based on a little hawk-sized UAV that Vallejo woman kept stashed away. I'm told she's been put away for a long, long time." Rob raised his voice a bit: "Kenny, remember the bird you saw on our fishing trip?"

"The 'humbug,' you called it—yeah. It was one of these, wasn't it?" he said, pointing toward the slope-soarer.

"So they tell me. It's no longer cutting-edge stuff in my group, but it sure did its job."

Kenny turned toward his father, his frown of concentration becoming a sly smile. "Any way you could get us one of those to play with?"

Rob laughed. " 'Fraid not. And you two can stop hinting at how nice it would be to have some parts from—where I'm working. You want to play with that stuff, kid, you get your aero degree first."

"And meanwhile, watch the damn plane," Gus ordered. As Kenny turned back to the job at hand, the older man went on quietly. "Corrie's dating again. Even if you didn't ask—figured you'd want to know."

Rob considered his reply long enough to make the silence discomfiting. "I wrote her," he said at last. "Told her she might as well." Softly, sorrowfully: "Neither of us is going to change much, Gus. She is what she is, and it would take a better man than I am to live with it. Besides, I'm, uh, seeing someone now, myself. It could get to be a permanent arrangement."

"Just one thing, Ro-bo, and I druther you said it's none of my friggin' business than to finagle the truth about it."

Rob turned his head, shielding his eyes from the summer sun, and regarded Gus with affection. "Let me guess: Was I seeing the lady before Corrie dumped me?" He waited for the nod and got it, accompanied by a sigh.

There could be no right answer to that. The truth would only deepen an old man's disappointment in his only daughter, fill his nights with despair over errors of nurturing that could never be corrected now; perhaps, never could have been avoided in the first place.

A lie, on the other hand, would leave Gus with the festering suspicion that Rob himself, whom Gus had gradually accepted as his closest friend and confidant, was the guiltier party. Though the old fellow might never mention it, he would thereafter regard Rob as a man who needed forgiveness—forgiveness that a man like Gus might never be capable of giving in its fullest measure.

You let him believe in his friend or his child. Life is full of shitty choices. "I'm no saint," Rob said. "And I would have had to be."

After a long moment Gus closed his eyes, nodded again, then looked toward the teenager who, for better or worse, was the girder that would keep the two men welded into a unit—even a flawed unit.

Gus raised his voice. "Okay, let's see if you can bring it down, Kenny. Even if you bust it, we can fix it together." He caught Rob's eye and essayed a smile, and Rob nodded understanding.